They Fought Like Men

by
Aiden James & Fiona Fraser

Published by Manor House Books

Cover Art: Blue Sky Design ~ Boston

Printed in the United States of America.

First Edition

BOOKS BY AIDEN JAMES

WITH FIONA FRASER
Toxicity
They Fought Like Men

CADES COVE SERIES
Cades Cove
The Raven Mocker
Devil Mountain

DYING OF THE DARK VAMPIRES
With Patrick Burdine
The Vampires' Last Lover
The Vampires' Birthright
Blood Princesses

THE JUDAS CHRONICLES
Immortal Plague
Immortal Reign
Immortal Destiny
Immortal Dragon
Immortal Tyranny
Immortal Pyramid
Immortal Victory

THE RODERICK CHRONICLES
Immortal Supremacy
Immortal Storm

NICK CAINE ADVENTURES
With J.R. Rain

Temple of the Jaguar
Treasure of the Deep
Pyramid of the Gods
Aiden James only
Curse of the Druids
Secret of the Loch
River of the Damned

CLASH OF COVENS
The Witches of Denmark
Witch Out of Water

THE GABRIEL FILES
With J.R. Rain
The Soul Taker
The Ghost Maker

THE SERENDIPITOUS CURSE
With Lisa Collicutt
Reborn
Reviled
Redeemed

NASHVEGAS PARANORMAL
With Patrick Burdine
Deadly Night
The Ungrateful Dead

THE TALISMAN CHRONICLES
With Mike Robinson
The Forgotten Eden
The Devil's Paradise
Hurakan's Chalice

Acclaim for Aiden James:

"Aiden James has written a deeply psychological, gripping tale that keeps the readers hooked from page one." *Bookfinds review for "The Forgotten Eden"*

"A variety of twists, surprises, and subplots keep the story moving forward at a good pace. My interest was piqued almost immediately and my attention never wavered as I forced my eyes to stay open well into the night. (Sleep is overrated.) Aiden James is a Master Storyteller, whose career is on the rise! Out-freaking-standing-excellent!" *Detra Fitch of Huntress Reviews, for "Immortal Plague"*

"Aiden James' writing style flows very easily and I found that Cades Cove snowballed into a very gripping tale. The Indian lore and ceremonies and the flashbacks to Allie Mae's (earthly) demise were very powerful. I think those aspects separated the work from what we've seen before in horror and ghost tales." *Evelyn Klebert, Author of "A Ghost of a Chance", "Dragonflies", and "An Uneasy Traveler" for "Cades Cove"*

"The intense writing style of Aiden James kept my eyes glued to the story and the pages seemed to fly by at warp speed.... Twists, turns, and surprises pop up at random times to keep the reader off balance. It all blends together to create one of the best stories I have read all year." *Detra Fitch, Huntress Reviews, for "The Devil's Paradise"*

"Aiden James is insanely talented! We are watching a master at work.... Ghost stories don't get any better than this." *J.R. Rain, Author of "Moon Dance' and "Vampire Moon" for "The Raven Mocker".*

AIDEN JAMES
FIONA FRASER

★ ★ ★ ★ ★

THEY
FOUGHT
LIKE
MEN

★ ★ ★ ★ ★

In Loving Memory of Sandra Seiberling. Her sense of humor and feistiness were much loved and are greatly missed.

The bitter conflict between the Union and Confederacy, spanning four terrible years from 1861 to 1865, brought the United States of America to the brink of annihilation. Families throughout the nation were torn apart by the Civil War, where soldiers died and their loved ones were left behind in a desperate struggle to survive.

A war based on perceived tyranny and rebellion gave birth to many contradictions, where deceit ran rampant on both sides. Within this environment, it is known that at least four hundred women enlisted as soldiers under the pretense of being men, from both the North and South.

Brave men who gave their lives for either side were not the war's only heroes, and this story is dedicated to these remarkable women.

~ Aiden & Fiona

Chapter One

Thursday, September 25th, 1862... Appleton, Tennessee.

The smell of burning wood had lingered in the air for nearly a week, interlaced with the stench of something else that had been consumed by the distant fires to the east.

Hattie Grey cast a wary look beyond the tree line that marked the edge of her father's small farm, situated just north of town. The late afternoon sun had begun its descent toward the west and she sheltered her eyes while fighting to keep rebellious strands of her long blonde hair in their place. Despite her best efforts, several wisps continued to lash her face, aided by a soft breeze carrying the pungent scent.

"Braxton Carter says the smoke's coming from someplace west of Elkton," drawled Hattie's father, Rufus Porter. He stood on the front porch of their modest farmhouse, pointing in the same direction as his daughter's gaze. "Most likely a good fifteen to twenty miles from here and probably on account of not letting them damn Yankees take a hog and a couple of chickens."

"I thought you said hanging a white sheet from the upstairs' window would be enough to get 'em to pass us by without losing anything." Hattie glanced toward the house, where she could picture hoisting the standard symbol of surrender across the shutters between two second-story windows. She frowned worriedly before returning her attention to the thick column of smoke in the distance.

"It can't hurt anything to hang it," Rufus offered, releasing a low sigh. "Hell, the boys from both sides ain't above thieving—especially when rations haven't been what they were supposed to be. Braxton told me neither of his boys are being fed right."

Rufus chuckled sadly, and it seemed to enhance the uneasiness Hattie saw written upon his face. Her father had always been able to hide such things until lately, when it had become obvious that the war between the North and South was nowhere close to ending. Likely, this was behind his recent advice for her to move north to Columbia, where her older sister, Stella, resided. *"It's calmer there, and I'd sleep a hell of a lot better knowing you were fully safe from the war,"* he'd told her.

Her father had always been one to look for the favorable side of things, and Hattie had noticed a steady erosion of that optimism in him, most clearly evident in his eyes. Normally bright emerald like hers, the dull sheen of doubt had noticeably dimmed them along with his jovial nature. She had always known her father to be a strong and determined man. Decorated for his bravery sixteen years ago, in the Mexican-American War of 1846, a leg injury sustained during that conflict hadn't slowed him down until shortly before this latest war had broken out. It was the only reason he hadn't enlisted to serve the Confederacy. He would never have voted to secede from the Union, but Hattie knew he also felt it was his sacred duty to defend Tennessee from the threat of 'Northern aggression.'

Rufus had raised his daughters to be upstanding women. Hattie and Stella were strong in their patriotism while remaining compassionate to their countrymen, regardless of what side a person took in the conflict that had divided America. When their mother died of yellow fever in the summer of 1855, following a trip to see Rufus' eldest brother in Memphis, he remained outwardly strong for his daughters and only wept in private for his beloved Lydia. Hattie recalled those days quite well. At the time, she was just ten years old and Stella was not quite twelve. Neither girl had ever lacked for anything, and their father's deftness at tempering his strictness with his natural benevolence had earned him great respect among the residents of Appleton.

"Our boys may be hungry out there, but they're not the ones stealing from people who barely have enough for themselves, Papa," Hattie retorted, immediately regretting her disdainful tone. "I'm sorry… I meant no disrespect."

Rufus nodded, and for a moment his troubled gaze eased. Hattie took it as a sign he agreed with her assessment of how the Federal troops had been far more demanding of the Southern populace's resources than the Confederacy's soldiers.

"I just don't think it's right that someone can come and take whatever they want," she added, more demurely. "I heard you and Mr. Carter talking about how the Yankees were burning some of the homes and farms they stole from. Jonas wouldn't stand for it, and I know you wouldn't either…"

It was all she could do to keep her emotions in check. Speaking her beloved husband's name tore at her heart. He had enlisted in the Tennessee cavalry in the summer of 1861, and since then she had only seen him twice—the past December at Christmas, and then for one night in late June, almost three months ago. His last correspondence arrived in early July, and he hadn't responded to any of the letters she had written to him since that time.

"True. I won't ever let that happen, Hattie," said Rufus, running his fingers through his thick blonde hair tinged with gray along the sideburns. "We've got enough to where we can share a little. Unless the Yankees want more than what's fair and reasonable. I'd just as soon fill their sorry backsides with buckshot."

She responded with an affirmative nod, but knew her nervous frown clearly announced she didn't share her father's confidence. After all it was just the two of them, with only a handful of farms smaller than theirs for several miles in any direction. If the Yankees did come through this area looking to steal anything, what would happen if her father's ire led him to grab his shotgun as he had just now threatened? Nothing good would come of it. Nothing good at all.

"Let's just pray they don't venture anywhere near here." Hattie paused to pick up the half-filled pail from the corncrib that she had laid down momentarily, after being distracted by the breeze and its acrid aroma. "I pray they'll just go back to where they came from."

Rufus murmured a quiet 'amen' as the worry returned, clouding his expression. The general consensus amongst everyone they knew was that the Yankees wouldn't be leaving Tennessee anytime soon.

"Why don't you pick a few of the last tomatoes on that vine over yonder and then I'll help you fix supper." He motioned to the vegetable garden's corner nearest to where Hattie stood. "Don't you worry none about the Yankees... we'll be fine."

He offered a weak smile and turned to go inside the house, seemingly invigorated and less hobbled by his leg than usual. Hattie wondered if this was an effort to show her that he could still handle things independently, and could take care of them both without any outside help. She waited for him to disappear from view, confirming his destination by the familiar loud crack from the old wooden screen door slamming against the doorframe, and then set out for the garden.

Distracted by her final chore that afternoon, she let the matter of the smelly plume of smoke go for the moment. If only she could do the same for her thoughts about Jonas. She tortured herself with a myriad of possibilities as to why his letters had suddenly ceased. No matter how hard she tried to think of other things, it had lately become a habit for her to torment herself on what the lack of correspondence meant.

Her friends and family, including Stella, assured her that Jonas would one day return when finally granted a full furlough. All her fears about his welfare would fade into relieved laughter as the two would again embrace as husband and wife, and she'd feel foolish for having agonized over his absence. That was what Mary Tarver, her very best friend in the world, had assured her. Even Stella had reminded her that her own husband, Captain Frank Cooper, had sent letters that were delayed in delivery by several months.

But late at night, when the world was quiet—save for the crickets and cicadas that never seemed to sleep, the doubts would assail her heart without a reprieve until exhaustion finally delivered her to the land of fragmented dreams. Sometimes Jonas was in them, riding a dark stallion as part of the Sixth Tennessee Cavalry, his latest regiment after the reorganization in Corinth, Mississippi, following the Confederate defeat in Shiloh. Although he never responded to her calls for him to wait for her to reach him in these dreams, he sometimes paused long enough to smile at her, the wind blowing back his dark unkempt hair from his face. His deep blue eyes regarded her with an ornery twinkle before he'd gallop away to rejoin his regiment preparing for another battle.

Oftentimes, she'd wake up with a start, chilled by cold sweat despite the summer's unforgiving heat and humidity that wouldn't subside until October....

Hattie peered over her shoulder at the house as she reached the tomato vine, hoping she had a moment to read the lines from the worn letter she kept with her always... Jonas' last correspondence. She carefully unfolded it, preferring to read the last lines in daylight, rather than illuminated only by a candle's dimness.

After another cautionary glance around her, she peeled the last page from the others, gently caressing the paper as if her husband's very essence could seep into her fingertips from the inked lines.

Never forget, my dearest love. You are forever in my heart and I think of little else when we're not fighting this regrettable war. I picture your face as I left you in the morning, just ten days ago. It's what keeps me careful and alive. How my heart yearns for thou that are so near and dear to me, my sweet wife. I will return to you when I can.

As ever your devoted and loving husband, Jonas Grey.

Hattie read over the words several times before carefully refolding the letter and placing it inside her bodice. Then she hurriedly gathered enough tomatoes to account for her time in the garden, making sure to leave the ones not fully ripe yet and discarding those destined to rot from insects, birds, and the rodents that cleverly avoided Papa's traps.

The last thing she thought about before stepping back inside the house were the cherished words of Jonas' letter and the assurances from Stella, Mary, and her father that her husband would return soon. Then she sent a whispered prayer heavenward, seeking protection for Jonas and to bring him home safe.

Chapter Two

Sunday, September 28ᵗʰ, 1862… Appleton, Tennessee.

"Hattie… I must say, *that* is the finest chicken stew I've enjoyed this year!"

John Tarver added a lip smack to further sell his enthusiasm for Hattie's cooking. Mary Tarver, his wife, echoed his praise while bouncing their three-month old infant, Nathan, on her knee.

The Tarvers had made the three-mile trek from their farm to Rufus Porter's homestead by wagon after church, and were gathered around the dinner table with Hattie's father. The heat from the kitchen made it much warmer inside the old farmhouse than out, but nature had seen fit to provide a comfortable breeze that Sunday afternoon. Rufus had opened all the windows on the main floor, and Hattie was grateful for the reprieve from the coals smoldering in the kitchen's fireplace.

"Well, it's nowhere near what you've come to expect from Mary's cooking, but I thank you for the compliment, John. Would anyone like more sassafras tea?" Hattie smiled, motioning to a pitcher she held.

"I'd like some, Hattie, if you don't mind." Rufus pushed his empty glass toward where she stood, next to Mary and her giggling bundle of joy. "How about you, John?"

"Thank you, Rufus. I'll take some, and surely Mary is ready for another glass as well."

The mood was light, although an underlying tension brought on by the earlier sighting of two new smoke columns to the east was also present. It was obvious to Hattie that the Tarvers were just as worried by the smoke plumes as she and her father. The faint odor wafting toward them seemed to be mostly of wood this time, and not livestock, as had been confirmed by Braxton Carter on Friday. Apparently, the Yankees were less inclined to destroy a family's means of survival on the Lord's Day.

But they are headed this way. The smoke appears thicker… closer.

"Thank you, Hattie," said Mary, after her glass was replenished.

For a moment, their gazes locked onto each other. Hattie could tell that Mary desperately wanted to share something, but was making an effort to hold her tongue. Her gray eyes misted as she looked away, leaving Hattie with a view of the soft blue ribbons woven through her dark brown locks—the same shade as Nathan's, though he had inherited his daddy's brown eyes. Clearly the child had ended up with the best qualities from both parents, sharing John's dimpled cheeks and his mother's pointed chin. Hattie hoped Nathan's cheerful disposition stayed true, since the war's strain on the community had embittered some residents, and children were rarely immune to the effects from their parents' hardships.

"I hear ole Jeff Davis wants to conscript every man and every boy old enough to hold a musket," said John, tapping tobacco into a hickory pipe that Hattie recalled at one time belonged to his great-grandfather. "Since Nate's gettin' easier to take care of, and my ma and brother, Jeb, live up the road just a piece from us, I reckon I can save myself a visit from the provost, Josiah Wims, by heading up to Columbia and enlistin' in the Confederate Army next month."

"Is that a fact?" Rufus raised his glass in salute. "Your pa would be quite proud. I wish George was still here."

"Me too." John raised his glass, tipping the edge toward Rufus. It appeared to Hattie that her best friend's husband fought to keep a tear at bay, knowing how close John had been to his 'pappy,' who had died several years earlier from consumption. "I aim to do him *very* proud."

"Surely you will, son," Rufus agreed. "Surely you will."

A moment of awkward silence followed as Hattie watched her father, currently focused upon the twin smoke plumes looming above the tree line and visible through their tall dining room windows. Both dark sentinels were in the same direction as the previous ones they had noticed a few days earlier. But as she observed earlier that afternoon, the latest evidence of fire seemed a few miles closer.

"Are you still plannin' to visit the Greys in a few days?" Mary asked her.

"I am," Hattie replied, grimacing worriedly. "As long as the fires stop by then."

"We could check on Milton and Eliza for you, since their farm sits just half a mile from us as the crow flies," John offered, glancing at Rufus and Mary before continuing. "I'm sure Jonas' folks would be just as obliged to have us call on 'em, rather than either of you havin' to hazard a trip."

Hattie nodded thoughtfully. "I appreciate that... but I'm looking forward to visiting with Eliza, especially since it's been almost a month since my last visit. As you know,

Milton's arthritis has made it hard for him to travel far from their place."

Hattie had grown quite close to Eliza Grey, who treated her more like a beloved daughter than a daughter-in-law. Eliza helped fill the void that had been there since Hattie's mother had passed away, nearly ten years earlier. Even if the distance had been twice as far and managed by foot alone, Hattie would gladly endure any hardship to spend time with Eliza, as well as with Milton.

"Maybe you and Rufus could stay with us for a while." Mary reached out to grasp John's hand when he whipped his head around to face her, but he seconded the invitation. "We've got the extra rooms, since my ma and pa are stayin' with Sally down in Florence, Alabama until November. And, John will soon be enlistin' in the army. It could be perfect. Then you could check on Eliza, and Milton too, as often as need be."

Mary held Hattie in her loving gaze. The proposal seemed too good to decline, since it could ease the loneliness of only having her father to talk to—especially at night, when Rufus would retire early after a long day of working the farm. The worry and heartache of missing Jonas often seemed unbearable at those times.

Hattie was prepared to accept the Tarvers' offer, but wanted her father's approval first.

"We'll take your invitation under consideration," he advised Mary, lightly stroking his graying beard, as if making up his mind right then. "We'd have to figure out what to do with the horses, pigs, and the rest of our livestock. I could have an answer for you by this time next week."

"That's plenty fair," said John, massaging his light brown whiskers similarly. "Besides, I'm not plannin' to leave for Columbia until around the fifteenth of October. It could be even later than that, since last I heard they might not be organizin' new recruits until November, and likely will be handlin' the bivouackin' and daily drills someplace else. That's what your neighbor mentioned the other day."

"Braxton Carter?"

"Yes sir. He said somethin' about Murfreesboro and some other town near Memphis. Murfreesboro would be easier to get to from here. But I intend to visit Columbia first, just to be certain."

"Hmmm." Hattie's father returned his gaze to the ominous plumes in the distance, frowning slightly. "When y'all are done with supper, I'd like to show you something in the parlor."

"We could wait a little while for dessert... although that apple pie baked by Hattie smells awfully temptin'," said John, rising from the table. He paused to regard his wife, who had returned her attention to entertaining Nathan. "How about you, my dear? Can you wait on dessert?"

"I'd like to help Hattie clean up first." Mary handed Nathan to John, and began gathering up the dishes until Hattie stopped her.

"I'll take care of those in a moment... I'll take the pie back into the kitchen for now, along with anything else that will keep for a few days," she advised. "I can tell from the look on Papa's face that he's ready to head into the parlor right now."

She smiled at her father, who nodded appreciatively.

"It won't take long, but I feel it's important."

He grabbed his cane from nearby and used it to help rise from his chair. Hobbling to the door leading to the kitchen, he held it open for Hattie to carry the pie and Mary to follow her with the leftover bread and butter. Then he motioned for John to join him in the small foyer separating the dining room from the parlor.

"This is mostly for your peace of mind, John," Rufus advised, leading the way into the parlor. He stepped over to an old secretary sitting next to the brick fireplace topped handsomely by a carved oak mantel, the only fancy mantel in the house. Rufus commented that the secretary had been in his family since before the Revolutionary War. "What I'm about to show you is an invention you'd be wise to consider adding to your home... If you wouldn't mind helping me move this aside, I'd be much obliged."

John helped him move the stately furniture piece, careful to not spill the inkwell or dislodge the pair of quills tucked inside a holder. A moment later, the oak wainscoting behind the desk lay exposed. Rufus pushed on a panel in the center of the wall, and it suddenly popped open.

"Well I'll be damned," whispered John, almost reverently.

Hattie and Mary had rejoined the men in the parlor as the secretary was being moved, and when Hattie saw the closet-sized room appear beyond the panel that her father set aside, it surprised her that she'd forgotten about the little storage space he had added to the parlor after her mother died.

"Most everything of value to us is stored here, and there's enough room for a few weeks' worth of food. As you can see, there are several sacks of grain and flour, and a few jugs of sorghum syrup, along with some other food items. I intended to fill it up by the first frost. But in consideration of what we'll likely face from the Yankee marauders—if they venture this far, there's enough room to hide a pair of women your size, Mary and Hattie, or even a grown man, such as John or myself."

"Why are you showing us this today, Papa?" Hattie eyed her father suspiciously. "You have a reason, and it's not just a precaution. Am I right about that?"

He smiled faintly and gave her an affirmative nod.

13

"If we're to spend time living away from this place, I would expect John and Mary to have something similar in their home," he advised, turning his attention to their guests. "Even if you don't want to take the trouble to build something quite like this, you need a place to hide your valuables and enough staples to get you through the winter. Keeping your livestock from the Yankees will be a lot harder, and based on what we're seeing in the distance, it might not be possible to get a fair shake in that regard. My heart tells me that we need to be fully prepared—even if we never see 'em in these parts."

"Papa, are you forgetting about the white flags they can hang from the windows and eaves?" asked Hattie. "Stella told me how it saved their home in Columbia from being invaded several times during the past year."

"Things are different in the bigger towns and cities, Hattie." Rufus' smile melted into a scowl as he regarded her seriously. "Sherman and Grant are said to be strict upon their men when there's a larger audience. Once the blue coats get further out, there isn't any discipline. Those fires we've seen ain't coming from any of the surrounding towns. They're coming from farms, some bigger and some smaller than ours, but all are in danger. Dangle a white flag from the rooftops if you must. But I damn well guarantee it won't stop an unscrupulous man from taking what he wants—especially when disregard for decency is motivated by hunger and contempt."

John promised to look into building a similar secret hideout inside his farmhouse that week. After everyone returned to the dining room to enjoy Hattie's apple pie, it was soon time for the Tarvers to return home.

"I know you're worried about Jonas," Mary said to Hattie, keeping her voice low as they finished cleaning up after supper. "My heart tells me the same thing I'm sure it's tellin' you, Hattie. Jonas is alive, and will come home sooner than you expect. The fact you haven't heard from him will have a logical reason, such as the Federals interceptin' letters that look suspicious to them, in fear that such correspondence might compromise their military maneuvers."

"I hope you're right," Hattie replied, accepting a warm hug from Mary. "I love you."

"I love you, too… Think about my invitation, all right?"

"I will, and I'll encourage Papa to give it serious consideration."

Rufus stood with Hattie on the porch as the sun hastened its descent in the west. They waited for the Tarvers' wagon to disappear from view before closing up the farm for the night.

"John liked your suggestion, Papa," said Hattie, after he added a fresh log to the parlor's hearth. "Mary says he'll take it seriously and build something similar to the hiding place you made." She added a hopeful smile that immediately faded when he shook his head grimly.

"I don't share her optimism, and I worry he could put them all in danger if he doesn't watch his outward zealousness to the Southern Cause. It's quite all right for us to privately consider these damn Yankees as the scourge of Satan. But if they come calling, he'd better stand down peaceably."

Hattie nodded quietly, wishing she didn't share the same apprehension. When she planned to visit Eliza that week, she intended to stop by the Tarver farm to check on Mary and Nathan, and encourage John to act on her father's advice about creating a hideout—if he hadn't already done so.

She tried to focus her thoughts on how wonderful it could be for her father and her to join the Tarvers, making a safe haven for them all. Yet, despite her best efforts to set aside her misgivings, the reality of towering smoke columns moving ever closer proved too difficult to ignore.

Something terrible was on the way.

Chapter Three

Saturday, October 4th, 1862... in a camp not far from Corinth,

Mississippi.

The Confederate forces led by Major General Earl Van Dorn would be traveling back to Tennessee soon. Finding a true moment of privacy had become a luxury for Jonas Grey, presently serving as second lieutenant for Company I of the Sixth Tennessee Cavalry under Captain James Lewis, and Colonel James T. Wheeler. Fortunately, a small bluff overlooking a quiet stream sat less than fifty yards from camp, and Jonas finally found an opportunity to sneak away to this tranquil spot shortly before midnight.

With the moon just three days shy of its fullness, Jonas was afforded plenty of illumination for his venture and had left his lantern back at camp. Even a dimly lit lamp could make him an easy target for the enemy. One couldn't be too careful these days, where a Yankee sniper's bullet could have any Rebel's name on it, and Jonas' officer stripes made him an even more desirable target... Peering through a tall pine's lower branches, the area ahead appeared to be safe enough. As long as he stayed low and didn't linger beyond half an hour, he figured he'd be all right.

Jonas needed this time in order to reflect on recent events in the war out west, and whether it was prudent to continue the effort that had decimated his original regiment to the point that only a handful of the men he had originally rode with remained. Hell, after the disaster at Shiloh, most of the cavalrymen from Middle Tennessee were gone. Sickness had claimed many of his friends, and the majority of the survivors had returned home, either sick, wounded, or both. Others had been buried on the battlefields that stretched across Mississippi, Tennessee, and Alabama.

Shiloh was followed by an earlier failed defensive stand at Corinth—a siege that had lasted from April 29th until the very end of May. The few small victories that followed were now nearly forgotten, especially after General William Rosecrans recently routed Van Dorn's army, first at Luka, Mississippi on September 19th and then again at Corinth in a battle that had just ended yesterday.

Defeat had become an increasingly bitter pill to swallow.

"I should've stayed home when I had the chance in June," he whispered to himself, lamenting the decision to return after thinking he would fulfill his yearlong enlistment in late July and then return to his beloved wife's side. But then Jefferson Davis eliminated retirements throughout the army, save for the highest-ranking officers. Conscription had become mandatory and enlistments permanent until the war's end.

The thought of possibly never leaving in one piece made him increasingly homesick, and frequently brought him back to the last time he was with Hattie, when he'd stolen away from his detail of guarding wounded comrades who were being escorted to Columbia, Tennessee. He had arrived home in the dead of night, and the moon was scarcely visible. Prudently journeying to Appleton under the cover of darkness enabled Jonas to avoid Yankee patrols continuously scouring the countryside for furloughed Confederates and deserters from both sides.

He had briefly ended up at the wrong farm, arousing Braxton Carter's pair of bloodhounds that pursued him to within a mile of the farm he shared with Hattie and her father. The intimacy between husband and wife that night had given him renewed strength and determination to survive whatever lay ahead, as he rejoined his companions the next afternoon. The men had already delivered the patients into Dr. Murdock's care and were on their way back to Mississippi by the time he caught up to them...

At present, while crouched low to the ground, Jonas climbed the rise overlooking the gurgling stream below. A cool stiff breeze forced him to button his coat up to his neck, and for a moment he considered an immediate return to camp. But the moonlight dancing on the water held his gaze, reminding him briefly of a bigger stream near his home in Appleton. *Sugar Creek...* a place where he and Hattie had spent many a summer afternoon during their courtship three years ago, and subsequent leisurely picnic lunches as husband and wife until the regrettable invasion of the South by the North.

The sound of a twig snapping quickened his heart. Jonas moved over to a fallen tree and quickly lowered himself to the dirt, where it offered protection from an enemy picket that could be hiding in the woods located on the other side of the stream, roughly forty to fifty feet away. After peering toward the tree line beyond the water and not hearing another report, he lowered his pistol and pulled out a locket from inside his shirt. The locket contained a daguerreotype, and under the moonlight's glow the portrait's features were clearly defined.

"I miss you so much, Hattie," he whispered. "What I wouldn't give to be with you right now…"

Another twig snap from across the way resounded, this one loud enough to confirm another man's presence… or a fairly large animal. Regardless, if the noise happened again, he'd either be forced to engage whoever or whatever was there, or leave this otherwise peaceful place and return to camp, where he should be anyway.

He waited for another minute before returning his attention to the only portrait he had of his wife. What he loved most about it was the slight smirk on her face. He remembered smiling at her from nearby, betting that her serene look could not be held and would result in blurriness. But he should've known her orneriness would've kept that tranquil expression mostly intact despite his coercive efforts. Hattie's obstinacy was the thing that had first attracted him to her, back when they were young teenagers. She had always been pretty too. Then when she had filled out toward womanhood, he felt lost in her presence—often not knowing what to talk about. Thankfully, she'd taken a shine to him as well, and they were married shortly after her seventeenth birthday, and not long before he'd turned eighteen.

Two years of marital bliss and then the war came.

It was his older brother Ezekiel's idea to enlist as cavalrymen, before they could be conscripted into the infantry. Zeke had taught him how to ride and shoot a rifle or pistol while in full gallop. The pair had hoped to be assigned to the same regiment, which they were, although in different companies. Neither had thought it would be an issue when they enlisted in July of 1861, over a year ago. But Zeke's company was spirited away to the northern part of Tennessee and Kentucky, and Jonas found himself more than one hundred miles away when Zeke was killed at Fort Donelson that past February.

Grieving from the news that came by letter from his mother, Jonas damn near quit that very day, and again after what happened at Shiloh less than two months later. But the thought of returning to Appleton as a deserter was enough to deter him, and once the cavalry's reorganization took place in Corinth that June, he found renewed incentive to remain when he was promoted to second lieutenant under his friend, James Lewis....

Jonas removed the last correspondence he had received from Hattie from inside his coat. Dated May 4th that year, he had asked her why she hadn't written him since then, when they were briefly reunited that sultry night in late June. She insisted that she had written, and he had hoped to find the letters waiting for him when he and his companions returned to Mississippi to rejoin Van Dorn's army. But the letters were still missing.

Since then, nothing else had come. But given the fact the previous letters remained unaccounted for, he tried to not let it worry him about Hattie's well-being. Rufus Porter, her father, was a strong man, despite a leg injury he had dealt with for years following the war in Mexico.

Getting another furlough—and hopefully one that would be for at least a week—wouldn't likely happen until the deeper snows came, and both armies were forced to bivouac for the winter. At least that was what Captain Lewis had advised him. Jonas was dismayed at the prospect of the war lingering deep into next year. However, Lewis also told him that General Van Dorn had indicated they might return to Tennessee in early November, with the intent of settling someplace near Columbia, and retire early for the winter. If that proved to be true, he might be able to return to Appleton in about a month.

My heart is always with you, Jonas. Fare well, my love, and please write soon. Hattie Grey.

These were the words he most reflected upon, since the letter's condition had deteriorated over the past five months. He dared not open it fully again in fear it would further separate into tattered pieces. Meanwhile, the solace he had hoped to attain proved elusive and his gut told him it was best to head back to camp.

Jonas allowed himself one last glance at the moonlight dancing upon the surface of the tranquil stream and then scurried back to the low-lit campfires scattered amongst his Confederate companions. He ignored the distinct feeling that a gun's sight was trained on his back... a feeling that didn't leave until he was within a few yards of his tent.

Chapter Four

Friday, October 10th, 1862… Appleton, Tennessee.

"Hattie, stay inside here for now. Looks like we've got eight or nine of the bastards mulling around outside!"

Rufus quickly secured the panel in the wall behind the secretary, and prepared to scoot the heavy furniture piece back to where it would allow Hattie just enough space to squeeze through once the panel was popped back open.

"Papa, please let me help! You'll need an extra gun to scare 'em off—"

"Damn it, daughter, this ain't the time to put up a fuss!" Rufus scolded, his voice muffled due to the wall's thickness.

Hattie heard heavy footfalls resounding from the porch, but focused more on a hushed reminder from her father about buried supplies behind the woodshed. She would definitely need them in the event the Yankee marauders set fire to the place and she was forced to flee.

"What about you?"

"I'll be fine."

Focused intently upon the thin sliver of light peeking through a twig-sized gap between the removable panel and floor, Hattie tried to ignore her growing terror. But she couldn't control the thundering of her heart as it thudded wildly within her chest.

She had been the first one to spot the blue coats entering the farm from her bedroom window upstairs. There had only been three to start with, and by the time she ran downstairs to tell her father about the trespassers, a fourth soldier had appeared from behind the barn. A covert glance through the kitchen window had revealed three more soldiers approaching the house from the corncrib. That's when Rufus rushed Hattie to the parlor's safe haven, having her scurry inside after she helped him push the secretary out of the way.

A bevy of regrets washed over her while reflecting upon the spurned offer to join the Tarvers. As she and Mary had agreed nearly two weeks ago, it wouldn't have been easy on any of them. However, a little inconvenience would have been worth the peace of mind gained from knowing that four trigger fingers were available instead of two. John hadn't heeded Papa's advice regarding precautions and her father made it clear he was immovable until John did. Rufus even offered to help him build a room just like the one Hattie presently hid within, but that idea was delayed by Mary's husband to the point Rufus finally gave up asking about it.

And now their farm had been invaded.

A knock on the front door drew a wary response from Rufus.

"What do you want?"

"We want to have a look inside… Open up and we'll be quick about it. We just want a little flour, molasses, some lard—that sort of thing."

"Your men already raided my barn. I saw them take my pigs, my best horse, and all but two chickens," Rufus replied. "Winter's coming and I'll damn near starve if y'all take anything else."

Laughter erupted from several men that had joined the first man on the porch, whooping it up as if from a good joke.

"Well, now… it appears as if there won't be the Southern hospitality extended to us that we've become accustomed to receiving."

Before her father could respond, the door crashed open. Deeper terror seized Hattie's heart, and she debated escaping from her hideout and coming to his aid. Reluctantly, she decided to wait. Something told her panicked mind that stepping out with a musket in hand would spell the immediate end of her father's life, and possibly hers too.

Meanwhile, a struggle ensued and she heard her Papa telling the intruders to give his gun back to him, followed by painful grunts in response to what sounded like punches, and the sound of something heavy landing on the floor.

They're beating him? Oh my God—I can't let this happen! I can't…

A violent slam of what she assumed was her father's body into the secretary interrupted her racing thoughts, followed by more laughter.

"So, where's your daughter?" The voice from the porch sounded much closer, gruff and menacing.

"She ain't… she ain't here," Rufus replied between panted breaths.

The sound of footsteps running upstairs was soon followed by the crash of toppled furniture from both bedrooms, and then heavier footfalls returned to the main floor in haste, as if their owners were angered by not finding anyone or anything of value.

"Nobody's up there. But a woman lives here, too—just like the bitch up the road told us!" announced a younger voice. A teenager, most likely.

"You hear that?" sneered the first man. "We know you've got a daughter, and we'd like to meet her. Maybe have a little fun before we take our leave of your gracious presence. Maybe cut the Gordian Knot like the great Alexander this time... unlike your good neighbors' fate. It all depends on you, Mr..."

"Porter. Rufus Porter," growled her father. "Like I said, my daughter's not here. Hattie left for Columbia two days ago, to join her sister in Columbia."

"You don't say?"

More laughter... accompanied by the sound of more punches. This time, the blows were accompanied by pained groans from her father.

In tears and covering her mouth to corral the whimpers desperate to escape her throat, Hattie regretted not defying her father's decision to place her in hiding. He needed her help, and the opportunity to come to his rescue seemed lost. She'd likely be disarmed before she could emerge from behind the secretary. Still, she debated doing it anyway.

"Well, Rufus Porter, we obviously don't believe you," continued the apparent leader of this unholy gang. "But while you consider just how difficult your resistance is making this for you, including your daughter when we find her, perhaps you'd like to share where you keep your valuables? Surely a man of your means is hoarding Confederate gold. Maybe a fine watch or two, or weaponry far nicer than that shotgun we'll be taking with us?"

Papa remained silent despite more blows from his assailants.

"Duncan, it looks like there are some silver utensils and a pitcher in one of the cabinets in the kitchen," a man called from the foyer, sounding a few years older than the boy from a moment ago.

"Grab what you've found," the leader replied. "Looks like it's time to move on."

"What about him?" asked an older, gravelly voice.

A sardonic chuckle was the initial response.

"Well... I believe we're done here with Mr. Rufus Porter."

A horrible feeling swept over Hattie, and she pushed on the panel to escape, but it wouldn't budge. An instant later, a gun blast ripped through the parlor, followed by the sound of what she feared was her slain father sliding to the floor. She felt the life drain from her soul as someone threw open the secretary's bottom drawers. Loose papers and her father's leather books landing on the floor added to the horrific realization that the man she loved more than anyone other than Jonas was no longer responding to the continued violation of their home.

Papa's dead? It must be! It's my fault—I should've been brave! I shouldn't be in here! He's dead because of me!

The loud crack of a book being slammed shut in anger caused her to nearly jump further back into the little room's dimness.

"Farm journals and nothing that's of any use," said the leader disgustedly. "Check upstairs once more, and then the barn and outbuildings. Gather what you can and burn it all to the ground."

"What about the daughter?" the younger soldier asked. "Where should we look next?"

"Son... you heard the man. We already checked outside when we got here. She's likely in Columbia, as he stated. Besides, no father worth a damn before God would give up his little girl if she were here. Not when I could tell he fully understood what would happen once we found her. Tell Luther when he's done setting fire to the barn to burn this place next..."

The rest of what was said faded from Hattie's awareness as she collapsed upon the floor. She no longer cared if her presence was discovered. But by then, the marauding gang was busy busting out windows to aid the flames that would soon consume her beloved home, and perhaps scavenging for more silver in the kitchen. No one bothered looking behind the secretary... and she soon realized at least one reason for that omission.

As she steadied herself to sit up again, her left hand touched something wet and slightly warm. She gasped and held her fingers against the small sliver of daylight beneath the removable panel.

Blood covered her fingers.

Papa!

* * * * *

Hattie almost waited too long to escape from the hideout that spared her life.

Frozen by fear and a level of grief she could scarcely contain, it wasn't until the smell of smoke penetrated the tiny room that she finally mustered the strength to leave. By then, the men who had murdered her father had exited the house, and from what she could determine from their shouts outside, they were busy setting fire to every standing structure on her father's property.

Expecting a struggle to forcibly remove the wooden panel that had kept her hidden, she was surprised when it gave way easily, falling loudly to the floor behind the secretary. Flames had already engulfed much of the parlor, and she immediately understood that any noises coming from inside the house would surely be perceived as part of the building's demise by the bastards lurking about outside. The problem for her, of course, was she couldn't stay put much longer without succumbing to the smoke and flames aggressively devouring the walls and ceiling.

Rufus' corpse lay slumped over at the base of the secretary. It appeared he had been shot point blank in the head with his own shotgun. Hattie's grief became more volatile as anger and a deepening thirst for revenge shook her to the very core. What remained of her father's face was unrecognizable, and she didn't allow herself to linger on what the Yankee monsters had done to him, despite feeling the urge to throw herself into the encroaching flames to join him in death.

Marshalling her strength, she rushed toward the back of the house, armed with the loaded musket and Bowie knife Rufus had thrust into her hands just before hurriedly jamming the wall panel back into place. She prayed that the fire had not yet spread to the kitchen, as the only viable way out for her at the moment appeared to be the small door exiting the back of the house, next to the kitchen fireplace. Hopefully, it wouldn't bring her face to face with her father's killers—men who had openly threatened to do more than simply shoot Hattie if they found her.

The fire had reached the foyer, and fresh flames licked at the kitchen's doorway. Part of the foyer's ceiling collapsed just as she made it inside the kitchen. There would be no other path to exit the farmhouse, leaving only the aforementioned door in the rear of the room or the broken window facing the smoke house and corncrib as her options. Dusk was nearing, and the fire's orange glow seemed to be everywhere outside. Hattie glanced briefly through the window, dismayed that all of the outbuildings were fully ablaze. Tall flames leapt skyward from the barn.

Our home has become the latest sentinel of death! Dear God, please let whoever sees the dark smoke from our farm pack what they can and flee before the Yankees pay them the next deadly visit!

Whispering a second prayer—this time for her own protection—she unlocked the small door, carefully opening it and peering outside in both directions. The immediate area sat empty, but she heard shouts from a heated argument between two men coming from the east side of the house, angrily debating whether to stay and recapture one of the horses that had gotten away. Hattie took the opportunity to run to a blackberry thicket roughly fifty feet away, scraping her arms against the thorns as she dove behind the bushes for cover.

For the moment, she had avoided detection… and just in time.

A soldier, seemingly not more than sixteen years of age, came around the side of the house holding a torch. He seemed surprised by the open door, whipping his head around suspiciously—as if looking to confirm that someone had just exited the house. Hattie crouched lower to the ground, praying fervently he didn't notice her presence, and even more that he didn't alert the others.

"Randall, where the hell are you?" someone called from the front.

"I'm back here!" the kid shouted.

"We're leaving, so get your ass back out front!"

The soldier paused to survey the area more carefully, finally tossing the torch through the small door as he ran to rejoin his companions.

Hattie released the breath she'd been holding, but kept motionless, still fearing eventual discovery by the Yankees. She didn't move until long after the whooping and hollering ended, and all that remained was the roaring fire that had since engulfed the entire house and everything inside.

The tears came as a powerful torrent, and she wailed into the early night. She had lost everything. Yet she would've gladly traded it all—including her honor to the Yankee mongrels looking for women to rape—in exchange for her father's life. Beyond devastated, she didn't think she could go on. The murderous band of evil men had taken it all from her.

A sudden snort from behind caused her to jump, whirling around with her father's knife held menacingly in front of her.

"Elsie," she whispered in relief, taking a tentative step toward her father's prized Saddleback mare, whose soft golden color looked almost red in the firelight's glow. "So, it's you who got away from the Yankees!"

The horse nickered in response, lowering its head as Hattie stepped closer. Elsie's dark eyes blinked twice, as if in confirmation of Hattie's assessment.

"There, there, brave girl… It's all right."

Hattie was fearful the encroaching fire would spook Elsie, and wished she had something to offer the horse to keep her calm. But when Elsie nickered again and stepped closer to her, Hattie grew more confident the ten-year-old mare wouldn't take flight. She gently reached for Elsie's neck rein, pulling her closer while lovingly stroking the mare's neck and snout.

She looked back at the house and farm, where every structure was on the verge of collapsing into piles of fiery embers. There would soon be nothing left of the only home she had ever known.

Although left with a horse to ride, riding bareback would be uncomfortable. She pictured fleeing to somewhere safe, and hopefully nearby. Perhaps Braxton Carter's farm had escaped notice, since it seemed from the conversation of the Yankees that they had picked her father's farm specifically.

Hattie's heart froze as she suddenly recalled what one of the younger Yankees had said.

Nobody's up there… but a woman lives here, too—just like the bitch up the road told us!

"Bitch up the road?" She muttered in horror. "Oh my God, *Mary!*"

Hastily forgetting the Yankee menace could still be close, she laid the musket in the brush and placed the knife high inside her left sleeve. She then coaxed Elsie low enough for her to mount and set out for the Tarver farm.

Riding with her arms wrapped around Elsie's neck, Hattie waited until she was a mile away from her burning farm before allowing the horse to run at full gallop. She reached the Tarver farm, well illuminated by the moon just two days past its fullness. If not for the darkened farmhouse, she might've believed that Mary, John, and Nathan had escaped the notice of the marauding Yankees. The front doors to the barn and house stood wide open.

After carefully dismounting and listening for signs of life— either from beloved friends or newly-hated enemies, and confirming the presence of neither, Hattie stepped over to an unlit lantern lying on its side and picked it up. Since highly unlikely that either John or Mary had left it out in the yard, where the chickens would normally roam but were now absent, it seemed logical to her that the Union murderers had been here before visiting her father's farm. Though they had spared the Tarvers' farm and house a fiery demise, she knew in her heart that the reasons were not borne of mercy toward her best friend since childhood, nor to Mary's young family.

She made sure Elsie's reins were secured to a post nearest to the front porch and then waited to light the lantern until safely inside the house. All remained deathly quiet, other than her soft footsteps and the creak of doors and the floorboards as she moved through the main floor. Unlike her Papa's place, John and Mary's home was a sprawling one-story building, presently littered with broken furniture. The front window was smashed inward, as if John or Mary had refused to open the front door, and their visitors decided a new entrance would serve them just as well.

Nothing of value had been spared, as a treasured china cabinet lay on its side, the doors and glass broken. Other furniture was broken, too, and as Hattie moved toward the bedrooms, she became aware of death's pungent odor.

Even before she reached the bedroom shared by John and Mary, her vision was blurred by tears and she realized all too well that her whispered pleas to Heaven for mercy upon Mary, John, and even little Nathan had gone unheeded... uttered far too late to make a difference in regard to the heinous acts that had happened here—perhaps several hours before her father's torture and brutal murder.

The bedroom door stood ajar and the first hint at the horrors to come was Mary's bloody pantaloons lying on the floor, just inside the doorway. Mary's body lay in a pool of blood, viciously stabbed to the point that all Hattie could see was blood, along with the expression of terror in her lifeless eyes and her mouth frozen as a terrified scream. Mary's left hand appeared to be reaching for something... and when Hattie saw what it was, her own screams that she had managed to stifle could no longer be contained.

Nathan Tarver, not even four months old, lay motionless; the bayonet that had pierced his tiny heart, still in place. And the tear-streaked expression of bewilderment told of witnessing much, if not all, that had befallen his mother and father. It was more than Hattie could bear.

But she had to know what happened to John, and her last upward glance to the bed cemented the terrible scene into her mind, likely forever.

Rope-bound to the bed's backboard, John's face had been beaten to the point his eyes were swollen shut and his mouth a bloody mess. It appeared he had also been stabbed through the heart, and Hattie's initial impression was that he had died first, though likely not before his beloved wife was violated. She shuddered at the thought she might be wrong and he could've been the last to go, perhaps punished for the stubborn arrogance that her father had worried about.

All of it was far too terrible to bear, and Hattie fell to her knees beside Mary and Nathan, wishing even more that it was her and not them who had suffered the wicked designs of these monsters from the north. But knowing it was far too late to change the evil visited upon Appleton's farming community that day, she gathered the two corpses nearer to her, rocking and weeping until the advent of dawn the next morning.

Everything that mattered was now lost… forever. Thoughts of wanting to die that very day were combated by only two things: More than ever, she missed Jonas, and would no longer be satisfied waiting to learn of his fate. But from even deeper within her arose a desire both foreign and welcome, as a bitter balm to her grieving heart.

One way or another, she intended to exact her revenge against the Yankees… and she would make them *all* pay for what they had taken from her. It would be her mission, and if necessary, her dying quest.

Chapter Five

Tuesday, October 14th, 1862... Columbia, Tennessee.

The late afternoon sun finally broke through an overcast sky as Hattie Grey reached the southern outskirts of Columbia. Traveling by horse shortened the fifty-mile trip north from Appleton by several days, despite taking pains to ensure she didn't overwork Elsie. Her father had planned to re-shoe the mare in the coming weeks, since it had been nearly six months since Elsie's previous shoeing. But along with working through the grief of losing him and everything else that mattered to her, Hattie was forced to make do with what she had to work with.

The previous Saturday and Sunday were the worst, as struggling through tears and the shock of such a terrible and sudden change to her world had left her emotionally paralyzed. Even so, she mustered the strength to bury Mary, John, and little Nathan Tarver in their front yard Saturday afternoon. Hattie marked the graves with crosses she made from pickets salvaged from a small fence trampled the day before by the Yankees. She carefully carved each name, making sure the inscription was deep enough to last until someone else could create proper headstones. Then, after she finished tapping down the dirt on Nathan's grave, she offered a prayer asking for peace and comfort be given to all three as they now resided in the 'bosom of the Lord' until Judgment Day. She concluded her funeral service with an equally fervent prayer for God Almighty to help her avenge these senseless deaths, along with the murder of her father.

By then, Hattie already had an idea on how best to make that happen. She gathered up suitable clothing from John's bedroom dresser and small closet, since his slight build was a better match for her than her father's stout frame. Fortunately, she wasn't anywhere near as voluptuous as Mary had been, and she managed to find suitable linens to bind her breasts. Hiding the true identity of her gender seemed doable, except for one aspect she had agonized over. Upon summoning sufficient fortitude, she located a pair of scissors from inside Mary's vanity and set out to finish the conversion of her appearance from female to male.

Whispering a promise that her long wavy locks would one day return, she bound her hair back with some twine found in Mary's kitchen. Then she inhaled a deep breath for even more courage and slowly began cutting just above the binding. It took a few minutes to cut through her hair's thickness, but finally the last section gave way and she brought her left arm down to see nearly two feet of hair in her quivering hand. She closed her eyes, took another deep breath, opened them and looked in the mirror.

She couldn't help the nervous laugh that bubbled up when she saw her reflection. Her hair now ended just below her jaw line. Hot tears welled up, but she clamped her mouth shut in a determined taut line to keep them at bay. Hattie focused instead on what still needed to be done.

The green eyes that her father had always said were as beautiful as her mother's now burned with purposeful anger. And, despite the loss of so much of her soft blonde hair that once framed the delicate features of supple lips, nose, and high cheekbones, she still carried the subtle allure of an attractive woman. But at least the butchery she had successfully performed made her appear much less womanly and passable as a young teenage boy.

She decided to wear a side part with her hair brushed away from her face. It wasn't easy, given her hair's wave that was much curlier without the weight to smooth it out. When finished, she wrapped the cut hair inside some cloth, also from Mary's kitchen, and put it inside her knapsack. She hoped to sell it to a wigmaker for money that she knew she'd need.

Hattie then took John's saddle and fitted it to Elsie. She also took some bread that the Yankees missed from inside a hidden larder, along with John's canteen and shotgun. It pleased her to discover how perfectly the shotgun rested in the holster attached to the saddle.

With only a few hours of daylight left, she planned to spend the night inside the Tarver's barn, with designs on leaving Appleton in the morning. She would never be comfortable sleeping in the house where Mary and her family were brutally murdered, and felt only slightly better about sleeping anywhere on the property.

But before the day was over, she wanted to check on Jonas' parents, Milton and Eliza Grey, as well as fulfill her father's wish for her to unearth the supplies from behind the woodshed that he mentioned shortly before his death.

Hattie arrived at the Greys' homestead, and had been distracted by what she'd tell her beloved in-laws about what had happened to her father and best friend's family. Not to mention, how would she explain her appearance? With a flurry of volatile emotions simmering just below the surface, she expected to lose her composure and bawl like a baby, as she had done multiple times since the previous afternoon. The emotional toll from it all had left her drained, and she planned to share her intentions on joining the Confederate infantry with Eliza before mentioning any of it to Milton. She could readily picture her father-in-law's disdain and thought it best to tell Eliza first.

She was so lost in her thoughts that she failed to notice the two bodies lying haphazardly near the steps to the front porch. When she realized Milton and Eliza had encountered the same bloodthirsty killers that took everyone else away from her, she slid off her horse and ran to them. Sobbing uncontrollably, she desperately checked for signs of life, even though insects had already invaded the corpses and the stench of death was near overpowering.

Both had been shot in the back, as it appeared they were trying to run inside their home when killed. Perhaps, they had hoped to barricade themselves inside from the hostile marauders that may have already killed the Tarvers by then, and decided to raid the Greys' residence next before moving on to her father's farm.

Darkness had set in by the time she finished their burial in the family plot out back. She gathered a few keepsakes from their ransacked home to forever remind her of this couple whom she loved so dearly, along with items that had been set aside for Jonas after Ezekiel's passing earlier in the year. She vowed to keep all of it—including their wedding rings—safely hidden until her hoped-for reunion with Jonas. The spot she chose for this was the very same hiding place her father had mentioned. Thankful the moon's light was bright enough for her to find the spot near the woodshed's ashes, she first dug up the supplies mentioned by Papa. Hattie exchanged the blankets, cooking utensils, and a loaded Colt pistol that her father had purchased shortly after he returned home from the war in Mexico with the items taken from the Greys' homestead. A sad irony for her was the recovery of a small bag of gold coins that her father had hidden inside the blankets, as it brought to mind the wicked taunt from the faceless Yankee who soon pulled the trigger that ended her father's life.

Could it have saved Papa's life had he told the man about the gold?

Her heart told her that it wouldn't have changed anything. Witnessing the slaughtered bodies of the other Appleton residents that were dear to her only confirmed this conclusion.

Hattie took one last look at the farmhouse's ruins still smoldering from the fire, wondering if she should try to retrieve her father's remains for burial. Though her mind urged her to do it, something told her heart that lingering here was dangerous… that it wasn't beyond a possibility the men hoping to find her yesterday could return at any time. Lord knew what they'd do if they discovered a 'young rebel' rummaging around here. She'd likely be shot or hung from a nearby tree before anyone realized her true identity.

Thinking along those lines, she hastily returned to the Tarver farm, where a restless night awaited her in the barn. Lying in a straw-filled stall, she considered all that had happened and the great unknown awaiting her, along with the fear this could be the very last night she'd ever spend in Appleton, Tennessee…

With nearly three days behind her, she was now on the verge of reaching Columbia and hopefully the recruiting station that John Tarver had talked about. She figured it wouldn't be difficult to find, but if it wasn't an obvious place, she could ask someone for directions once she arrived inside Columbia's city limits.

There was also the issue of letting Stella, her sister, know what had happened in Appleton, where they both were born and raised. Hattie's sister had been estranged from their father for the past several years. Rufus was much stricter with his oldest daughter, and the final straw for Stella came when she eloped with Captain Frank Cooper, after falling for the dashing army officer during a visit with mutual friends in Clarksville, Tennessee. Rufus wasn't pleased that the two planned to marry so quickly, as Stella and the former West Point cadet had only known each other for several weeks prior to their announced engagement. His anger worsened when the pair suddenly decided to elope to Georgia instead, and returned as Mr. and Mrs. Frank Cooper.

As independent as Hattie considered herself to be, Stella was even more so, and had frequently butted heads with Papa while growing up. Against his wishes, Stella traveled to Clarksville shortly after her eighteenth birthday, to spend what was supposed to be a week with a niece of Braxton Carter, Bessie Watson, who presently attended a small women's college in the city.

At the time, Hattie could see Stella's point of view just as easily as their father's. The visit to northern Tennessee ended up lasting more than a month, once Stella met Captain Cooper. He had recently returned from New York to rejoin his family in Columbia. While visiting a fellow cadet in Clarksville, he was introduced to Stella. The couple soon fell madly in love and spurned advice to wait on getting married. With the prospect of her fiancé facing a long-term assignment in the United States army on the east coast, Stella accepted his request to elope before accompanying him to Washington, D.C. in the spring of 1858 for his initial assignment. Hattie could tell that Rufus took it much more personally than Frank's parents, and Stella elected to stay in Columbia with them instead of returning to

Appleton when the war broke out. By then, Frank had resigned his post to take a similar commission with the Confederate Army, and Stella's decision not to visit Appleton until after the war ended had driven the rift between father and daughter even wider.

Hattie remained on good terms with her sister, despite hardly ever hearing from her after what had happened between Stella and Papa. But now, she knew Stella would be completely devastated by the news of their father's passing. Worse, Hattie didn't know how to tell her without revealing her ruse as a man hoping to become a soldier. As Papa and most anyone else she knew would do, she expected Stella to try and talk her out of her plans to join the Confederate Army disguised as a man—as Mr. 'Henry' Grey. Moreover, it wouldn't be beyond Stella to expose her for the pretense alone—and certainly would do so under the impression that it would be for Hattie's own good.

It left her unsure of what to do—especially since her main focus at present was joining the Confederate fighting cause, come hell or high water. Still, she intended to let Stella know somehow, and likely in a way that would hurt her older sister much worse, due to Hattie's avoidance of telling Stella directly in light of the aforementioned risks.

"Can I help you find somethin' there, young feller?" asked an older man, with a long graying beard. He sat in a rocking chair on the depot porch as Hattie gently guided Elsie over the train tracks, just south of downtown Columbia.

Hattie looked up sharply and almost responded as she normally would, in a sweet angelic voice. But she caught herself in time.

"I just arrived from Appleton, down in Lawrence County," she replied, in the deepest voice she could muster, feeling her face flush when her voice cracked. "I'm looking for where I can sign up for the war."

The man studied her for a moment, shaking his head while pointing the stem of a long pipe in her direction.

"Son, that's mighty noble of you," he said, finally. "Especially knowin' how things are in these parts. The Good Lord's mercy is upon you, 'cause you're comin' here just two months after the Federals left us alone. Otherwise, they'd have strung you up for talkin' that way... I know where Appleton is. You're not likely to appreciate what I have to tell you next, but you've got a long journey still ahead."

"Oh."

That's all she could muster, since she thought for sure that John Tarver knew where the latest recruitment was taking place. She suddenly recalled that Jonas had originally gone to Camp Cheatham, near the Kentucky border—another several days ride by horse from Columbia. A sickening weight pulled on her gut and she began to worry her intentions might prove even more foolhardy than she had feared and for naught. Then she remembered the other two places John had mentioned.

"What about Murfreesboro?" she asked, hoping to not sound as desperate as she felt. "Have you heard of any recruitment for the war going on out that way?"

The old man nodded.

"Seems I've heard somethin' about that, but it's only fixin' to happen soon from the talk goin' on 'round here," he advised. "I heard somethin' about one of General Bragg's men roundin' up some boys to begin their drillin' next month. A commander from these parts named John Calvin Brown is overseein' the outfittin' of the new regiment. The Yankees imprisoned him up north until August, when he was exchanged for a pair of Union officers. 'Reckon you could venture out that way and learn more 'bout it."

Murfreesboro would be almost as far as Camp Cheatham…
but Hattie recalled something her father said about Cheatham
being taken over by the Union after the fall of Fort Donelson. It
seemed a safer bet that Murfreesboro was where she should go.

"Son, you can make it to Murfreesboro in two to three days
by horse from here, I reckon." The old man pointed his pipe at
her again, offering a near toothless smile. "But you'd be best
served to get your rest and wait 'til tomorrow evenin', or
another night to head that way. Them Yankees patrollin' the
back country won't hesitate to shoot a man or string 'em up if
they's suspected of supportin' the Southern Cause."

Hattie nodded, picturing what they'd likely do to a woman
with the same bent.

"Where can a feller get a room for the night and some
supper?" she asked.

The old man slowly stood and pointed toward town.

"There's a hotel on Market Street, toward the northwest
side of town, and there's a saloon across the street from it.
They'll likely refuse you liquor, but tell Beatrice Tanner that
Billy Robbins sent you and she'll get you fixed up with a hot
meal."

He laughed, and with a shake of his head replaced his pipe
in the corner of his mouth as he sat down and resumed his
rocking. She smiled politely while trying to picture the
directions the old man gave her. Hattie's plans had changed, as
her time in Columbia would likely be just a day or two before
setting out for Murfreesboro.

As she returned her attention to navigating the rails that
bisected the main thoroughfare into the city, she waved
goodbye to the old man. Then she headed up Main Street to
reach Market Street, veering to her left when she reached the
intersection and heading toward what sounded like a loud
ruckus. The commotion emanated from the "Two Oaks

Saloon", which sat across the street from the hotel described by Billy Robbins.

Boisterous men with exposed pistols strapped to their thighs stood on the porch outside the saloon's entrance, watching her approach. Hattie's heart raced with excitement, as she drew closer to a realm she had been excluded from previously. No chaste woman who wished to be considered of high moral regard would have dared to enter such a rowdy establishment.

Even though she had already embraced the idea of no longer being viewed as such a woman, it was a pretense she could still back away from. It wasn't too late, yet, to call off the entire affair and creep away as a grieving daughter, left to wait on her husband's safe return from a war that had already decimated her world. She could do that still… or she could step into a realm where danger was the only certainty. A place dictated by the whims and moods of unruly men—either coming from or going back to fight in the war.

Yes, danger… but also freedom once they see me as a man!

The thought became a silent mantra as she guided Elsie to a vacant post and stepped down, mindful to do it like her beloved Papa would. As she secured Elsie's reins, Hattie pushed the thought of her father from her mind. This couldn't be the place for tears. Then with chin up and the fire of Yankee hatred flowing through her entire being, she walked resolutely to the saloon's entrance, pausing only to quietly nod to the men who eyed her with some amusement.

She stepped inside… ready to fully embrace anything and everything that came her way as Mr. Henry Grey.

Chapter Six

Sunday, November 9th, 1862… Not far from Oxford,

Mississippi.

The frost-covered banks of the Tallahatchie River glistened in the early morning sun.

Jonas Grey found it mildly ironic that he continued to be drawn to such places, as the incessant pull caused by thoughts of his beloved wife and their cherished memories of Sugar Creek had become both a salve and a prickly briar to his lonesome heart. Granted, the Tallahatchie wasn't anywhere near as pristine as Sugar Creek, but still he embraced the crisp morning air of mid-autumn in northern Mississippi. He inhaled deeply before releasing his breath slowly… allowing for a moment of quiet revelry.

Much had changed in the past month, as not only had General Van Dorn not brought his cavalry back to Tennessee, but the general had also suffered the embarrassment of being demoted to an advisory role under General John Pemberton. Jonas' heart sank at the realization that there wouldn't be a return to Tennessee any time soon. As his friend, James Lewis, pointed out, Appleton was roughly one hundred and seventy-five miles away from their current location and would take a week's horse ride just to reach his home.

It might as well be five hundred miles, so long as I am prevented from visiting my wife. If only I could be approved for two week's leave, to check on Hattie and Rufus… and then Ma and Pa, too. Just a ride out east and then back here again, after making sure they're all right.

Meanwhile, the Confederates were on the run, as General Rosecrans and other Union forces continued to pursue Van Dorn after defeating his army at Corinth five weeks ago, on October 4th, and again the following day in a bloody confrontation at Hatchie Bridge, just over the border in Tennessee. To Van Dorn's credit, and a reason for Jonas to have gained a slight admiration for the diminutive general, his regiments had since vigorously pestered General Grant's supply lines throughout northern Mississippi. The decisive moves were an improvement over the hesitancy and over-confidence Van Dorn had been known for.

Despite multiple skirmishes with the Union and the ever-present danger of Yankee surprise attacks in retaliation for Van Dorn's actions, Jonas decided to approach the general about an overdue furlough. Distracted by an ever-increasing worry about Hattie and his family, which Jonas felt had greatly undermined his sharpness in battle, he beseeched Captain Lewis to speak to Van Dorn on his behalf. Not surprisingly, Jonas' commander refused to make the request—largely on account of the general's inflamed outlook following the recent damage inflicted upon his reputation.

"You'd be best served to wait a few more weeks, until we're done raidin' and have bivouacked for the winter," James advised, just two days earlier. "There'll be plenty of time for a furlough then, and gettin' one that'll last a month or longer."

But Jonas wasn't nearly as confident in that prediction as Captain Lewis. In spite of Van Dorn's recent demonstration of passionate leadership, his reckless temperament had resulted in high casualties to his assigned armies during the past eight months—a problem that hadn't abated. The skirmishes from the latest retreat through Mississippi had brought a new wave of death. Nearly every day he had lost more friends, and he couldn't picture Van Dorn letting up unless Grant's army retreated north of the Mississippi border.

That'll never happen....

Dried bloodstains on the sleeves and breast of his officer's coat told of several close calls during the past week, and there hadn't been much reprieve from the Union Army. Some of the blood came from slain comrades, but most belonged to Yankees killed in hand-to-hand combat when his company had been ambushed several days ago, just south of Abbeville.

So far, he'd been lucky—*damned* fortunate, truth be told. Being a Confederate officer, even on the low end of the pole, meant having a bull's eye on one's head, chest, and back. His latest hat bore fresh holes from Minié balls that had barely missed their mark. And after seeing so many men die in the past year, it wasn't likely he'd continue to emerge unscathed. Definitely not, if the war extended as deep into 1863 as James had heard mentioned in passing by the general and his colonels.

To date, Jonas had only been injured by a bayonet wound to his arm, at Shiloh in April, despite several bullets ripping through his coat and a former hat during the two days of fighting and the subsequent retreat that brought them to Corinth the first time. Miraculously, the lone bullet that did hit him left only a bruise after it glanced off the metal buckle of his holster.

Throughout it all, his thoughts were never far from Hattie and their home in Appleton…

As he gazed out onto the river's surface, he considered the advice given months ago by Clarence Tuttle, a private who hailed from Chattanooga and was a damned fine horseman: *"This war ain't for us or about us. Our sacrifice is for the rich plantation owners and nobody else, Jonas. I'm leavin' at the first chance, and you should too! Go home and take care of your wife and the rest of your kinfolk—same as what I plan to do. And I don't give a damn if they come after me or not… Whether I stay on or leave, I'm as good as dead. I'd rather take my chances with a bullet to the back from the provost than gettin' picked off unawares, likely the next time that wee little bastard, Van Dorn, sends us unprepared into battle!"*

Jonas wondered what had become of Clarence, who slipped away while they were headed down to Louisiana the past summer. Did he encounter the shame from dishonor that had kept Jonas from considering desertion? Jonas knew his own execution would be likely—either at home once the provost or 'home guard' found out he was there, or along the way. But, all he wanted to do was check on his family and then come back.

"I've got to make it home somehow, and as soon as possible… something's wrong," he whispered to himself, his chilled breaths rising into the air. "Hattie ain't responding to my letters, and I've seen the farms burnt to the ground here in Mississippi. It's coming to Tennessee soon, if it hasn't hit by now. I'll be damned if I let that happen to her and Rufus, or my folks!"

Both the Union and Confederacy took food and supplies from civilians, which had become an unfortunate necessity of the war. However, the Yankee raids left barely enough for the afflicted to survive. He had heard that things were getting worse all over. The enemy demanded more and more, while leaving even less for a victimized family to live on, and here lately, destroying their barns and houses…

The sound of a horse snorting startled him, and he was surprised that he hadn't heard the approach coming up from behind.

"Sorry, Lieutenant, you're requested back at camp." A tall horseman, Private Jim Bailey, tipped his hat as his long blonde hair fell forward. The meditative charm of the Tallahatchie had been broken. "Captain Lewis seems to be in the same foul mood from last night. Best not to test it."

"I suppose you're right," Jonas replied, releasing a tired sigh. "I'm coming."

Hattie's last letter from many months ago had been in his hands, and he carefully refolded it before returning it to his saddlebag and remounting his horse. The two men headed toward the tent line less than a quarter mile away, traveling mostly in silence peppered with conversation about the day's work awaiting them. All the while, Jonas' worries about Appleton remained at the forefront of his mind, along with the sinking feeling in his gut that his waiting to go home was already a grievous mistake.

Chapter Seven

Saturday, November 29th, 1862... Camped for drilling

just outside Murfreesboro, Tennessee.

This day promised to be different than what had become routine since late October, when Hattie arrived in Murfreesboro.

Nearly six weeks had passed since she found the camp for new recruits that the old man, Billy Robbins, had confirmed and Beatrice Tanner further assured would be there. By the time November arrived, she had also become used to the name of Henry Grey, and in many ways now thought of herself in masculine terms. But leaving Columbia almost didn't happen.

After coming close to being thrown out of "Two Oaks Saloon" when mistaken for a local vagrant youth who had stolen some pies and liquor from Mrs. Tanner, Hattie ended up striking a friendship with the middle-aged woman who had lost her oldest son to the war. Had it not been for Mrs. Tanner's determined efforts to interest Hattie, as Henry, in Beatrice's youngest daughter as a possible bride, Hattie might've stayed longer.

Being away from Appleton had given her time to better collect her thoughts and seriously consider what she was about to embark on. Joining the war as a real man was daunting enough, and during the week she spent in Columbia, she had seen the empty and haunted stares from those who had returned from the battlefields after losing an arm or a leg—sometimes both. Her unspoken assessment about these men was that they had lost much more than just a limb. Something eternally important had died in their eyes. From their words and her gut feeling, the war they had volunteered for wasn't the one they found waiting for them.

These wretched souls had obviously gone into the conflict with certain convictions and expectations that had been shattered. Would it be the same for her? Especially, since her desire to join the cause was fed by Yankee hatred and a desire to find a husband that had seemingly disappeared from the face of the Earth.

But on the morning of October 24th, she awoke with renewed fire and conviction to pursue her original course. By then, she had found her sister's home, located just north of Columbia. After thanking Beatrice for her kindness, Hattie set out to make up for two previous feeble attempts to engage Stella face-to-face. She gathered enough nerve to approach the front yard of the Cooper Italianate mansion. Having decided it was best to compose a letter and hand deliver it to one of the Cooper's house servants, she waited for one to emerge and successfully obtained a young girl's attention—long enough to entrust the letter to the girl with a gold coin and the understanding that only Stella would receive the letter.

The servant was only the second Negro that Hattie had met in her lifetime, and she was struck by the girl's beauty and affable warmth of personality. At first the girl refused the coin, but Hattie insisted, since she was ashamed to not have the courage to tell Stella in person what had happened to their father, amid fears her disguise as a man would only worsen the wound and add confusion. Not to mention, the chances of ending up in the Columbia jail for her masquerade was very real—or at least being detained by the provost until Hattie had renounced her scheme.

The risk of missing out on the only way she could realize her desire to find Jonas, or what had become of him, while also avenging Papa's death was too great. She hoped to make amends with Stella after the war ended, and silently prayed the Lord would whisper this intent to her sister's soon-to-be grieving heart.

Hattie had considered watching the front door from a safe vantage point, to see if Stella came to the entrance at the servant's behest. However, she figured it might be less painful to not be present in the event her sister actually emerged instead of Harrison Cooper, Stella's father-in-law, as had been the case when Hattie had ventured this far in her earlier attempts to make contact with Stella. *It's better for now to leave things in mystery, and trust in God Almighty to make things right in His time...*

She also debated leaving Elsie with Stella, given the tender condition of the mare's hooves. Upon recalling that Stella didn't bear the same fondness for animals that she did, Hattie thought it best if she journeyed to Murfreesboro and leave her father's cherished horse with a suitable farm that took a liking to Elsie near the city's outskirts.

The weather was cold and damp, making it difficult to cover as much ground as she had when traveling from Appleton to Columbia. She reached the western outskirts of Murfreesboro, Monday afternoon, October 27th. Hattie had found a small farm, less than two miles outside of town, where an elderly couple was quite grateful to receive a healthy working horse, since their horses had been confiscated by the Union Army several weeks earlier. Elsie's charms seemed to immediately capture Martha Wilson's heart, and her husband, Herschel, advised he was pleased to learn that Hattie's father had bestowed loving care upon the mare for many years. It left Hattie with a good feeling and she prayed that her father's spirit would be equally pleased, as she had done her best to tie up as many loose ends as possible before her enlistment.

She found a boarding house that evening, and it took much of what was left of the money buried by her father. Fortunately, Hattie received good news at supper that she would earn eleven dollars per month once she enlisted. The news came from the boarding house's proprietor, Abel Simms. Mr. Simms advised he had a nephew who enlisted earlier that year, and his dour expression lit up when he heard that one of his guests for the night, Henry Grey, intended to join the Southern Cause the next morning.

"You're just in time, Henry," Mr. Simms advised, while Hattie and four other guests dined on cold pork roast at a large dining table set in the house's front parlor. His narrow face was free of any lines or wrinkles until he smiled, which then revealed deeply dimpled cheeks partially hidden by an unkempt beard. "I heard just yesterday that General Calvin Brown's staff will be here soon, and some boys are already drillin' just outside town."

"So, it's not too late to sign up?" Hattie asked, mindful to keep her voice sounding as deep as possible.

"No, sir," Abel replied. "It's never too late to be recruited, and most of the boys your age and older have already been conscripted. Bein' from a nice quiet place like Appleton has made your wait to be notified longer than most, I reckon. So, consider yourself officially told this evenin' that you must join our noble cause against Northern aggression!"

Abel laughed lightly and was joined in the revelry by the other men sitting at the table. Only the wife of one abstained, and Hattie felt uncomfortable under her scrutinizing gaze, forcing what she hoped was a shy grin while avoiding anything beyond a mere glance at the woman. Meanwhile, she pushed Abel's comments about Appleton from her mind, since it would never again be a 'nice quiet place' after the murdering Yankee marauders had changed the town forever.

When it was time to turn in for the night, Hattie was left to share a bedroom with a boorish man named Frank. If she had known this arrangement awaited her, she likely would've saved her money and found a tree to sleep under. As it was, Frank tossed and turned for much of the night, keeping her up for most of it. She felt terrified he might roll over onto her side of the feathered mattress at any time, and inadvertently discover she wasn't a teenage boy after all.

When morning came, she allowed herself an extra cup of coffee at breakfast, and then set out for the campsite where Abel and another man directed her, just outside of town. Filled with anticipation, Hattie recalled the jubilation that Jonas, Ezekiel, and the other local young men who volunteered for the war in July 1861 had expressed before heading north to Camp Cheatham.

I'm here—I finally made it! I see the men going through the drills beyond the long double row of tents. There's the line of new recruits just ahead. It's finally happening! I'm here and it's...

As she stepped up to the line, greeted by a handful of blank expressions, it soon dawned on her that the rapturous excitement expressed by her husband and his older brother— along with every other Southerner she knew at the time that had joined the war effort—was missing. Not a single face wore an expression even close to delight. *Maybe it's the dreary cold*, she thought, *or they had to come from miles away, like me.* Yet, having an aversion to long travels and being outdoors contradicted what it meant to be a foot soldier. She wasn't fond of the cold, either, and she knew having insects crawl over her in the spring and summer would be annoying at best. But these aspects were expected, and considered a cost associated with finding Jonas while taking down the enemy that had stolen her life.

Even the attending officers seemed indifferent, and the lack of passion for the war hit her in the face like a bowl of frigid water.

"They all seem like undertakers 'round here," said a young voice from behind her. Unsure if the kid was addressing her or not, she merely glanced over her shoulder. "I know you seen it, too. They's actin' like the Yankees done won the war, and we're here just wastin' time, with no more purpose than gettin' killed."

"I had hoped for a better spirit," she said.

"Me too… but Pa says I can't come home 'til the killin's all done and the very last Yankee has skedaddled back north of Kentucky," said the kid, a blonde with hazel eyes who looked all of fifteen, if that. "The name's Lester Smith."

He held out his right hand for Hattie to shake.

"Henry Grey. Pleasure to meet you, Lester." She gripped his hand with the strength she'd often witnessed from her father when greeting male acquaintances.

"Same to you."

He smiled sheepishly, and she nodded before turning her attention back to the front of the line, where it appeared a local doctor was examining the mouth of a short stubby man in his mid-twenties. Hattie had heard much about the physical examinations required of new recruits, and was relieved to learn that what used to be a bare-chested exam in early 1861 was now an abbreviated routine that included checking a recruit's eyesight, condition of their teeth, and having them jump and bend to check the joints. The examination would end with a handshake test to make sure the grip was strong.

Ever fearful of discovery, Hattie ended her exam with an even stronger grip of the doctor's hand than she had given young Mr. Smith, and it seemed to surprise the physician. She didn't linger, moving on to a tent that was open on both sides. The recruits ahead of her were reading documents placed before them and signing what she assumed was their name at the bottom of the page. Although quite literate, she barely read the contract that indentured her soul to the Confederate Army for the duration of the war. With nowhere else to go, she had no intentions of leaving any time soon.

Next came the issuing of a full infantry uniform, coffee cup and cooking hardware, blankets, and a small tent for which she overheard an explanation that it would double up with another soldier's half to make a single tent large enough to support two grown men once the flaps were buttoned together. As she expected, the guns she brought would have to suffice. Ammunition for the musket and pistol were provided only for that day, along with a stern warning not to waste it and that additional bullets and powder would be rationed daily until it was time to leave camp and officially join the fighting.

The little tent that would be joined with another half brought unpleasant thoughts of the night before—especially if she were forced to share close quarters with one of the larger men joining up that day. The issue dominated her thoughts as she gathered her other supplies and emerged to the brisk afternoon that awaited her at the recruitment tent's other side. A staff sergeant directed her and the other recruits to where they would bivouac, with drills set to begin for the group later that afternoon.

"Hey, Henry," said the kid from earlier, running to catch up to her. "Would you be opposed to sharin' your dog-tent with me?"

Obviously, Lester Smith was as leery about sharing his half of a tent with one of the older men in their group of nearly twenty recruits as she.

"I reckon it'd be all right."

In truth, she felt relieved and somewhat drawn to the slender boy who stood slightly shorter than her. Almost like a younger brother of sorts. Even so, she intended to keep her guard up, fully aware that her pretense would be especially vulnerable while familiarizing herself with this new environment.

Within the hour, the run-through of basic drills began with the sergeant assigned to teach the latest new arrivals. The session lasted until dusk, with the promise of resuming after breakfast the next morning…

Six weeks later, the daily routine of drilling with her fellow infantrymen had turned what at first seemed confusing into second nature. For eight to twelve hours every day (except for Sunday, when it was cut to six hours), Hattie and her new cohorts drilled as squads and in company formations. All of it was necessary to get accustomed to orders and properly falling into formations, such as marching in a column and the correct version of a 'company front'. By the end of November, she had become quite comfortable with how to face properly, dress the line, and interact in step with her fellow soldiers.

Having read the Revolutionary War memoirs that her father kept in the parlor's old secretary, along with the journal of his own experiences from the Mexican-American War, she understood not much had changed in terms of tactics and strategy during the past few centuries. In addition, Rufus had taught her how to properly use a gun at the age of twelve. All of it made tasks, such as how to properly guard mount and efficiently load and prime a musket, easier for her than it was for many of the older recruits.

When the moment came to be introduced to her new commanding officer, William Thomas Powers, Hattie could hardly contain her excitement. She'd finally see action in the war, and soon. Captain Powers, who preferred to be addressed as 'Billy', had been part of Crews Battalion, Tennessee Infantry, since January that year. But after casualties and illness decimated the regiment, the Ninth Regiment of the Kentucky Mounted Infantry absorbed what was left. Eventually, another reorganization brought the former first lieutenant his current promotion to Captain, as head of B Company in the newly formed Twenty-Third Battalion, Tennessee Infantry.

Under the auspices of General Brown, Captain Powers arrived with nearly a dozen seasoned veterans whom Hattie assumed were there to help assimilate the new recruits into the Twenty-Third. Powers studied a document handed to him by one of the camp's drilling sergeants. After roll call had finished, the captain regarded her with steel blue eyes while commenting about Appleton, stating he had once rode with a fine cavalryman named Ezekiel Grey. He wondered aloud if 'Henry' was of any relation to 'Zeke'.

"He was my cousin," Hattie lied, fighting to retain a calm outward façade while her pulse quickened. *Does this man know Jonas? Maybe he knows where my husband is! Maybe....*

"Well, he was a damn good soldier... a mighty fine man." Captain Powers shook his head as if reminiscing about Jonas' deceased older brother. "Died too young, like so many. I hear he had a brother also join the cavalry, but I've never had the privilege of knowin' him. Hopefully, you'll do your family just as proud, young Henry."

He saluted, to which Hattie responded in kind. She smiled as well... until she caught one of the captain's companions staring at her. The soldier frowned while studying Hattie, and though it certainly wasn't the first time she had been regarded suspiciously by a fellow soldier during the past month and a half, there was something off... something different about this person.

It wasn't until Hattie decided to meet this soldier's sullen gaze straight on that she became aware of a very inconvenient revelation. As the soldier's eyes locked onto hers, they communicated the truth silently... but also purposefully in the way only females could do.

The soldier was a woman.

Chapter Eight

Friday, December 5th, 1862… Murfreesboro, Tennessee.

Considering potential obstacles that she might encounter in her search to find Jonas, while exacting revenge for those she lost in Appleton, Hattie never expected to come face-to-face with another woman pretending to be a male soldier. Such a reality was the furthest thing from her mind, leaving her completely unprepared to deal with it.

Maybe I should leave. I could slip away and try to find another recruitment site and start over.

During the past month and a half, she had gained valuable infantry skills that could benefit her while also providing a stronger ruse as a man. But slipping away and rejoining the Confederate Army elsewhere would likely mean going to Memphis or possibly another state.

And, how in the hell would that work? For one thing, I no longer have a horse!

Even if she could reclaim Elsie, and miraculously discover that her beloved mare now had healed hooves and new shoes from a blacksmith, traveling to Memphis meant a journey of almost two hundred and fifty miles to the west. Not to mention, there might not be any recruiting going on when she got there—or anywhere else for that matter.

Despite the powerful urge to flee, what kept it from becoming something she'd act upon was the realization that where there was one woman, and now verifiably two, surely it meant there were other women elsewhere disguised as male soldiers. There could be a wide variety of motives for joining up, either with the South or the North. And the most frightening aspect she now understood was they'd all likely know one another's true sex from the moment their eyes met.

Hattie had no doubt the woman soldier she sought to avoid in the Twenty-Third Battalion was just as thrilled as she about sharing space in a small regiment. The men around them appeared oblivious about a potential catfight that could erupt at any time, as the hostility Hattie felt emanating toward her from the dark-haired woman with intense brown eyes had yet to abate nearly a week after Hattie's introduction to Captain Powers.

It wasn't until the morning after the announced assignment of General Brown's army to General Braxton Bragg's much larger force that the unspoken distrust between them was finally broached. It happened shortly after daybreak, Friday. Hattie had just taken care of her personal business and was returning to the tent she shared with fellow private, Lester Smith, when another veteran soldier stepped out from behind a frost-covered juniper bush to block her way.

Malcolm Bates had introduced himself the afternoon following the Twenty-Third's arrival, questioning why the two youngest boys among the recruits had been allowed to bivouac without an adult soldier present to keep an eye on things.

"Seems you two could use an experienced soldier to keep you straight," he had said to Hattie back then. "You'll stay safe and out of trouble with me watchin' your backs."

Hattie had never before experienced a predatory feeling like the one emanating from this grizzled forty-ish man with cold gray eyes. The gooseflesh on her arms and along her neck had stood on end as he waited for her response.

"We'll be all right," she had replied, curtly, worried this man might approach the company sergeant, Joe McCracken, or Captain Powers himself to override her rebuff. Even so, she held her ground. "But we're much obliged."

She recalled forcing a bright smile, to which he nodded in silence, while his gaze regarding her was like a wary copperhead whose nest she had just disturbed....

Now, just five days later those same cold eyes regarded her hungrily. She worried Malcolm somehow knew she wasn't really a teenage boy. He leaned against a large elm with his right leg blocking her path. Picturing several ways this might play out, she prepared herself for the worst while intending to move past him. He stood a good six inches taller than she and, by her guess, outweighed her by forty to fifty pounds.

If he blocks me, I'll push through... But if he grabs me, I'll have to pull my knife and bring it to his neck. Hopefully, it won't take more than that to get him out of my path.

"No, I don't think so," he growled, as she moved to step past his feet while glaring at him sullenly. "You and I need to have a little talk."

His menacing haughtiness disappeared in mid-sentence, and the intimidating confidence was suddenly replaced by a look of surprise. He glanced warily over his shoulder.

"This ain't your concern," Malcolm snarled at someone unseen by Hattie. Whoever it was had come up quietly behind him. "Go on, Louis. Get on out of here—"

The sound of a pistol being cocked shut him up, and he raised his hands while a nervous smirk pulled on the corners of his mouth.

"No, I don't think so, Malcolm," said this person named Louis. "I've got a different proposal for you. How about you get your own ass on out of here, and I won't tell Billy Powers about your sleepin' while on picket the other night? Keep your goddamned eyes to yourself and your mouth shut tight, or you can count on a little rendezvous with Sergeant McCracken's bloodied whip. Understand?"

Hattie had heard that falling asleep during guard duty was an offense punishable by either thirty lashings or worse. Their new commander, General Braxton Bragg, was rumored to have hung some pickets for failing to stay awake. Malcolm grumbled that he understood.

Meanwhile, she couldn't hide her own surprise in regard to the mysterious visitor's voice, as Hattie immediately recalled hearing it several times in passing during the past week. The alto timbre, much deeper than hers, carried a slight feminine edge. *Sweet Jesus, it's the other woman in camp... What do I do now?* While quietly debating on which menace was worse, Private Bates stormed angrily back to camp. Hattie found herself up close and personal with the soldier she had desperately sought to avoid, Private Louis Templeton.

"So, Henry Grey, it appears we finally have a moment to discuss the difficult quandary we've found ourselves in," said Louis, holstering the pistol. "Perhaps you can enlighten me about who you are. And, I do mean who you *truly* are?"

"What do you mean?" Hattie asked, warily.

"Don't play coy here, missy!" Louis hissed, her eyes flashing in sudden anger. "You might be able to fool the men with your ease in handlin' a musket, but you're no more a man than—"

"Yes I *am* a man!" Hattie shot back, feeling a surge of rage rise from deep within her. "You don't know *anything* about me!"

Louis pushed her up against the tree, covering her mouth with a grimy hand while peering around the tree as if fearful someone else might show up and interrupt the interrogation. Hattie was amazed at the soldier's physical strength, as the woman's brawn rivaled that of Jonas and her father. She felt frail in comparison, and ashamed when Louis easily thwarted her efforts to free herself and then try to draw her knife from its holster on her belt.

"Now, we're goin' to try this one more time," Private Templeton whispered. "Who... are... *you?*"

Hattie refused to answer, but felt the sting from burning tears elicited by the anger that continued to bubble up from within. Her assailant's own heated stare softened, as Louis nodded knowingly.

"All right. If that's the way it has to be, I'll go first." Louis released a low sigh before glancing around the tree again. When apparently satisfied the pair were in no immediate danger of being discovered, she eased her grip on Hattie, and took a few steps back. "My real name is Lucinda. Lucinda Marie Templeton."

She waited for a response from Hattie, who continued to hold out, massaging her sore arms that were likely bruised from being roughed up a moment ago.

I can't tell her who I am... it's too dangerous! Tell her, and I'll lose the power of my secret!

"I've been in this war since near the beginnin'," Private Templeton continued. "There have been others like you and me, and the ones that have kept to themselves and resisted the friendship of those like us have invariably been discovered. You can't hide every aspect of your womanhood, no more than the rest of us. So, you can either continue to go it alone and be out of my hair in a month or two... Or you can sleep better at night, knowin' you have at least one ally in Captain Powers' regiment. How about it?"

Hattie's response was a blank stare, while her mind raced.

This woman talks as if there are many more like us. If so, how many? What in the hell have I got myself into?

Hattie's adversary laughed quietly while shaking her head.

"All right... Be difficult," she said. "If you're anythin' like me and the few other gals I've come across since the war started, I'm guessin' your real name is somethin' similar to Henry or the name of a dead relative held dear. Ain't I right about that?"

Hattie leaned back against the tree, glaring at this impudent woman... this *Lucinda*. The soldier's one-week presence in her life had hampered the already difficult adjustment from orphaned daughter and possible widow to infantryman. Her gut told her things could get even worse if she cooperated... or perhaps better? There was no way to know for certain.

"Ah, I do believe I've hit a nerve in that regard. So, is it the name of your pa? Maybe it's a brother, or a cousin or uncle? After all, it sounded kind of true when you said your cousin was Billy's pal, Ezekiel. Maybe you're his kid sister, instead, with a name like Harriet, Hazel, Helen, or—"

"Hattie!" she blurted out in a hissed whisper, stopping herself from saying anything else to avoid an emotional deluge of tears threatening to follow. She bit her tongue and waited for the painful surge to retreat before going on. "Hattie Grey. Are you satisfied?"

The soldier she now knew as Lucinda, and not Louis, Templeton laughed and shook her head.

"Satisfied? Ah, hell no!" She smiled roguishly. "But it's a start. For the time bein', you don't make life uncomfortable for me, and I'll do the same for you, Hattie Grey."

She extended her hand to shake, but Hattie was unwilling to reciprocate.

"I'll not bite, and hell, who knows? We might take a likin' to each other someday and protect each other's backs." She stepped toward the path leading back to camp. "I imagine they'll be lookin' for us soon, so pull yourself together, soldier. See you around."

Lucinda offered a congenial grin before slipping out of view.

For a moment, Hattie couldn't move. It was as if the wind had been knocked out of her. Her secret was gone… but as she thought about it, she realized it was truly inevitable at some point. Oddly, it surprised her that she felt a little relieved. The fact her surreptitious actions would no longer be a mystery to Louis "Lucinda" Templeton was offset by the fact they shared the same furtive existence.

And there are others. We equally have as much to lose or gain.

The thought quickened Hattie's resolve and gave her renewed hope that things could work out. It brought a slight smile as she hurried back to camp. She wasn't alone.

Chapter Nine

Sunday, December 14th, 1862... Savannah, Tennessee.

Saturday's sleet-filled afternoon and the news of burgeoning Yankee patrols had deterred Jonas from his quest to return to Mississippi, forcing him to head north and seek shelter in Savannah, Tennessee. The delay was followed by snow on Sunday amid reports of an impassable Union presence hovering along the Mississippi and Alabama state lines.

"You should wait until they clear out, son, since they've been hangin' any stray Rebels they come across," advised Elmer Langford, whose saloon Jonas had stepped into Sunday afternoon for a reprieve from the weather. The older gentleman with light gray eyes, and a goatee that reminded Jonas' of his grandfather's beard, allowed Jonas to stable his horse behind the saloon. "I believe we've lost enough young men already... you can stay here until it's safe to move on."

"Much obliged," Jonas replied, grateful but unable to muster a smile on account of the shattered state of his heart and soul. "I'll press on in the morning."

Elmer nodded thoughtfully. "I see you're a cavalry soldier, Lieutenant," he said. "I also hear that Earl Van Dorn's down in Mississippi. Is that whose army you're with?"

"Yep," said Jonas, wishing he had taken the offer of whiskey instead of a hot cup of coffee. "And it appears I'm going to be returning to camp a few days later than promised."

"So, you're returnin' from furlough?"

"Uh-huh."

"I see." Elmer stepped over to one of the front windows, wiping away the condensation to peer outside. "The snow's still comin' down steady. We could have ice if it changes back to rain tonight."

Jonas nodded without looking up from his cup, where the warmth wafted up to his face. His nose and cheeks tingled after being exposed to bitter cold for more than an hour while he futilely sought a passable road to resume his quest to reach Mississippi. But after discovering two more Yankee patrols combing the area, he returned to the main square, hoping to find shelter and protection from the elements, as well as from the enemy scouring Savannah's southern perimeter.

Had he encountered the same Union surveillance on the way to Appleton a week earlier, he would've had no choice but to immediately return to Water Valley, the latest campsite for General Van Dorn's army under the watchful eye of General Pemberton. In hindsight, he now cursed his good fortune in encountering only a smattering of Yankees by comparison, along with clear weather all the way to Appleton. His arrival home could've been delayed by at least another week had he pressed on through the same opposition he encountered on his return trip to Mississippi; a journey that followed the same route until it became obvious he would likely perish by gunfire, the end of a rope, or nature's unpredictable wrath.

Maybe I should've just let it happen. Things might be better on the other side of Death's Veil... or at least easier.

"Well, if you decide to stay until the weather improves, I've got plenty of cured pork and beef to share, since it's just me." Elmer stepped over to the end of the bar where Jonas nursed his coffee. "You can use the spare bed in back to sleep, and there's plenty of hay for your horse."

"I'm grateful for your kindness, sir." Jonas looked up from his cup, mustering a weak smile. "When the weather lets up, I'll have to find a way to reach Mississippi before the Yankees discover my presence. Have they been in here as of late?"

Elmer shook his head. "Not since Albert Franklin Beaufort returned to Columbia."

"General Beaufort was here recently?"

"Less than a month ago... and a nephew of mine told me just yesterday mornin' that the general is on the move again, having left Columbia. Johnny followed the cavalry halfway to Clifton, before he broke off to head south to Lawrenceburg."

"When was that?" An idea suddenly occurred to Jonas, and though it might not work, it seemed like a better idea than chancing the gauntlet waiting for him south of town.

Elmer shrugged. "I suppose it was the day before yesterday. Friday."

If Beaufort traveled with artillery, which Jonas had heard was a battle aspect favored by the general, then maybe there was a slim chance he could catch up to his army.

"Your nephew's certain that General Beaufort was headed to Clifton?"

"Yes, sir," Elmer confirmed, nodding as if he pictured the previous day's conversation. "Johnny said one of the men mentioned General Beaufort wanted to cross the Tennessee River and felt that Clifton was the best place to do it this time of year."

"Well, how about that." Jonas' smile widened at the irony he might soon meet the war hero he admired from afar, until he considered the general might also be the man to either imprison or execute him on the spot. Regardless of his fate, Jonas felt it would be better left in the hands of his Confederate cohorts. He sent a silent request heavenward for a clear morning, and turned his attention to what Elmer Langford had in the way of cured meat, pleased his appetite that had been absent for the past few days now returned.

In spite of dreary skies the following morning, the worst of the weather on December 15th appeared to have moved east. After Elmer loaded him down with enough cured pork, beef, and coffee to last a few days, Jonas parted ways with the saloon owner, grateful again for his fortuitous hospitality. He headed north to Clifton, preparing himself for what he would tell General Beaufort, if in time to intercept his army's progress to the west. Surely, he'd have to explain why his two-week furlough—the longest he had been granted in over a year— proved inadequate. Jonas would have to tell the general the truth and prayed he wouldn't suffer an emotional breakdown while doing so. Maybe there would be mercy, or maybe not, in respect to the heartbreak regarding the recent and still raw news of his beloved wife's death, along with the loss of his father-in-law, best friend, and his own parents—all murdered by a gang of Yankee marauders.

When he had arrived in Appleton on December 9th, after leaving northern Mississippi on the 1st, Jonas was dismayed that it took an extra day beyond the seven days he had hoped it would take to reach his home. Although nowhere near as difficult then as now, getting past the Yankee patrols he encountered upon leaving Water Valley had proven harder to elude than expected. It was the factor that almost prevented the furlough in the first place. Colonel James Wheeler finally agreed to sign off for him, after Jonas and James Lewis presented Jonas' impassioned plea to check on his family, following newly confirmed reports of pillaging taking place in the southern region of Lawrence County, Tennessee.

Jonas was further dismayed to see several buildings burned to the ground in what had been the town's square. One of the home guards, Billy Gibbs, caught up with him before he headed for Appleton's northern outskirts, where the Porter farm and his parents' homestead were located.

"I assume you have your furlough proof, Lieutenant Grey?" Billy eyed him solemnly while extending a gloved hand to receive Jonas' permission proof for his return home.

"Well, hello to you too, old friend," Jonas replied, his words clipped curtly in response to the cool welcome from his former childhood pal. "I'm approved to be here with Colonel James T. Wheeler's blessing, as you'll soon confirm."

He retrieved the document from his saddlebag and handed it to the guard. Meanwhile, his alarm about what had caused the fire damage pushed its way to his mind's forefront. He waited impatiently for Billy to review the furlough pass and hand it back to him.

"What happened here?" Jonas asked, after he returned the document to its protective home. "Just a guess... but I assume the storehouse next to the general store didn't burn to the ground on account of a lightning strike."

"That would be correct." Billy nodded. "Old man Johnson forgot about a lit stove in the storehouse, and by the time the fire woke him and his wife, the flames had already claimed much of the building."

"You don't say?" Jonas couldn't hide his contempt—especially since he never recalled Amos Johnson keeping such a stove in his storehouse. He also noticed a smaller building used for storing livestock feed across the street from the

Johnsons' store was burned to the ground as well. "If the fire happened as you stated, and wasn't caused by a ricocheting bolt sent to the Earth by Zeus himself, then it appears some other miracle spread the blaze to the only other storage building owned by the Johnsons. Unless terrible misfortune found them again soon after the first incident."

"It was indeed two fires, with the other being unsolved," Billy responded testily, his green eyes flashing angrily beneath the shadow of his dark bangs. "You can talk to Amos yourself, if you doubt the truth of what I'm telling you."

He pointed to the general store, which was already closed for the day.

"Maybe I will. But if you'll excuse me, I'm here to visit my wife and family."

Billy moved to stop him.

"Jonas… you'd be best served to not head out that way. A wave of sickness swept through there last month. It might not be wise or safe—"

Jonas cut him off, eyeing him suspiciously. "That'll be for me to determine, Billy. In the meantime, shouldn't y'all be keeping an eye out for Yankee mischief?"

"That's *exactly* what we're doin'."

The growing uneasiness that had been with Jonas since early October made it impossible to wait any longer to check on his family's welfare. He pushed past Billy, spurring his horse to full gallop.

Despite the horse's weariness after being ridden mercilessly for much of the past week, and his own exhaustion compounded by minimal sleep since leaving Water Valley, Jonas rode as swiftly as possible to reach his father-in-law's farm. Billy pursued him from a safe distance, but close enough to where Jonas remained an easy shot, if gunning a man down in the back suited him. Jonas had already witnessed where the war created enemies among best friends, and he felt certain that whatever deceptive reason Billy or any other home guard had for trying to stop him from reaching his home, it could be one worth killing for. It would be regrettable if Jonas were forced to shoot the man who was once quite close to him and his older brother, Zeke.

As soon as the burned-out remains of the farm came into view, Jonas' heart sunk. Not that he had expected things to be like they were during his brief stay in late June. He had known instinctively for a while that something was wrong... something not quite right back at home. Witnessing the burned-out buildings in town reminded him of what he had recently seen in Mississippi. Even so, seeing the blackened piles of charred lumber that had once been the barn and the house he shared with his beloved wife and her father ripped asunder his burdened heart.

He slowed his approach while hearing the hooves of the guard's horse coming up fast behind him. Halting and then sliding off the hearty stallion picked for him by his pal, James Lewis, Jonas' legs felt as if they'd give way at any moment. The nightmarish scene surreal, he staggered toward the house, all the while ignoring the calls from Billy for him to hold up and wait for him.

At first, he didn't see the gravesite, and almost missed it due to the haphazard pair of crosses made from walnut branches scavenged from the woods nearby. *No names... not even that simple honor given to my wife and Rufus. Just four sticks hastily tied to form two markers.*

He fell to his knees between the twin burial mounds, while a rush of uncontrollable emotions and thoughts cruelly assaulted his mind and heart.

"They were dead before the Yankees came and plundered what was left," Billy advised from behind him. His horse's nicker and snort confirmed he had yet to dismount. The war had heightened Jonas' survival instincts, and he quietly unbuckled his pistol's holster and began to slide out his Remington revolver. "Doctor Steadman says it was most likely cholera, and nearly every resident on this side of Appleton was infected. Many died... includin' just about everyone along this road."

Jonas couldn't immediately respond, while tears blurred his vision. Tortured memories of his happiest days on Earth—all with Hattie—overrode all else.

"Have you visited my folks' place? The Tarvers? The Edwards and Carter homesteads?" Jonas finally asked, his voice reduced to a shaking murmur.

"Braxton Carter survived, as did George and Bessie Edwards," said Billy, his tone unsettlingly steady. "But the young Tarver family, and sorry to say, your parents, all succumbed and were buried before we were notified about the fatalities."

Fatalities? He talks like Van Dorn... as if my family and friends were merely victims of some evil they had volunteered to face.

"And were the other buildings burned to the ground like what happened here?"

Like they were in town?

"No, Jonas," Billy replied after a moment of silence, as if collecting his thoughts. "Apparently, the Yankees were scared off before they reached your folks' homestead and the Tarver farm. Likely, they had learned of the pestilence that claimed a dozen lives in total. We consider ourselves fortunate in this region, as the Yankee looters and the cholera outbreak have both moved on since."

Jonas snickered in his misery. He readily recalled the farms he saw destroyed in Mississippi, along with reports of destruction and murder throughout the southern region—and even worse deeds—that went far beyond what was considered acceptable behavior in civilized war.

"Do you truly expect for me to believe that the good people of Lawrence County—and here, especially in Appleton—are fortunate the looters didn't linger to cause more harm than you've described? And, as for the cholera outbreak… it doesn't just show up and leave, as if it had an appointment elsewhere to keep!" Jonas was unable to remove his gaze from the pair of graves next to him, but rose to his feet. "And, do you take me for a fool who would believe that the destruction of an unoccupied farm—as you claim this one had become prior to the Yankees' arrival—was merely an aberration, when their obvious purpose in doing so has been to make homeless the residents within?"

There was no response… just the click of a revolver being cocked. Jonas immediately understood he had crossed a line forged in secrecy and deceit. As he peered over his shoulder toward Billy's horse, standing less than ten feet behind him, he asked again if the guard viewed him as a fool in order to disguise the sound of his own pistol being readied for firing.

"It didn't have to come to this. You should've stayed away." Billy aimed his pistol at Jonas. "You should've—"

Jonas' instincts took over. Resigned to the likelihood of his demise, and ironically upon the spot his beloved had been laid to rest, he drew his gun and fired. His quickness caught Billy off guard, and the bullet struck the guard in the left shoulder, knocking Billy from his horse. Jonas was on him before he could take aim again, striking Billy's gun from his hand while throwing him to the ground. Jonas brought his Bowie knife up against his adversary's left carotid artery.

"No more bull!" he hissed, pinning Billy to the ground with his knees upon the guard's chest. "If you want to go on living, you'll tell me the truth about what happened!"

"I don't know what you're talkin' about—*owww!*"

Jonas jabbed the tip of his knife into the weeping wound in Billy's shoulder.

"All right! All right!" he screamed in agony.

Jonas let up, but held Billy firmly pinned beneath him.

"Tell me everything you know, or so help me God, I'll kill you!"

What proceeded from the guard's lips left far more questions than answers, and during the next several hours, Jonas confirmed as much as possible from what Billy Gibbs revealed under duress. The gravesites for Hattie and Rufus contained only skull fragments and a handful of other bones, since the fire had consumed everything else. Doc Steadman's examination had determined the bones were likely those of Rufus, although it remained possible that the tibia—which crumbled upon the physician's touch—might've been Hattie's, given the fact she stood almost as tall as her father.

The graves for his parents and for the Tarver family were already completed by the time the home guard contingent arrived to assess what the Yankee pillagers had left in their wake. The mystery of who had taken the time to bury the dead with their names engraved on the crosses hadn't been solved. Obviously, it had to be someone who knew them all... Bloodstains on the porch of the Grey homestead, and the heavier blood stains in Mary and John Tarver's bedroom told of the wickedness visited upon these families and two others further up the road.

Billy pleaded for Jonas to not pursue the murderous gang of Yankees, for fear they would come back and bring even more carnage and destruction. Not to mention, Jonas' corpse would likely be hanging from a tree somewhere in the vast Lawrence County wilderness to the west, where the enemy had headed next.

Jonas wondered if swinging from a rope wouldn't suit him best, although he didn't wish for evil to return to Appleton. While leaving Billy tied to a large pin oak until the next morning's sunrise, he debated on what to do next. The very reasons he had joined the 'Cause against the North' were now gone, buried forever with those he loved. From there, it became a contest between suicide and murder... someone would pay for what had happened. Either it was going to be him—now that he had nothing to live for—or more Yankees, having already slain dozens in battle during the past year and a half.

The verdict, for now, was to go on living. But God help any and all Yankee soldiers that crossed his path. He vowed to spare none.

He released Billy the following morning, December 10th. The home guardsman's shoulder injury had worsened, leaving him disadvantaged in defending himself. Still, Jonas decided to keep his weapons anyway. After making sure Billy's horse continued on to town with him tied to the saddle, Jonas took a less traveled route toward western Tennessee...

Now he was headed north to Clifton that Monday, December 15th, and rain fell relentlessly the entire way. Even so, Jonas expected to arrive before nightfall. He worried Franklin Beaufort's army might already have reached the Tennessee River by then... but as he approached the town he saw the Confederates were in the early stages of crossing. There was still time to engage them, and he sought the provost pulling up the rear.

As he had hoped, Jonas was escorted at gunpoint to the general's presence. General Beaufort appeared to be keeping a watchful eye upon the creation of two flatboats near the river's edge for the intention of ferrying his men and horses across the river, while several canoes had begun carrying men to an island that wasn't much more than a sandbar. A low fire had been lit there. Other than the provost's torch as he escorted Jonas, all other firelight was absent. Jonas wasn't sure at first if this was on account of the rain, or if, as the provost had mentioned, Beaufort was mindful to keep out of sight for any Union gunboats in the area.

The general seemed agitated when Jonas was brought to him, and likely on account of the painstaking task of crossing the river under such foul conditions that would take longer than originally anticipated.

"Who in the hell is this, James?"

"Sir... it's one of Van Dorn's riders," the provost replied, clearing his throat.

Jonas noticed that the young man, who was only slightly older than himself, seemed much more nervous than he had been just moments ago, when demanding to see Jonas' furlough document. *Surely this boy has yet to experience the loss of the most important thing in the world to him and still thinks everything else matters.*

"His name is Jonas Grey and he's a lieutenant reportin' to Colonel Weaver," James continued, when the general nodded in silence, while seemingly shifting his entire attention in the dimness upon Jonas. "He was supposed to return to Mississippi by tomorrow, but says he couldn't get past the Yankees gathered near the border. He says he came up north specifically to find you, sir."

Beaufort let out an amused laugh, and Jonas wished he could make out the general's features in the diffused glow from the torch, to gain insight as to whether it was a good or bad thing in his regard.

"So, is this true, Lieutenant Grey?" he asked, after a moment's silent deliberation.

"Yes, sir," said Jonas, evenly. "While I am at your mercy, General, please know that I had no intention of not returning to Mississippi as I promised Colonel Wheeler and my captain, James Lewis. Despite carrying a heavy heart, after visiting my home in Appleton, only to find my beloved wife, her father, my parents, and others dear to me ruthlessly murdered by Yankee marauders, I made haste to return to camp. But I was rebuffed at every occasion. Even though I'd gladly die if I could take a handful of the damned rascals with me, the odds never favored me killing more than one, and in all likelihood, myself dying in the process..."

Jonas couldn't finish, as the depth of bitter sorrow threatened to overwhelm him.

I will not weep—not in front of this man who fears not death or any man, and who bravely laid his life on the line for his men at Shiloh!

"I'm very sorry to hear of your loss, Lieutenant Grey. Tell me... how long were you with Van Dorn?" Beaufort took a step closer, his shadowed face no longer hidden. His bright blue eyes regarded Jonas with a mixture of curiosity and what Jonas would normally view as admiration, had it been a lesser man standing before him. He dared not assume anything at this point.

"Since shortly after Shiloh. In Corinth, when the reorganization brought me under Captain Lewis. I was promoted to second lieutenant at that time."

"And how many Yankees do you suppose you've killed since joining the war?"

Not nearly enough!

"I can't say for certain, since I stopped counting after fifty, and that was by the time we left Corinth," said Jonas. "It might be around eighty by now. But it sure as hell ain't enough!"

The general chuckled, and clapped his hands together in delight.

"Well, how about that, Lieutenant Grey. Seems to me like you might be too good a soldier to serve under that son of a bitch, Van Dorn. You can stay and serve with us, and for good measure, I'm promoting you to first lieutenant under Charlie May, since Pete Sears, his previous first was killed just this past week."

Jonas was taken aback, and couldn't help his slack-jawed response to General Beaufort's kindness and willingness to forgive his truancy. He accepted the offer to join his cavalry, while being determined to not swoon like a spring primrose at dawn. He shook the general's hand before being introduced to Captain May. Jonas was unsure how his new commander would feel about him joining his company under promotion, but soon learned that Charlie was a rare confidant of Beaufort's, who by then had gained far more enemies than allies throughout the Confederate Army since the war began.

After Charlie gave a quick introduction to the rest of Company C from the Third Regiment, who were huddled along the bank of the Tennessee River amid freezing rain that showed no signs of letting up, Jonas felt guilty about the lined slicker he wore. He asked Captain May if the reason General Beaufort had chosen to head west as winter approached might be to eventually bivouac someplace near Memphis for the winter, instead of Columbia.

"To shut things down like they do up north, or how we've heard Bragg and Johnston are obliged to do out east?" He laughed, and Jonas felt foolish for even mentioning it. "No sir... we ain't slowin' down—not at all! Hell, we're just gettin' started. General Grant had better protect his supply lines, 'cause we'll be callin' on 'em all very soon!"

The rest of the company laughed and it all sounded sweetly refreshing to Jonas. He marveled at the bravado shared by all the men, in spite of the prospects of being soaked to the bone that night from the incessant rain compounded by the bitter cold. He began to wonder if perhaps he had finally found a place to 'belong' in this war… a place that might even one day become a home of sorts, since he no longer had one.

The pain of losing his precious wife, family, and friends would likely never heal, but there was now a genuine distraction. A diversion that came with the chance to kill those who took everything away from him.

Let the Yankees beware… I'm still coming for 'em!

Chapter Ten

Friday, December 26th, 1862… Murfreesboro, Tennessee.

Christmas Day had come and then mercifully passed.

While some soldiers spoke glowingly of letters that had recently arrived from loved ones waiting at home, Hattie was left with only painful recollections of holiday merriment with her father and missing husband. With so little to celebrate, she began to believe more and more that the two were now likely reunited in Eternity.

During the past three weeks, much had changed for her, as it had for all of the surviving recruits. Two new soldiers were no longer part of the Twenty-Third Battalion. One followed through on a whispered threat to desert by leaving three days prior to Christmas. The other, an older man named Joshua Talbot, died of dysentery. Three other men had contracted the same illness but were still among the living, although they were removed from the battalion until their expected recovery in January.

In the meantime, news arrived early Friday afternoon that General Rosecrans was on the move toward Murfreesboro with half his army of eighty thousand men. General Bragg's army would've enjoyed an advantage of seven thousand soldiers had Jefferson Davis not reduced his Army of Tennessee by ordering nine thousand troops to march west, in an effort to help stave off General Ulysses S. Grant's deeper invasion of Mississippi. Despite the questionable decisions made by the high-ranking officers of the Confederates and their Union counterparts, it seemed as if fate had stepped in, drawing the two evenly numbered armies together. Captain Billy Powers declared it "inevitable" that the North and South would soon meet in a "memorable and bloody confrontation".

Hattie's gut told her the captain's forewarning was likely correct. Her feeling of dread far surpassed what she had felt from the towering smoke columns preceding the murderous gang of Yankees' arrival to her father's farm three months earlier.

"It does seem most likely, despite the revelry goin' on up yonder," commented Lucinda to Hattie and Lester Smith as they huddled around a small fire, discussing the latest report from Captain Powers. "Plum shameful, ain't it?"

She pointed toward a plantation located not far from where the Twenty-Third was camped in frigid conditions, next to a ravine with several other regiments now under Bragg. Along with lights upon a hill, rapturous music ferried by the chilled wind marked where a Christmas celebration continued for the third consecutive night. Only the soft, heated sizzle from the fire's glowing embers dampened the urge for Hattie to venture closer to the hill for a better view and listen.

Lester mentioned he had overheard Sergeant McCracken tell another private that most of General Bragg's staff had spent much of their time inebriated at the main house in the distance, behaving like they had "nary a care in the world". It was as if the war had been placed on hold indefinitely. Despite ongoing festivities at this particular plantation, General Bragg had remained conspicuously absent. During the past two weeks, Hattie had heard how officers and infantrymen alike equally despised the general, and she surmised that feeling probably was mutual.

From her perspective, the celebration in the distance that night didn't seem quite as boisterous it had on the two previous nights. Perhaps it was because Christmas had officially ended. More likely, though, the mood had become subdued after scouts returned with confirmation that the Yankees were undeniably on their way to Murfreesboro.

"I heard General Bragg took time out earlier today to execute a deserter from General Breckinridge's Orphan Brigade," said Hattie, ready to move on from the conversation concerning their superiors' excessive Christmas celebration on the hill. "Sergeant McCracken was talking to Captain Powers about it. The soldier was late coming back from a furlough."

She rubbed her hands together over the coals, massaging her fingers that often tingled, bringing the worry of frostbite. Plummeting temperatures the past week made keeping warm a challenge, and Hattie had marveled at the sight of shoeless soldiers in an Alabama regiment camped not far from where the Twenty-Third's B Company was bivouacked. Some of the soldiers' toes had turned black. *How can they even stand up for long—let alone march anywhere?*

The images of bloody footprints in the early morning snow on Christmas Eve were still fresh on her mind. And, yet the shoeless soldiers continued to drill and prepare for several hours at a time alongside Hattie's regiment without voiced complaints.

"I heard about the execution... Braxton Bragg is such a heartless bastard." Lucinda frowned, glancing over her shoulder to make sure none of the other soldiers were close enough to eavesdrop. "I had hoped things might've changed since the last time we were under his thumb, but had a bad inklin' three weeks ago when we got here and I saw the long faces. Then after we received our first shitty rations, I knew for certain the son of a bitch was still Lucifer incarnate."

Lester grinned, his green eyes shining in the firelight.

For Hattie, the humorous point brought to mind one of the advisements Lucinda had given her just two weeks prior, soon after their hostility to one another had thawed to allow pleasantries that had since blossomed into a guarded alliance.

"You'll need to take good care of your things," Private Templeton had advised, pointing to the shiny shoes on Hattie's feet. "Like those new shoes. They won't last long, and you'll likely have to pull a pair from a dead Yankee by spring. The Confederacy ain't about to issue another pair to you any time soon. Just statin' a fact."

Lucinda went on to explain to both Hattie and Lester that day how life would change when they were no longer under the protection of the recruitment camp. Rations of food and ammunition wouldn't always be something they could depend on—especially the food, where what had once been enough to sustain a foot soldier for two days out of a three-day allotment, it was now barely able to nourish a soldier for one day. Being hungry had become expected—especially under cruel generals such as Braxton Bragg. Lucinda laughingly told the pair that they would soon learn to properly forage for the rest of their diet, or hope a nice fat rat happened along their path.

Hattie grimaced in thinking about a cooked rat on her plate, but was grateful for the advice anyway. She was much more appreciative of what Lucinda later shared in private about the 'necessary five vices' to ensure she was viewed as a male soldier: drinking, smoking, chewing tobacco, swearing, and gambling. Working the farm in Jonas' absence had toughened her up some, but it would take more than strong muscles and calluses on her hands to sell the illusion of being a man.

The tension between the two women became less and less noticeable, and they were able to share confidential facts about themselves that steadily became more personal.

"Why are you here?"

Hattie initially clammed up in response to this question. It had become easier to make it through her days by pushing all thoughts about her previous life from her mind. But Lucinda's persistence eventually won out.

"Yankees killed my father and best friend," she finally told her, while feeling the sharp edge of an invisible dagger pierce her heart. "And, my husband is gone."

"You said before that your husband joined the war... right?" Lucinda responded quietly, as if trying to restrain her ruffian nature in hopes Hattie would continue to talk.

Hattie nodded weakly. "He did. It was the summer before last... He and his brother joined the cavalry, got separated, and Zeke died—as you heard me confirm for Billy."

Lucinda offered a slight smile. Hattie could tell she wanted to hear more, so she continued to talk... unsure of how much she could stand to reveal, and knowing she would shut down if the pain became too great.

"I haven't heard from Jonas since early July," she said, pausing to allow a lump in her throat to pass. "Our farm was burned to the ground. They killed his parents' too, and I couldn't stay."

"So, you're here to make amends on their behalf? To kill the sons of bitches for what they did to your kin?"

Hattie nodded again, unable to speak. Up until then, she only knew that Lucinda grew up in Shelbyville, Tennessee, about sixty-five miles northeast of Appleton. Lucinda told her it was fine to say no more, and proceeded to tell her why she had joined.

"Pa likes to get drunk, and when he does he'll go lookin' to hit someone. He especially likes to hit his own kin, no matter how old or young." She bit her lower lip as if needing help in preventing her own emotional dam from bursting. This surprised Hattie, given Lucinda's 'tough as nails' exterior, though it also made sense. "My older brothers both joined at the war's outset, but for different sides. Frank joined the Confederacy in Columbia, and Jeff headed to Knoxville to join the Union Army. They never have seen eye to eye on anythin' since they were young boys fightin' over which rooster to hit with a slingshot. I'm two years younger than Jeff, who's a year younger than Frank...."

"So why did you join?" Hattie asked, when Lucinda's voice trailed off, with a far-away look in her eyes.

"I got bored after they left," she replied, snickering. "I damn near got myself killed at Shiloh, after thinkin' I could skip all the drillin' nonsense. As soon as I left home, I headed south, not knowin' where to enlist and fearin' discovery by one of the doctors who liked listenin' to a feller's heart. You know that can't work out too well for the likes of us. So, I had to find a different way into the Confederate Army, eventually sneakin' into an outfit from northern Alabama that was on the way to Corinth to join up with General Albert Sidney Johnston. The captain had just been killed, and the regiment I joined didn't have a new name yet, since it was the remnants of four regiments from previous skirmishes.

"We were unprepared, despite the drillin' we did manage, and when we were routed on the battlefield at Shiloh, I concealed myself with another regiment, this one from Tennessee. I changed my lie of joinin' the Confederate Army at Florence, Alabama, to Columbia, Tennessee instead, and

86

claimin' I was from Lewisburg, since it's a day's horse ride from Shelbyville. Next thing I knew, several other soldiers and me were reassigned to Billy Powers' company in the Twenty-Third Battalion, Tennessee Infantry. So here I am, lookin' to kill Yankees and prayin' to the dear Lord it ain't my brother, Jeff."

Lucinda laughed, and Hattie found it hard to resist smiling at Private Templeton's self-effacing sense of humor. Although it would still take some time to know if she could fully trust her, or anyone else, she steadily warmed up to Lucinda. Once Lester also took a liking to the straightforward soldier, the three became known teasingly as 'the young-un brats of Company B'. The trio stuck together for the most part, and the troops at large regarded them all as teenage boys that hadn't reached puberty yet. Not a one of them bore whiskers, although Lester had a pair of wiry hairs growing on the tip of his chin. The light wrinkles on Lucinda's forehead from a year of marching and fighting in the sun had made her appear to be the oldest, which in truth she actually was, since she'd celebrate her twenty-first birthday in January. Hattie was slightly younger, as she would turn twenty-one in March. Neither one believed Lester's claim of being sixteen…

"I know y'all have heard the news about General Johnston's arrival from the east just before Thanksgiving, and probably figured he'd be leadin' us by now." Lucinda's advisement pulled Hattie back to the present and the dying coals of the campfire. "It appears he's decided to give Braxton Bragg enough rope to finish hangin' himself first."

"Do you think General Bragg's wantin' to take us down with him, by leavin' us unprepared?" Lester asked worriedly.

Lucinda chuckled while reaching over the fire to pat him patronizingly on the shoulder.

"You both have been drillin' for damn near two months, so you're prepared as best you can be," she assured them. "No new soldier steps into battle knowin' what to expect, so there's always a chance of dyin'. But don't fret none... ole Louis will be there to keep y'all from gettin' yerselves killt!" She laughed again, as did Lester, who seemed to understand the latest jest was a playful poke at the way he talked.

As for Hattie, she expected a few jitters to be there when it came time to engage the enemy, as was natural for the human condition. Yet, as she pictured in her mind a horde of blue coats swarming toward her and her companions in the next few days, her unease faded. Instead, she found herself eagerly looking forward to the moment she could exact a measure of revenge... and hopefully lay to rest her broken heart.

Chapter Eleven

Wednesday, December 31st*, 1862… shortly after dawn at*

Stones River.

The Confederate and Union armies had been facing each other since the previous night, after General Rosecrans' Army of the Cumberland arrived at Murfreesboro on December 29th. By then, the revelry of Christmas had finally been forgotten, and the soldiers of the Twenty-Third braved freezing rain and sleet amid a thick fog that at times obscured the depth of the enemy's forces now gathered along the west side of Stones River.

General William Joseph Hardee had issued commands to his subordinate generals, J.P. McCown and Patrick Cleburne, to attack the Federal right flank and swing around the Yankee line in a right wheel, in order to drive the enemy back to the river while simultaneously cutting off their main supply routes at the Nashville Pike and the Nashville & Chattanooga Railroad. This information, in the most basic terms, had reached Captain Powers and had then been disseminated to his officers and infantrymen in the late evening of December 30th—with the current plans for a morning attack dependent upon how things looked at dawn.

As predicted, the Union Army's position hadn't changed by morning. The sun began its ascent above the frosted hillsides and fields surrounding the river, and the regiments presently reporting to these two generals were quickly readied for a daybreak attack. The Twenty-Third Battalion had been temporarily assigned to General Cleburne's division and would be part of the wave to follow General McCown's initial offensive against the Union's position.

Hattie awoke an hour before dawn from restless sleep to find Lester and Lucinda stirring nearby. Lucinda had built a small fire for coffee only, as the order to be ready to march at sunrise had spread through the entire camp. The bitter cold had made for a wearily long night, with a spirited competition in the evening hours between the bands from both armies providing the only noteworthy distraction. The contest had ended with nearly all of the musicians and soldiers joining in a spirited rendition of "Home Sweet Home." Most of the men smiled as they sang along, and even Lester and Lucinda joined in that brief moment of quiet joy.

But for Hattie, the instruments and voices carrying the melody brought rekindled pain, as refreshed memories of her father and other loved ones so recently lost renewed the attack on her defenseless heart. Even long after the music had died and given way to an icy wind laced with stinging raindrops, she pictured the last days—both good and bad—with her father and Mary, along with a giggling little Nathan clinging to his mother's shoulder. The discomfort of sleeping amid rocky terrain was countered during every waking moment by heated anger that fueled her heart and core to the point her frozen extremities were scarcely noticed.

"Y'all ready?"

Lucinda posed the question to both Hattie and Lester, just before Joe McCracken and two other sergeants moved through the ranks, ensuring that each soldier was dressed and ready for battle.

"Yes," Hattie replied, after looking over her shoulder at Lester, who merely nodded. He seemed nervous, and she wondered if her demeanor would've been the same as his if not for the powerful lust for vengeance flowing through her entire being.

Lucinda observed Hattie with a glint of curiosity in her eyes, seemingly aware of the urge to kill simmering just below the surface.

"Remember to keep your wits about you, and don't shoot before you aim." Lucinda took a bite of hardtack and placed the rest back inside her haversack. "As I've been tellin' y'all, this ain't gonna be like what you're expectin'. It never is the first time. Not for anyone."

Hattie nodded, silently wondering just how useful the past two months of drilling would prove to be that day.

"Don't lunge carelessly either," Lucinda advised.

"Looks like they's startin' to move out ahead of us, Louis." Lester pointed to where the first regiments moved toward the large empty field below them, where the line would form. "I'm ready."

He clutched his loaded musket while rechecking his cartridge box.

"You should've already counted what you're bringin' to battle, Lester," Lucinda chided. "I'll try to keep an eye on you and Henry here, but once the fightin' starts, we're likely to get separated. Watch out for each other if you can... No one else will have your backs once things get bad, I promise you that."

91

As the lines for Cleburne formed in preparation to follow McCown's forces, Hattie steadied her breaths drifting above her head in the wintry air while she waited anxiously for the order to move forward. Initially, she had correctly envisioned how it would go that chilly morning, other than a winter sun replacing the night's mixture of sleet and rain. As the organized march moved to double steps and finally gave way to a frost-crunching sprint across the field toward the enemy, the sudden eruption of gunfire and shrill yells from the attacking rebels appeared to catch the half-dressed Federals off guard, and many of them scrambled in panic to arm themselves. From her view, it appeared the Confederates had quickly gained the upper hand in the harried confusion seizing the Union camp less than two hundred yards away.

By the time the first wave reached the camp, the enemy's flimsy line crumbled. Even so, bullets whistled past Hattie's head. Despite the revelry of a rout, and the fact most of the Yankees were retreating in a panic toward the north where Rosecrans' army had come from, sharpshooters protected by the rocky hillside picked off a number of Confederate soldiers. Suddenly, the infantryman directly ahead of Hattie flew back as if he had run into a stone wall. The man, a kindly forty-one-year-old from Columbia, named Thomas Hays, lay on the frozen ground, nearly tripping her. Warm moisture oozed off the back of her hands and face... She realized in horror, after a glance at what was left of Private Hays' face, that the bloody mess had been her comrade's head.

Badly shaken by what she'd just witnessed, it took the brisk excitement of routing the enemy to keep her focus on the task at hand, and she joined her comrades in chasing down stragglers in retreat. Hattie's third loaded cartridge returned the fate delivered to Private Hays to an equally vulnerable blue coat near the edge of the Union defense line, where numerous Yankee soldiers lay sprawled upon the ground.

Moving up the hillside, Hattie lost track of her regiment, finding herself amongst the Alabamians whose hardiness had garnered her admiration. Still, she glanced around looking for Lester and Lucinda. It appeared that most of Cleburne's forces were pursuing the retreating Yankees as they headed north. But she thought she saw the color guard for her company moving through the rocky maze just ahead. She ran to catch up to him, and as she approached a large boulder, a Union soldier carrying a rifle with a clean bayonet stepped into her path.

Her heart raced with anticipation. She pictured killing a Yankee in hand-to-hand combat, and hopefully it'd be a soldier as ruthless as the fiends who had murdered her father. She savored the image of exacting retribution upon such a monster, wondering if she'd feel the vindication she longed for, along with a measure of peace.

But then their eyes met.

Dear Lord, it's just a kid!

In some respects, the young soldier reminded her of Lester... a boy, and one not much older than her fellow recruit. The kid seemed far too frail and frightened to even be present in this hellish place. The soldier's light-blue doe eyes, almost gray, reminded her of Stella, and his upper lip quivered as if he'd start bawling at any moment. She hadn't expected her fury to wane, but she lost the callous disposition to dispatch him and move on. Their eyes remained locked as he whimpered.

"You'd be wise to turn around and find a place to hide over yonder," she told him, compassionately. "Go now, and you might survive—"

Suddenly, the kid's expression changed to one of rage and he lunged at her, swiping madly at Hattie's mid-section with his gun tip bearing the razor-sharp bayonet. It sliced her coat, and surely would've done serious damage to her abdomen if he'd possessed a steady hand. Hattie had moved in too close to effectively wield her own weapon. She believed for certain she'd soon be reunited with her father, Mary, John, and their precious infant—along with Jonas' parents and her own mother, long since deceased. Perhaps Jonas would be waiting on the other side of Death's Veil, too. But just as the young soldier prepared to eviscerate her, a grime-covered hand holding a bloody bayonet tip appeared in her right periphery, thrusting the blade into the soldier's throat. The kid fell to his knees while the crazed anger in his eyes turned to surprise and then bleakness as he took his last struggling breath.

"What in tarnation's gotten into you, Henry?" hissed Hattie's benefactor. "If a soldier's armed and wearin' Union blue, you'd best assume he's intendin' to kill you!"

Hattie didn't know how to respond; shocked it wasn't her dead body lying in the mud instead of the Yankee boy resting by her feet. It took her a moment to recognize an infuriated Lucinda beneath the sanguinary bath that covered her face and arms.

"He was just a kid," she mumbled.

Lucinda rolled her eyes. "So is Lester, and he can hardly wait to tell you about his first felled blue coat. Come on, we need to catch up to the others." She motioned to where their regiment was headed north with most of General Cleburne's forces.

"I thought we were supposed to pursue the Yankees up the hill?" Incredulous, Hattie couldn't believe the Confederate leadership wouldn't want to make sure the Federals' presence on the hill was snuffed out.

"You should already know them damned Yanks have dug themselves in behind the rocks all up and down the hillside," said Lucinda, disgustedly. "If we linger here too long, they're apt to pick off the entire lot of us like a bunch of goddamned crippled gobblers at a Christmas turkey shoot!"

A bullet ricocheting off a nearby pine tree gave persuasive emphasis to Lucinda's point. Crouched low, she and Hattie scurried down the hillside, zigzagging to avoid bullets from sniper fire. Until the very moment they rejoined Cleburne's army, Hattie refused to cast a single glance over her shoulder... silently praying to be spared the fate of the late Thomas Hays.

Chapter Twelve

Wednesday, March 25th, 1863... Brentwood, Tennessee.

The morning's bright sunshine had given way to a familiar gray and gloomy dullness by early afternoon.

Heavy clouds promised a windswept assault of rain, sleet, or snow against General Beaufort's cavalry—and perhaps a combination of all three. Despite braving the volatile elements of late March, life serving under the mercurial general had remained refreshingly exciting for Jonas. Much like the erratic Tennessee weather as the season moved from winter to spring, every day came with new adventures and a sense of satisfaction that the efforts of Beaufort's cavalrymen were actually making a difference in the war.

Unlike General Van Dorn's tendency to attack without a well-conceived plan, General Beaufort's approach included schemes that maximized his men and resources. Sometimes that meant doubling up on attacks against Union strongholds—specifically against their supply lines and stockades in Middle and West Tennessee. Other times, the shrewd general and his hell-bent staff would find unique ways to fool the Federals into believing a much larger force of men was present.

Jonas had witnessed Beaufort's army swelling to as many as four thousand men, when fed by other cavalry regiments in the region, before shrinking back down to several hundred riders, along with a small artillery battery. He chuckled privately at the premise that some might think this meant hardly a fair fight could be had against much larger Union forces. But anything was possible for this group when led by a fiery leader who had long perfected a gambler's bluff.

In all the raids and confrontations Jonas had participated in since being assigned to Charles May's regiment in December, the Yankees often seemed convinced they were fighting a Confederate force vastly superior in size—only to discover in disgust that it wasn't the case. It was the thing that amused Jonas most, other than the general's penchant for jovial laughter when the Yankees thought they had Beaufort and his men cornered, only to find the ornery 'Wizard of the Saddle' had already moved on to his next target.

The mischief of harassing General Grant's army by attacking supply lines from Kentucky down to the Mississippi border had been a way of life for Jonas from the moment Beaufort invited him to join his famed Elite Company. Life on the run had made it a hell of a lot easier to push aside his broken heart, although late at night his beloved Hattie haunted his dreams. It seemed especially cruel to him that sometimes the visions of her wouldn't merely be based on cherished memories—something expected and easier to restrict to the ruins of his battered soul on the mornings that followed these torturous nightmares. The mockery of images unfamiliar left him with conflicts to work through during idle moments each day.

They're just dreams. Sometimes she's running toward me like I remember her, with her soft blonde hair bouncing on her shoulders and wearing the loving smile that's destined to torture me forever. Then suddenly it all changes... She's carrying a musket and her face is distorted by rage unfamiliar.

Jonas would often awaken in a cold sweat upon catching this unseemly glimpse of Hattie. Most of the time, he simply passed it off as just a nightmare borne of wartime angst, since the troublesome images were similar enough to what other cavalrymen had sometimes mentioned when discussing their dreams. To escape thinking about such things, he immersed himself in the camaraderie prevalent among his fellow riders in Company C and the rest of the Third Regiment. The men fought hard for their fearless general and each other, and were rewarded during the occasional lulls in action. Playing cards and pitching horseshoes were popular among Jonas' peers, and he soon excelled at both pastimes. He wasn't above sharing in a round or two of whiskey with his new buddies either.

And, as of two days ago, Captain James Lewis and Private Jim Bailey had arrived as part of a handful of Van Dorn's regiments temporarily assigned to Beaufort to assist in tearing up the railroads and telegraph lines near Brentwood.

His former captain seemed as much in awe of the general as Jonas had been upon meeting Beaufort at Clifton, and both James and Jim quickly gained the respect of Captain May and several members of Jonas' new company. James reminisced about their very first shared sighting of Beaufort, at Shiloh the previous April. He and Jonas had watched from a nearby wooded area as the wild and reckless colonel led his cavalry on a charge into enemy lines, seemingly determined to take on the whole damned Union Army by himself. Beaufort's cavalry couldn't keep up, and the isolated hero penetrated the lines as a lone Confederate who soon found himself surrounded by angry

Yankees screaming for one another to "shoot the goddamned son of a bitch!"

Jonas agreed the Good Lord must've taken a strong liking to the fearless colonel, as Beaufort shouldn't have survived beyond that April evening. The fact he escaped, despite being shot through the hip during the confrontation, could only be viewed as a miracle. *"That's one crazy bastard,"* Lewis had reverently mused at the time, after handing Jonas his spyglass to take a look. Jonas then watched in awe as Beaufort grabbed a Yankee soldier to use as a shield, dropping the man on the ground once he was safely out of sniper range and racing back to his cheering cavalry.

Beaufort's remarkable bravado remained the man's hallmark, in Jonas' estimation. His finest moments often came when things looked the grimmest. Jonas mentioned the general's heroics at Parker's Cross Roads on New Year's Eve to Captain Lewis, where Beaufort's cavalry suddenly found themselves completely surrounded by the enemy. Outnumbered more than two to one, Jonas thought for sure the Federal forces would cut them all down—especially since the prevailing rumor was that the Union Army preferred a dead Franklin Beaufort over all other Confederate generals and the same fate for his Elite riders, referred to as the Beaufort's "detestable vermin."

"I believed for certain we'd be gathering at St. Peter's Gates that day." Jonas chuckled as he recalled the event. "And hell, maybe General Beaufort thought the same thing too... But suddenly his eyes lit up and he told us to 'charge 'em both ways!'. At first, the command sounded more fatuous than a pair of squirrels fighting over a pecan cluster in front of a white-tailed fox. But the men who'd been riding with him since '61 set out after the Yankees from every direction, thereby creating the illusion we had five times as many riders as were present. And by God, instead of being dead or captured, we made it all the way back to Lexington that night."

"I can only imagine, and I envy you, Jonas," said Jim, shaking his head, as did James and two other former Mississippi cohorts of Jonas, lieutenants Daniel Martin and George Summers.

At that moment, the five of them were sitting around a fire with three other members of Beaufort's Elite Company, including a former slave named Levi Jones, whom James kept eyeing suspiciously. Jonas finally broached the matter.

"I can tell you're surprised that a man of color rides with us. Ain't that right, Jimmy?"

The question took Jonas' former commander aback, and he exchanged an embarrassed look with Jim before affirming Jonas' assessment with a nod.

"Just never seen a Negro doin' a rider's work is all," he said, avoiding Levi's gaze. "At least not on our side of things."

Jonas nodded thoughtfully before responding, shooting an amused glance to Private Jones that was returned with a subtle smile that matched a playful glint in Levi's warm hazel eyes.

"Private Jones is personally responsible for the fact I still walk among the living," said Jonas, returning his attention to his former cohorts. "I would've taken several blind shots at Clifton and again at Huntingdon if not for his keen eye and sense for the enemy's presence. Initially, I had a similar perspective to yours, Jimmy, even though I'd only dealt with a handful of Negroes in my lifetime. Nobody in my neck of the woods can afford owning slaves, as you know. But Beaufort set me straight about it, and if you'd paid attention to what's going on around here, you might've noticed that his cavalry presently has more than two dozen men like Levi Jones, with eight of them serving in the Elite ninety."

"You mean colored?" Captain Lewis sought to confirm.

"Yep. And I'll say it right here—same as General Beaufort told me three months ago. You'd be hard pressed to find better soldiers, and none braver." Jonas paused to look over at Levi again, who nodded silently with a tip of his hat. "I trust my life to Levi, and I'd take a bullet for him too, if need be."

"You'd do that?" James sounded incredulous.

"Absolutely," Jonas responded evenly. "And, I'd do it without hesitation."

…That conversation took place Tuesday evening. As if portentous, Jonas' assessment of Levi's loyalty and ability as a marksman was proven true Wednesday afternoon. After riding out to Brentwood with generals Beaufort and Frank Armstrong and launching a successful attack against the Union garrison just south of town, General Beaufort decided to push their luck and attack the Federal stockade just two miles further south.

The mood amongst the men was jovial after capturing several supply wagons and nearly eight hundred Union prisoners. But after burning the bridge across the Little Harpeth River and heading west to their present encampment, Union cavalry under General Green Clay Smith soon pursued them.

At first, Beaufort's cavalry expected a small skirmish when the Yankees caught up to them, just a few miles from the stockade. However, the Union Army had recently outfitted some units with repeating rifles, and Smith's cavalry were included in that selection. Within the hour, Jonas watched Yankees armed with the new rifles pick off several comrades, and by the time Beaufort ordered the retreat, they had lost nearly half of their bounty of supplies and prisoners collected that afternoon. Fortunately, Colonel James Starnes, along with his assigned cavalry that Beaufort sent to the area the night before, recaptured most of what was lost to General Smith. But the shock of encountering superior Yankee weaponry would take some time to sort through.

Almost lost in the confusion was Levi Jones' rescue of both James Lewis and Jim Bailey, who had gotten separated from their regiment during the skirmish. Both were cornered and facing arrest at the hands of several Union cavalrymen, when Levi and another Company C rider surprised the Federals from behind. James told Jonas that Levi was forced to step into harm's way in order to get a clean shot at the apparent leader. Once that one fell from his horse, the other three fled.

"I owe you a debt, Private Jones," James told Levi, once they returned to camp and were gathered around a fresh fire. "Jonas was right. You had our backs, and I'm much obliged."

Jonas could tell Levi was quite pleased to be vindicated in regard to Captain Lewis' doubts, though he said very little in response.

When it came time for James and the others to rejoin Van Dorn's army that weekend, he brought the incident up once more when he pulled Jonas aside.

"We could use a man like him. As for you, Jonas, I bet General Van Dorn would welcome you back with open arms to his cavalry," he said.

"Nah, this is where I belong now, Jimmy," Jonas replied. "Maybe we'll get a chance to ride together again, since I heard Van Dorn's reassignment will keep him here in Tennessee for an extended period. From what I presently understand, Beaufort will attend mostly to the western side of the state... at least for now. But I reckon you and I will meet up sometime, my friend. And, if not, may the Good Lord keep you, Jim, and the others safe."

It felt a bit strange to say goodbye to one of the few good friends Jonas still had in this world. But it also felt right. For better or worse, he had willingly chosen to follow General Beaufort along with his new comrades for the duration of the war.

"It suits me," he whispered to himself.

Jonas watched the four horsemen head southeast toward Spring Hill, until they disappeared with the rest of the former Mississippi regiments behind a tree line at the edge of a meadow dotted with thistles and buttercups, a quarter mile from Company C's latest campsite.

"This is home… for now."

Chapter Thirteen

Monday evening, June 22nd, 1863… near Wartrace, Tennessee.

Nearly six months had passed since General Rosecrans pushed the Army of Tennessee down toward Tullahoma after rallying to defeat General Bragg's forces at Stones River. Ever leery about Rosecrans bringing another attack with the superior size of his Army of the Cumberland, Bragg stationed fifty thousand of his troops along the Duck River, from Shelbyville to Wartrace.

Hattie had expected another bloody confrontation between the two armies by spring, while Lucinda anticipated Bragg's full replacement by General Joe Johnston. Yet, other than minor skirmishes to the north of Shelbyville, life had been relatively peaceful… and Bragg remained in command. Neither development was good for an army where idleness served to remind soldiers of what they lacked, rather than the aspects to be thankful for.

Hate for the loathsome Bragg was on the upswing, after sufficient food rations and other important commodities—such as proper clothing—had been routinely denied to the infantry during the bitter winter months on through the humid heat of spring in Middle Tennessee. The soles of Hattie's and Lester's shoes had worn through, with several holes in each, due to excessive drilling that seemed designed to keep the soldiers occupied more than anything else. Rumor had it that enough new shoes to outfit the entire army under Bragg's command were available to be picked up at Chattanooga, and had been since March, less than three days' journey by wagon. Yet, for whatever mysterious reason, the general refused to order delivery of the shoes—or any other clothing items.

Lucinda says Bragg wouldn't be inclined to get shoes for his own momma, unless the delivery also came with a firestorm from Jehovah to burn up Rosecrans' entire army!

In the meantime, foraging had become a prime necessity. Although, due to the length of their encampment, the area farms had been taxed beyond what they could give without the local residents facing the same hardships. As a result, Hattie was about to experience her first full indulgence of rat. Her previous small taste had given her a much better appreciation for such army delicacies as groundhog and possum.

"It's all good eatin'!" Lester enthused, half done with his meal when Lucinda served up Hattie's portion of a long slender rodent for supper that night. The critter reminded her of the vermin her father would shoot and toss into the woods whenever rats invaded the corncrib at his Appleton farm. "They's better fried, I'll admit. But, damn, Louis—you's gettin' better and better as a cook. This-un's much better tastin' than the last one we had. Henry's sure to love it too!"

He beamed with delight while digging into the rest of his portion, which to Hattie appeared to be the rat's abdomen and chest. Lucinda took the shoulders and head, leaving Hattie the hindquarters. While the other two had already dug in hungrily, she stared at her portion, unable to do much more than to push aside the critter's tail from the small dried-up potatoes Lester covertly recovered from a recently executed soldier's rations.

Her previous experience eating the lowest of rodents, just two weeks prior, had only required her to try part of a leg... tolerable, but only because she was weak from hunger. Since then, the hard tack had improved, though slightly. Still, she preferred it by far to the noxious fare lying on her plate with the tail hanging over the edge.

"You gonna stare at your supper all evenin', Henry?" Lucinda eyed her puckishly; perhaps knowing Hattie was on the verge of losing her appetite. "You'd do best to just get it over and done with. Grab the tail and then munch it on down!"

Lucinda smacked her lips after devouring a larger bite of rat than Hattie could envision herself consuming.

Hattie finally took the advice to pick up the tail. Much to Lucinda and Lester's delight, the tail split open in her fingers, leaving her holding the critter's skin as the hind meat fell back onto her plate in a disgusting plop.

Never in her previous life would she have stooped to eat something so disgusting. But Bragg's insensitivity to disease brought on by malnourishment meant the only way a soldier would survive in relatively good health was to consume whatever critter came along their path.

Even so, it took another moment to work up the courage to do it, which usually meant for her to mentally evacuate her present surroundings and focus on a much better place... a place she once loved and shared with Jonas.

Sugar Creek.

She closed her eyes, picturing a warm spring day before even a hint of war had reached their peaceful community. She and her beloved husband rested beneath a lofty oak with branches extending above the creek's tranquil flow. She recalled the steadiness of his beating heart as she laid her head upon his chest... Jonas' hands, so strong, gently caressed the back of her neck and shoulders.

A blissful moment in time, she could remain there forever. She *would*, in fact, if only it were possible, even by miracle alone.

The rat's flesh was coarse, and she swallowed what she could without choking. She washed it down with water from her canteen, filled just that afternoon from a small brook feeding the river, which she and Lester had recently stumbled upon less than a mile from camp.

"See? It ain't so bad, huh?" Lester laughed merrily, and Lucinda joined in.

"That's truly some nasty... *shit!*" Hattie spat out the uncomfortable curse word, along with the remains of what refused to go down her throat. "No more rat for me—*ever again!*"

Lucinda quietly shushed her when the other soldiers huddled around nearby campfires cast disparaging looks their way.

"At least you'll be better off for tomorrow, if the rumors prove true that the Union Army is finally ready to engage us again," Lucinda advised, teasingly. "You'll need your strength, Henry, and if General Bragg decides to march us toward Chattanooga, where supposedly headquarters awaits his return, I daresay you'll be indulgin' in more interestin' delicacies than what we shared tonight." She smiled, but it was almost a grimace, as if she could picture the critters she'd been forced to subsist upon in previous campaigns before she and the other veteran soldiers arrived in Murfreesboro the past November.

"I hear there's plenty of chipmunk and squirrel in the Chattanooga hills," added Lester, wearing a hopeful look. Hattie envied his primitive appetite and the ability to picture simpler happy times, even if it was just a fleeting moment of suppertime bliss.

"The Yankees seem more than content over yonder to leave things as they've been... even more so than Bragg. What makes you think it will be different now?" Hattie's question drew a surprised look from Lester and a knowing smirk from Lucinda. "I'm serious, y'all. We've been called upon to be ready to fight for damn near every day since March, only to find the enemy hasn't ventured forth an inch. And other than a few shots from their artillery to let us know they haven't forgotten about us, there's not been much else."

Lucinda walked up to her with a pot of coffee, which was in reality more chicory than anything else, motioning for Hattie to dump the soured water from her cup. She filled it half way.

"Somethin's different this time... it's just a feelin' in my gut." Lucinda glanced at Lester, the weak onset of dusk loomed in the distance behind where he sat. A beautiful sunset of orange and purple hues had invaded the horizon to the west. Protected at the moment by a thickly wooded ridge, Hattie pictured the damage a bombardment from Union artillery could soon do to the low ridgeline dotted with tents at present. It could happen at any time... or perhaps not. "Maybe Bragg finally realizes the tedious life of non-fightin' for damn near six months has compromised his army. If only the bastard realized we've been soft since the day he had us flee Murfreesboro with our tails tucked between our legs! Months of picket duty, card games, and overall idleness has just made things worse."

Worse? It's made things excruciatingly maddening! Morale is terrible and the men talk about how things would be different if Joe Johnston was in charge. Yet Johnston seems to be in no hurry to replace General Bragg and personally take over... Why?

"I can tell you're thinkin' my assessment is a load of manure, Henry. But, even if we don't wake up tomorrow with an order to march to battle, I goddamn guarantee you it's comin' soon!" Lucinda paused to offer Lester the last of their supper round of coffee. "Hell, standin' on picket has gotten to the point where we're becomin' fast friends with them damn Yanks. We go much longer, they might as well call off the war!"

Lester's slight grin told Hattie that he felt similarly. Both he and Lucinda were jaded, and yet held out more hope than Hattie in regard to resuming the war with the Federals. Maybe this was due to the reports of continual fighting going on out west in Mississippi and back in Virginia. In a way, it reminded her of the malaise that had been in Appleton at the war's outset, when other parts of Tennessee had already sent volunteers and the young men in her town were waiting for their opportunity to contribute to the war effort. The men were anxious to 'go kill some Yankees' and perhaps be fortunate to come home with some kind of lasting reminder from the war— such as a gunshot wound or missing limb.

Hattie never quite understood why anyone would want that sort of proof of valor. But it was prevalent among many of the men in Appleton, and she suspected it was the same everywhere else, too. Except in regard to Jonas and his brother Zeke. They simply wanted to ride together and join the effort to push the Yankees back up into Ohio, Pennsylvania, or wherever else the bastards came from that had invaded the South. The brothers had hoped to get it done quickly, envisioning a return to Appleton in just a few months after heading north to Camp Cheatham in July of 1861. Jonas had promised to come home long before Christmas that year.

She wondered how Jonas would've reacted to having to wait this long to engage the enemy. She grimaced forlornly at the thought he might've moved on by then, to go to the fighting if it wasn't going to come to him... She tried to picture his reaction to having to wait six months since Hattie's last real battle with the enemy—hers and Lester's only significant war experience. The light skirmishes that took place in January through March, as they moved back toward Tullahoma, weren't enough to keep the blood rush of excitement going through her, and it seemed to be the prevalent perspective throughout the Confederate camp that stretched for roughly ten miles along the Duck River. As the fervor died, along with the focus on actively engaging the Union Army that had pursued them from a safe distance, so did the sense of urgency she'd been borne into while in Murfreesboro and that had fueled her angry heart on up to the confrontation at Stones River.

It had become obvious to Hattie that her comrades had forgotten the horrors of that bloody battle, which she vowed to never forget. No one—not even Lucinda—spoke of it anymore, and it truly seemed as if none of her fellow infantrymen could recall losing their footing on the blood-soaked fields, half-frozen and covered with corpses of men and horses from both sides to the point it was nearly impossible to avoid stepping on the dead.

Maybe it was the tragic turn of events, when what appeared to be a Confederate victory on New Year's Eve inevitably became a defeat at the hands of Rosecrans' army by January 4th. In an apparent effort to ease the plight of dejection that had spread throughout Bragg's forces, Captain Powers had told his company a few days later that the Confederate focus had shifted to protecting Chattanooga, and that the army had 'merely fallen back' to secure a solid line of defense to keep the Yankees from reaching that pivotal stronghold. "Lose Chattanooga and lose the war in Tennessee" had been the admonishment, along with a passionate picture of the Union's desire to sit in the catbird seat above Georgia and northern Alabama. Billy added that this assessment came courtesy of

Colonel Tazewell Newman, who had been privy to a conversation between generals Cheatham and Bragg....

"Just be ready to rise early," said Lucinda, pulling Hattie back to the present with a gentle nudge. "And if I'm a few days off on what's comin', at least the three of us won't be caught unawares should the Yankees show up in our camp with bayonets drawn or musket's blazin'. You understand that can happen, right?"

"Yes," Hattie replied. She forced a compliant smile.

"Good... we should probably turn in early, once the stars are out," said Lucinda. "Looks like Billy and Joe told everybody else the same thing." She motioned to the rest of the Twenty-Third, as well as the other regiments camped nearby. Almost everyone appeared to be preparing for an early day tomorrow.

Shortly after dusk, Hattie laid out her bedroll near where Lester and Lucinda lay gazing up at the clear sky. She joined them in studying the stars, silently picking out the constellations that her father had taught her as a young girl. Despite the disenchantment that had eroded confidence in her decision to join the war effort, she promised herself to not give in to complacency or lethargy—regardless if it was caused by a lack of food, supplies, and here lately, meaningful purpose dimmed by a cruel general. Nothing would affect her mindset going forward. Nor would she allow anything to erode the tender hope of finding Jonas... regardless of whether he was alive or dead.

Chapter Fourteen

Sunday morning, September 20th, 1863... Chickamauga Creek,

Georgia.

"Jonas! ...Charlie's been hit!"

The shout that had risen above the din came from Levi Jones. For a moment Jonas had lost track of Levi's position, as well as Captain May's, while moving through the woods towards Lafayette Road. Surrounded by confusion brought on by an endless barrage of bullets and grapeshot coming from the Union line just ahead, Confederate soldiers were falling in bloody heaps everywhere he looked.

It's a goddamned slaughter pen we've stepped into... The scouts couldn't have been more wrong about what they saw at dawn!

Roughly half of General Beaufort's cavalry had been sent as dismounted cavalrymen to march with General Breckinridge's infantry lines toward the Union Army's position, which for the most part hadn't changed since the scouts' reports reached Breckinridge, and then Beaufort, shortly after dawn. At the time, no one anticipated that the Federal troops under the direction of General George Thomas would be able to construct formidable breastworks within two hours of sunrise.

Charlie had suggested Company C, along with a few other Third Regiment companies, was best suited to be among Beaufort's regiments assigned to support Breckinridge's infantry that had been significantly reduced during the previous day's fighting. Several other regiments had been picked for this effort, since Beaufort intended to utilize his best riders later that morning and on into the afternoon. But Beaufort's most tenured captain argued that Company C was among the least exhausted of the bunch and still eager to fight—despite enduring two other dismounted encounters with the enemy since late Friday morning.

"Charlie? Levi? Where the hell are you!"

A flurry of whistling bullets whizzed by Jonas' head as he tried to raise his voice above the roaring boom of guns and cannon fire, forcing him low to the ground to avoid being hit. Meanwhile, recent acquaintances and established friends alike continued to fall around him. Their agonized cries filled the air thick with smoke, as the combined and uneven Confederate lines emerged from the woods. From there, the men trotted toward the road. As darker smoke drifted toward him, Jonas detected part of the reported breastworks just ahead, less than one hundred yards away.

Shit! They look impenetrable... We should've sent an artillery bombardment first!

Levi was crouched on the ground next to a fallen tree, grimacing... but Jonas soon determined he had only been grazed in the shoulder. Charlie May sat propped up next to him against the tree, writhing in pain and fury while desperately grasping his right thigh. A wave of Confederate soldiers stepped over the tree to either side of the pair, seemingly oblivious as they sought to keep from joining their fallen comrades—most of whom lay motionless upon the blood-soaked grass and soil. Jonas slid down next to Levi, keeping his head below the tree's upper edge.

"Goddamnit—you two go on and fight!" Charlie ordered angrily. "I'll be all right… y'all can come get me when the battle's over!"

For a moment, Jonas considered obeying Captain May's command, carefully raising his head and preparing to aim his loaded musket at the Yankees beginning to venture toward them from behind the breastworks. *The bastards have more repeating rifles—we'll never get close enough to take the road!* Carrying on the fight and seizing the recently built defenses, along with the thoroughfare the Federals seemed obsessed in protecting, was what General Beaufort expected from his men. Yet, as Jonas thought about the friendship he and Charlie had nurtured, he hesitated on leaving him. Like Levi, Charlie had saved Jonas' life on several occasions.

He glanced at Charlie's thigh, noticing the spread of blood moving towards his knee through his trousers.

"If we leave you now, you're going to die!"

"Lieutenant Grey, I just gave you a goddamned order and you will obey it—*ahh shit!"*

Charlie tried to raise himself in an apparent effort to face Jonas directly, but fell back against the tree and grasping his leg with both hands.

Jonas and Levi exchanged worried looks and confirmed with a nod what was to come next.

"Save your strength, Charlie—we're taking you back to camp!" Jonas pulled the captain's legs in closer to the tree just as a bouncing cannonball careened over it, knocking Jonas' hat off. "You can take up my insubordination with General

Beaufort if you so choose, but I'll be damned if we let you bleed to death!"

Levi nodded when Jonas shot him another glance.

"The hell you say!" Charlie protested, trying to rise again. Levi stopped him and held his right leg fast while Jonas used his knife to quickly cut away the trouser pant leg to just above the bullet wound. "What in the tarnation are you two doin' to me?"

Levi wouldn't answer, and instead kept his focus on holding Charlie's leg in place. Jonas also ignored the question, using his bayonet to tear a portion of his shirt as he attempted to stem the blood streaming from Charlie's entrance and exit thigh wounds.

He's been shot through clean! No obvious shattered bones… that could be good if we get him back to camp in time!

"I'm making a tourniquet to keep you in the land of the living—despite your stubborn determination to do otherwise," said Jonas, finally, just before ducking again when another ricocheting cannonball obliterated the torso of one of Breckinridge's infantrymen that had just stepped over the tree. Blood showered down upon all three of them. "It appears the Good Lord ain't intending for you to die today—at least not here. I reckon the wound's treatable, as the bullet passed through cleanly. Looks like it missed the main artery too…. The blood flow's heaviness is from the bullet's entry and exit holes combined, but I think we've got 'em fixed enough to get you to the surgeon."

"Provided I don't get shot again—or get you two killed while stupidly tryin' to save my ass!"

"I guess we'll know the truth about all that shortly, Captain," said Jonas. "Here goes nothin'!"

Jonas paused briefly to check the weeping wound in Levi's shoulder, and when satisfied that his original assessment of it not being serious was correct, the pair lifted Charlie to where Jonas could secure his grip around the captain's waist. The three headed back to the woods, with Levi hovering protectively behind Jonas and Charlie, his loaded musket at the ready until after they had safely reentered the woods.

Jonas ignored the scornful looks from Breckinridge's men and a few of Beaufort's cavalrymen as well. A reprimand for not fighting through as directed could be forthcoming, but leaving Charlie's fate to God Almighty's mercy in a world where compassion and miracles had long since expired seemed like an execrable idea. This was especially true when it involved the 'brethren' from his regiment, where men like Charlie and Levi were not only close friends, but family too.

They were the only family he had left on God's formerly green Earth.

And like my former family, the Angel of Death seems to have a preference for us Rebels... doggedly coming to collect our souls sooner or later.

* * * * *

"Goddamn it, Henry! Stay focused on the enemy before us, and *nothin'* else!"

Lucinda had just pulled Hattie out of harm's way as a Yankee's bayonet barely missed her neck. Her only redemption was shooting the soldier dead before he could take a second swipe, this time at Lucinda's back.

"You're welcome," Hattie quipped solemnly, after the pair dove for cover in a nearby thicket. At the moment, they were roughly one hundred yards from where Jonas and Levi were presently carrying their injured captain to safety.

General Brown's Brigade, which included the Twenty-Third Battalion and four full Tennessee regiments, had recently been assigned to General Alexander Stewart's division. That morning, Stewart ordered three brigades in unison—including Brown's troops—to attack the Union line intent on holding Lafayette Road. Major Tazewell Newman and Captain W. P. Simpson had led the Twenty-Third's initial charge against Union General John Brannan, and it appeared that all five regiments under Brown were on the verge of breaking through Brannan's defenses.

After more than a solid day of exhaustive warfare, it seemed as if the Confederate Army was about to gain the upper hand. Hattie's and Lucinda's fellow soldiers, whose faces were awash in sweat and the blood of comrades and enemies alike, whooped and hollered as Brown led them into the day's deepest penetration thus far. Lester was among the first to cross the road... it should've been a moment of complete triumph. Yet despite mustering her own joyous whoop, it was cut short by a sudden longing that descended swiftly upon Hattie's unsuspecting soul and mind, battering her heart with a raw mix of emotions that pummeled without mercy.

Thoughts of Jonas... and he's in trouble? What in the hell? Why am I suddenly thinking about him? For Christ's sake, I've trained my mind to only think of him at night, when I'm alone and it's safe enough to do so! This isn't fair—definitely not now, damn it!

As if anticipating him to unexpectedly appear, she whirled around with her eyes searching wildly in every direction, until her gaze was drawn to an area just northeast of where her battalion had been positioned.

General Cleburne's men were there, and beyond his troops remnants of Breckinridge's Orphan Brigade approached what looked like Union breastworks. All were engaged in furious battle, both hand to hand and with guns fired from close range.

So, why is my attention being pulled to them? There are no mounted cavalry present, and if there were, it would be General Wheeler's men, who have been with us for a while now. Or, perhaps new riders under the famed Franklin Beaufort.

If Jonas was still among the living, he'd likely be fighting somewhere out west. Although, she had also heard that General Grant was on his way toward the east, with a rumored destination of Chattanooga. It might mean that Jonas and whomever he served under was headed east too. But before she'd allow herself to get her hopes up, it would be true only *if* he were still alive. God alone knew if her beloved husband had, or hadn't, suffered the same fate as the general he last served under. *Earl Van Dorn.*

She had learned from Lucinda that General Van Dorn had been shot and killed this past May, inside his headquarters south of Nashville. The news saddened her—mostly because she thought she might never learn of her husband's fate, since she had seen where brigades and regiments had been reorganized or disbanded upon a key leader's demise. At best, Jonas had likely been absorbed by some other cavalry under a different general… and at worst, his fate was now lost to her forever.

Stop it! Damn it, Hattie, quit thinking like that! Besides, you know full well Jonas isn't anywhere near here! DON'T do this to yourself—NOT now!

That's when she glimpsed the latest wild-eyed Yankee coming at her, his hands covered in blood as he charged her with his rifle's bayonet poised to kill. That is, until Lucinda intervened, saving her life once again.

"You think this is a game?" Lucinda screamed, livid and justifiably so.

"Of course not!" Hattie glared at her while their Twenty-Third comrades charged toward the hole in the Union line. The pair would only have a moment before being noticed inside the thicket—either by their comrades or the enemy. "I don't know what just happened... I sensed something strange and then thought maybe it meant somebody was close by."

"Who? Your missing husband?" Lucinda asked derisively.

Hattie had learned to deeply admire her female counterpart, to the point they had become quite close during the past ten months. And although she sensed Lucinda's devotion to her was stronger than how she felt in return, Hattie viewed her as the sister she had wished Stella would've been. Someone close, and with whom she could share her deepest fears and secrets. She could do that with Lucinda... and yet, at that particular moment, she resented the fact that Lucinda had grown to know her so well.

Wounded by her remark, Hattie merely nodded.

"You think he's here... fighting with us somewhere nearby?" Lucinda's tone was less harsh, though she still eyed her in disbelief. "Honestly?"

"No." Hattie shook her head, frowning. "He's probably in Mississippi. Or, maybe he's chasing down the Yankees to the west of us under General Grant."

Lucinda nodded slightly, casting a wary glance around them. "Billy said something last week, something about Grant's army was now headed east... We better get going, or we might miss the best action we've had to date."

There was disappointment in Lucinda's tone, and Hattie tried not to think about it too long, worried she might once again find herself distracted and ineffective. Following Lucinda and her chilling 'Rebel Yell', Hattie ran to keep up. Focused mostly on the Yankees ahead, who were desperately trying to close the breach, she glanced again at Breckinridge's troops in the distance. Too hard to make out anything other than gleaming bayonets in the late morning sunlight amid thick smoke from muskets and cannon fire, she wondered again why she thought about Jonas. All she could do was utter a muted prayer for his protection—wherever he was—and try to stay alive another day.

Chapter Fifteen

Sunday evening, September 20ᵗʰᵗ, 1863... shortly after dark at

Chickamauga.

Lester Smith had spent the better part of supper glorying in his role of helping General Brown's Brigade route the Union Army at Lafayette Road. Hattie and Lucinda listened politely, knowing the kid, who still looked two years shy of his purported age of sixteen, could use the boost in confidence. In the present moment, it mattered little that what appeared to be a decisive victory in the day's battle soon changed, as General Brannan's determined Yankees eventually turned back the tide of Confederates, leaving Brown's troops further away from the road than where they had been when the day's fighting began... During the past few months, Lester had become increasingly withdrawn. The reality of a long pointless war seemed to eventually take its toll on every soldier, but Hattie noticed how the empty forlorn faces belonged to those with deeper sensitivities—including Lester—as compared to the boorish brutes among the ranks.

Despite Lester's difficult life at home before joining the war, the boy from Manchester, Tennessee was one who at first embraced living in the moment, just as the less sensitive infantrymen were wont to do. Yet, Hattie had noticed early on his tendency to linger, looking at the dead longer than anyone else in their small regiment when they marched past the bodies being lined up for burial, or when they came upon individual soldiers that had died within a few hours of the Twenty-Third's arrival to a battleground.

No one did that unless they carried at least some empathy for their fellow man. Lester kept much of what he felt to himself, which in Hattie's estimation could only worsen the emotional pain and loneliness inevitable when immersed daily in this hellish environment.

Unlike Lucinda, Lester had also been noticeably reticent with what he shared about his previous life, other than dropping hints about his rigidly strict upbringing. Back in July, Lucinda finally managed to get him to reveal that he was the third oldest of four brothers, and the only one sent to fight in the war to defend the Confederacy by his father, Buford Smith. It seemed callous to Hattie that Buford insisted on any of his children to fight a war when he was physically able to do so himself. But even stranger was Buford's decision to send one of the younger boys instead of Lester's older brothers, Lelan and Simeon. According to Lester, his eldest brother, Lelan, had turned twenty-one the month before Lester showed up in Murfreesboro with his father's musket and Bowie knife in hand.

Despite Buford's curious decision, Lester's feathers would get easily ruffled when Hattie or Lucinda said anything remotely disparaging about his father. As for his mother, Martha Mae, she had died soon after the birth of the youngest brother, Paul, leaving the four boys to an ill-tempered and impatient man to rear. Hattie couldn't help but wonder how his life might've turned out far differently if his momma was still around.

"I'd say he turned out all right," Lucinda had told Hattie back in early summer, after the mostly happy-go-lucky kid told them the first sordid details about his upbringing. "Hey, his shitty existence ain't no worse than yours or mine. He'll be just fine."

For the most part, Lucinda was right. Lester had adjusted to army life quickly and he soon became one of Captain Powers' favored 'stand-ins' for whenever Sergeant Joe McCracken was busy with other assigned tasks. That extra attention, along with his friendship with the two gals he thought were teenage boys, seemed to help Lester push away the sorrowful longing Hattie sometimes discerned in his deep hazel eyes....

"Well, you done real good, kid," said Lucinda, when dusk had given way to darkness and he had finally finished detailing his exploits.

She stood up from their dying campfire to retrieve a few small wood pieces to keep it going a while longer. Despite orders to keep the embers low, which ignored the fact everyone knew the Union Army had left for good and was likely halfway back to Chattanooga by then, Hattie felt certain that all the soldiers stuck spending the night on the battlefield were grateful for whatever warmth they could get. The night before, General Cleburne's men and others were forced to sleep on this very same place of death—among many of their fallen comrades that had yet to be removed. The weather had been bitterly cold then, and unlike tonight, those soldiers were forbidden from striking the smallest flame for fear of being easy targets for the Yankees hidden behind temporary fortifications along Lafayette Road.

"It's just too bad we couldn't keep the Yanks runnin' on their heels all the way back to Chattanooga," Lucinda continued, upon her return.

"I thought General Bragg intended to retake the city?" Hattie had heard this claim mentioned while on picket duty just two nights earlier. "If so, we should've pursued them all the way there."

"Billy's in agreement with you, Henry, as am I," Lucinda advised. "However, from what I can tell—and have heard it stated several times the past few hours—our illustrious leader is bettin' the Federals will be back, and we shall see yet another day of fightin' at dawn. That's why we're camped out here tonight among our own dead and dyin' men."

True. A good portion of the Army of Tennessee remained camped throughout the long battlefield, where most of the fighting had taken place over the past two days. The dead and dying from both armies lay spread out amid tiny campfires dotting the darkness for as far as Hattie could see in either direction along Lafayette Road. There had been a fairly strong effort earlier that evening, by the nurses and some Southern soldiers, to try and ease the suffering of both the Confederate and Union wounded. Yet, even so, the men they couldn't reach and the ones they couldn't save still lay in the darkness, moaning as they waited for their agony to end.

It seemed ghoulish to plunder the bodies for useful items, such as unused cartridges and shoes with intact soles. But the three of them had grown impatient for the wagon to come around with whatever was left of these same items gathered from the battlefield earlier that night. By the time it would arrive, surely it would've been picked over by the larger regiments.

After supper, they set out to claim what they could from the deceased soldiers located not far from their campfire, accompanied by other soldiers from their battalion.

The stench from those who had passed away, earlier that Sunday along with those who fell on Saturday, soon became overwhelming. The threesome didn't make it very far before turning back. Hattie bit her lip to keep from squealing after walking on top of corpses so plentiful that touching the Earth's surface rarely happened. When she did feel the muddy soil beneath her bare toes, it came with the sickening realization that the grime clinging to her feet consisted mostly of congealed blood.

In a way, it was sadly ironic for Hattie. She recalled how shocked she was to see barefoot soldiers back in December, scarcely picturing how such misfortune could befall an infantryman. Yet here she was, nine months later facing the same affliction. The affect upon her was profound, since she now had a better understanding on a personal level of what the brave Alabama regiments had long endured.

Although her feet hadn't become infected with gangrene, her heels and toes, blackened from dirt and the usual grime from going almost a month since her last stolen shoes had worn out and been discarded, ached mightily. She and Lester had followed Lucinda's lead in creating moccasins from tree leaves and plants in the areas where they marched, though these provided short-lived relief. Bleeding sores on both calloused feet sent twinges up her shins with almost every step, but Hattie kept the discomfort to herself. Unlike in December, when the Alabama troops stood out from many of the other regiments due to their shoeless condition, at present most of the Confederates in attendance were barefoot. From what Hattie recalled from the past two days of exhaustive fighting, many Yankee soldiers were also fighting without footwear.

The three of them managed to collect several cartridge boxes and two pairs of shoes that fit Hattie and Lester on the way back, after stumbling on a cluster of corpses less than thirty feet from their smoldering campfire. Lucinda stated she would try to find a pair that fit her in the morning. For the moment, something else had drawn her attention. A pair of local women, inappropriately dressed in what appeared to be evening gowns, seemed to be looking for something near the road... or most likely, someone. The women were accompanied by what looked like a Confederate colonel, although difficult to say for certain due to the soft glow from a single lantern carried by one of the women.

"What the hell they's lookin' for, you reckon?" Lester squinted in the trio's direction. "I believe I saw 'em lookin' 'round earlier, only over there... down yonder." He pointed to an area further south.

"Well, it's got to be somethin' important," said Lucinda, following his gaze, as did Hattie. "More than likely, it's *somebody* rather than a thing... Probably lookin' for an acquaintance among those fallen would be my guess."

One of the women pointed to what might be a body, situated next to something much larger. *Maybe it's a horse?* Meanwhile, the colonel shook his head. What looked like a sergeant, who hadn't been visible until then, stepped up from behind the group and bent down to whatever the object was. The colonel took the lantern from the woman holding it and held the light source lower, near where the other man stooped. It soon became clear that the colonel's subordinate was turning over a corpse. The woman who had held the lantern let out a heartrending shriek and immediately fell to her knees sobbing.

Hattie couldn't tell if Lucinda and Lester experienced anything akin to sympathy for this woman's grief at that moment... but she did. The woman's anguished cries into the night, at the obvious loss of someone deeply cherished, were what she had long expected to have happen to her, should she ever find Jonas dead on a battlefield. In that moment, her heart felt as if it had stopped beating, and she could almost literally feel the woman's misery—along with the hopelessness of knowing she would have to carry on her life without the most important thing in it.

Her man is dead!

"Well I'll be goddamned!" Lucinda suddenly hissed, pointing to an area roughly fifty feet away, to the right of their campfire, and not quite halfway to where the officer, his assistant, and the other woman huddled around the grieving debutante. "That son of a bitch is laughin' at 'em!"

"Who you talkin' 'bout?" Lester asked. "Oh, shit... it's Malcolm Bates! Why's he actin' like a damned fool? Looks like the colonel's motionin' for him to get his ass away from there!"

Private Bates' laughter grew louder and the colonel yelled punishment threats at him when the disrespect continued unabated. Hattie couldn't believe Malcolm's cruel blustering, nor the audacity to trade insults with a superior officer. Then again, Malcolm might've been drunk or realized he wasn't fully visible to the colonel or his assistant from where he peered at them from behind a broken wagon wheel. He retorted with a few more malicious taunts before trying to scurry away like the yellow cur Hattie had made a point to avoid. For the most part, Malcolm had left her and Lucinda alone, following his embarrassing encounter in December. But occasionally he still tried to engage Lester in conversation.

After the colonel and his assistant led the two women back onto Lafayette Road and away from the battleground, and everyone else had returned to peacefully minding their business at camp, Hattie, Lucinda, and Lester began settling in for the night. Sleep wouldn't be easy, and a soft breeze brought more of the battlefield's pungent smell their way. Surely, it would only get worse as the night wore on.

"At least we can't see 'em in the dark," said Lester, quietly, as the three 'youngun brats of B Company' lay on their bedrolls. "Or it might be a hell of a lot worse."

Hattie refused to picture anything worse, largely because she didn't want to allow her mind to visualize new horrors. But after witnessing ever-increasing calamities as the war continued, she already knew it'd likely be impossible to imagine anything as grim as what awaited her and her Confederate comrades in the near future.

In the meantime, she ignored the odor of death as best she could, focusing on Lester's and Lucinda's light snores and the few stars visible during that overcast night. But despite all efforts to try and return to the one happy place she relied upon inside her mind, where she and Jonas would lounge carefree along the shaded banks of Sugar Creek, her thoughts were relentlessly drawn back to the woman in the fine blue gown. Again and again, Hattie was forced to revisit that forlorn creature as she clung to her beloved beau's lifeless body while wailing inconsolably into the northern Georgia night.

Chapter Sixteen

Wednesday morning, November 25th, 1863...

Missionary Ridge, Chattanooga, Tennessee.

The victory over the Union Army at Chickamauga seemed to bring the very worst out in General Braxton Bragg during the following two months. First was the mistake of believing the Army of Tennessee could outlast the Army of the Cumberland, which had successfully retreated to Chattanooga in the aftermath of General Rosecrans' defeat on September 20th. Seizing the opportunity to cut off the Union Army and its supply lines gave the Confederate commander a false sense of superiority, and Bragg foolishly believed his army could withstand the ravages of hunger while anticipating far worse conditions for Rosecrans' troops.

Yet somehow, despite their hardships, Rosecrans' army hung on long enough to receive reinforcements coming from the west under General Grant. He also received additional troops from the southeast, courtesy of General Sherman and others. Soon, the Union forces in and around Chattanooga were restored to full strength, and the tenuous grip that General Bragg failed to capitalize upon would soon prove to be a major blunder with far-reaching consequences. Once Grant replaced Rosecrans with General George H. Thomas, Bragg's control of the situation slipped through his fingers like sand.

The defeat in October at Brown's Ferry weakened the siege, and then the demoralizing Confederate loss at Lookout Mountain just yesterday evening had left the entire Army of Tennessee humiliated. At least that was Hattie's and Lucinda's take on things, largely based upon what they'd witnessed with their own eyes.

Forced to march through blustery conditions in sub-freezing temperatures late Tuesday night, the remnants of the Twenty-Third Battalion didn't stop until they reached Missionary Ridge in the wee hours of Wednesday. Now serving under General Breckinridge as their corps commander, as part of Major General C.L. Stevenson's Division, only their Brigade General, John Calvin Brown, remained the same after the casualty-devastated Twenty-Third had been combined with the Forty-Fifth Tennessee Regiment—yet another unit hit with heavy losses at Chickamauga. The two regiments that together had lost over a third of their combined infantry in September, and had suffered more losses since then, now barely counted as a single regiment.

As the troops began the process of entrenching themselves along the ridge to be ready for battle at daylight, Hattie wondered if further reorganizations would soon come. More losses had hit Breckinridge's army on Tuesday, both during the confrontation at Lookout Mountain and during the retreat northwest to Missionary Ridge. Morale among the soldiers of B Company had never been lower—definitely true from her perspective, as she mentally reviewed the past twelve months since her enlistment. Tormented by perpetual hunger, the latest three-day rations had nearly disappeared shortly after they were given this past Monday morning. The Twenty-Third's survivors had been reduced to a cold, dirty, and lice-covered team of embittered infantrymen.

"How long do you think it'll take for the Yankees to figure out we're up here?" Hattie asked Lucinda, through teeth chattering as the pair shivered in the inescapable chill.

Hattie had taken a dead Yankee's wool blue coat the previous afternoon, ignoring Private Templeton's loathing look in response. Lester had done the same. All three had followed the lead of the majority in Brown's Brigade in recent weeks, where they had resorted to tying rags torn from deceased soldiers' garments around their feet, after the deepening cold made the previous options to protect their extremities from frostbite impractical. Finding salvageable shoes that would last longer than a week had become an increasing rarity, bringing the realization that the enemy faced similar hardships in regard to footwear. As had been the case last winter, some of the soldiers preferred to go barefoot rather than deal with coverings that would either continuously fall off their feet, or proved to be a grave liability when the rags became wet.

Lester drew close to both women in a non-subtle attempt to shield himself from the frigid breezes flowing over the ridge.

"Once dawn arrives, I bet Captain Simpson will give the okay for us to build a small fire," said Lucinda, pulling up her frayed gray jacket's collar to try and block the latest gust's assault. "I've got enough chicory coffee left in my haversack to warm us up a bit."

Hattie nodded her appreciation, knowing the small bits of crumbled hardtack they each carried would have to provide enough nourishment to get to nightfall. There was always the hope of replenished rations when not under the threat of immediate attack. If today could be better than yesterday, and somehow, she and her companions succeeded in keeping the enemy from pushing them back further, then maybe supper would bring new rations that could temporarily take care of the hunger cramps seizing her stomach.

She looked forward to the fire in a few hours—if it proved to be allowed this time, which wasn't assured. It wouldn't happen if an attack from the Union Army was imminent, or if her battalion was directed to move again. Both possibilities were strong.

On the way to the ridge she had stepped into an icy brook, seizing her feet and legs with renewed surges of pain that didn't let up until numbness set in.

If only I can warm my feet for a little while, maybe the damned rags would dry out before it's time to fight again.

Nothing was certain anymore. Amid all the changes facing her battalion, now under Captain Simpson's supervision after Major Tazewell Newman was wounded at Chickamauga, the only constant reality was being turned away again and again by the Yankees. Despite the urgings of his staff, General Bragg in his acute stubbornness wouldn't relinquish Chattanooga. After learning about this futile stalemate through officer grumblings, it became obvious to everyone around Hattie that General Grant had gained the upper hand. It was just a matter of time before the Federals made good on their intentions to permanently drive the Confederate Army out of Tennessee.

Stopping the Union onslaught would have to happen here at the ridge. All the men and a few other women she and Lucinda had recently come upon, also disguised as boys, bore the same destitute look in their eyes. Defeated... and yet Hattie knew the spirit of the Army of Tennessee would be rekindled the moment the Yankees came after them again. It had been the case with each encounter that had followed the victory at Chickamauga. Yes, the Rebel fire still burned in the infantry's collective souls... if only they possessed the physical stamina to last.

We must somehow find the strength… I fear the devil Bragg won't feed us again if we lose!

Seeking a distraction to not think about the bitter cold, Bragg's inhumane treatment of his troops, and the fact that the sunrise was still a few hours away, Hattie thought about a recent conversation between her, Lucinda, and Lester. It was on a clear night two weeks ago, though without the near-full moon that had illuminated their nocturnal journey to the ridge. She recalled how the stars seemed almost close enough to reach out and touch.

She and her companions were hungry that evening, too. Hattie's makeshift shoes were drying next to a small fire while she tentatively massaged her bleeding feet, which somehow seemed to take her mind off how famished she felt. She was thinking about deserting, and had for days. In fact, they all talked about it that night at supper. Lester mentioned it most, but even Lucinda admitted thinking about it as well. In hushed voices, they discussed plans as if it would be easy enough to simply leave. Since Hattie had nowhere to go, she and Lucinda joked about either heading south to the Gulf of Mexico and take their chances there, or journeying out west. But Lester solemnly reminded them about the difficulty of avoiding the provosts and home guards "collectin' bounties on yeller-bellied deserters".

"You honestly believe they'd send anyone to find our sorry asses?" Lucinda had playfully chided. "A provost might well shoot or hang us on the spot, but rest assured, there ain't ever goin' to be a single damned penny put on *our* heads!"

Lucinda's response brought to mind the executions General Bragg had insisted upon—some under highly questionable circumstances. In particular, Hattie thought about those soldiers punished for foraging to find food under their present conditions, where three-day rations had rarely made it past the first day, and usually disappeared within hours of disbursement. If the search for further nourishment made for an unexcused absence, it could get a soldier whipped or shot.

Although either punishment was highly undesirable, Hattie and Lucinda viewed whipping as potentially the most humiliating option. Forced to strip down to their underclothing, or naked, the whip would not only reveal their true sex, but depending on the general's mood upon learning of the deceit, Bragg might insist on carrying forth as if the women were men. Three strips of leather attached to a wooden paddle would deliver the sentence. Thirty-nine strikes had become the consistent number meted out—and that had been the way things were handled long before Hattie's enlistment. But in effect it was one hundred and seventeen lashes, due to the triple shot of leather ripping into a soldier's backside—or front, if the victim turned to protest during the administering of a judgment.

Hattie shuddered at the thought of the one whipping sentence she'd recently been required to witness. The soldier belonged to the Forty-Fifth Tennessee, and for missing the morning drill session while foraging, his punishment was delivered that very afternoon. The man's screams still resounded in her mind as if freshly witnessed. But she fully believed he preferred this punishment to sitting on his own coffin while awaiting death by a firing squad—a process that could take several hours for the condemned to think about their impending demise. Lucinda had correctly surmised that Bragg possessed a perverse sadistic streak, which showed up most when a soldier was about to be publicly punished....

"I wish Captain Simpson would've let us take some shots when we had 'em surrounded, back inside Chattanooga," Lester lamented. "I'd have taken out the Yankee boys mindin' the cannons. Hell, we might be sittin' 'round a roarin' fire in the city right now, with the generals and colonels up in the hills, dancin' with them fine plantation ladies like they did in Murfreesboro last Christmas."

Lucinda smiled admiringly and added a supportive nod.

"I wish they would've let you do it, too, Lester." Hattie reached over and patted his shoulder firmly. "But, General Bragg made it clear he'd penalize us for wasting any ammunition—even though you're right. We sure as hell could've taken out the Yankee's artillery regiments, and who knows what else."

Lester and Lucinda nodded and looked away—a clear indication they were done talking about what might've been. Another missed opportunity had come and gone, along with the best chance so far to remove Bragg from leading the Army of Tennessee. Billy Powers had shared with Lucinda and Lester that when Jefferson Davis came for a visit in October, every general—including the recently added Franklin Beaufort, who would leave soon after—had hoped for Bragg's removal. Captain Powers said that nearly every general present had signed a petition to dismiss Bragg for incompetence, and every one of them expected that was why Davis showed up during Chattanooga's languishing siege.

But to almost everyone's astonishment and disappointment, Davis left Bragg in charge after giving his subordinates the floor to air their complaints. Since then, several generals had been relieved of their command, and General Beaufort had been sent back west. The shake up made no sense to Lucinda, who had a better eye for the devious workings behind the army's orderly façade. Hattie and Lester felt dismayed as well. With the backing of Jefferson Davis, Braxton Bragg appeared reinvigorated, and therefore entrenched as their commander for the foreseeable future…

The Union's attack came later Wednesday morning than expected, amid spitting snow. As Hattie anticipated, Brown's Brigade and the rest of Stevenson's division rose to the occasion. Along with the troops of Cheatham, Gist, and Cleburne, they turned back the Federals' first few attempts to ascend the hill to reach the top of the ridge. Together, the combined forces had inflicted enough casualties upon the enemy that Lucinda and Lester joined Hattie in her assumption that any further Union assaults against the Confederates perched atop the ridge would be much more subdued. For much of the day, they were able to hold their ground easily, and on more than one occasion, several regiments were sent in pursuit of the Yankees scrambling down the hillside in panicked retreat after failing to reach the ridge's apex.

Toward nightfall, however, the pesky Union General Thomas Wood's troops had finally managed to break through the middle of the Confederate line to the south of Breckinridge's position. Soon after, Union troops began to collapse the northern and southern line locations. While the latest development portended yet another demoralizing Confederate defeat was on the horizon, the Twenty-Third and Forty-Fifth had joined the effort to keep the effect of Wood's middle surge from decimating the southern section of Stevenson's line.

Hattie and Lester had just heard the dreaded order to fall back from the battlefront. However, it appeared that Lucinda either didn't hear it or chose to ignore the latest acknowledgement of defeat. Hattie sought to relay the message again to Lucinda as she staggered back from the fighting at the edge of the ridge, nearly slamming Hattie in the gut with the butt of her musket.

"What in the hell's wrong with you?"

Lucinda's dingy face carried a deathly pallor, and she only gave Hattie a look of confusion in response. She then muttered 'sorry' while lowering her weapon.

"Captain Powers and Sergeant McCracken just pulled us back. We need to leave now!" Hattie gently grabbed Lucinda's arm when she cast a longing look back toward the edge of the ridge, where the Yankees now outnumbered their Rebel companions. Some of their fellow infantrymen from the Twenty-Third were surrendering. "We can't save them—"

"That's not it, Henry!" Lucinda interrupted her. "My God, it happened... *just like I feared!* I need to go back and check for sure!"

She pulled away and started to head back toward the line, where the Yankees were presently overrunning their previous defenses and would surely capture Lucinda, or shoot her dead. Hattie grabbed her arm again—much more forcefully.

"You don't need to do anything other than get your ass out of here with me and Lester!"

"I shot him, Hattie!"

"Who?"

Lucinda's imploring look was enough to reveal the man's identity before the name could leave her lips.

"Jeff? You're sure you just now shot your brother?" Hattie couldn't hide her shock, made worse by Lucinda's tearful nod. "It could've been someone else. You know how things are... everyone looks alike these days. Hell, almost half our army is dressed in Union blue it seems, and I shot a Yankee just yesterday dressed in gray."

Lucinda shook her head, much more adamantly than when she nodded a moment ago. She wept inconsolably and began to collapse upon the ground. Hattie tried to hold her up, while keeping a watchful eye toward the line that continued to disintegrate.

"No... no, I know my brother. Despite the beard and the fact the Yanks ain't bathin' any better than us, I'd swear it was him! ... God help *me! ...I do believe I've killed him!"*

Frozen to where she stood, Hattie was at a loss as to what to do next. She pictured Jeffrey Templeton climbing the hillside, only to be shot by his sister pretending to be a man. Meanwhile, at present Union soldiers continued to swell over the ridge, hollering "Chickamauga! Chickamauga!" as they came.

A volley of gunshots made the next decision for her. The first shots came from the Yankees steadily closing in on where she and Lucinda stood, since Hattie had yet to lay down her musket in surrender. But before she made a move to give in, Lester yelled for her and Lucinda to stay down. To her amazement, he responded to the Union shots with a repeating rifle he had picked up from a fallen Union soldier that afternoon. As the Yankees ducked for cover until more could join them in pursuit of prisoners, it bought Hattie enough time to drag Lucinda out of immediate harm's way.

If not for Lester's bravery and devotion to her and Lucinda, as he continued to fire toward the enemy with a loaded pistol which he had also picked up earlier, they likely would've been killed or captured that evening. As it was, it took both him and Hattie to get Lucinda back on her feet and away from the battle, staying focused on the task of catching up with the rest of their fleeing regiment headed back toward Chickamauga.

Pursued by gunfire, none of the three engaged the enemy any longer. No one looked back either. Wincing as bullets struck the trees around them and tore up the ground near their feet, the assault didn't let up until the three had scrambled down the opposite hillside, and the rest of their regiment was finally in sight.

By then, Lucinda had regained much of her composure, and Hattie sensed the resolute confidence returning to her friend from the moment the first raised muskets from the marching Confederate Army came into view. Lucinda likely had already buried her grief beneath the façade that had served her well up until then, although Hattie understood it was far from dealt with. Not to mention, she still wondered if it truly was her brother that Lucinda had shot while the Yankees swarmed the ridge. After all, it wasn't like they'd had time to shake hands or strike up a friendly conversation.

Soon, the trio had safely rejoined the line, and the sound of gun blasts behind them steadily faded. Another battle had been lost, and this one came with an extra personal tragedy beyond the usual casualties. But dealing with it all, including the return of their fatigue and dire hunger, would have to wait... at least until they reached their next destination. *Chickamauga Station.*

Chapter Seventeen

Monday evening, February 22ⁿᵈ, 1864… nestled in the woods

near Okolona, Mississippi.

After a long day spent battling Union forces under the direction of General William 'Sooy' Smith in northeast Mississippi, spirits were mostly high among the riders that served General Franklin Beaufort's cavalry. All in all, the grueling efforts of Beaufort's men earned a badly needed Confederate victory—made sweeter by the fact they accomplished the feat against a foe that outnumbered their cavalry three to one.

As had often been true since Jonas joined Beaufort's Elite Company, the general's brilliance as a strategist had once again played a key role in keeping Smith's cavalry confused and on the run. But Monday hadn't started out that way, and Captain Charles May had later agreed the initial attack, shortly after dawn, seemed less than assured of success when Beaufort's first charge soon faced a dismounted cavalry that had constructed barricades around their positions.

Whoa! Perhaps we should dismount as well?

Jonas whistled to Captain May to draw his attention to the fortified Union line ahead of them, shrouded by a morning mist that had yet to evaporate. But Charlie shook his head, determined to follow Beaufort's lead to attack the line, even though doing so left the Confederate riders fully exposed. Despite the likelihood of immediate casualties, in blind faith and raw courage the rest of the Third Regiment picked up the pace to keep up with their leader. Not that Jonas feared much, since dying in a valorous moment would mean he might awaken in Hattie's arms in some version of Paradise. Lately, he pictured her loving smile most often when galloping toward the enemy poised to kill with rifles and cannons at the ready, when the chances of him and his companions receiving mortal wounds were greatest.

The plan that morning had been to force the entire Union cavalry to retreat, since the general's scouts returning two hours before dawn had reported that Smith's rearguard was already retreating. Most likely this was due to what appeared to be a large contingent of slaves that had recently fled from plantations burnt to the ground throughout the region by General Sherman's army. Jonas had overheard Beaufort and his younger brother, Colonel Jeffrey Beaufort, discussing the migration of the disenfranchised Negroes seeking refuge with the Union Army and had thus begun heading northwest toward Pontotoc during the night.

It made sense that Smith's men wouldn't remain camped just south of Okolona for much longer, less than two miles away from General Beaufort's position on Sunday night. Nearly all of the general's officers agreed that these Yankees would surely seek to rejoin the rest of his army on the move at some point. Jeffrey Beaufort had engaged the same army Sunday afternoon, near the swamps of the Tombigbee River.

His older brother, Franklin, had joined the fight soon after and was able to force Smith into a retreat to his camp, while the Yankee commander's rearguard at that time remained in the swamplands to fight against Jeffrey's group until finally forced to retreat two hours later. Satisfied Smith's army was settling in for the evening, Jeffrey and his men returned to where General Beaufort's troops were bivouacked.

After the general consulted with his colonels in the early hours of Monday, the decided upon plan was to launch a frontal assault against General Smith's army while probing the strength of either flank. Once the weakest points were determined, they would exploit those flaws and tear apart the Union lines. It seemed highly probable that Smith would fully retreat to Pontotoc at that point, based upon what the scouts had picked up from conversations among the Union troops Sunday night....

After the initial charge failed to break the Yankee resolve, General Beaufort ordered additional passes as the morning sun began its frost-melting ascent in earnest and was soon rewarded for his patience. The Federal line began to crumble, and it appeared the contest would end before afternoon. However, when Smith's forces reformed on a ridge less than a mile from their original position that morning, the Union began to rally. Then, tragedy struck unexpectedly.

Jeffrey Beaufort was in the process of leading his brigade against Smith's reformed line when suddenly a fragment from an exploding cannonball struck him in the neck, throwing him from his horse. Franklin was in the vicinity when it happened, and despite fierce enemy fire, he rushed to where his brother lay dying on the battlefield. As had often been the case, the general ignored his own welfare as he rode out to where Jeffrey had fallen.

For Jonas, it brought to mind a telling moment at Chickamauga five months earlier, back when the general crossed Reed's Bridge alone. Beaufort had ventured that brisk Friday afternoon to within one hundred yards of the enemy, seemingly unfazed by the bullets and grapeshot aimed in his direction as he surveyed the enemy's position. Then he returned to his cavalry and a stunned infantry regiment from Murfreesboro witnessing the event, and who had finished rebuilding the bridge just before the audacious Confederate leader ventured across it. Jonas doubted he'd ever forget the infantrymen murmuring among themselves in awe as they watched the physically imposing 'wizard' casually guide his service horse back over the bridge, as if the Union Army was miles away instead of still within rifle range of putting a bullet or two in his back.

But on this day five months later, Jonas and his companions were the ones deeply affected. This time, it was the general's depth of soul as a human being, where his vulnerability proved every bit as compelling as the man's brazen fearlessness. Jonas understood immediately that very few of his comrades, if any, had ever seen Franklin Beaufort shed tears. Jonas was struck by the general's devotion and outpouring of grief as he knelt beside the body of his younger brother, holding his head in his lap as he wept.

Jonas and the rest of the Elite Company covered for their beloved leader while Charlie and Levi ran out onto the battlefield to bring him and his brother's body back to safety. Beaufort angrily waved them off, placing his brother's hat over Jeffrey's face and telling his adjutant to remove his brother's body when safe enough to do so. Then he remounted his horse and returned to where his cavalry waited.

"Prepare to attack!" he commanded. With his eyes filled with tears and his face flushed by rage, Beaufort raised his saber in his right hand, which Jonas had watched him sharpen that very morning. He then placed his other hand upon his cherished Colt revolver and immediately led a furious charge against the Union line.

A rain of bullets and renewed cannon fire greeted the latest Confederate assault, but Beaufort would not be denied. His cavalry broke through the line, cutting through blue coats underestimating the general's vehemence. The fighting was the bloodiest Jonas could recall up to that point, and not just from watching Beaufort use his saber to cut through the dismounted Yankees during the battle. The rest of his cavalry—Jonas included—also engaged in hand-to-hand combat that left their ragged gray coats heavily streaked in crimson.

The event seemed almost surreal in its violence, amid the ground-shaking boom from cannons and close-range explosions from rifles and muskets pointed in all directions. Neighing cries from horses and the hair-raising timbre of the famed yells from Jonas and his companions were peppered by the death screams from mortally wounded men on both sides. The carnage, though numbering far-fewer casualties than Shiloh or Chickamauga, was the same in Jonas' eyes, and made more poignant by the event that inspired the unbridled fury: the death of Jeffrey Beaufort.

Jonas expected Smith's army to turn tail and run when faced with the Confederate's renewed passion fed by malice, and he doubted any of his cohorts would've blamed the Federals for doing so. No cowardice, but an understanding that a much more inspired and determined force than the Yankees had first encountered that day was now bent on their full destruction.

Yet, Smith's army fought on—despite retreating as they continued to trade gunfire and resort to their swords when cornered. Their defiance seemed to further anger Beaufort, who remained in harm's way. Twice he was nearly killed, and Jonas was near enough to witness both occasions. The first involved an artillery explosion that blew his horse out from under him. Scraped up but not seriously injured, and despite the delivery of instant death to his horse, the general would mount up again—only to have the second horse shot from under him as well.

By then, the fight and flight behavior of Smith's army had moved them a few miles from where the battle had started. The early afternoon sun hovered brightly above the ongoing contest. Meanwhile, Jonas and Charlie confirmed with each other the foregone conclusion that the Yankee retreat would continue without needing any more prodding beyond what the Confederates had already applied. Captain May was among the officers encouraging Beaufort to consider calling off the pursuit and not pressing the general's luck, especially after having two horses shot from under him.

"Goddamn it, Charlie, there's still a war going on! I'll be damned if we give up fighting today!" He shouted angrily. "And, that goes for the rest of y'all trying to talk me out of chasing these sons of bitches out of here! So, get me another horse—bring me *King Phillip!*"

From what Jonas had gathered during the past fourteen months riding with Beaufort, Captain May was one of the general's closest friends. But Jonas had never seen Beaufort this upset with any of his officers before. Usually, that level of wrath was reserved for his superiors, such as General Braxton Bragg. Beaufort had never forgiven Bragg for raiding his cavalry, shortly after Jonas joined in December 1862. At that time, Beaufort hadn't forced a handful of officers and experienced riders to comply with the order, after they refused to leave on the threat he'd have to shoot 'em. Since then, Jonas had witnessed several occasions where Charlie and the others could sway Beaufort to step back and reevaluate a situation when there was good reason to do so. The general had repeatedly shown an admiration for those who could match wits and intelligence with his own, and if an alternate idea made sense, he'd pursue it.

Not that day.

As if aware further arguing would be pointless, or downright dangerous, no one said another word and waited for Beaufort's personal servant to retrieve the stallion he prized above all others.

"Those fellers out yonder have no idea the mischief comin' their way," Charlie told Jonas, as the horse the men affectionately called "Iron Grey" was brought and saddled up for Beaufort. The men's nickname for the beautiful white saddle horse with a black mane and tail came about mostly on account of King Phillip's seeming hatred and open hostility for any man dressed in blue. "I just pray the Good Lord will overlook our testin' fate with a critter that hates the Yanks even more than we do!"

It didn't take long for Captain May's hushed observations to be proven true. As expected, the general and his beloved horse set out in haste to make up for the time lost waiting to resume the rout of Smith's army, with Charlie, Levi, Jonas, and everyone else belonging to Beaufort's cavalry struggling again to keep up. They soon reengaged the Yankees, who were foolishly lingering where they'd left them. Jeffrey Beaufort's brigade and another regiment from nearby also joined the charge that cut deeper gaps into the Union battle lines. The retreat that followed took both armies on an eleven-mile running battle. As the Federals withdrew, they fell back through a series of defensive positions that included plantations and hastily erected roadblocks.

Beaufort led the charge until his cavalry was engaged to his liking. Jonas found it hard not to smile at the instances where King Phillip bared his teeth and aggressively nickered whenever a Union soldier would attempt to confront the general.

Finally, toward the end of the afternoon, Smith attempted one last counter attack, forming his remaining forces into three battle lines and charging upon the Confederates. Beaufort's men responded with gunfire to disrupt Smith's men at a range of less than fifty yards. The second volley was enough to dissuade Smith from making a third attempt, and his men fled in earnest toward Pontotoc.

Beaufort immediately ordered the end of the pursuit, as his army was running low on ammunition by then. Levi joked to Jonas that Charlie's earlier worry about "the third time bein' a charm" to fell their leader might've come true if the enemy had any inkling that Smith had three times more men than Beaufort that day.

Dusk rapidly approached. Jonas, Levi, and Charlie were laughing with their Company C comrades when screaming pleas for mercy suddenly interrupted their revelry. The cries came from an area less than two hundred feet away, and were answered by musket shots. Jonas had whipped his gaze around to follow Levi's eyes, taking notice that his buddy's smile had disappeared.

What in the hell? It looks like Captain Jacobs and his sergeant just executed a handful of escaped slaves that must've strayed away from Smith's army!

"General Beaufort ain't gonna be happy about this—I'm tellin' you straight, Levi," said Charlie, quietly, while holding out his arm to prevent Levi from approaching the two men walking back toward the rest of the cavalry. "Let him handle it, my friend. I'd just as soon not have to kill them boys myself, if you don't mind… If you go pickin' a goddamn fight, you'll leave me little choice but to get involved."

It was a stark reminder for Jonas—and certainly Levi, too—that many of the men serving under Franklin Beaufort didn't share the general's egalitarian views. Prejudice remained a hidden undercurrent among some of the men, though most understood that Levi and the other Negroes had proved to be indispensable to the cavalry's success. They all carried their own weight, and in battle none showed an ounce of cowardice—the only two traits Jonas cared about. Not to mention, he and Levi had grown to be good friends who genuinely respected each other.

Reflecting on this and the other day's events, the silver lining had been the disruption of Union Commander General Sherman's activities in Mississippi by sending Smith's army scurrying back north—which had been Beaufort's directive and intention. But it came at a terrible price for the commander Jonas respected above all others.

Under the light of a full moon, Jonas had thought he had found a quiet spot where he could be alone and gather his thoughts. Instead, he stumbled on Beaufort quietly mourning his brother's passing. Respectfully, he didn't approach the general and moved back toward camp, settling on a small clearing in the woods where a sizable boulder offered a place to sit.

The air chillier than it had been under the canopy of tall pines from which he emerged, it prompted him to fully button his coat. But the clearing's sereneness offered what he sought, and he could feel a quiet calm settling upon his soul as his wispy breaths rose above him. Despite the moon's brightness, the clear sky offered an opportunity to view many of the constellations. He lingered on them, recalling summer nights in Appleton… nights sitting on the porch of Rufus Porter's farmhouse with his beloved wife leaning against him as they took turns pointing out the various groupings of stars and their proper names.

His heart began to ache and he forced himself to think of something else. Usually, it would be a recent event, and most often it would be the face of a Yankee he had killed—always picturing the fiends who had murdered his family in Appleton, or who had been the ones who killed his brother Zeke at Fort Donelson.

Jonas had personally dispatched nearly a dozen Union cavalrymen that day, and lately the satisfaction he felt in exacting revenge against surrogates in place of those who killed his loved ones had become less and less gratifying. But he held no desire to leave the long bitter conflict, and certainly he would never desert the only army and general he had ever loved since joining the war more than two and a half years earlier.

The main reason he stayed on was that he had nowhere else to go… at least no other place he desired to be. He'd been offered a furlough during the past December, and despite being in Tennessee when it came from Beaufort, he turned the opportunity down. There wasn't any town or city he could picture visiting, even though a few of the other men granted a leave were headed to Columbia, Tennessee, where Hattie's sister, Stella, resided. He especially had no desire to be around family, since all it would do was remind him of what he had lost by not being home in Appleton to defend Hattie and everyone else who had died.

"You can't keep blamin' yourself," Charlie had told him, back at Christmas. "If you'd been there, you'd be deader than a possum caught in a hornets' nest, Jonas. Shortly before you joined us, we'd heard stories about these bands of Yankee vermin that sometimes numbered twenty to thirty men—far too many for you to fight off on your own."

But the guilt and sense of profound loss would still find him when he wasn't vigilant in protecting himself. All he wished for was peace… but most nights his thoughts would invariably turn to Hattie. He tried to picture her as happy and serene in Heaven, wondering if she could somehow see him, and if that's the reason he felt prodded to fight on, and to live. That his survival somehow still mattered to her.

"Nice night. Isn't it, Lieutenant?"

Jonas whirled around.

He had thought for sure he was alone and regretted not paying better attention to his surroundings. He had passed the provost tent that sat roughly thirty feet from where one of today's 'prizes' was being held for what General Beaufort hoped to exchange for two of his officers captured by the Yankees in December during the aforementioned furlough.

"I know how Sherman thinks," Beaufort had commented earlier that evening, when Jonas was in earshot of the general's latest conversation with Charlie. *"And offering him five officers for my two should be enough. Just need a couple more Yankee officers and we'll be ready to do some dealing."*

Captain Willard Burdock, originally from Indiana before the surviving members of his regiment were assigned to Smith's army last fall, had been captured shortly after Jeffrey Beaufort's death. General Beaufort hadn't been made aware of this development until just before supper, and it elicited his only smile that night.

"It is… more for me than you, I'd imagine, Captain," Jonas replied, evenly. "I figure those cuffs ain't much fun to wear in weather like this."

He'd just as soon kill a Yankee than allow the bastard to share their rations. But this was another peculiar trait of

Beaufort's, as he insisted on treating prisoners of war well, and in most cases with far better care than his men could expect to receive if they were captured. The captain's cuffs were attached to a chain that was wrapped around a large cedar's base, and the glow of a small campfire sat less than ten feet away from the tree in an area Buford could reach.

"Your commander is kinder than the majority of Rebs in his position, it seems. He may be a scoundrel, as General Sherman has stated, but he is most definitely a gentleman, too."

Jonas wanted to tear the man's partially visible smirk from his face, but restrained himself. In the dimness, Captain Burdock shook his head, eyeing Jonas as if he didn't fear what he might do. But, strangely, there wasn't contempt in his shaded gaze… just amusement.

"I can tell you're vexed by the apparent contradiction in what you might face, if it were you being kept prisoner by General Smith," Burdock continued. "Depending on how you responded to the presence of the Negroes would prove telling in whether your handcuffs' comfort would be of pertinent concern, or not. My commander was especially worried about what Confederate soldiers under the command of Franklin Beaufort would do to these wretched souls seeking our army's protection."

"You think we're all a bunch of Simon Legrees's?" Jonas replied, his tone testy. "You don't know the half of how things are run in General Beaufort's cavalry. Hell, there's damn near fifty Negroes among us, with more than twenty fighting each day. All were promised their freedom at the war's outset if they joined him in the war effort. He'd tell you himself that they're as brave as anyone else here."

"Fifty former slaves?" Burdock chuckled. He turned himself to better face Jonas, allowing a thin ray of moonlight to fully bathe his left side, revealing an emerald eye that bore an ornery twinkle. "I saw the colored soldier who rides with you, and it appears he enjoys a level of respect lacking toward others not as dark as him. I overheard the provost named James mention to one of your men that six slaves recently freed from a Tupelo plantation were executed this afternoon. Where was your general's favor for them? Or does he only have compassion for those slaves who served him on his Memphis plantations prior to the war?"

Jonas found it harder by the moment to not react with a violent strike against this insolent man with the laughing gaze. Only his respect for Beaufort's orders to leave all prisoners unmolested kept him from delivering a blow.

Besides, what grounds do I truly have to be this irritated? He's just a Yankee asshole possessing a sassy mouth and asking questions I'm in no position to answer....

"I suppose you should ponder the appropriateness of those questions and ask General Beaufort yourself, the next time you see him—should you be so inclined." Jonas tipped his hat after offering his own smug grin. "When you say your prayers tonight, be thankful you're not someone else's prisoner. 'Night, Captain."

Jonas returned to his company, smiling at the thought he might've gotten the better of Burdock at the end of their conversation, based on the man's fading smile after hearing Jonas' closing rebuke. Still, the Yankee captain's questions needled him as he lay in his tent, waiting for sleep to come. It likely meant a restless night ahead, and yet also a rare reprieve from the usual rehashing of his failure at Appleton.

Hattie... wherever you are, please forgive me.

Chapter Eighteen

Wednesday evening, March 30th*, 1864… Dalton, Georgia.*

New shoes, new uniforms, warm coats and daily food rations had done much to restore morale throughout the entire Confederate Army of Tennessee. The changes toward a better existence for the beleaguered infantry had officially begun on December 16th, 1863, when General Joseph Johnston finally took over for General Braxton Bragg, after Bragg managed to lose the entire state of Tennessee to the Union that year.

The official transfer for the role of acting commander, from a brutally abusive leader to one that was 'compassionately' stern, came just in the nick of time. Open talk of desertion had spread to where Hattie, Lucinda, and Lester were among the hundreds of soldiers quietly considering leaving the army as soon as Christmas arrived. Those who were unhappiest no longer worried about being punished for their grumbling remarks, as the latest defeats at Lookout Mountain and Missionary Ridge capped off a disastrous Chattanooga campaign for the South. By December, Jefferson Davis finally had had enough of Bragg's endless excuses and empty promises, and it was just a matter of time before he made the move that had been rumored for the past eleven months.

The surviving remnants of the Twenty-Third Battalion's B Company had pieced together much of what went on inside Braggs' headquarters' walls as the reins to the army were turned over to Johnston. Most of the gossip and more reliable information came from conversations overheard between Captain Powers and Captain Simpson, who in turn had heard it from General Brown. No doubt, the rumor trail had been fed by the open hostility between Bragg and his subordinate generals to whom Brown answered. Hattie figured that Lucinda's analogy of how 'shit flows downhill, and quicker as it nears the bottom' was the most appropriate metaphor to explain how so much information made its way to the common soldier. Likewise, she found it easy to believe that if the war effort had always been a well-managed affair—as it had been the past few months under "General Joe"—no one under the rank of colonel might be the wiser concerning the inner workings of the Tennessee army's higher command.

"At least they's been treatin' us better these days," said Lester. They had just finished supper that night and lounged around a warm blaze, enjoying the fact there were no campfire restrictions and hadn't been for quite some time. Such rules wouldn't apply until the war resumed later that spring, likely in May. "But it looks like I'm gonna have to buy some shoes from the commissary, unless Sergeant McCracken takes pity on an orphan."

"You're planning on telling him that your pa and brothers are dead?" Hattie asked, surprised Lester would engage in such a ruse, ignoring for a moment the fact that hers and Lucinda's identities were forged in falsehood.

"And why the hell not?" countered Lucinda, smiling coyly at Hattie before turning her attention to Lester. "The way I see it, fate took you home to a den of thieves who ain't any better than strangers, Lester. Worse, even... Fate took your shoes, and now it's up to you to finagle another pair. If it were me, I'd work up the best sad story anyone can concoct and commit it to memory so it rings true tomorrow when you visit the commissary... I'd be glad to help you, if you'd like."

"You'd do that?" His face suddenly lit up.

Lucinda shrugged, grinning wickedly as she affirmed with a nod.

Lester's ill-fated return home came during a month-long furlough to Manchester, Tennessee, that was cut short after getting into an argument with his father and brothers over the money paid to him the past sixteen months by the Confederacy. What Lester hadn't spent he kept safe in a saddlebag, and since he had a bad feeling about taking more than thirty dollars home with him, he left the rest in the care of Lucinda and Hattie. As he had worried, his father demanded what he hadn't already spent when he arrived home—roughly twenty-one dollars. Lester refused to give him more than ten dollars, explaining he might need the rest to get back to Dalton.

That answer wasn't acceptable to Buford Smith, who didn't believe Lester's claim that the bulk of his Confederate wages were presently in 'safe keeping' down in Georgia. His brothers didn't believe him either, and though he spent much of his time visiting his Aunt Bessie, his mother's sister who lived a couple of miles away from his father, the tension between him and his siblings finally boiled over into fisticuffs just three days after he arrived home on March 20th.

Robbed of everything but a few coins that added up to less than a dollar, Lester returned to Dalton looking gaunt and famished, and had worn out the new shoes issued to him in January....

"What if General Johnston finds out?" Hattie kept her voice low, as other soldiers made their way past them. It would be time to retire soon, as the morning would bring a renewed schedule of drilling, despite the fact that she and Lucinda had also been granted furloughs and were fortunate to draw the same time frame, set to begin in the afternoon. "Even though he has been far more merciful than the 'cloven foot of tyranny' that used to run things around here, you've seen his response to stealing from the locals. You sure you want to test his ire with a lie, should he discover this story's not true? I'd just as soon pay for your shoes, Lester, to keep you safe."

Lester grinned, but shook his head in response to Hattie's offer. "Henry, you need to hang onto yer money. Same for Louis. But I like the plan of playin' Joe McCracken for pity's sake. Aside from hittin' the side of my face with a snowball that had a rock in it back in January, he owes me five dollars that ain't been paid back yet, from when I lent it to him at the backgammon contest last month."

Hattie recalled both events and knew the latest incident bothered Lester the most. The backgammon tournament was held in a larger tent belonging to one of General Brown's colonels, and involved a dozen so-called 'backgammon experts' from among several Tennessee regiments. The winner was a Lieutenant from the Twenty-eighth. Sergeant McCracken had fumed for a week that he'd been cheated out of a rightful victory and the sixty-dollar prize—all the while refusing to make good on his promise to repay Lester for spotting him the entry fee. Hattie had overheard Joe tell Lester, *"The money's comin' back to you, just as soon as we get this sorted out with General Brown,"* But after two weeks passed, Lester told her he'd just as soon let the matter go, rather than worry about it. Hattie figured the disappointing furlough experience and the loss of an additional twenty dollars prompted him to reconsider the unpaid debt.

"I'll pay the five dollars and also get you some shoes," Hattie persisted. "I haven't much need for anything beyond decent meals and a dry place to lay my head at night…"

She couldn't finish, as a sudden rush of emotions suddenly seized her heart and interrupted her train of thought. *Jonas! My God, how I miss him!* Meanwhile, Lester and Lucinda regarded her with surprised looks.

"It's all right, Henry. Nothin's gonna happen to Lester," Lucinda said gently, eyeing her in a way that made Hattie worry she might be stealing a peek behind the wall that had momentarily failed to protect her delicate psyche. "Joe Johnston keeps things organized and neat as a pin around here—that's true. But for all his strictness, he doesn't seem inclined to punish a soldier without good reason. He's more like the good and noble 'Pa' that Lester and me have missed out on knowin'. If anythin', Sergeant McCracken will be the one at risk for detention."

Hattie nodded in silence, fighting to regain the upper hand on her emotions and refusing to think about the man she hadn't forgotten… the beloved husband she still prayed nightly to be reunited with. Instead, she focused on General Johnson's punishment methods that reflected a much kinder disposition than General Bragg's bitter spirit. Detention could mean simple imprisonment under the camp provosts' supervision, since they were the only ones employed by the new commander. Gone was the rearguard that would wait for deserters to flee the lines, as some had done at Chattanooga. Johnston's visible philosophy seemed to be based on trust: treat your men well and they'll never be inclined to desert.

Gone, also, were the three-pronged whips and chain poles utilized for Bragg's spectacles of terror. They had been replaced by the pillory and guard barrel, which brought more humane humiliation, even though a prisoner would be uncomfortably confined and left in public view of every soldier passing by. For a woman masquerading as a man, these latest methods of punishment presented less chance of getting exposed... unless a menstrual cycle occurred while bound in the pillory stocks, or held fast in a guard barrel. That could be equally mortifying to being stripped bare to receive the famed thirty-nine lashes that had permanently left the Army of Tennessee, along with the demon of a man who seemed to relish any form of punishment to make examples of the rank and file when he wasn't belittling his officers.

Despite the more humane treatment of soldiers, executions for criminal acts hadn't ceased with the new regime—just the opposite. More men were put to death than before, but now it was for true crimes ranging from thievery to spying for the Yankees. Yet, no spectacle was made of any man—not even the guilty. Hattie had only heard the details as related by those who were called to participate in the firing squads that dispatched up to a dozen culprits at a time—including one entire company that had been caught pillaging local farms, a crime that threatened to erode the local support the Confederacy desperately needed to thrive...

"Besides, y'all will need yer money for the trip north to Shelbyville tomorrow afternoon, when yer furlough begins," said Lester, rising to his feet and dusting ashes from his trousers. "Seein' how they's plannin' to drill the rest of us more now that the days are lastin' longer, I'm goin' to hit the hay a lil' earlier than usual. 'Night, y'all."

Lucinda suggested she and Hattie should follow Lester's lead and also retire soon. While she dampened their campfire's flames, Hattie silently reflected on the journey they planned to pursue by foot the next afternoon. Likely they would need new shoes soon, as well, unless they happened upon an opportunity to purchase a horse or mule along the way, or came across a wagon or two willing to oblige a pair of furloughed soldiers.

Furloughs were another fighting privilege that had been denied by Bragg that was promptly addressed by Johnston. Hattie's and Lucinda's time away from Dalton was part of the final wave of leaves granted, since the commander wanted to make certain all the furloughs were completed by the end of April, before preparations to resume the war began in earnest.

Lucinda planned to visit the 'kinder side' of her family back in Tennessee, and had suggested the trip north almost immediately following hers and Hattie's discovery they'd been granted the same thirty-day period, along with six other soldiers from their combined regiment. Their other furloughed comrades were soldiers from Murfreesboro under the Forty-Fifth banner. Hattie and Lucinda would travel alongside the other infantrymen until they reached Manchester—Lester's hometown. At that point, the pair's path would take them another twenty-five miles due west, while the Murfreesboro boys would continue north.

Hattie had expressed her reservations about visiting anyone who could possibly expose her true identity, but Lucinda assured her that the visit to Shelbyville wouldn't include a visit to Lucinda's immediate family. Instead, they'd spend two weeks visiting with her father's aunt, who had faithfully corresponded the past two years with her grandniece. It had greatly amazed Hattie that "Auntie Harriet" supported Lucinda's presence on the battlefield to affirm the Confederate cause, and had periodically sent baked goods to Lucinda, addressed to Private Louis Templeton, that she willingly shared with Hattie and Lester.

"Are you ready to turn in?"

Lucinda's voice from behind her brought Hattie back to the present.

"I believe so."

Hattie finished burying the fire and followed Lucinda to the tent they sometimes shared with Lester. Larger than the smaller tents she and Lester had shared for the better part of last year, the new tent was large enough to sleep several soldiers. Fortunately, no one had been assigned to turn their trio into a foursome as of yet. Most of the time, Lester preferred the old tent that he now had to himself, stating Hattie's snoring sometimes kept him up. Only during the most frigid nights would he join her and Lucinda.

As Hattie settled into her bedroll, she could tell that Lucinda was eyeing her in the dimness.

"What's the matter?"

"You weren't choked up about Lester's shoes, were you now?" Lucinda teased with a chuckle.

"No." Hattie said nothing else, but she realized her tone gave away more information than she intended.

"You were thinkin' about Jonas," Lucinda accurately surmised. "Just like when I caught you starin' at Joe Wheeler's cavalry earlier today, and you wouldn't tell me what's up."

"Maybe I was," Hattie admitted reluctantly.

"You forget that I know you better than sometimes I think you know yourself, Hattie Grey... Do you miss him?"

Lucinda's tone carried a mixture of curiosity and longing that gave Hattie pause to answer.... But she knew eventually she wouldn't be able to hide the truth kept secret in her heart. Even so, it was a struggle to keep from crying as she thought of Jonas, made worse by the expectation of supplying a believable answer for Lucinda.

"I do. Every single day."

Hattie could say no more; greatly relieved she avoided anything beyond a sniffle in her reply.

Lucinda responded with a low sigh, and then maddening silence as Hattie waited for more.

Is she going to chide me for how I still miss Jonas, and carrying on as if it has only been weeks since he and I last held each other... instead of nearly two years?

"You know? I'm guessin' he ain't dead... and I believe someday you'll find each other again."

This time, Lucinda sounded sad, although not as forlorn as Hattie feared she herself had sounded a moment ago. Along with the sadness was a trace of something else. *Perhaps, something akin to envy?* Maybe... but hers and Lucinda's separate lonely existences in this war had long been countered by their companionship, along with a friendship that had seemed unlikely in their early days and had since grown to be profound.

She might think I don't care about her deeply, but I do. I love her too... just not in the same way I love Jonas.

Hattie reached over to Lucinda, gently touching her arm. She could feel her companion's probing gaze again, despite being unable to discern any of her features.

"Thank you," Hattie whispered.

It's all she dared to say, and hoped her heartfelt emotion in her tone revealed how important Lucinda was to her. Lucinda didn't verbally respond, but soon grasped Hattie's hand and gently squeezed her fingers.

After lingering a moment, Hattie withdrew her hand. She waited, listening for Lucinda's usual routine of pulling up her blanket to her neck and turning over on her side. Content that her intended message was understood, Hattie's thoughts turned to the upcoming journey north. Furlough was as close to freedom as a soldier could hope for in a war that seemed to have no end. She looked forward to it… but also wished somehow this moment of liberty would lead her to Jonas. Or, at least to find out something—*anything*—about what had become of him.

Chapter Nineteen

Early Tuesday evening, April 12ᵗʰ, 1864... Fort Pillow,

Henning, Tennessee.

"Today was regrettable... a terrible mistake," Jonas whispered to himself, shaking his head in dismay. "We should've just gone straight to Kentucky as originally planned...."

Cold rain drizzled from a lifeless sky, as the depressing notion repeated tirelessly in his mind, refusing to leave him at peace as he sought to make sense of what he had participated in earlier that afternoon. Dusk rapidly approached, but its advent did little to alleviate a scene fraught with carnage that surrounded Jonas. He solemnly surveyed both sides of the Mississippi's eastern bank beneath the bluff where the beleaguered Fort Pillow sat empty.

Union dead are everywhere, and some still holding the rifles and muskets they refused to lay down. Others are unarmed, and most are black soldiers... And yet the rascal, Bradford, who betrayed them through cowardice, and just might be the one responsible for Hattie's death, still lives!

Despite the river waves, dyed red, lapping at the bank, Jonas could still clearly picture Major William Bradford flailing as the undercurrents threatened to pull him out to deeper water. The cowardly Union officer tried to hide in the chilled murkiness after he'd fled the fort that had been left to his charge after Major Lionel Booth was killed by a sniper's bullet from one of General James Chalmers' sharpshooters. The yellowbellied Yankee 'second in command' finally came out of the bitter Mississippi that was filled with drowned Negroes who couldn't swim, pleading for mercy—a stark contrast to the fiend's reputed love of pillaging and burning farms throughout West Tennessee.

Levi Jones was the armed Confederate to initially greet Bradford as he crawled onto the riverbank, and Levi was also among the first to point out the fleeing major to General Beaufort from the bluff, behind where Jonas now lingered. The Confederate cavalry's leader had been elsewhere when the slaughter ensued, keeping a watchful eye on a Union gunboat upriver from Fort Pillow. By the time Beaufort realized pandemonium had taken over inside the fort, there was little he could do to prevent the soaring death count inflicted upon the Federals pinned inside their collapsing defenses.

Jonas thought about how a fateful series of events had fallen like dominoes since late March, after Beaufort had been given a directive to head north from Mississippi to Kentucky, in order to remount and refit a new division of Kentucky cavalry. Beaufort's current cavalry's path took them through Jackson, Tennessee, and it was there that the projected course had been fatally altered.

Most of Jonas' mounted cohorts had noticed an increased hostility toward Beaufort's army from the populace that had been frightened into Union allegiance. Those patriots to the Southern Cause who refused to fall in line were under continual threat from bands of robbers and horse thieves. Worse, these marauders were raiding the countryside under the support of the Union Army. Jonas' blood boiled at the news that the ranks of the bloodthirsty criminals largely responsible for the ongoing mischief were filled not with honorable soldiers but deserters and other traitors to the Confederate effort.

It wasn't until seven of Beaufort's Tennessee riders were killed while returning to their hometowns to recruit new soldiers to ride with the general that the matter became much more personal. The murdered cavalrymen included one of Jonas' close friends, fellow lieutenant Willie Dodds. Willie had the unfortunate fate of encountering a regiment of renegades led by Union Colonel Fielding Hurst of the Sixth Tennessee Cavalry. Hurst and his crew had been plundering towns and farms throughout southwestern Tennessee, and were believed to be the slayers of all seven members of Beaufort's cavalry.

Willie's death was the most distressing for Jonas, and the details that came to Beaufort, as related by Charlie May to Jonas and Levi, filled their hearts with fiery heaviness that continued to burn two weeks after the fact. Willie had successfully made the journey to his father's home in Henderson County. However, Hurst was in the area and learned of the young lieutenant's whereabouts from a scout that had caught wind of Willie's arrival. The Yankees intercepted him less than a mile away from his father's farm as he headed toward Lexington.

"A friend of Willie's daddy came to tell Beaufort what had happened, and was the one to find Willie's discarded body in a ravine," Charlie had said. Jonas recalled his captain wincing as he shook his head sorrowfully. Though not nearly as close as Jonas was to Captain Pierce's second lieutenant, Willie's brutal death still brought angry tears to Captain May, as well as to anyone else who had come to know Willie in a personal way. "Sorry to be the one to tell you both, but since he's been especially close to y'all, I figured you should know what Colonel Hurst and his flickerin' Yankee scum did to Lieutenant Dodds."

Jonas shook with rage and sorrow at the news, and it stayed with him for days as he quietly grieved over the loss of his friend. The details might've been better left a mystery, he soon decided, after learning that Willie's handsome face had been skinned away, and his nose lopped off. Jonas allowed Charlie to continue telling him and Levi what Beaufort had been told, and it appeared Willie was kept alive through this abuse, which included having his jaw disjoined and his privates cut off. Jonas pictured Willie resisting bravely, perhaps openly questioning the manhood of his oppressors. Something the sharp-witted William Dodds would've said to the Yankee vermin surely was what inspired them to keep him alive until they had finished slicing up his torso, arms, and legs, before finally bludgeoning his head—most likely with Willie's musket butt, based upon what the witness had shared with Beaufort.

No person should ever be treated in such a vile way— unless it's the Devil himself!

After Willie's murder was disclosed to the Elite Company and the rest of Beaufort's troops, the general promptly made a declaration that there would be no mercy extended to anyone belonging to this gang of wicked blue coats, vowing to kill them all if they crossed his cavalry's path. Yet, due to his previous orders to head north, avenging Lieutenant Dodds and the other six men recently lost to these monsters would have to wait until their business in Kentucky was completed. Even then, it would be unlikely that they'd be able to pursue Hurst and his gang of scoundrels to end their reign of terror and depredation.

Many of the men wanted to forego the trip to Kentucky and immediately chase down Hurst and his crew; and then string 'em up in the woods where they were believed to be hiding. *"Let these goddamned sons of bitches rot as they swing in the wind!"* But cooler heads prevailed, at least for the time being. Within days of Willie's death, a group of women traveled from Henning to see General Beaufort in Jackson. They soon confirmed more disturbing reports about a second group of Yankee marauders under the direction of Major Bradford, who was yet another traitor born and bred in Tennessee. This time, the menacing gang's exact location was soon revealed, and had been confirmed by other concerned citizens residing in Jackson.

Fort Pillow.

The fort, which had two years earlier belonged to the Confederacy, had since fallen on hard times, according to the locals. Still, it proved useful to the Federals when they had launched their successful campaign against Memphis in June of 1862. Since then, the fort had become an afterthought for the most part, despite being used occasionally as a Union cavalry stopover. According to the locals residing in the area of Fort Pillow, Bradford's cavalry had been holed up there for the past two months.

Captain May and others reminded the general that while Bradford's cavalry of marauders wasn't as prone to murder as Hurst's group, they had done much damage to the area, stealing anything of value and routinely burning the farms they raided. It had reminded Beaufort of Jonas' tragic tale of what had happened to his farm and family in Appleton.

"Jonas... I know what you're thinking and I'm considering that as well," Beaufort had told him, in a rare personal conversation soon after the ladies that came to visit with the general had left to return home to Lauderdale County. "It's possible this could be the same culprit who visited harm to your hometown and family. Major Bradford was known to be in Middle Tennessee in the fall of '62, as likely Charlie has informed you. I promised those fine ladies here this afternoon that I'd pay a visit to the fort. When we do, you'll have to agree to not take matters into your own hands. There's a right place and method for vengeance... but not when it can put your fellow soldiers in harm's way. Am I clear on that?"

Jonas gave Beaufort his word to not act rashly, and to wait for an approved opportunity to exact vengeance, and only then if it appeared there was no potential harm to come to his fellow cavalrymen. What he didn't promise was to wait until Bradford could be brought before a Confederate court. If this despicable man was found to have had anything to do with his beloved wife's murder and the deadly injuries delivered to the rest of his family and friends, then he had no intention of letting Bradford live to see another sunrise after capture. Thankfully, Beaufort didn't push beyond the initial promise, saving Jonas the awkwardness of having to tell him what he'd honestly do if given the chance...

The meeting with the distraught ladies of Henning took place two days ago, and this morning Beaufort had given the welcomed order to follow General Chalmers' assault upon Fort Pillow. Heavy rainfall prevailed throughout much of the morning, and to the Confederate's dismay, Bradford's plundering cavalry were not the only Union forces occupying the fort. Two artillery units under the direction of Major Booth were also present, and instead of Bradford, Booth was the current commanding officer.

The biggest surprise to greet the Confederates that morning had been the fact that both artillery units were composed entirely of Negroes. This news had incited some of the men to worse anger—despite the presence of blacks among the ranks of Beaufort's cavalry as well as in Chalmers' army. At issue was how previous encounters with black soldiers fighting under the Union flag had gone. Several of Jonas' companions in other companies riding with Beaufort had watched comrades die at the hands of angry blacks, even after surrendering. "No Quarter!" had been the cheer, and the white Union officers and soldiers had stood by and let the wanton brutality happen.

This was also a concern of Beaufort's, as Charlie had mentioned to Jonas that the general had recently written a letter to Union General Cadwallader Washburn, one of General Sherman's officers, weeks earlier to warn the Federals of dire consequences to former slaves who continued to harm Confederate prisoners, as well as shout threats of not allowing Rebel soldiers the opportunity to peacefully surrender during battle. As a result, if pressed into hand-to-hand combat with belligerent Union blacks, Beaufort feared his men would lose their composure, resulting in even greater harm upon Negro captives.

Jonas had already witnessed the failure of keeping some of Beaufort's cavalrymen, who carried deep-seated prejudices, from harming recaptured slaves down in Mississippi. Now, things were already progressing badly that morning, and where Jonas had heard the racially charged insults from the same cavalrymen and others in response to the yelled taunts from the Negroes in the fort, between cannon blasts. By then, the Confederates had completely surrounded Fort Pillow and outnumbered the fort's occupants five to one. However, that fact had little effect on the pair of artillery units shouting insults against the increasingly agitated army surrounding the fort. It left Jonas fearful he might soon witness an eruption of terrible violence against the black's donning Union blue when the fort eventually surrendered.

And these Yankees will most certainly surrender, as they are badly outnumbered and will eventually run through their supplies of cannon and grapeshot. Then what will happen? Nothing good, and if they wait too long, there won't be a damned thing anyone can do to prevent what's coming... If only they had the good sense to surrender now, before all hell breaks loose!

But Booth steadfastly refused to offer up the fort in surrender.

Beaufort kept up the siege on the fort, with sharpshooters and artillery bringing the primary assault. Jonas figured, as surely did Beaufort, the fort's commander would come to his senses before regrettable tragedy struck. Yet, the two sides continued to trade cannon shots and gunfire deep into the afternoon. By the time Beaufort finally grew impatient and issued a final demand for surrender, Major Booth was dead and his subordinate, Bradford, was then in control.

"They can't hold out forever, Charlie, and it's asinine for them to keep harassing us so," said Jonas, his slicker soaked through from the waiting game that by then had lasted through several heavy downpours. Bradford had requested an hour-long ceasefire, which was accepted by Beaufort and then suddenly cut much shorter by the general, who now demanded the fort's full surrender within the next twenty minutes. Otherwise, the entire Confederate Army gathered there that afternoon would invade the fort. As was often the most effective threat, Beaufort had issued a 'no mercy to be shown until full surrender' ultimatum to Bradford. "Someone's got to give in. You and I sure as hell know it ain't going to be us."

"My guess is they're tryin' to hold out until more reserves arrive," Charlie replied, adding a perturbed chuckle. "Based on what I gathered a short while ago, one of our sharpshooters caught sight of Marshall's gunboat steamin' down river toward the fort and told General Beaufort about it. You already know his mood has been testy today… we best be ready to charge at any moment."

The order to charge soon arrived, and when it did, Beaufort was absent from the front. But it didn't matter in terms of expediency. The combined forces of Beaufort and Chalmers stormed the fort, and the mass of confusion and violence that ensued was the most unbecoming Confederate moment Jonas could ever recall witnessing. Nothing was as it appeared to be from outside the fort, and the Union soldiers within seemed to be caught in drunken disarray. They were no match for the swarming Rebel infantry and cavalry pouring into the fort after they easily overran its protective outer defenses.

The actual fighting lasted less than half an hour, the bloodbath instantaneous. Fought in confusion from the moment Beaufort's men entered the fort, it appeared to Jonas and Levi, as well as to others in the Third Regiment, that most of the Union soldiers were trying to surrender. However, enough of the infuriated Negro Yankees continued to fire their weapons, revoking the possibility of attaining a peaceful resolution. To make matters worse, Beaufort had apparently retired to a nearby hill to watch the assault while surveying the progress of Union Captain James Marshall's gunboat. Surely, he was unaware of the melee going on inside the fort's main section, and Jonas felt dismayed that he and his Confederate cohorts had underestimated Major Bradford's unruly influence upon all of the Union troops inside the fort.

Jonas didn't see the major's cowardly departure, but he did notice the stream of white soldiers fleeing through a sizeable hole in the rear of the fort as it filled rapidly with angry Confederates. The blacks were the ones who stayed behind…

many of whom fought bravely. But faced with overwhelming odds against their survival, more and more began to surrender, dropping their guns and lifting their hands above their heads.

Jonas was soon horrified to watch his companions gun down these pitiful soldiers pleading for their lives. Some fellow dismounted cavalrymen took things even further, ramming their bayonets through the hearts of the helpless Negroes and the few white Yankees now trapped inside the fort.

Lieutenant Grey wasn't about to stand for such dishonorable bloodshed, and after exchanging looks of disbelief with Levi, he made a move to stop the massacre. Charlie also shared their horror, but moved to block Jonas.

"Stay out of my way, Captain! This ain't at all what I signed up for, Charlie!" Jonas brushed past his superior officer, raising a pistol and pointing it at the head of a fellow rider from General Beaufort's cavalry. *A fellow Elite... and one who's making the biggest mistake of his life!* "Tommy, stand down! Do it now, or I swear to Christ you'll be answering to God Almighty in the next minute for what y'all have done!"

Corporal Thomas Means paused to glare at him. "What in the hell's gotten into you, Jonas? You heard what the blue coat scoundrels did to Willie! And these... *these* slaves that have risen up against us, are just like the rest of the Yankee scum who murdered our friend!" he sneered in anger. "They deserve to die! They'd kill us without mercy—*you* heard them shout that shit at us all the damned day long!"

Jonas had indeed heard the taunts. And, yes, they had offended him... But he also had the advantage of watching Levi, and though he wasn't a mind reader, he could tell that somewhere deep inside his good friend, Private Jones held a kinship of pain and suffering that the Yankee Negroes shared with him. Jonas understood it went deeper than just similar skin color… and despite Levi being one of the best marksmen in Beaufort's cavalry—if not the *very* best among the Elites— he couldn't hit a damned thing all that day. Charlie had even remarked about it once, chiding Levi for pulling up before his aim was true.

Jonas liked Tommy, no doubt. But he loved Levi, and since this was the closest man he had to a brother these days, his loyalty overrode all other considerations. Jonas cocked the pistol.

"Lay it down, Tommy," he entreated, less harshly. "Don't make me do it—"

"What in the hell is going on here? *Stop!*"

A booming voice they knew well and respected above all others resounded from behind where Company C and many others in the Third Regiment presently stood. Everyone under Charlie's command had held off killing any more Yankees until the standoff between Jonas and Tommy could be resolved. Meanwhile, the rest of Beaufort's men were still killing the blacks they viewed as traitors to the Confederacy.

"Stop this insane madness, goddamnit—*do it now!*" Beaufort shouted in anger.

Normally, his first command was all it would take, since no one dared test General Beaufort's resolve when he was enraged. At least that had been the case for as long as Jonas had ridden with him.

Just not today, so it seems!

While still shouting "No quarter! No quarter!", more than a dozen cavalrymen ignored Beaufort's command to stop. But not to be denied, the general moved in front of them all, waving his saber to push them back and firing his pistol into the air above his head.

For a moment, Jonas thought for sure they were about to lose their beloved leader. Men he had come to know well during the past sixteen months had suddenly become strangers in their madness. Yet, before they gunned down the general who'd placed himself between his men and more than a dozen Yankees cowering behind him—most being former slaves from Tennessee and Mississippi, the Elite participants and Chalmers' infantrymen reluctantly lowered their weapons.

"These men behind me, and those who have survived this unfortunate confrontation will be given full quarter!" Beaufort ordered. "I hear our guns being fired behind the fort—Relay the same message immediately to the rest of the men!"

Peace was steadily restored inside the fort… but the dead were many, and very few were dressed in gray. As for the killing that was supposed to cease outside the fort, and especially toward the river below the bluff where Fort Pillow sat, confusion remained. Jonas soon learned this was largely due to some of the black soldiers, in terror as they fled, firing back at the Confederates perched atop the fort's upper walls, despite the presence by then of a white flag having replaced the Union's stars and stripes.

After the battle ended, Jonas had taken a tour around the fort by himself, in order to get a better feel for what had happened. Trying to clarify 'why' would take longer. There would be wounded feelings he would face—like Tommy's. He knew also that Beaufort would likely long reflect on what had taken place this dreary day near the banks of the Mississippi, if for no other reason than the burning tears Jonas caught a glimpse of as Beaufort exited the fort, keen to find out where the coward Bradford had made off to.

When Jonas reached the reddened banks of the Mississippi, he suddenly thought of Captain Willard Burdock. Beaufort had hoped to use the Union captain as part of a prisoner exchange with General Sherman, to win back a pair of officers taken prisoner during their December furloughs. Yet, even though

Beaufort was willing to give six officers that included Buford for just the two Confederates, Sherman declined the offer and the captain was then taken to Castle Morgan, in Selma, Alabama.

Jonas missed the antagonistic verbal jousts with Burdock, and most had dealt with the contradictions present in Beaufort's army, mostly in regard to the treatment of Negroes. It certainly wouldn't have been an uplifting discussion, but Jonas would've liked to hear the captain's take on what had transpired that afternoon.

Likely nothing reassuring... May the Good Lord bless and protect the cynical bastard!

Jonas hoped that as Beaufort's cavalry rode toward Kentucky that night he could somehow find a way to better understand what had happened that afternoon, and possibly gain a better perspective. The facts of the matter couldn't be changed, and he didn't expect to find immediate forgiveness from God Almighty. Killing outside of the civilized rules of war couldn't be something easy to forget either. Even so, perhaps he and his comrades could attain a balanced understanding and vow to do better next time.

It proved to be Jonas' only prayer that night.

Chapter Twenty

Wednesday evening, shortly after dusk, April 27th, 1864...

just outside Chattanooga, Tennessee.

Hattie and Lucinda hid beneath a railroad bridge less than a mile west of Chattanooga. Much of the area they had traveled through during the past two days was familiar territory to them, having traversed the area while under the command of General Braxton Bragg. But the landscape and overall feel had changed throughout the region since the previous fall.

"How in the hell did Lester avoid bein' captured on his way back?" Lucinda wondered aloud, before carefully peering up toward the rails above the bank where they sought shelter— both from the rain and Union patrols. "I don't know if we'll make it back down into Georgia without gettin' captured first, or shot, and we should've figured that followin' this route back to camp was a mistake. Hell, it ain't like the Yanks just reclaimed Chattanooga yesterday."

Lester had told them that he had taken the same path—a shortcut leading back to Dalton, Georgia from Manchester,

Tennessee. Although he had mentioned the Union patrols, he'd stated that they had 'paid him no mind' since he was dressed like the civilian boys his age. Lester had kept the pair of trousers and shirt that he'd worn to Murfreesboro, from when he was recruited, inside his knapsack. He had rolled the clothes tightly, and Hattie recalled Lucinda teasing him after they fell out of his knapsack while marching to Tullahoma the previous spring. At the time, she had questioned why he believed the clothing would be important enough to keep, given he needed the room for more important items, such as cooking supplies and the stakes for his tent.

"Cause one of these damn days this war will be over and I might need to look for a church," he had replied, defensively. "I already know for certain that I've done killed eleven Yankees these past few months. When I'm seekin' forgiveness for them, and the many more I'm gonna shoot dead, Pa says I'd better be dressed right proper and not shame myself or him when I'm kneelin' before the Lord."

At the time, Lucinda couldn't restrain the same urge to laugh that Hattie managed to keep from escaping her throat, beyond a slight giggle. It wasn't the first instance where either gal had offended the youngster by their reactions to what he'd say, but Hattie could tell Lucinda's taunts that day had angered as much as hurt him. In the end, Lester stubbornly kept his civilian clothes.

Now they were the ones looking foolish.

Like their six male Confederate companions who had accompanied them into Tennessee, and who had advised they'd be taking an entirely different route back to Georgia once they parted ways in Manchester, Hattie and Lucinda had dressed in their most recently army-issued shirts and pants while traveling to Shelbyville, Tennessee. They had left the gray caps and coats back in Dalton, Georgia, but it wasn't enough to keep them from looking like the Confederate soldiers they were as they moved through enemy territory. Upon realizing their attire had drawn unwanted Yankee suspicion on the trip into Tennessee four weeks ago, the group decided to continue their journey strictly at night.

They managed to avoid any serious confrontations with Union patrols from that point forward, except for one near-capture just outside the small town of Sewanee early one evening. Fortunately, the dozen Yankee cavalry riders gave up the pursuit when the eight Confederates on furlough hid behind a blackberry thicket in a small ravine. Despite carrying pistols, they were at a distinct disadvantage, given the fact that the Yankees appeared to be fully armed, with some soldiers carrying repeating rifles.

The group continued on to Manchester by traveling even later at night and with heightened wariness. Hattie and Lucinda sustained this practice after parting ways with the others, and kept up their keen vigilance until safely inside Harriet Mather's home in Shelbyville. During their stay, Lucinda's great aunt made sure the ladies' presence in her modest farmhouse remained a secret—going so far as to have them dress as women with slave head-wraps around their heads to conceal their shorn locks—just in case a Yankee patrol happened to stop by during their stay.

But when it became time to return to Georgia, memories of their near encounters with the enemy had dimmed to where the pair had chosen to decline Aunt Harriet's offer to provide feminine attire for each one to wear until after they had safely crossed the state line and neared their regiment's campsite. Lucinda openly worried that dressing as women could provide a damaging reference point, should they encounter any of their Rebel companions before a change back into their male personas was possible. In the end, that fear of their true identities being discovered prevailed—despite how fortuitous such disguises would've been in their present predicament…

"Maybe we should take our journey directly south. We can head toward Chickamauga and then head east to Dalton from there," Hattie quietly suggested to Lucinda, who vehemently shook her head.

"No, they'll be down there, too," she replied. "And likely worse… I reckon the Yanks are all spread out from here to within a mile of where the Army of Tennessee is situated right now."

"The campsite in Dalton, near the ridge?"

Hattie pictured the spot where B Company had pitched their tents, along the southern edge of Rocky Face Ridge.

"Yep. And hopefully they haven't moved to anywhere else yet." Lucinda stepped back beneath the bridge. "Regardless, we might find ourselves in the thick of a fight when we get back. And if not, you can damn well bet it'll be comin' soon."

Hattie nodded in the growing dimness, able to easily imagine the scene Lucinda described. The Yankee forces they had viewed four weeks earlier, using a pair of field glasses carried by Private Irwin, had confirmed the Federals' presence just a few miles away from Dalton. By now, they could be much closer to the Confederate camp.

"Maybe we should've taken Billy Power's advice and taken the train to Selma instead… or found a couple of horses and rode down to Atlanta," said Hattie. "I doubt there'd be many Yankees down that way just yet."

She laughed sadly, wishing she had pushed for a different locale to explore for their shared furlough. Hattie had never been to Selma before, and Atlanta might've offered an even better experience, as she had heard and read about the bustling *Gate City of the South* back in Appleton. Her father had been there several times, the last visit taking place just before the war against the North broke out.

"Hey, don't worry none." Lucinda drew closer, surely reacting to Hattie's sinking demeanor. She peered into her face, close enough to where Hattie could detect a similar melancholy and mistiness in Lucinda's soft brown eyes. "We'll find a way back and probably end up laughin' about all the worryin' we've done since yesterday."

Lucinda added a smile that Hattie could tell was forced.

She's a damned liar... I can tell she's plenty worried!

"It's not just that," Hattie confessed, releasing a defeated sigh. "I had hoped we'd find time while we were in Shelbyville to ask around a bit—after we had spent a few days with your dear auntie, of course."

She shook her head, thinking about how the Union presence extended into Shelbyville, too.

We never had a chance to try and find out anything about what was going on out west. That's where Jonas probably is right now, maybe in Arkansas or down in Mississippi. I heard there's fighting even farther away, in places like Missouri or Kansas. Or, maybe....

The bleak truth of the matter was Jonas could be anywhere. Rather than vacillate daily on whether he was alive or dead, Hattie now clung to the possibility Jonas remained among the living... somewhere. But it took everything within her to not allow a desperate mind to mercilessly niggle her heart.

"Did you think he'd know where to find you, even if he had some crazy reason to be in Shelbyville?"

"Who?"

"Goddamn it, don't play me like that! You know who I'm referrin' to... *Jonas?* He's the only thing you've ever been pinin' for, though justifiably so." Lucinda's probing gaze studied Hattie's eyes, and she grinned knowingly. "Sometimes, you've just got to trust in Fate, God, or whatever else you believe in to make what your heart's tellin' you should be there to one day come true. But you should also know by now that it sure as hell ain't gonna show up *when* you're expectin' it to happen. Life don't work like that, Hattie…. *Shhhh!* Someone's comin'!"

It took a moment for Hattie to hear what Lucinda picked up in the dimness, and then the faint clicking of boot heels steadily became louder. A full company of Yankees marched in quickstep along the railroad above, traveling from the west. Hattie silently prayed for the patrol to hurry past them, and hopefully stay upon the tracks and not venture down the embankment. Without any suitable places to hide in close proximity, hers and Lucinda's presence would be easily detected and their capture assured. Hattie joined Lucinda's panicked scanning of the area, hoping to find someplace to conceal themselves amidst where they'd previously looked—perhaps a spot neither one had seen until then. But there weren't any.

The footsteps grew louder, accompanied by a sergeant's shouts, and then suddenly slowed, followed by a barked command to halt. Hattie started to reach for her pistol, but Lucinda touched her arm while shaking her head.

"Don't do it," Lucinda whispered. "They'll shoot without givin' us a chance for surrender if either of us show we're armed… Hey, I just noticed something."

Lucinda pointed to a crevice at the top of the embankment and motioned for Hattie to quietly move up with her toward it. Meanwhile, it sounded like heavy feet were moving toward both sides of the bridge. Just as the two women reached the crevice, presently cloaked in darkness and quite possibly home to any number of rodent vermin, several soldiers dropped down into the mud and made their way beneath the bridge.

There wasn't time to do anything other than scurry into the crevice. Hattie followed Lucinda's lead, pushing her legs and as much of her body into the hole as possible. Thankfully, the deepening dusk had cast much of the area around them in shadow, but where they still enjoyed a fairly clear view of the four Yankees investigating an area less than twenty feet below. Three of the men were dressed in rain slickers and carrying rifles.

Hattie's heart thudded heavily within her chest. A glance toward Lucinda confirmed she was just as alarmed.

"Malcolm? James? ...Any sign of the two 'Johnny Rebs' down there?"

The voice came from above. It sounded gruff and much deeper in timbre than the one that had bellowed the marching commands a short while earlier.

"Nah... although it does look like someone was here earlier," the soldier not wearing a slicker replied, kneeling as if trying to get a better look at the area where Hattie and Lucinda had stood moments earlier. "I bet they've moved on."

Hattie began to feel hope that they might get lucky.

"We could probably use a lantern down here," said one of the other three Yankees, a stout, stocky man squinting into the dimness below where the two women hid.

The unseen man above them hissed and started cussing while stating they should've brought a damned lantern down there with them in the first place. However, worse news soon followed for Hattie and Lucinda.... The man told another soldier to 'get a lantern lit' and join the others below.

"I believe we're just wasting time down here, James," said the first soldier, as he turned to face the Yankee that had requested a lantern. His voice was louder this time, as if he intended his rebuke to be heard by everyone in the area, above and below the bridge. Hattie also noticed what looked like stripes in the dimness, upon this soldier's shoulders. *He's a lieutenant, which likely means the irritated soldier above us is the captain of this bunch, or maybe even higher ranked.* "Captain Reynolds... if you feel better about spending more time down here, then so be it. But I'm willing to bet tonight's supper that the two Rebs we saw earlier are headed toward the Georgia border as we linger here. Or, perhaps they're skirting past Chattanooga. But, of course, sir... it's your decision on how long you want us to spend down here."

Please just go! Please, please....

The stillness from above, as the captain silently debated on whether to take his direct report's advice, or not, was nerve-racking. Each second seemed to stretch on mercilessly.

"All right, Malcolm," said the captain, finally. To Hattie he sounded unconvinced. "I intend to catch the trespassers before they slip through to Georgia. And since we know they were in this area, I'll have Frank join your effort to flush them out should they have indeed headed south from here. The rest of us will stay the course back to the city. Either way, we'll find the pair and have them hung before morning."

The lieutenant named Malcolm and the soldier named James gave their word to the captain that they wouldn't stop pursuing the Rebel pair until they reached the state line. Several lanterns were lit from above, and while avoiding being splashed by dripping rain, Hattie and Lucinda watched a heavily bearded soldier through the cracks between the railroad's ties grab two of the lanterns before descending down the embankment to join the other soldiers.

Hattie wasn't able to stifle a slight gasp when one of the lanterns briefly flooded hers and Lucinda's hideout with light. Yet, as a mysterious instance of luck that made little sense to either of them at the time, all five men were looking toward the area south of the bridge when it happened. None of the

Yankees gazed their way again until the moment they were exposed in full illumination had passed.

Perhaps the one named James had heard the gasp, as he hung back for another minute while the soldier named Frank stepped away with the pair of lanterns, handing one to the lieutenant. The four moved beyond the bridge's edge and out of Hattie's and Lucinda's direct view. However, the lone soldier stood staring in their direction, squinting again but more intently, as if he could see something. He called to Malcolm, while the rest of the company perched above resumed their march, moving at quickstep pace once more.

"What is it, James?" The lieutenant sounded even more perturbed than the captain had earlier.

Hattie heard a low sigh as the soldier shook his head. "It's probably nothing. I'll be right there."

Soon, all of the Yankees moved on... but it wasn't until after midnight that Lucinda and Hattie ventured out from under the bridge. With the news that they had been seen by someone, getting out of Tennessee became the only priority that night. Neither one believed their status as women would spare them from the gallows, or worse.

The sky was mostly clear by then. Once the moon fell away from brightly illuminating the surrounding landscape, the pair emerged. The five Yankees that had nearly discovered their presence hadn't returned. Lucinda suggested the chances of not getting discovered would be better served following Hattie's earlier suggestion to head directly south.

Perhaps they would remain unseen in the early morning dimness. Hattie pictured the Federals wearily making their way back to rejoin their comrades in Chattanooga and not returning to the bridge. But she and Lucinda couldn't afford to wait and find out if the enemy would return or not. Forced to proceed much more cautiously, it likely meant that the trip home would take an extra day at least, maybe longer, and depend on how much ground they could make up before exhaustion forced them to take rests. General Johnston would hopefully be merciful once they explained their reasons for being late in returning from furlough.

No matter, they were lucky… *damned* lucky.

Hattie sent up a silent prayer of thanksgiving, hoping that merciful fortune would continue to smile on them a bit longer… all the way back to Dalton, Georgia.

Chapter Twenty-One

Friday evening at sunset, June 10th, 1864... just outside

Baldwyn, Mississippi.

By the time summer approached in 1864, there had been many skirmishes and a few notable battles for Jonas to remember. But never had there been a rout quite as one-sided as what happened during that afternoon's confrontation with Union General Samuel Sturgis' army... at least not one he could readily recall. The Federals' combined infantry and cavalry, at roughly eighty-three hundred troops, was more than twice the size of General Beaufort's cavalry, which had swelled to thirty-five hundred for this particular campaign. Despite a morning and early afternoon standoff, Sturgis and his men had been forced to flee toward Memphis, Tennessee by sunset. The Yankees left Mississippi a lot lighter in men, artillery, and supplies.

Jonas could tell that Beaufort was especially pleased with his crew, as his men had captured more than sixteen hundred prisoners. The large number of captives would surely make a difference the next time Beaufort approached General Sherman and his subordinate generals to consummate a meaningful trade. The pot had been very much sweetened by the addition of eighteen artillery pieces and several wagons loaded with supplies. Of course, Beaufort's men intended to keep the best of the artillery booty for future engagements with the Yankees, as well as the food and ammunition inside the wagons for immediate distribution—all with the general's blessing.

After the tension that had lingered for weeks, following the Fort Pillow disaster, this victory was a badly needed boost for the men of the Third Regiment, who had nearly come to blows on several occasions during the return trip to Mississippi after the Kentucky regiment was outfitted and ready to ride for battle. Things became even more tense when plans to invade Middle Tennessee, in order to intercept and destroy General Sherman's supply lines from Nashville that were intended to support the Union Army's southern thrust towards Atlanta, were thwarted by an apparent order from Sherman given to Sturgis for a counter-invasion of Northern Mississippi.

Beaufort needed a significant victory, and quickly. Jonas and the rest of his Elite riders didn't let him down.

Yet, while everyone else was in a celebratory mood afterward, Jonas could only share their relief from a hard-fought battle that seemed to reunite them all as a single formidable force to be reckoned with. For that he was grateful. But heaviness weighed upon his heart, and it pulled relentlessly upon his soul.

They would be heading south toward Okolona that night, after supper. Amid the revelry, Jonas slipped away to a small creek he had stumbled upon earlier, in the aftermath of the last cavalry charge. The air was still thick and humid, as the day's heat had yet to pass. However, by the ravine that framed the creek's course, it felt cooler. Even his horse seemed to appreciate this moment's reprieve from summer's arrival.

At first, he didn't perceive this remote setting's allure, which wasn't much more than a gurgling brook beneath a mature oak's shade where he presently stood, to be anything more than a call to something familiar... a place where he could hopefully find succor for his weary soul. But as he knelt next to the water's edge, a sudden deluge of images and emotions seized his entire being.

Hattie... Oh my God, how I miss her! This sense of loss... it's far too great for me to bear much longer! It finds me... always. No matter where I am... it finds and tortures me so!

For a moment, the fading sunlight drifted through the oak's leaves being pushed to and fro by a sultry and gentle breeze. The rays dancing upon the water once again brought to mind memories of Hattie and him, lost in love, and in a time of fragile innocence destined to be brutally violated by war. All that was good had been exchanged for a world of emptiness and eternal torment. It seemed exceedingly cruel and unjust that if he failed to protect his thoughts he could expect his broken heart to endure fresh wounds.

Sugar Creek! Cursed, I am forever drawn to that wonderful and yet devilish place! Why does it haunt me so? When will I ever be free of such pitiless thoughts and memories of my beloved?

Overwhelmed, Jonas lowered his head and wept bitter tears that would not stop. Sobbing like a young child, as if unable to control the onslaught in any way, he was unaware that someone else had joined him in this seemingly innocent place that had cleverly deceived him. He turned his head, though unable to control the damage done by this spot he had mistakenly believed to be a sanctuary. Nor could he define through his tear-filled gaze who it was that dismounted from another horse and now stepped toward where he knelt in profound sorrow.

"Jonas... it's me. Levi," said the figure bending down toward him.

Mortified, Jonas sought to wipe his tears upon his forearms covered in sweat, despite an earlier cleansing to remove the blood and grime from the day's battle.

"I must look pathetic, and hardly worthy of your respect," he whispered hoarsely. "But..."

"You'll always have my undyin' respect, Lieutenant," said Levi, dropping to his knees beside Jonas. "Captain May sent me to find you, as we'll be packin' up soon. But you and I have some time, since he gave me an hour to find you and come back. He didn't know where you were. It took me just a few minutes to find this place."

Jonas realized that Levi must have noticed his reaction when seeing it earlier, and figured this would be the spot where Jonas would go to 'reflect'. *A bad habit of mine, since it seems I can't get through a goddamned day without needing to cleanse my mind of all the shit that happens!*

All Jonas could do was nod in response to Private Jones' words and continue his futile attempt to wipe away the tears still clouding his vision. Levi placed a piece of cloth in his right hand that took Jonas a moment to recognize what it was... a handkerchief. One made of fine quality linen, and embroidered along the edges.

"Go on and use it, Jonas," said Levi, quietly. "It ain't ever been used, as I've been savin' it for the day when I'll have a good reason to cry. It ain't happened so far."

"Thank you."

Jonas dared not say more, as the flood of tears had yet to recede, prevented from their fervent flow only by his dogged determination to not cry before a subordinate—even if that man was his best friend.

"You're welcome."

That was all either man said for what seemed like an eternity to Jonas. Yet, he could tell from the mosquitoes and mayflies landing on the creek's surface that only a minute or two had passed before Levi spoke again.

"You didn't have to risk your life for my brothers at the fort up yonder. You could've been like most of the others, but that ain't who you are, Lieutenant. Yes, we're friends, but I've got other friends here, and they don't view me like you do. You've always treated me like your kin... as a man. A *complete* man, and not just a Negro. I'm no former slave in your eyes, is what I'm meanin' to say."

Jonas' long dark locks had fallen forward and he brushed them back from his face to better regard his friend. Levi's expression was one of grave seriousness, and though the man was one whose word Jonas could trust, he sensed what Levi chose to tell him could've just as easily been never shared. Yet, for some reason Levi felt comfortable enough to entrust Jonas with his private observations. Jonas felt incredibly honored and would've smiled had his heart not ached so badly.

"You're the only kin I've got..."

Again, Jonas could say no more, and mercifully Levi nodded.

"I feel the same way, Jonas," he said, before casting a wary glance around them. When apparently satisfied their privacy remained true, he continued. "My only other kin is General Beaufort. Colonel Jeffrey used to be kin, too... God rest his soul. Mr. Beaufort, I mean Franklin, and his wife raised me from a boy, and Jeff treated me like a brother. Franklin told me after he purchased me from a bad master that I had a 'look of determination and intelligence.' I was made a house slave that very day and soon was charged to look after young Willie on the plantation. Franklin bought my brother, Isaac, too."

"So, you were a purchased slave of the Beaufort family?" Jonas asked, as his personal storm began to retreat. Caring about the business of others had proven time and again to be the best salve to help him forget his own misery. "And you worked for the general on one of the big plantations he owned near Memphis?"

"Yes."

"Then your freedom comes from joining up with him and Jeffrey at the war's outset, I suppose. That's what I've heard he extended to all of the forty-four slaves that joined up at the outset of the war."

It seemed to be the logical conclusion for how Levi got involved in the war effort, although in almost eighteen months, he had never shared anything about his past. It left Jonas to assume Levi was perhaps one of Beaufort's field slaves, held no higher in esteem than any of the other forty-three that had joined the Southern Cause. But Levi's claim of being treated special by the general, and regarded like kinfolk to his recently deceased younger brother, put everything Jonas had previously assumed in a completely new light.

"I was already freed when I agreed to come with Franklin and Jeff, a month after Governor Harris granted them a cavalry," said Levi. "There are many slaves owned by the general's family and some, like me, were granted their freedom in private before the war came. I've been free since June of 1858, but stayed on, willin'ly workin' alongside those who weren't free. Most times I worked in the big house, but sometimes in the fields at harvest. I've learned to read some, too."

"I figured as much... Can you also write?" Jonas recalled Levi peering over Charlie May's shoulder more than once, when the captain would receive a letter from his home. Unlike a few of the whites in their company who were verifiably illiterate, the slight lip movements were a telltale sign that Levi was following Charlie's gracious recital of his wife's generous sense of humor, staying a step ahead of what Charlie told those gathered round him.

"Some… but a Negro actin' like he knows too much ain't a good thing," he replied, grimacing. "When Franklin became colonel, he told me I'd have to watch my mouth, and ignore what some men said. I understood all that, but it gets hard watchin' men who view me as a fellow Confederate go and kill other Negroes like they're nothin' more than used-up dogs or horses."

"Escaped slaves and Union soldiers?"

Levi nodded.

"You know I've seen it, too… and it ain't right." Jonas rose to his feet, dusting off the knees of his trousers. He grabbed his hat that was perched upon his horse's saddle horn and prepared to remount. "I could've killed Tommy over it. And I can't say that I won't shoot a friend if it happens again. Maybe it'd be different if I grew up like them, but I'd sure as hell hope not. No one owned slaves where I grew up, and I'd only seen a few before the war when I'd travel to Columbia, and the one time I was in Chattanooga with my pa and brother."

Jonas bit his lip to keep from thinking about his deceased family, knowing it was just a hop and a skip to reach the realm of his dead wife once more. Levi grabbed Jonas by the arm before he climbed onto his horse.

"Just remember this, Jonas. We've all lost someone… some before the war, and some durin' it. I lost my ma and pa, too, though at a young age. And, after Mr. Beaufort agreed to purchase me from a man who beat all of his slaves—children included, and some to death—I still lost my brother, Isaac, to yellow fever two years later."

He released Jonas' arm, and prepared to mount his horse.

"You being an orphan as a kid... Do you think that's why the general and his wife took you in like they did?"

Jonas climbed onto his horse while Levi nodded thoughtfully.

"Maybe it was that. Reckon I can't say, and I've never asked." He mounted his horse and took the reins, ready to return to camp. "I won't ask him ever. But I was a boy who learned quick back then, and it helped me to ride a horse by the second try. Then Jeff taught me how to shoot a musket and pistol, both while standin' and ridin'."

"So that's how you got so damned good at it, huh?"

"I believe so."

Levi laughed, as did Jonas, feeling more like himself again.

"Franklin and Jeff told me I'd be a cook until folks had gotten used to my presence," said Levi, as they trotted back toward the field where they had battled the Yankees just a few hours earlier. "I did cook for about a month, but they came and told me that some of the whites 'couldn't shoot worth shit' while on a horse, and moved me to the cavalry. I've been here ever since."

"You're too modest, my friend." Jonas patted the neck of his steed, letting the horse know they'd be moving to a full gallop in a moment. "You're one of the best shots we've got, and you already know you're the most respected Negro in the Elite Company. Hell, you just might be the most respected rider, period, as I can't name anyone else any better. You damned well know that the general views you no worse than he does any of the rest of us, too."

Levi chuckled and tipped his hat to him.

"He's fond of you, too, Jonas," said Levi. "And remember this… Don't ever say sorry for the emotions you're strong enough to show. It's what makes you a man. It takes a hell of a lot more courage to stand naked than it does to hide who you are in shame. Take it from someone who's done both in this life."

Those were the last words spoken that night in regard to Levi's private past and Jonas' moment of exposed anguish. The pair sped back to camp together and soon were headed south with the rest of their regiment, while the entire cavalry continued to bask in the glory of their victory. Jonas hoped it would prove to be the beginning of better fortunes for them all, though something inside told him much more needed to fall in their favor before such a wish could come true.

At least it's a start, which is all anyone can ask for.

Chapter Twenty-Two

Sunday, in the wee hours following midnight, June 26th, 1864...

Not far from Kennesaw Mountain, Georgia.

"Do you see them still?" whispered Hattie, leery of lifting her head above a small bank within a ravine near the Confederate line. She had already done so twice. The last time she raised it, bullets struck the ground a foot away, sending a stinging spray of dirt into her face.

"Yep... they're still comin'," Lucinda advised, lowering her head quickly after peering above a black walnut's protruding root. "We'd best get movin' again."

They had been running for much of the past hour to escape a trio of Union pickets that had ventured from their posts to chase them, after shouts of *"Stop those damned Rebel spies!"* erupted from General Edward Hobson's camp late Saturday night. Dodging bullets to within a mile of where their regiment's campsite sat, just south of Marietta, Hattie and Lucinda hoped to somehow elude their pursuers long enough to safely navigate the final distance before dawn. The three

Yankees were fully armed, each with rifles and pistols. Meanwhile, Lucinda was down to her last bullet in her pistol and Hattie had just two bullets in hers. Since covert surveillance missions meant traveling light in terms of concealed weaponry, the pair was limited to just two knives and one pistol apiece. Until that night the limitation hadn't been an issue. But they had never killed a Yankee inside a Union camp before.

Dark cloud cover kept the stars and half-moon at bay, but it wasn't enough to keep the lantern-carrying Federals from following their trail with ease. The past hour had been a terrifying race to avoid being shot, following an unexpected opportunity to exact revenge. Hattie wished the euphoric moment had lasted longer... but it quickly dissipated the moment their clandestine presence was discovered. A death scream muted too late, which preceded a sergeant's throat being slit by Lucinda, was enough to rouse the sleeping regiment whose captain had been murdered moments earlier by Hattie.

It was foolish... stupid! Yet, a part of me has been redeemed. Still, hellfire surely awaits should I perish this night!

"Follow me!" Lucinda whispered, pointing to a small ridge just beyond what appeared to be a clearing in the dimness, closer to the protected boundary that separated the Union and Confederate encampments. "It looks like there's a better position just beyond the openin' in the trees... maybe sixty to seventy yards from here. I recognize it from earlier tonight, and we should be within a Rebel sharpshooter's range. Just as long as our own pickets have been payin' attention to the gunfire that's followed us this far."

As a fresh barrage of bullets tore up the shadowed ground around their feet, while also splintering tree limbs at a height that could've been a core hit had the marksmen's aim been truer, Hattie chased after Lucinda. Neither one slowed until after they had sprinted to the clearing's eastern side. The sharp crack from a pair of bullets ripping apart a branch just above Hattie's head sent her sprawling into the brush along the base of the tree line.

"Over here... hold on!" Lucinda dragged her to a large hackberry with a trunk base wide enough for them both to hide behind. "Are you all right?"

Hattie nodded, peering around the trunk toward the area they had just vacated.

The cloud cover had loosened above, allowing enough light to illuminate their pursuers cautiously venturing into the clearing. A subtle snap of a twig thirty to forty feet to Hattie's left caught the attention of one of the Yankees, who raised his pistol and pointed it at a dim figure whose details she could barely make out... other than the long barrel of a musket. An instant later, the crack of gunfire erupted with a flash that briefly illuminated the face of a familiar picket who immediately ducked, leaving only a cloud of smoke to tell of his presence a split-second before.

In the clearing, the pistol wielding Yankee—a rough-talking youth who had added taunts of 'yellowbellied rebs' to the bullets sent Hattie's and Lucinda's way in the ravine—fell backward amid a gush of blood erupting from his head. The other two Yankees immediately fell back, sending random shots toward the wooded area from where their cohort's kill shot had come. The response was immediate, as several more flashes from other Confederate pickets that had joined the first confirmed the pair of Yankees' decision to retreat was prudent.

"Louis, you do realize y'all was supposed to do your scoutin' on the quiet side of things," said an amused voice from the darkness, a few feet behind Lucinda. Another familiar face, this one a member of the Forty-Fifth Tennessee Regiment, stepped into view. "Captain Simpson said y'all should be back soon, and then we heard the gunshots, along with them damned Yankees hollerin' like they's about to corner a pair of scared rabbits for supper."

"More like a pair of ornery razorbacks, and more than able to hold their own," Lucinda retorted. "Nice to see you, too, Jimmy... Where's the captain?"

The soldier nodded smugly, pointing absently behind him. "Back near the line, I reckon. We're here to do the dirty work, don't you know... Anythin' good?"

Lucinda laughed and patted him on the shoulder as she and Hattie moved past. "Not for your lowly ears, Private," she teased. "I'm sure once the news gets back to General Brown and on up to Hood and Johnston, you'll hear about it soon enough."

"So, you boys ain't sharin' nothin', huh?" Jimmy called after them. Several other pickets mulled about nearby. "I'll keep it in mind the next time you're short a dollar and got a winnin' poker hand."

"Hell, it's the same shit as you're wont to do whenever it's been y'all's turn to scout the enemy," Lucinda shot back before she and Hattie picked up their pace to get back to camp.

They had indeed heard something good... something that sounded quite useful. And it came from the same lips that soon met a deliciously delivered demise.

I believed at first he was just a drunken officer foolishly 'shootin' the shit' around a small campfire with his subordinate. And, surely the sergeant with him was his most trusted assistant. Perhaps they were both present when Papa died....

What had been a standard surveillance assignment from Captain Simpson, under the direction of General Brown and auspices of generals Stevenson and Hood, ended up delivering some very valuable information about General Sherman's intended initial attack, set for the morning of June 27th. General Hood had suspected something was coming in the next few days, and had sent in a few scout tandems to try and get a timeframe of when to expect the next confrontation. Hattie and Lucinda not only learned this information, but the drunken captain went on to announce that General Sherman intended to deploy a full-frontal assault just after dawn on the 27th. In terms of important knowledge, Lucinda couldn't believe their good fortune and whispered a directive to Hattie to prepare to sneak out of General Hobson's camp.

"There ain't gonna be anythin' more obligin' than the date, time, and intentions of a planned attack by the Yanks," she had said, as they hid in the shadows near the officer's tent and small fire where the two men sat 'shootin' the shit' Yankee style.

Hattie fully agreed in that regard, especially since it involved a plan supposedly devised by General Sherman himself. If they had left then, she would've been spared Lucinda's ire that almost got them apprehended inside the camp. It would've also prevented Hattie's fears of facing God Almighty at the Seat of Judgment for killing an unarmed man unable to properly defend himself.

What it wouldn't have done, however, was reveal the long dreamt-for identity of her father's killer.

"So, as I've told you, Vernon… Sherman devises to implement an asinine strategy on the morning after tomorrow," slurred the heavy-bearded, middle-aged man to his sergeant companion. "The general's genius, that he is fond to brag about, will likely come under dire suspicion. Or, if he continues to be favored by the Devil himself, perhaps he will continue to add to a fabled legacy with another victory for the

Great and Sovereign Land of the United States... Hear, hear! Fate might well allow William Tecumseh Sherman one more edification... one more time to cut the Gordian Knot like the great Alexander..."

Hattie didn't hear a word beyond the unique phrase she had last heard uttered shortly before her father's murder. It replayed cruelly in her mind long enough to determine that the man sitting less than twenty feet away from where she and Lucinda crouched behind a supply wagon was in fact the very same man who took the life of Rufus Porter.

The man is drunk, but his voice sounds exactly the same! Sweet Jesus, what should I do?

Lucinda nudged her, urgently motioning for Hattie to join her in retracing their steps out of the camp... to retreat from a golden opportunity that would very likely never happen again. She was saying something, as well, but all Hattie could hear were the taunts delivered to her father before his face was obliterated by his own shotgun. *Very likely by this man, and definitely done in his presence!*

Hattie knocked away Lucinda's hand as the Union captain stood up, telling the sergeant named Vernon that he had to go relieve himself of some "very good Kentucky whiskey". Mindful to stay low, she followed him from a safe distance, ignoring Lucinda's hissed command to "Stop messin' around!" followed by a desperate plea to get their asses out of there.

The optimum time to attack the captain would've been during the full two minutes it took to empty his bladder upon a tree. Especially with Lucinda coming up fast behind her... but Hattie couldn't kill him like that. Something about seeing her father's face in her mind, believing he was somehow aware of what she planned to do, and wanting her to behave like a lady kept her from shoving her Bowie knife through the officer's heart from behind.

"What in the hell are you doin'?" Lucinda hissed angrily in her ear. *"You're gonna get us killed—"*

Hattie put her free hand over Lucinda's mouth and shushed her. To her knowledge, this was the very first time she had ever stood up to her beloved friend, and it caught Lucinda off guard. Hattie silently indicated she just needed five minutes, if even that, and then they could leave.

The captain glanced over his shoulder toward where the two Rebel spies crouched in the shadows. But then he returned his impaired focus on finishing his personal business. When he began closing his trousers, Hattie mouthed to Lucinda to not interfere... that this wasn't her concern.

"The hell you say!" she mouthed back.

"Just trust me, damn it!"

Before the captain had turned around and could stagger back to where his companion waited, Hattie pounced upon him. She knocked him to the ground, climbed onto his chest and brought the knife up to his neck while covering his mouth. Effectively pinned, a look of panic spread across the fiend's face.

"Don't speak!" she hissed.

"You all right over there, Duncan?" Vernon called to him, from the area of the fire the two had been tending.

Duncan? My God, this is indeed the bastard responsible for Papa's death! That's the name spoken in our house—I remember it now!

"Don't you dare answer," she whispered coldly to the man held fast beneath her weight upon his chest. "And you damned well better listen to what I'm about to tell you, Captain."

She loosened her hand slightly to where he could still breathe.

"You're just a boy," he replied in a heavily muffled voice. "You'll be hanging by dawn for the mischief you've chosen to engage in—"

"I said don't answer, *Duncan!*"

Hattie clamped her free hand tightly over his mouth to keep him from saying anything else. She brought the knife up against his jugular, whispering that if he attempted one more word she'd proceed to cut his head off.

"You're going to listen to me—and it'll take just a minute for me to say what needs to be heard. Then yours and my business here tonight will be done. Understand?"

He eyed her blankly, but nodded.

"Good... Do you recall a quiet little town in southern Tennessee near the border of Alabama? A place where you and your men raped and murdered a woman, and then butchered her infant child and husband? Along with an older couple and some other good folk—do you remember?"

The captain shook his head.

"Liar!" she spat at him.

"Henry, better hurry—someone's comin'!" Lucinda whispered from behind her.

"Duncan?" Vernon called, from near the stake to the tent the two men apparently shared. Hattie, Lucinda, and the monster named Duncan were just around the corner. "You over there sleeping in a drunken stupor again? The colonel won't be pleased when he finds out you've consumed more liquor than allowed."

Hattie allowed herself a glance back to where Vernon's voice emanated from and then resumed her 'conversation' with his superior.

"Oh, but you do remember, Duncan—I *know* you remember the man named Rufus Porter. A good and noble man that you *murdered* with his own shotgun!"

The captain blinked twice, and his eyes glanced wistfully to the far corner of his tent, less than thirty feet away from where he lay pinned to the ground by one menacingly angry Rebel spy.

Likely praying his good buddy Vernon comes to his rescue real soon… Just not soon enough!

"Do you remember the daughter that wasn't there?" Hattie asked, bringing her face close to his to further mute her whispered voice. "Huh? Remember the name, Hattie?"

Recognition suddenly appeared in the face of the Union captain whose unique first name and his curious fondness for obscure classical literature were irrefutable facts that linked him to the destruction of her world, and now brought her an unexpected encounter—an event so sweetly gifted by Fate for the attainment of full resolution. *And that finality can only happen if I am served my revenge!*

"Damn it, Duncan!" Vernon's exasperated sigh announced he was about to step around the edge of the tent and would be in clear view of his captain's dire predicament momentarily. "Guess I'll have to pick you up once again…"

Duncan squirmed in sudden desperation, and Hattie's time to glory in a delectable offering of vengeance was over. Not only that, the tables might be turned at any moment.

"I swear to Christ if you landed in your piss again, and I have to clean you up…. Well, this time I'm going to have to say something to the general, too. *What the hell—*"

Hattie didn't see the sergeant round the corner. Even if it meant a bullet would soon pierce her heart or brain from behind, taking her from this world of violent cruelty, she wasn't about to let the bastard named Duncan live another moment. There could be no mercy for a fiend who, instead of serving a noble cause, chose to burn farms, rape women, and kill families—either by execution or destitution.

She slid down just enough to expose the man's chest and raised her Bowie knife, plunging it into his wicked heart. She drove the blade in deep, to where a crimson surge flooded the handle and her right hand. But Hattie paid no mind to it, focused instead on watching the man's empty soul and malevolent existence be vanquished from his eyes. When the look of horrified recognition morphed into one of frozen terror that further ebbed toward mere lifelessness, she prepared for her own execution... But while waiting for a pulled trigger to follow the sound of a firearm being cocked, a shrill cry rang out into the humid Georgian night.

Acute awareness of her foreign surroundings suddenly returned, and she rolled off the officer's corpse. She recalled seeing a lantern in her periphery as she exacted her revenge, along with the lengthened shadow of an arm raising a pistol. Fortunately, the gun never went off, or the ensuing mayhem could have been worse. Seeing Lucinda's bloody knife in the glow from the fallen lantern told part of the story, and the man writhing on the ground with a gaping wound in his back and chest, along with an ear-to-ear slit below his jaw told the rest.

Lucinda had delivered the blow to Vernon that Hattie had not given to Duncan from behind. Unfortunately, a shrill scream escaped from the sergeant's mouth as his heart was pierced, before Lucinda succeeded in slitting the man's throat to quiet him. He was still in death's throes as the pair scurried along a path they struggled to retrace, moving through a camp now wide-awake.

Two dead Yankees, and these killings would never be seen as anything but cold-blooded murder... at least from a Union point of view. But in Hattie's mind, and what she hoped would be the view of God Almighty, this was an example of biblically warranted retribution followed by a slaying of necessity at the hands of Lucinda. Not to mention, both sides in this war merely killed each other at every opportunity to do so.

In truth, the logistics and vileness of the deeds mattered less and less as the pair fled for their lives over the next hour. Only after delivering the 'important secret' they had learned via eavesdropping to Captain Simpson, who immediately traveled to visit General Brown, did the two women fighting as men get a peaceful moment to reflect on all that had happened...

"I understand now why you did it," said Lucinda, as she and Hattie sought to catch what little rest they'd get that night. The edge of dawn would surely bring a full day's work for The Army of Tennessee, assuming what they had learned that night proved to be true—or at least believed by Hood and Johnston. If so, the latest battle loomed on the horizon just a day away. "I would've done the same... I just wish you'd told me why you were so determined to linger. Even just the name of your Pa would've given me a clue. Instead, it seemed like you'd lost your damned mind out there. Shit, Hattie, if you'd just mentioned a bit more details about what happened back in Appleton months ago or even last year, I might've figured it all out on my own."

"Sorry... I'm not so good with sharing details like that, I'll admit. Still, tonight when it happened, I wanted to tell you then, but didn't know where to start," Hattie explained. "There wasn't enough time to tell you everything, and the opportunity that presented itself would've long disappeared by the time I finished explaining it all. But I am sorry for endangering you like that."

She stared at the top of their tent in the dimness, picturing what had happened in Appleton almost two years earlier, and hearing Papa's pleas and the terrible sound of the shotgun blast from close range in the parlor, followed by blood seeping into her hiding place. An experience she'd managed to bury as something in the distant past was once again fresh, as if it had happened earlier that night.

"Well, like I said, I'd have done the same thing." Lucinda rolled over on her bedroll, and Hattie could tell she was looking at her. "But there'd better not be any more goddamned secrets that can get us killed out there. All right?"

She laughed lightly and turned back to her preferred sleeping position before Hattie could answer, signaling that she was done talking… for now.

"No more secrets, Lucinda. I promise."

Hattie meant it, and though there was no immediate acknowledgement, she believed they'd reached an accord about it all. And despite finally avenging her father's vicious murder, Hattie felt uneasy about the way it went down. While it seemed like fate, it also felt messy and incomplete… as if acting carelessly as she had done would in turn spawn new consequences. The moment of exacting revenge wasn't clean by any means, and it bothered her.

Someday, I might have a new debt to pay. Instead of getting even, I might've just made things a hell of a lot worse.

It was the last thing she thought about before she fell asleep, and it remained fresh on her mind when she awoke to a busy day already in progress just a few hours later.

Chapter Twenty-Three

Late afternoon on Friday, July 22nd, 1864… just east of

Atlanta, Georgia.

The end of a difficult week, which began with the sudden demotion of the beloved Confederate Commander, Joe Johnston, in favor of John Bell Hood, culminated in a battle that might've been won had the change not been made.

Surely, the official loss of Atlanta wouldn't have been near as decisive, based on how things had gone under Johnston's guidance since early May. Meanwhile, the new leader for the Army of Tennessee seemed determined to foster riskier tactics without considering the cost in casualties—the very opposite of Johnston's approach. By this stage of the latest campaign in the war, the Rebel forces in Georgia had shrunk by nearly a third from the force that reengaged the Yankees back in May. Since then, morale had steadily teetered towards despair again, and the past week's leadership change came on the heels of ongoing reorganizations of regiments and brigades made necessary by the ever-increasing losses sustained by the Army of Tennessee.

Hattie and her remaining Twenty-Third Battalion cohorts understood the need for change... It was just too bad that General Hardee turned down a rumored offer of assuming the role of commander, leaving Jeff Davis to settle for Hood. Along with Lucinda and Lester, Hattie had long learned to adjust to what each new day brought to them, regardless of the end result being good or bad. As such, the trio accepted the positive spin of retreating from Dalton to Atlanta in order to protect dwindling ammunition, food, and other supplies—knowing it revealed a deeper truth as to which side had gained the upper hand. It certainly couldn't be the army on the run.

Not being able to hold a position for longer than a few days had been the aspect Lucinda had noticed most. Hattie and Lester could only nod in agreement when she would grouse about the South bending over backwards to lose the war.

"It'll be no better under General Hood, and likely worse," she had told them, just two days prior. "They say he ain't been right in the head since losin' his leg and the use of his good arm."

Hattie reflected on how things had gone from feeling hopeful in early April to feeling overmatched, worse than ever, by July. It started when she and Lucinda made it back from their furlough on May 1st, one day later than expected. The pair were forgiven due to what had happened to the guys from their combined regiment on the same furlough trip to Middle Tennessee. Half of their six companions that traveled to Murfreesboro didn't return. George Irwin helplessly watched Melvin Tubbs and two others be captured by a Union patrol and summarily executed on their way back to Dalton—same as what almost happened to Hattie and Lucinda. For Hattie, the news proved to be a harbinger for the continued misfortune that had transpired since their return from Tennessee.

Even the pair's successful scouting excursion in June ended up not mattering much, in light of how the battle waged on June 27th turned out. General Sherman did launch the full-frontal attack gleaned from the drunken conversation they had spied upon. Yet, somehow, despite Hood's and Johnston's delight at learning of the highly unusual tactic from the Union Commander, who was often overly conservative in his approach, the battle waged near Kennesaw Mountain still resulted in the Army of Tennessee retreating further south towards Atlanta.

The loss at Kennesaw proved to be a testament for the ever-shriveling, shrinking violet the Confederacy in the West had become. Nevertheless, the gals and their young male companion understood it wasn't so much cowardice on the part of Joe Johnston that resulted in the steady southern drift to Atlanta. Instead, it was the fact that nearly twenty thousand troops had disappeared from his corps since May 14th at Resaca. Being badly outnumbered and trying to match brawn with the enemy could've led to a full rout of what remained of the South's only buttress against the North, west of Virginia. Rather than succumb to a single critical loss that might've ended the Confederacy's hope for independence from the Union, it appeared that Johnston chose to continue the strategy of drawing the enemy into battle and then falling back in hopes of eventually wearing out Sherman's troops.

Hattie believed this approach actually worked at times, though it also seemed as if the Federals sensed they were gaining a strong advantage that increased with each push of the Army of Tennessee deeper south. And now they were at the climax, since Atlanta had been under continual bombardment from Sherman's army since Wednesday.

"Maybe that's the benefit of waging war in someone else's backyard as opposed to their own," Hattie suggested to both

Lucinda and Lester that morning as they hurriedly ate their breakfast. "We have so much more to lose than the Yankees."

By dawn, it had become discouragingly obvious that the Federals had stepped up the skirmishes the night before in preparation for a full day of battle set to begin shortly.... Then, after more than seven hours of trading gunshots and artillery fire that Friday, the exhausted and hungry soldiers under General Brown, and two other commanders, were about to be called upon to engage the enemy in hand-to-hand combat as the sun hastened its descent toward the western horizon.

"Sergeant McCracken's on his way." Lester pointed to the officer who shared the role of preparing the Twenty-Third and Forty-Fifth units to march with two other sergeants. Joe McCracken appeared angry as he readied the line to depart from their temporary fortifications. "Looks like we're about to finally take the fight to them damn Yanks."

Lester smiled, strapping on his Springfield rifle to go along with the latest Union carbine he'd picked up from the battlefield earlier that afternoon. With a pair of pistols tucked into his belt and his bayonet gleaming in the late afternoon sun, Hattie thought he looked the most ready and excited for the upcoming direct confrontation with the Federals out of all the infantrymen forming the last of three grand columns. Lucinda adjusted his hat for him, stepping back in admiration just as the sergeant arrived. Lester smiled bashfully for an instant, before taking on the most serious look Hattie could ever recall seeing from him. McCracken patted Lester on the shoulder as he walked by.

The line formed quickly, with Lucinda and Hattie following Lester and one of the original members of the Twenty-Third, Joshua Tibbets. The older man wore a look of weariness that was common amongst the infantry, despite most everyone responding with an outward show of excited determination that afternoon.

There are so many of us emerging at once—we must look a powerful sight! There's an energy crackling in the air, and the men are beginning to holler in preparation of our advancing attack. All of us moving in step with the drills General Johnston insisted upon, as if our farewell tribute to him happens now!

Amid cannon fire, grapeshot, and bullets from Yankee sharpshooters, the three columns of nearly two thousand soldiers under the direction of generals Brown, Clayton, and Stevenson, and following the order of General Cheatham, marched with precision toward the Union entrenchments set up along the southern edge of the Georgia Railroad. When close enough to engage the enemy, the order was given to move from accelerated quicksteps to a full run.

The exhilaration of the battle's onset quickened Hattie's heart to where it churned like a runaway train inside her chest. Being stuck in the middle of the rush of screaming Rebels bearing down on the Union defense lines, the rows of Union blue-clad soldiers unloading their guns at the approaching Confederates was obscured by the mass of soldiers ahead of her, until finally within one hundred yards of the enemy's position. The columns began to disintegrate with a growing number of running soldiers picked off in mid-stride by gunfire.

With every direct hit—whether by bullets, grapeshot, or shrapnel from exploding cannon balls bouncing haphazardly through the lines—the air around her rained familiar crimson amid terrified screams from those hit by the vicious shower of death thrown upon them from just ahead. But they didn't slow down, running through the increasingly treacherous footing that worsened as trampled-down weeds and grass glistened in blood from fallen Confederates that made solid footing a tenuous affair.

Death is everywhere! It never ever ends... Men I've known and others mere familiar faces are falling around me. Yet, look! The Yankees ahead are beginning to die just like us!

Suddenly, what was left of Brown's column veered north, and the Twenty-Third and Forty-Fifth immediately followed Colonel Anderson Searcy toward the railroad, dipping into a ravine filled with overgrowth along one side of the train tracks. The terrain was cumbersome and dangerous, and yet it offered cover and an immense advantage over the Yankee marksmen who missed wildly. Hattie glanced back toward the columns to the south, where the Confederate wave had survived the initial onslaught and soon reached the Union's unstable line. With bayonets and swords drawn, Rebels and Yankees embraced one another in a deadly dance to determine which army would give ground first. Their gleaming blades glistened beneath an impartial sun, which seemed all the more determined to flee the summer sky and avoid witnessing the carnage wrought by each army's embittered hatred toward the other.

The order came to climb the ravine and cross the railroad tracks to where the Yankees were entrenched. The benefit of cover now lost, Hattie and her Confederate comrades prepared to invade the trenches. Bayonets at the ready, she and Lucinda prepared to follow the line pouring into a sea of blue-clad soldiers caught unprepared.

As the Union redirected artillery to attack the wave of grey and brown clad soldiers still pouring into the Yankee position, Lester launched into his unique Rebel Yell, which being punctuated by a litany of colorful swear words directed at the enemy often drew amused looks from his cohorts. Even old man Joshua Tibbets cracked a near toothless grin.

The Federal soldiers took offense—as was often the case. However, normally the two armies would be on level ground, thus making the insults hurled both ways fairly equal. Being perched a good ten feet above the angry sea of blue scurrying to grab their weapons while the Confederate infantry chased them down with bayonets at the ready had given Lester and others a false sense of superiority. Bullets soon tore through the ranks of Brown's Brigade that had yet to descend into the melee of soldiers in hand-to-hand warfare. Joshua caught a bullet that passed through his cheek before another ball landed between his eyes, dropping him upon the tracks in a crumpled heap.

Lucinda and Hattie managed to elude getting shot, though bullets whizzed by their heads.

"Is that all you yeller Yanks got to offer?" Lester yelled toward the blue side of the conflict heating up below them. Hattie caught a glimpse of him jawing some more, when Lucinda pulled her out of the path of a cannon ball that bounced up from the base of the train tracks, soaring over their heads before hitting the side of a rail and careening elsewhere.

"Ah, y'all can do better n' that!" Lester persisted. "I said, is that all—"

Gunfire knocked off Lucinda's hat, and she pulled Hattie down with her, just as Lester's latest taunt abruptly ended. It wouldn't have been the first time the youngster's bravado was muted, and as usual, the boom of the big guns and perpetual crack and pop sounds from rifle fire drowned out most everything else, other than the screams and battle cries going on below. But it was the sudden look of horror on Lucinda's face that sent a wave of panic through Hattie, as Lucinda looked beyond her, to where Lester had drifted after Joshua fell.

"Don't look back, Henry!" Lucinda pleaded, grabbing Hattie's arm to pull her along as both prepared to jump into the fray. Hattie wasn't ready to descend yet, adjusting her bayonet and nearly losing the blade from not having it fastened correctly upon her rifle's barrel. "Please just trust me—*don't* do it!"

But Hattie had to look, and surely Lucinda knew she wouldn't be able to stop her.

She peered over her shoulder as she descended the small hill the railroad traversed, with Lucinda by her side, preparing to engage a handful of Yankees at the ready, their bayonets positioned to pierce hers and Lucinda's hearts should a misstep fail to protect them from harm. In that brief instant, Hattie saw Lester was gone.

Frantically looking over both shoulders in alarm, just before she had no choice but to address the man trying to kill her on the Union's behalf, she couldn't find Lester anywhere. It wasn't until she sidestepped one Yankee and drove her bayonet into the gut of another that she realized she did see him... or at least what was left of the boy.

A body was lying on its back atop the rails near Joshua's corpse, and though it didn't register at first, she soon recalled the way Lester had his pistols crossed in his belt. He had liked to imitate a lithograph of a pirate from a Robert Louis Stevenson novel his deceased mother had left to him as a small child. It was something he had shared when Hattie had questioned him about the curious habit this past spring.

The decapitated Rebel bore that trait, and it might be the only surefire way to identify Lester's body when the battle ended and it became safe enough to try and retrieve him for burial.

She began to weep, though at the same time, the anger drove her to fight ferociously. Lucinda fell behind for a moment, but managed to catch up when three Yankees cornered Hattie after she took down a pair of others.

"We need to step back!" Lucinda chastised her, after Hattie outfought and killed one of the men while wounding another. The third man retreated when faced with two bayonets. "You shouldn't have looked!"

"The hell you say, Louis!"

Lucinda grabbed her arm again, this time in all likelihood to keep Hattie from wading any deeper into the predominantly blue crowd. Meanwhile, the Yankees seemed to be withdrawing, perhaps headed south to where the rest of the Union Army was situated, a few hundred yards away.

"It served no purpose for you to do that—and you know it!" Lucinda scolded, once she had pulled Hattie back, amid their cohorts pushing past them to pursue the enemy seemingly on its heels. "Once again, you almost got yourself killed—and me too!"

Hattie could offer no response… no rebuke of any kind, despite the burning anger that raged within. Meanwhile, grief threatened to take her down, leaving them both vulnerable to a likely exit from this world.

Maybe it'd be better. Lester was like a brother to us both…. Other than Lucinda, I have no one else now… Jonas? For all I know, the thoughts that torment me daily might be of my own making. Perhaps he awaits my arrival where Lester's soul has now been welcomed.

"Snap out of it, Henry! You hear me? *Shit!*"

Lucinda slapped her across the face, just hard enough to bring her back to the present.

"You're in distress," she told her, quietly. Hattie watched Lucinda look around cautiously while putting her arm around her and forcing her head down. "Act like you're wounded. Don't give me any shit about it, either. Hell, shudderin' is like gettin' stunned by a bullet grazin' one's head, or a rifle butt to the gut takin' the wind out of a soldier. Either way, you ain't any good to the army you're in until you can get your wits back—you hear me?"

Hattie couldn't speak, still overwhelmed by a level of anguish she'd only known twice before, back in Appleton, where the separate losses of both parents carried near debilitating sorrow. Lucinda took her back to the base of the train tracks, repeating, "Injured soldier comin' through!" almost as a chant, until the rest of the army had moved past them. As the pair trudged up the small hill to the rails, all that remained were the Confederate dead and wounded.

Lucinda wanted to keep moving, until safely out of range of errant gunfire and away from being caught and possibly shot by a provost. Hattie managed to remind her that General Johnston didn't keep a battle provost like General Braxton Bragg had done, and General Hood had yet to make that implementation. She made a murmured promise to do whatever it took to keep them both safe, but only after finding a place to bury Lester.

Hattie chose a burial spot beneath an unusually shaped elm near the railroad. The tree bore a twisted bough that looked easy enough to find at a later time, either for the purpose of merely visiting the grave or removing Lester's bones to take home to Tennessee once the war eventually ended. Both women quietly wept by the side of his grave until the return of the bewildered army that had just learned another retreat was in progress. Sergeant McCracken seemed to scarcely notice the pair's truancy, while announcing the command to fall back had reached Colonel Searcy and Captain Powers by way of General Brown after it had been issued to the brigade's leaders from the Army of Tennessee's new commander.

"Sherman's sendin' an artillery attack against the citizens of Atlanta as we stand here," said McCracken, his eyes tearing as the sullen anger from earlier returned to his countenance. "They're sayin' it's too late to stop it... too goddamned late to stop *any* of it."

Chapter Twenty-Four

Early evening, Wednesday, November 16th, 1864... just outside

Florence, Alabama.

After a successful campaign of ruining the Union supply lines to Nashville during October and culminating in a major victory at Johnsonville just five days earlier, Jonas and the rest of Franklin Beaufort's Elite Company left Corinth, Mississippi on November 10th and headed east to Florence, Alabama. The request to return to the Army of Tennessee had come from General Beauregard to General Richard Taylor, who then ordered Beaufort and his men to assist General John Bell Hood in his campaign to reclaim Nashville with the intent of driving General Thomas' forces deep into Kentucky. The ultimate goal, according to what Jonas had learned from Charlie and other officers who had Beaufort's ear and confidence, was to eventually cut a swath all the way to Cincinnati, Ohio. It seemed entirely possible, given that General Sherman had relinquished control of the Union Army north of Chattanooga to Thomas' supervision, while he turned his full attention to the fiery destruction of the state of Georgia.

Jefferson Davis supposedly was excited by what appeared to be a glaring mistake of overconfidence by the Federals. If the Army of Tennessee could successfully invade the North, it could well change the South's fortunes. Support from England and other European nations had steadily waned, as news of Sherman's efforts to burn every city and town his army encountered in Georgia had given the impression that the war involving America's divided nation was nearing its end. A prevailing impression, internationally, was the Confederacy was steadily losing ground in the east while hanging on by the thinnest thread of hope in the west.

What Jonas and his cohorts cared about, of course, didn't have a damned thing to do with what the rest of the world thought about the war. They wondered aloud if this was the smartest course to take. Granted, the orders given would be followed regardless... but Jonas wasn't alone in thinking it might be wiser for Beaufort's cavalry to avoid unnecessary skirmishes in and around northern Alabama. Instead, they could be at full strength to assist Hood's forces after his army had cleared the Tennessee state line in the journey north to Nashville.

"It just don't make any goddamned sense as to why we need to risk our necks like this," Charlie had complained privately to Jonas and Levi. "I mean, we've done all right for over a year not worryin' about anybody gettin' needlessly shot at. We've done more in this past month to hurt Sherman's and Thomas' efforts than ole 'Peg-leg Hood' has managed to accomplish down there in Georgia since July. The army's lack of leadership remains the same, if you ask me... The thing about Bragg, Johnston, and from what I've seen and heard so far about John Bell Hood, is they all got shit for brains. I damn well guarantee Sherman would piss himself if Jeff Davis came to his senses and made Beaufort commander of the whole damned army instead of these other idiots."

"I reckon you're right about that," Jonas recalled replying that evening, as he, Charlie, and Levi hovered around a small fire at their camp near Corinth. At the time, they were losing the battle to keep the faltering flames alive, sheltering the struggling blaze as best they could from an unrelenting assault from chilled rain. "Maybe Beaufort will get a chance to present a better point of view to General Taylor. Or maybe Beauregard and the others down in Alabama will finally experience an epiphany."

"A what?"

"It ain't important, Charlie... Let's just say I hope someone comes to their damned senses before we move out—and I'm not talking about what Beaufort thinks about it. We can already assume he keenly realizes what'll work well and what'll lead to disaster.... But, he'll follow orders too, until things reach the point where it should be obvious to everybody else that a different approach is necessary. They say Beauregard is a smart man... Maybe he'll ponder it more and then change his mind."

It wasn't intended as a joke, but Charlie and Levi burst out laughing, and once Jonas caught the humor of it he joined in heartily...

Now in Alabama, a week had passed since that fireside chat in northern Mississippi. After braving sleet and treacherous roads, in addition to other perilous hazards to reach Florence, Beaufort's cavalry had finally made it to the place where the Army of Tennessee was camped... two damned days ago on November 14th.

Charlie had been proved correct about the foolishness of not simply waiting for Hood's army to cross into Tennessee.

Beaufort's cavalry had lost nearly forty men during the small skirmishes they encountered during the sixty-mile ride from Corinth to the northern edge of Hood's encampment. The road conditions and fighting had lengthened the time it would normally take to get there, but as it turned out they could've—and very likely *should've*—left several days later.

Hood seemed to be enjoying a leisurely pace in getting his troops across the Tennessee River. The vast majority of infantry and artillery regiments were still camped on the southern side of the river. Observing the lack of progress from the river's northern shore, Jonas had been near enough to hear Beaufort cuss up a storm when he learned that the Army of Tennessee's latest commander had waited to give the order to cross the river until the day before Beaufort's arrival.

Previously, it had been indicated by General Taylor that the Army of Tennessee would be ready and waiting on the northern side of the river to begin an immediate trek north. Worse, it soon became known that this procrastination was symptomatic in regard to Hood's recent behavior. In contrast to the grand plans to invade the North, which Hood had proposed with eagerness to both Jeff Davis and Pierre Beauregard, the Confederate commander seemed to have since gained a better understanding of the difficulty in fulfilling such a proposal. Especially when his fighting force was outmanned by Thomas' troops by more than ten thousand soldiers.

According to Beaufort, this whole scheme was Hood's idea, and yet the man doesn't possess the knowledge or resolve to see it through to fruition!

"We traveled sixty miles to get here and still have twice that distance to make in order to reach Nashville," Thomas Means observed, after joining Jonas at the river's edge, where the Third Regiment's top lieutenant gazed across the water toward a thousand campfires. Jonas pictured Hood's infantry trying to warm themselves, though surely the small fires offered meager protection from brisk gusts coming off the river. "But there they all sit... waitin' on God knows what to get movin'. If they were to leave now, they'd be done crossin' by tomorrow afternoon and still have the opportunity to travel by day and night to reach Nashville in just a few days, since the moon's still bright... But sure as shit it ain't about to happen."

"Yep... I reckon you're right, Tommy."

Jonas worried that lingering in Florence for much longer would prove disastrous for his overall mood, too. Often a bit melancholy, the view of the campfires across the blustery river had made him think of Hattie more than usual. Not so much the warm memories at Sugar Creek as it was more her gravesite in Appleton. Despite trying to force himself to switch thoughts to more pleasant times with his beloved wife, now two years deceased, it was like his mind had been taken over by a disobedient mongrel dog that refused to obey even a single command. Jonas silently cussed himself, but it had no effect on the end result. *Her untimely passing haunts me still!*

"At this rate, we'll be stuck here waiting on them to get off their asses and get moving for at least a few more days," Jonas continued, drawing in deeply from his pipe, the tip flaring for an instant. "I sure could use a fresh bottle of whiskey... maybe a couple." He chuckled sadly.

"You think Beaufort will stand for much more of this shit?"

Tommy sounded as worried as Jonas felt. Jonas shot him a tired grin in the dimness. Recently promoted to second lieutenant, Tommy had made it a habit of following Jonas on his daily sabbaticals—largely as an excuse to sip from a flask he carried in his coat or to smoke. Although irritated by the invasion of his privacy at first, Jonas had learned to accept it, and now even looked forward to having Tommy's companionship. To his surprise, it seemed to pull the edge off his broken heart that seemed incapable of healing from the loss of Hattie.

Levi sometimes would join them, as well as Charlie. Jonas was pleased that the tension between him and Tommy had steadily ebbed over the summer and that their friendship had survived the near-deadly standoff at Fort Pillow. And though Tommy had always seemed respectful towards Levi, it appeared he now made a better effort to extend a bit more respect towards the other blacks still riding with the Elite—which numbered just a handful after losing Napoleon Carter during the last skirmish they encountered, roughly twenty miles to the west of Florence.

"It's hard to say what he'll do." Jonas paused to allow Tommy a moment to light up a cigarette he had pulled out from his jacket—likely one of a handful Lieutenant Means had rolled from the remains of a tobacco pouch he had salvaged from a dead Union colonel earlier that month at Johnsonville. The Yankee officer had also been in possession of a finely carved pipe—much nicer than the one Jonas carried. But neither Tommy nor Jonas could stomach the thought of their lips touching anything where an enemy's lips had been previously. "We saw him stand up to Bragg at Chickamauga, and I could tell he was a bit reluctant to leave the raids in order to do this. But, now that we're here, I reckon it's quite likely he'll be patient for a while longer."

A sudden gust from the river belted them. The two men retreated to the slight protection beneath a large pin oak that had yet to shed its leaves, despite the fact an early winter seemed to be in the offing for the region.

"Goddamn, tonight's wind is actin' somethin' fierce, Jonas! Anyway, I'd wager all the money I've got left in my saddlebag that Hood won't be sneakin' up on the Yankees at this rate...."

More n' likely, they'll have plenty of time to rest up while waitin' for this sorry army to reach Nashville... maybe by Christmas." Tommy laughed.

True. Any pretense of clandestine intentions by heading north into Tennessee again had long been forfeited by rumored delays that at present were going on two months. Jonas chuckled again, this time more robustly at the thought that Sherman obviously knew what Hood's plans were, and apparently thinking so lowly of them that he'd left less than half of his corps in Tennessee while taking the bigger Union contingent with him to wreak havoc further south. Either way, the Confederates were significantly outnumbered. By then, Jonas, Tommy, and the rest of Beaufort's cavalry were used to being outnumbered. The difference in leadership and strategy, however, allowed Beaufort to beat unfavorable odds. Jonas had yet to see anything that indicated Hood could do the same.

"As I said, General Beaufort surely is steamin' mad about it all," said Tommy. "Hey... it looks like we might have to head back soon, Jonas. Here comes Levi... likely Charlie's lookin' for us."

"I reckon you're right about Beaufort's displeasure." Jonas pulled up his slicker's collar to fend off the increasingly bitter chill swirling along the river's edge. The cloud cover above carried a slight pink paleness, indicating snow might be covering the ground by morning. "But I might add he has shown remarkable patience. It'll take every ounce of it in dealing with Hood's continued vacillation."

"Ain't that the truth." Tommy sighed while putting out the flame from the second cigarette he had just started. "I realize it ain't ideal conditions. But goddamn, man, if our general was in charge, we'd have been halfway to Nashville by now. Beaufort has the patience and perseverance of a saint!"

"Maybe more like Job from the Bible," said Jonas. "But I'm also willing to bet that if Hood keeps straddling the fence, like they say he's been doing for weeks now, then we might see that patience come to an end in a most inglorious way."

"Toward General Beaufort?"

"Oh, hell no," Jonas assured him, waving to Levi. "Only one general in these parts can look forward to being shamed, and perhaps *by* Beaufort… Guess we'll have to wait and see what the weather brings in the morning. If the sun's shining, things could get quite interesting."

Tommy took his leave of Jonas' presence, advising he'd see him back in camp. Jonas had elected to brave the cold a while longer. Tommy offered Levi a cigarette before heading back to where Beaufort's cavalry was bivouacked on a small bluff above the river.

Levi and Jonas leaned against the oak's stout trunk, sharing the night's last smoke together. Observing the flickering campfires across the river, the small talk between them proved to be another soothing distraction, and Jonas found himself thinking less tormenting thoughts. Instead of images of the gravesite at Rufus Porter's Appleton farm, he focused instead on Levi's observation that the tiny fires dotting the opposite shoreline resembled a summer's night sky in Memphis. The twinkling lights did remind Jonas of stars…. It made it a hell of a lot easier to get back to happier thoughts of Appleton, and his mind's oasis along the beloved creek where happiness could once be found.

Happiness with Hattie… May the Good Lord be merciful and allow that kind of bliss to find me again… someday.

Chapter Twenty-Five

Mid-afternoon, Tuesday, November 29th, 1864... Just south of

Spring Hill, Tennessee.

"You sure this will work?" Hattie asked, as she and Lucinda lay hidden in a thicket near a badly rutted country lane.

"It's got to... just trust me, Hattie."

Lucinda added a confident smile that belied the worry in her eyes. The pair had been watching the progress of General Cheatham's Corps, as the Army of Tennessee marched north to a village known as Spring Hill, after leaving Columbia early that morning. As part of the plan to escape the Twenty-Third Battalion, Lucinda had suggested they try and stick with the general they knew best, John Calvin Brown, who had recently been promoted to Major General and placed in control of Cheatham's old division.

"It appears the Good Lord's takin' a merciful outlook and has provided a path to escape what has befallen us," Lucinda had said last night, when it became apparent they were no

longer safe. *"General Brown's taken charge of General Cheatham's troops, leavin' his old brigade and General Reynold's infantry as a consolidation under Colonel Palmer. Billy told me a while back that the colonel is a man with high ambitions. He intends to become a general soon—despite how things have gone for the army as of late. He won't trouble himself to go lookin' for us, at least not while he's got much bigger fish to fry in commandin' two brigades."*

But Hattie wasn't convinced providence had smiled upon them. She remained fearful of discovery and increasingly certain the pair's desertion would soon be realized by the other commanding officers leading the Army of Tennessee's march to Spring Hill. If her hunch proved correct and they were caught, she and Lucinda would likely be executed somewhere along this God forsaken road. Lucinda's planned excuse of claiming they wanted to continue fighting in the campaign to reach Nashville, and that she and Hattie couldn't abide their regiment's cowardice in staying behind, wouldn't save them. In truth, the Twenty-Third had been temporarily retired at camp, just beyond Columbia's city limits, due to continued decimation of the battalion. The same reprieve was given to Tennessee's Forty-Fifth Regiment. The combined fighting force had suffered enough casualties during the past few months to warrant a rare 'exemption from battle' granted by General Hood.

The removal surprised Hattie, since her understanding was that every soldier was necessary if they were to have any chance of defeating General Thomas' Union forces, presently stationed in Nashville. In addition, General John Schofield and his Yankee army of twenty thousand men were presently in a race against Hood's army of thirty thousand to reach Nashville first. If Schofield was the winner, the prevailing consensus among officers and common soldiers alike was that the

Confederate war effort in the west would end, since they'd be outnumbered two to one at that point.

The exhausted and largely demoralized Army of Tennessee would not only be badly overmatched, but would face the further disadvantage of bringing an attack against a well-fortified Union fortress in Nashville. All of the folly could've been avoided by a better sense of urgency on the part of John Bell Hood—a man who began his tour as commander in July, and at that time appeared to be more like Joe Johnston than Braxton Bragg. Since then, however, General Hood had become reviled almost as severely as General Bragg.

None of that mattered much to Hattie or Lucinda at the moment. The decision for them to pursue the marching troops deployed to Spring Hill by Hood, which represented less than half of his full army, had been made that morning, just a few hours after the march began. Spurred on by the arrival of a trio of provosts that had shown up at Captain Power's tent with a bloodstained Bowie knife, it was just a matter of time before the weapon was tied to Lucinda, due to the engraved initials of 'L. T.' upon the handle. And, if that fact was miraculously ignored, assuredly a few of their Twenty-Third cohorts had noticed that one of two such knives Private Louis Templeton carried in his belt had been missing the past two days.

Lucinda had assured Hattie that she could readily deflect any initial suspicions about the knife being the very same one she used to pierce the heart of the lecherous Malcolm Bates three nights earlier. But Hattie felt Lucinda was foolishly ignoring how the pair had faced growing scrutiny following Lester's death four months earlier. Not to mention, neither woman could honestly swear that no other infantryman had seen them near where Malcolm's body was finally found, yesterday morning, November 28th.

"Here comes Maney's Brigade," Lucinda whispered, pointing excitedly. "Just as I figured… it looks like two of the regiments are in the same sorry shape they were in last I saw 'em, back in Columbia. You remember what I told you, right?"

Hattie nodded, increasingly certain this was a bad idea.

Something doesn't feel right… We're not supposed to be here!

"When I give the signal, we'll emerge and slide into line with the Twenty-Seventh Regiment of Tennessee."

Lucinda waited for Hattie to nod again before she returned her attention to the army kicking up the road's dust. She pulled a branch back to get a better look toward the rear of the column of weary soldiers that had been on the move since dawn— several hours longer than she and Hattie had spent running to catch up to them. The army's actual journey north had started before daybreak. Shortly after the contingent chosen to march that morning had left camp, the provosts made their way to the tent line belonging to the Twenty-Third Battalion.

At present, Hattie finally detected the tattered Tennessee regiment that had captured Lucinda's attention. The troops marched just ahead of Tennessee's Fourth Regiment, and both regiments had been severely decimated in Atlanta. Hattie began to understand Lucinda's confidence in believing the pair could blend in with such a rag-tagged and visibly defeated group, where they would most likely avoid immediate questions as to why two 'dirty-faced youngsters' from another regiment had joined the journey intended to ultimately seize Tennessee's capital.

Despite her lingering worries about invading the regiment as it double-stepped toward Spring Hill, the road-weary expressions upon the soldiers' faces throughout the infantry seemed to further support Lucinda's assumption that their presence would largely be ignored. Hattie began to believe that having two more experienced warriors along for this latest expedition against the Yankees might outweigh the fact that neither one belonged to the Twenty-Seventh or any other regiment on the road right then.

Still, it's so damned risky... What if we fall behind trying to fit in? We could end up falling out of the line or cause problems for other soldiers. The infantry's pace is brisk!

Hattie was exhausted from the race to catch up, and she could tell that Lucinda was just as winded and surely felt weak from hunger as she. Only the fear of being imprisoned, shot, or hung for either desertion or the murder that inspired their flight from camp kept Hattie going. Doubtless, it was equally true for Lucinda.

And it's my fault this has happened! I should've kept a better eye out for Corporal Bates...

Ever since Lester had perished on the battlefield just outside Atlanta, Malcolm Bates had turned the watchful attention he had given Lester toward Hattie instead. It was unwelcome—as always had been the case, even for Lester— and had made her feel more uncomfortable in his presence than before. Malcolm would sneak up behind her, usually at unexpected times, and almost always when away from everyone else, including Lucinda. Though no soldier was clean, as time for bathing was a rare luxury and lice were rampant, Malcolm's odor was more noxious than most. The only virtue Hattie could consider in his regard was that his imminent presence was always preceded by his repugnant scent.

Hattie bore no regrets that Malcolm was dead... and she only mourned the fact that Lucinda had been forced to murder the man when he managed to sneak up on Hattie during a most intimate moment.

Such an event had long been one of her greatest fears as a soldier, and the very thing that would usually expose the presence of a woman disguised as a man in the infantry. Lucinda had reportedly witnessed similar events happening twice prior to Hattie's arrival two years earlier as a new recruit. Those instances had resulted in the exposure and removal of the women pretending to be male soldiers. It was a key factor in forging their initial friendship, as each needed the watchful eyes of the other for protection and long-term survival in an environment created exclusively for men.

Hattie hadn't realized that the additional buffer of Lester had further sheltered her from a predator like Malcolm. But by September she understood that the man who had somehow lucked into an undeserved promotion, following the Army of Tennessee's defeat in Atlanta, had designs to horn in on hers and Lucinda's friendship. In hindsight, she realized that Malcolm had long held unseemly designs on her, and perhaps pursued the same intentions with Lester that he never talked about.

Fortunately, Lucinda's coolness and disparaging hostility to Malcolm's presence, which ignored his promotion to become hers and Hattie's direct superior, provided enough protection to where his inappropriate actions were limited. Hattie expected him to have charges of insubordination brought against Lucinda, but the fact he never had done so told her that Lucinda's claims of possessing 'damaging information' on Malcolm must have been true. Regardless, she worried about an eventual reprisal against Lucinda, or herself.

There were a few close calls, when Hattie would leave camp to take care of her personal needs in the nearby woods. She had seen Malcolm thirty to forty feet away acting as if he were looking for something… or someone. But as far as she could tell, her presence had gone unnoticed by him. Either he would take care of his own 'needs', while she remained still and quiet as she waited for him to finish, or venture far enough away to where he was no longer an immediate menace.

Malcolm Bates had become an unfortunate aspect of her military career, post-Lester. But his presence was survivable... until everything changed on the night of November 26th.

As had been a delicate aspect of pretending to be a man for the past two years, menstruation had proved largely inconvenient—and just as much for Lucinda as Hattie. Cleverness was key, and fortunately when a soldier's clothing was often streaked with blood, a compromised moment wasn't impossible to hide.

In retrospect, it could've remained that way for Hattie— even with a man whose unnatural interest and affection for young teenage boys needed to be continually accounted for. Just a few days shy of the new moon, Hattie couldn't rely on moonlight to aid in cleansing herself. As midnight approached, the camp had seemed deathly quiet, despite pickets posted in the distance keeping an eye out for any unforeseen activity from Schofield's army. She counted on her combined regiment's exhaustion to provide the privacy she needed, as the Army of Tennessee hadn't reached their present location until well after nightfall.

She had just finished cleansing herself and pulling up her trousers when she heard footsteps quietly approaching. Panicked, she pushed her back against the chestnut tree she had chosen that night on account of a large protruding root she could sit upon. Her breaths rose rapidly into the night air, and she cursed silently, knowing they and the soft glow from her lantern—still perched at the base of the tree—would give her presence away, and likely had already done so.

The footsteps drew closer, each step carrying the report of boot soles stirring fallen leaves along the path Hattie had recently followed.

"Who's there?"

She hated the nervousness in her voice that she worried could raise the timbre from boyish to feminine, exposing her true identity as a woman. Regretting that she had left her Bowie knife in the tent with Lucinda, she opened the blade to the much smaller pocketknife she kept on her person at all times. Knowing it would be of little protection, her first worry was appearing foolish if it turned out to be Sergeant McCracken, or even Captain Powers, although their tents had been dark when she'd slipped away from camp after waiting for the closest picket to turn his attention elsewhere.

The footsteps stopped.

Hattie peered around the chestnut's trunk, again silently cursing her nervousness that kept her from picking up her lantern. She couldn't see anything beyond the tree… and her instincts told her that no one was there. She began to wonder if she had heard a deer or some other nocturnal critter, and began to relax.

But as she turned her attention back to where her lantern sat, suddenly a shadow stepped in front of it. She managed to stifle a gasp as the figure closed in, and regret washed over her as a familiar stench filled her nostrils.

"Well, well… what might you be doin' out here at this late hour, Private Grey?"

Malcolm laughed haughtily, spewing a fresh blast of his noxious breath into her face. A man larger than Jonas in height, he proved to be stronger physically than she had previously assumed, given his cowering before Lucinda and her taunts. When she tried to move past him, he easily prevented her escape, shoving her against the tree.

"Not so fast, Henry... we've been needin' this 'talk' for quite some time."

He snickered when she failed to push him away, and as if he knew she would try to kick him, he pressed his left knee against her right leg. All the while he drew nearer... as if positioning his face to caress hers.

"It ain't so bad," he whispered meanly. "Didn't Lester ever tell you about him and me? Hmmm? The things he'd do to keep ole Malcolm satisfied... Who'd you think put the good word in for him with Joe McCracken, to get special privileges? You think it was your buddy, Louis? Let me tell you somethin'... Louis don't know shit! Louis don't know the half of what got me promoted to corporal, neither. 'Twas a long time comin' after all I'd done for the younguns like Lester Smith. God rest his wretched soul!"

Hattie looked up at his shadowed face in horror. The smug delivery told her more than the statement itself, and she suddenly felt weak in her knees. *This monster violated Lester? How so? But it feels true... God help me, I'll kill this bastard!* She wanted to lash out at Malcolm immediately, and with a venomous rage that swiftly simmered to a boil within her. Yet a small voice in her mind warned her to wait... that her opportunity for escape could be jeopardized. The chance to avenge anything Malcolm had done to her beloved 'little brother' would only come to her if she bided her time. If she could just *wait!*

She couldn't control the anger, and though Malcolm held her arms fast, she managed to free her right hand still gripping the pocketknife. Hattie lunged at him, and she briefly saw surprise in his pale gray eyes, visible under the lantern's soft glow. But the knife's blade got caught on his coat and he knocked it out of her hand.

Enraged, Malcolm shoved her against the tree again, this time his hands lingering on her chest. A look of astonishment quickly morphed to a deeper leer than she had ever witnessed from him. Hattie struggled as he pinned her arms with one hand and tore at her shirt with the other. The look of shock and anger gave way to an expression that chilled Hattie's blood.

He knew.

"Goddamn, you're a *woman!*" he whispered gleefully. "Well, hell… you're all *mine* now!"

Hattie fought harder, but he seemed to have become immensely stronger, effortlessly preventing her from pushing him away. She tried to scream, but his grimy hand covered her mouth. She closed her eyes in a vain attempt to muster enough strength to try and kick him away. Again, it failed, and she listened helplessly as he unfastened his belt, followed by the sound of his trousers being pulled down. Then he returned to fondling her breasts, now exposed, with one hand while kissing her face. He kept his hand over her mouth and used the other to furiously pull down her trousers.

Other than losing her father and beloved husband, the very worst thing she had ever feared beyond being discovered was being raped. Discovery had happened, and the sexual attack was about to ensue. Hot tears of anger and humiliation began to flow. As he finished removing her trousers far enough to allow access to the most private and tender part of her body, she braced herself for the inevitable horrific pain… both physical and emotional. She tried to ignore the stream of depravity he spoke into her ears when not trying to mash his whiskered vile lips close to hers through his dirty fingers. She wanted to die right then.

Malcolm let out a yelped grunt and suddenly fell away from her. It took Hattie a moment to realize that not only had he not succeeded in his attempt to ravish her, but the muted cry was from Lucinda's Bowie knife plunged from behind to the hilt, skewering his heart.

"I'm sorry." It was all Hattie could muster.

Lucinda shook her head sorrowfully.

"I should've protected you better, Hattie. *I'm* sorry."

Hattie wanted to tell her it could never have been her fault. But she couldn't say anything. A profound mixture of relief and humiliation washed over her, and she fell to her hands and knees, retching. When finished she stood, shaking as chills seized her entire body, while somehow managing to pull her pants up.

For an instant, she caught a glimpse of Lucinda's pensive face in the lantern's glow, almost hearing the silent debate as to what to do about Malcolm. He lay in a dead crumpled heap at the base of the chestnut tree with the Bowie knife's handle protruding from his back. Naked from the waist down, he'd somehow managed to kick off his trousers and boots during the assault.

There wasn't a prolonged discussion on what to do with the fiend's body. Hattie figured it would've been a messy situation no matter what they had tried to do that night. Burying Malcolm might've been the best decision. Yet, had they been caught by some other camp straggler or one of the pickets on duty, Malcolm's death could've been viewed as premeditated, and the truth obscured by ill-timed circumstance. At the very least, Lucinda likely would've faced a court martial for murder, as explaining the truth would not have been an option.

They left Malcolm exactly where he fell and slowly made their way back to camp.

When they were safely back inside their tent, both women retired to their bedrolls without saying a word. But when Hattie's muted whimpers escalated to tears she could no longer hold within, Lucinda moved to her bedroll, holding Hattie until well after the dawn's first glowing embers began to appear on the eastern horizon.

Talk of leaving their regiment hadn't come up until the following afternoon, when news reached the Twenty-Third from Billy Powers that they and the Forty-Fifth would be given at least a week off from fighting, and likely longer—courtesy, most unexpectedly, from John Bell Hood.

At that time, no one had stumbled onto Malcolm's body. But by nightfall, Lucinda quietly mourned the fact she had chosen not to bury him, stating she had assumed the army would continue the intended course to reach Nashville in the next day or so. Then when Captain Powers broke the news that Corporal Bates had been murdered in 'cold blood', it came with a commitment from General Hood to 'track down those responsible and bring them swiftly to justice."

The plan to leave was a decision that both Hattie and Lucinda agreed upon. However, the choice to try and assimilate into yet another regiment—Lucinda's third, and Hattie's second—wasn't mutual...

"Let's go!"

Lucinda motioned for Hattie to follow her as she emerged from the thicket. Almost nonchalant in her approach, she fell in line just ahead of the Fourth and scooted up into the Twenty-Seventh. The reaction from both regiments seemed neutral until Hattie also joined in, causing a few of the infantrymen to glance toward the area they had appeared from, perhaps expecting more Confederates to follow. When it became apparent that the pair of haggard soldiers were alone, most of the soldiers turned their weary gazes to the task at hand, seemingly much more concerned with the accelerated pace to reach Spring Hill.

Hattie traded a brief glance with a lieutenant whom she could tell recognized her face, as she also was familiar with him from the few times she had seen him in the company of Captain Powers. She offered a faint smile that he responded to with a slightly raised eyebrow.

Shit! I bet he knows our regiment was supposed to stay back in Columbia... We might soon be in some serious trouble!

She glanced at Lucinda, who mumbled, "stay at ease," without turning to look at her. Hattie settled her attention upon navigating the uneven road ahead, soon welcoming the distraction. Despite expecting the officer to turn toward her again, and with a more scrutinizing gaze than before, he didn't shoot a glance Hattie's way until they had reached the southern outskirts of Spring Hill. By then, the troops at the front of the line were preparing for battle. Amid Union cannon fire in the distance came swift reports that a Union brigade positioned just ahead had recently repulsed General Franklin Beaufort's cavalry.

Lucinda and Hattie traded surprised looks. Neither one had expected a full battle that day, as the understood objective was to make enough progress by nightfall to prevent Schofield's army from reaching Spring Hill in its quest to make it to Franklin, and then continue on course to Nashville in the morning. An even bigger goal, according to what Lucinda had gleaned while eavesdropping the night before on a disgruntled Billy Powers, who was quite unhappy about being pulled from active service, was to fool Schofield into thinking the Confederates remained near Columbia. The hope behind the ruse was to surround Schofield's army and then force a much-needed surrender.

Obviously, based upon the cannon reports and the increased sense of urgency going on with Cleburne's men ahead of them, that plan had failed. The Union Army, or at least a significant portion, wasn't in Columbia. Instead, they awaited the Confederate Army's arrival in Spring Hill. Regardless of whether or not this meant Schofield's troops had escaped the trap devised by Hood and his generals, or if Union reinforcements had been deployed from Nashville, a battle loomed just the same.

"The web-footed grunts are always the last to know a goddamned thing!" Lucinda fumed quietly. "But we better get ready, Henry. Looks like there's some confusion goin' on up ahead… We'll be formin' battle lines at any moment."

Hattie nodded, solemnly wondering if this was why she had felt ill at ease. The sight of men dying around her from either army was nothing new, and as such, she had grown callous to most of it during the past two years. Without the full Army of Tennessee, the immediate conflict wouldn't carry the carnage of Stones River, Chickamauga, or Atlanta… unless the Union Army in Spring Hill at that moment was a far greater force of men than General Hood or anyone on his staff of officers had anticipated facing that day.

It feels wrong, regardless, and getting worse by the minute! We truly shouldn't be here… not any of us!

Chapter Twenty-Six

Wednesday morning, November 30th, 1864.... The march to

Franklin, Tennessee.

The feeling of dread that had plagued Hattie since Tuesday morning continued to worsen. Despite Lucinda's assurances that their lot had actually improved, Hattie's anxiety kept her from sleeping a wink Tuesday night. It mattered little that Lieutenant Isaac Cooper, the officer with whom she had exchanged knowing looks right before all hell broke loose along the southern edge of Spring Hill, had later given Hattie and Lucinda a reprieve for their defection from the Twenty-Third Battalion. When he strode up to the campfire where she and Lucinda were sharing supper and small talk with soldiers from the Twenty-Seventh Regiment of Tennessee, Hattie set her plate down in anticipation of being arrested. But instead of an armed escort to a provost, the handsome lieutenant who reminded Hattie of her beloved Jonas pulled the pair aside. He told them they could remain as 'actives' for the battle, although he couldn't promise that discipline wouldn't be forthcoming for their unauthorized presence.

"It's your own damn fault for worryin' so," Lucinda had quietly chided her the following morning at breakfast. "They need us to fight today, pure and simple."

A greater sense of excitement pervaded throughout the camp than the previous evening, as everyone prepared to give chase to General Schofield's troops that had somehow slipped past the entire Confederate Army during the night. From what Hattie and Lucinda had gathered from their new cohorts, General Hood was livid upon hearing the news of this development when it arrived, shortly before dawn. He apparently could be heard screaming from inside the Oaklawn mansion where he had set up his Spring Hill headquarters the night before, which was situated just a couple of miles away from Columbia Pike—the very road taken by most of Schofield's army.

But along with the keen sense of anticipation Wednesday morning came the realization that the advantage sought by the Army of Tennessee had been irrefutably lost by daybreak. The trap set for Schofield—and Hattie had heard by then that the network of safeguards supposedly managed by generals such as Cheatham and Beaufort were extensive—had not only failed to stop the Union Army's progress toward Nashville, but had also missed the opportunity to sound an alarm as the Yankees marched right past Confederate campfires throughout the night.

"You mean, they need us to chase after the Yankees, who are more than five miles up the road," Hattie observed.

"I reckon the entire Union Army is twice that far by now." Lucinda responded with a begrudged chuckle as she dumped the rest of her chicory on their small campfire's coals. "And by the time we catch up, the Yanks will have a bigger advantage. We might not get close enough to see em' until after they've reached Nashville. If that's true, it'll be too goddamned late to accomplish anythin'… other than dyin', I suppose."

"Maybe we should stay behind… maybe this ain't such a good idea after all."

Lucinda whipped her head around, regarding Hattie in disbelief.

"Are you insane?" she hissed angrily. She looked around guardedly and then pulled Hattie aside, acting as if the pair gathered up their tent spikes, which were already inside Hattie's haversack. "You can't be serious. There's no way we can *ever* go back! All that's left is what lies ahead."

Hattie said nothing in response, shaking her head sadly.

"Oh, so you think they'd take us back with open arms?" Lucinda eyed her sullenly. "Hell, they might just do that. But only to wrap those arms around us real tight and then take our dirty asses to the nearest tree to be whipped and hanged!"

The conversation ended with a huff from Hattie's closest cohort—the only soldier left from the small group she had long trusted, and the one person in the entire Army of Tennessee whom she cherished. The infantrymen that had grown fond of Lester the past two years, and subsequently became friendly to her and Lucinda, had increasingly kept to themselves since July—a fact Malcolm Bates readily exploited. It didn't help matters that Lucinda had become less and less approachable to their fellow soldiers in the Twenty-Third Battalion, as well as the Forty-Fifth Regiment… Hattie worried that Lucinda's emotional distance might one day include her, too—perhaps resulting in Private Templeton leaving the Confederate Army for good. If the most recent reports that had reached the Twenty-Seventh proved accurate, and Schofield's army remained in Franklin to set up breastworks and other defenses, Hattie worried she might find herself alone by dusk. Lucinda had saved her life repeatedly, and Hattie mourned the fact she had never been able to adequately repay the favor.

I might never get a chance to repay her, if she up and leaves the army!

Soon after, they were back on a road headed north, this time following the Union's course taken the night before along Columbia Pike. For the next several hours, the Army of Tennessee's pace to Franklin was even more brisk than the day before. Hattie sensed a determination to fight among their new regiment and the rest of Maney's Brigade that was lacking the previous day, when Hood's army skirmished against the Federals in Spring Hill. Perhaps it was the burning rage that had spewed forth from their commander's lips after the missed opportunity to box in Schofield's army and force their surrender. Regardless of the reason, Hattie hadn't seen this level of enthusiasm among the Rebel infantry since late spring in Atlanta.

Shortly after one o'clock that afternoon, the front edge of the Confederate lines reached the outskirts of Franklin. The Union Army was entrenched along the southern edge of town, as reported earlier, which apparently came as a surprise to General Hood and a disappointment to the staff of generals serving under him. From what Lucinda and Hattie finally pulled from Lieutenant Cooper, the confirmed Federal stronghold inspired a raging debate at Hood's latest headquarters—a mansion located not far from Winstead Hill, which loomed directly behind where General Brown's division was now camped.

By mid-afternoon, the Twenty-Seventh, along with the rest of Maney's Brigade, had been waiting for nearly two hours for the next command. Presumably, it would be a call to march on the Union forces that had spent much of the day preparing for the Confederates' arrival.

"What in the hell's keepin' us from goin' inside the town and flushin' out the Yanks?" Lucinda shook her head disgustedly, when Isaac Cooper's pocket watch chirped an alert that three o'clock had arrived. Her irritation reflected the growing restlessness that had infected the Confederate line. Many of the men fidgeted anxiously where they stood, with more kneeling while they all awaited an announcement of some kind. "The only thing waitin's gonna do is give those bastards a bigger upper hand!"

Lieutenant Cooper also shook his head. But Hattie sensed the lieutenant's frustration came from Lucinda and members of his regiment talking as if they wished to launch themselves thoughtlessly into harm's way. The latest news had come just an hour ago from one of General Cleburne's officers, advising the Yankees had indeed erected breastworks and other fortifications that were already partially in place from a previous occupation of Franklin. Despite being ignored for well over a year, refortifying what was already present had provided the Union with a formidable defense.

Hattie heard the lieutenant hiss under his breath that unless the Confederates could find a way around the breastworks and other hazards, casualties could be very high. He claimed to have heard this from Colonel Hume Field himself, who stated that the advisement first came from the lips of generals John Brown and John Carter.

"So, it's true?" Hattie asked. "The Yankees dug themselves in and have spent the rest of the morning, and afternoon so far, just waiting for us to arrive?"

Her heightened apprehension made her willing to chance a scornful response. To her surprise, he regarded her thoughtfully, as if measuring what to safely reveal.

"Yep... Colonel Field said a crescent-shaped fortress of sorts now protects the Union Army, and it's further enforced by an abatis made from osage orange trees on one end and a grove of locust trees on the other," he confided. "It don't seem fair that the Good Lord has provided the Yankees with extra hazards to use against us, considerin' they already have plenty of artillery and repeatin' rifles to defend against any frontal assaults. If General Beaufort and General Cleburne can sway General Hood into tryin' to flank Schofield's army—which Colonel Field said is a strategic move that's been discussed since this mornin'—while also preoccupyin' the bastards with our sharpshooters, then maybe we can draw 'em out for a fair fight. But if not..."

Without a need to state or affirm the obvious consequences, Hattie tipped her hat to Lieutenant Cooper and headed back to where Lucinda had joined several members of the Twenty-Seventh in a quiet poker contest. All the while, the sun continued to descend toward the west. Four o'clock would be arriving soon. The weather had been sunny and unseasonably warm throughout the day, and Hattie wondered if the delay would lead to regrets in missing out on a perfect afternoon to engage in battle. That random thought struck her as odd, since the unpleasantness of war seemed best suited for the hellish extremes of winter or summer.

But just as it seemed the wait for what was to come might not end before nightfall, the order came for the entire infantry to prepare for a brazen march upon the Union position, presently determined to be less than two miles away. Surprisingly, the eagerness from earlier returned to the ranks—fed in part by the appearance of generals Cheatham, Cleburne, Brown, and others preparing to personally lead their troops into battle. Not surprising, though, was Lucinda's cynical outlook on what had transpired in the senior officers' meeting with John Bell Hood.

"Looks like we're gonna find out just how strong the Union's defenses are before sunset," she observed dryly, pointing to her left. "I see Colonel Field over there talkin' to Lieutenant Cooper and the other officers. They're lookin' none too happy. I reckon we should go find out what the fuss is about."

The seven officers gathered around an animated Hume Field were shaking their heads as if dismayed. One of the sergeants protested loudly, to where his *"Ain't that some shit!"* comment pulled the attention of a number of soldiers already moving toward their regiment battle alignments. Before Hattie and Lucinda made it to where they stood, Colonel Field left to join General Brown, who was in the process of aligning his division in a manner similar to General Cleburne's infantry. Meanwhile, Lieutenant Cooper and the rest of the officers, including his immediate commander, Captain Thomas Kizer, stormed toward the infantry line of the Twenty-Seventh.

Cooper ignored Lucinda's and Hattie's initial inquiries about what had upset him and the rest of Colonel Field's direct reports, other than to snidely tell Lucinda, "Well, looks like you're gettin' your goddamned death wish after all!"

Along with his sergeant's assistance, the lieutenant quickly organized the Twenty-Seventh, relaying General Brown's order to form in columns to protect as many men as possible from being picked off by Union artillery. The entire Army of Tennessee had been directed by General Hood to march directly to where the Union Army waited, and then launch a furious attack against their line of defense once the breastworks came into full view. The plan also called for all four brigades under Brown's direction to deploy into their normal battle lines upon reaching the range of small arms fire. The same orders were given to Cleburne's division.

The methodical approach would change to a quickened pace for the Twenty-Seventh when Sergeant Ezekiel Patterson's command to 'double-quick' was given.

"So, we're really going to do this?" Hattie whispered to Lucinda. "General Hood intends to kill us all!"

"It so appears." Lucinda offered a wan smile.

The mischievous twinkle in Lucinda's eyes was the first genuine sign of warm familiarity that Hattie had seen from her beloved friend since before the unfortunate incident with Corporal Bates, just a few nights prior. She couldn't help but smile in return, and then it was time to get serious. The invasion of Franklin was now set to begin, and Hattie would recall later how it was the only instance the two exchanged smiles that day.

General Brown's Division occupied the western side of Columbia Pike, while General Cleburne's Division held the eastern side of the thoroughfare. They were near-mirror images of each other, except for the battle flags. Cleburne's group carried the Irish blue flag with a white moon, and Brown's color guards hoisted red flags bearing the battle version of the St. Andrew's cross. The twin divisions corrected their alignments to face General Cheatham. Cheatham's Corps marched between Brown's men and Cleburne's, with the intent of assaulting the center of the Federal works. When apparently satisfied with his entire army's preparedness, Cheatham gave a nod to a flag bearer that also held Brown and Cleburne's attention.

The flag dropped, and the march into the most precarious and deadly situation Hattie had yet to witness was underway.

While the initial course was steady and the pace smooth, with the bands launching into a merry rendition of Dixie, it didn't take long for all of that to change. Within half a mile of the infantry's approach, as they trod downhill across an open field, the air above the town's edge suddenly rumbled with man-made thunder. The first grapeshot canisters and exploding shells ripped through the front of all three divisions. Hattie tightened her grip on her rifle, keeping her worried eyes trained on the trail of soldiers a few hundred feet ahead of the Twenty-Seventh that were moving to fill in the gaps where their comrades had been marching just moments before, but were now completely obliterated from the ranks by artillery fire.

My God, we're going to die—it's surely going to happen today!

The pace remained steady while the gaps needing to be filled required more and more men. Soldiers less than fifty feet away from where Hattie and Lucinda marched side by side began leaving their positions, hurrying to fill the voids that could've been worse had the lines not been pulled tight.

Meanwhile, the cannon bombardment steadily increased. Sooner than expected, the Yankees attacked the Rebel aggressors with small arms, prompting the command from Sergeant Patterson to "double-quick". Immediately, Maney's Brigade joined the others under Brown in deploying to the standard line of battle, and the legendary yells and cries soon filled the air.

Hattie and Lucinda raised their voices in exhilaration as well, and gave chase so that they could keep up as the mass of determined Confederates sprinted toward the Union lines. The rain of blood that had accompanied nearly every significant confrontation between the North and South came early, but then suddenly quieted when the assault discharged from behind the Union fortifications lessened to allow a pair of Yankee brigades to drift out onto the field ahead of the Confederate wave. Still a mile away from the breastworks, the Union troops' presence seemed to hinder the artillery teams, likely unwilling to injure their own soldiers now directly in the line of fire.

Brown and Cleburne urged their troops to hurry, surely seeing the opportunity to cover valuable ground with minimized losses. The Union brigades were quickly overwhelmed, and only able to fire a single volley before retreating toward the breastworks. The Rebels' surge soon swallowed the fleeing Yankees, with nary a shot coming from the formidable wall of earthen clay and wooden planks that in some places rose to nearly ten feet above the ground.

Hattie grimaced as she and Lucinda stumbled over the dead—equally divided between both armies at this point, with many of the bodies gashed by sabers and bayonets. The injured and dying men they had first encountered during the rush to reach the Union line were mostly Confederates, whose bodies had been maimed and mangled by artillery fire.

For the briefest moment, it appeared they had an unhindered opportunity to reach the breastworks directly ahead. Brown and Cleburne's joint infantry picked up the pace, swarming over the Union survivors desperately trying to make it to safety. Just as it appeared the Confederates could reach the breastworks in under a minute, a horrible feeling seized Hattie's heart. Union marksmen unleashed a relentless barrage of bullets from behind the breastworks. The sudden assault caught the Rebel troops less than forty feet ahead of her by surprise, lifting dozens of soldiers into the air before they landed hard on their backs, never to stir again.

There wasn't time to regroup. Bravely, those who survived the onslaught pressed on, despite the fact many a Confederate officer now lay dying upon the blood-soaked ground, where the grass and weeds had been trampled down in the wake of the attack. Hattie had glimpsed Cleburne knocked from his horse earlier, and Brown was missing. But it was the death of

Lieutenant Cooper that almost stole her courage to press through a gap in the breastworks, first forged by General Granbury's Texans, who seemed to have no understanding of fear and self-preservation.

In the fading sunlight, Cooper had taken over when Captain Kizer was wounded by a shell explosion. As the young lieutenant swung his saber to direct the Twenty-Seventh to follow the flow of soldiers invading the breastworks' breach, his face exploded from what was likely a pair of Minié balls that struck the back of his head simultaneously.

Perhaps it was the fact that she had grown to admire the man over the course of the past day… or more likely, because Cooper favored Jonas more than any soldier she had encountered until then. Whatever the case, it nearly brought Hattie to her knees as she stumbled toward his corpse.

"No! Henry get back up and follow me!"

Lucinda urged Hattie to come with her to where the Texans had broken through the Union defenses. The Confederate lines had largely dissolved as the fighting turned viciously fierce. To survive the bloody melee, where swinging bayonets and swords could indiscriminately kill foe and friend alike, Hattie zigzagged behind Lucinda, engaging the blue coats only when they blocked the path originally created by Cleburne's Texans. Hattie was almost stopped again when they came across the body of General Hiram Granbury, kneeling with his hands upon his face. A circular exit hole in the back of his head told the story of the final moments for one of Cleburne's bravest generals.

I've got to keep going! I can't let Lucinda down… Lester, wherever you are, this is for you, too!

To make it through the breach, Hattie and Lucinda were forced into hand-to-hand combat against a trio of Yankees blocking their path. Wild-eyed with rage, the men spewed violent taunts with an unholy level of hatred fed by years of war. They bore down hard as they prepared to skewer Hattie and Lucinda with their bloodstained bayonets. But the pair's grit and refusal to give an inch provided enough of an edge. Hattie's well-timed pistol shot between the eyes of a young Yankee private ensured they'd survive a while longer when his partners fled in surprise, apparently having spent the last of their ammunition.

For the next hour, though progress was slow but steady, it appeared Cheatham's army would drive the Union opposition away from their fortifications. More and more Confederates continued to pour into the breach, following the scant illumination of dying twilight and the small fires from broken lanterns that lay scattered upon the ground. A beautiful one-story home stood in the background, lending a moment of wonder to Hattie, as surely a family had to be present. A family most likely forced to surrender their property to General Schofield, or one of the other Union commanders—perhaps before the family had even finished eating breakfast. Hopefully, someone was keeping them safe, similarly to how her father had saved her life when the band of Yankee marauders had come to call on her farm two years earlier.

Yet, despite the tantalizing promise of victory, instead what had seemingly become the Confederacy's fate for much of the past year soon took over. Once again, fortune had become the fickle mistress it had so often been toward the Southern Cause. When it happened that evening, darkness had fully engulfed the landscape, save for where several new fires burned in the front lawn of the stately home that for the most part had miraculously remained intact, despite dead soldiers piled everywhere around the house. Many were lying haphazardly over the back-porch rails that Hattie had gained a glimpse of during the push-pull of gaining and losing ground with the enemy. As dusk turned to full darkness, Hattie could scarcely believe the Union Army had somehow regained control of its makeshift fortress, where two sections of the breastworks were presently engulfed in flames.

The deadly dance continued between warriors from both sides, haggard and exhausted, and where each misguided thrust of a bayonet or sword could mean death in the response. When Hattie had ammunition, she was certain she had killed nearly two-dozen Yankees before she ran out of cartridges and bullets, and perhaps Lucinda had taken out even more enemy soldiers. Yet the vast majority of bodies that covered the ground, to where it had become impossible to not be standing upon a corpse at any one time, were clad in butternut and gray.

We're going to lose horribly yet again! More Yankees keep emerging from behind the house, as if they've been in hiding this entire time and are now ready to join the battle!

She and Lucinda had joined with several stranded soldiers from Alabama to form a fighting circle. But the most recent influx of Yankees promptly took out three of the young men, leaving just one, along with Hattie and Lucinda, against the refreshed blue rush headed their way. Somehow, Lucinda eluded a pair of bayonets, and Hattie followed her signal to retreat back through the breastworks' breach—hopefully to safety. More than a dozen Confederates were coming up fast from the other side, which would give them a better fighting advantage against the Union soldiers in pursuit.

Lucinda stepped through the hole, and turned to make sure Hattie was right behind her—which she was. Suddenly, Private Templeton lurched backward, and to Hattie's horror, the flickering flames from the burning timbers in a nearby breastwork revealed a swath of shadow rapidly spreading along Lucinda's lower left side. She fell to her knees as Hattie reached out to her in horrified disbelief.

Oh my God—NO! This can't be happening... Dear Jesus, don't let it be real! It simply can't be true!

But as she reached Lucinda, who collapsed into her arms, she confirmed that the shadow that continued to spread across the lower portion of her shirt beneath her coat was deep crimson in color... *blood.*

"I'm sorry, Henry," Lucinda whispered, her tone hushed and unrecognizably hoarse. She gazed up into Hattie's face; her brown eyes softer than Hattie ever recalled seeing them before, with a bewildered glint. "Looks like my turn in this dance is over." She smiled weakly.

"No, it's *not!*" Hattie protested. "We need to find a doctor—let me fetch a surgeon and you'll be all right. You're going to make it through this, Louis. You *have* to make it!"

The manner in which Lucinda had been pushed back made Hattie assume it was a bullet wound, though in the dimness it could've been almost anything. Rather than ask if she knew if she'd been shot or stabbed, Hattie gently pushed aside Lucinda's coat near the injury. She let out a pained howl as Hattie tried to remove her shirt. But knowing that time was of the essence, Hattie pushed through Lucinda's protests while guiding her out of the fighting path, which was far from easy. While resolutely ignoring Lucinda's heartrending groans, Hattie brought her to a ripped-apart stump of a tree nearby, likely torn asunder by a shell earlier that evening.

The battle continued to rage on around them, but the spot would have to suffice. The poorer light proved adequate for a quick view of the damage to Lucinda's abdomen. Hattie initially hoped it was a bayonet or knife wound, even though any damage to the midsection of a soldier in this bitter war was likely a death sentence. She had seen only two Confederate infantrymen survive out of hundreds that were wounded in this manner. Most died slowly, and in increasing agony... Her heart was breaking at the thought of Lucinda dying this way—acerbating the profound sense of loss hovering around her. Hattie didn't believe she could carry on without the only 'tried and true' companion she still had in this cruel and unforgiving world.

Yet, the damage was wrought by something else. Thankfully, the wound was small, likely caused by a Minié ball.

It could be a hell of a lot worse, but depending on where the bullet went next, it could still be severe. I need to take a look at her back, but she's losing so much blood. Her face is paler than a moment ago...

"What is it, Henry?"

Lucinda studied her face, but all Hattie could do was shake her head and weep.

"Goddamn it, you're goin' to have to stay strong and carry on—"

"No, you're *not* gonna die! I *won't* let it happen!"

Hattie stood up amid the battle's chaos, screaming for a litter to be brought over. But of course, with the fierce fighting still in progress, no one would dare carry a stretcher into this bloody mess. Besides, men were dying all around her—why should anyone favor Lucinda's life over another? Especially when there were officers among the fallen.

Lucinda tried to sit up, but fell back, coughing up a small stream of blood that lingered on her chin. But she managed to grab Hattie's leg and pull her down out of harm's way.

"Henry... don't call anyone... *Please don't!*" she pleaded. "This is what I've always wanted... to die as a man, on a battlefield like all the other brave soldiers that have come and gone before me... You call some goddamned surgeon, and you know what? They won't be able to save me, but... but they'll sure as hell know my true identity. My death will be a disgrace... I *must* die with honor!"

Hattie didn't know how to respond, since she didn't agree at all. But, in truth, Lucinda was dying before her eyes. Grief threatened to incapacitate her, and she tried to force herself to think only of what was best for Lucinda, wanting to comfort her as best she could. Hattie gently stroked her face, regarding her in such a way that she hoped Lucinda would understand just how much she loved her... Love was the only thing she could give.

What about hope? Lucinda could be with Lester soon... Maybe I'll be coming along shortly, too. Maybe I should just stand up and tell the Yankee bastards to finish the damned job they've done in ruining my life! By taking everything—Papa, Mary, Lester, and now Lucinda—and perhaps Jonas, too— they've destroyed me entirely!

But then the urge to save Lucinda overrode all else, and Hattie did stand up again. No longer caring whether she lived or died, she whirled around, frantically searching in the dimness for anyone who looked like they might be a surgeon or assistant to such.

"Henry, watch out!"

Hattie turned in time to see a bayonet headed for her chest. Even if she had wanted to avoid the blow, it would've been impossible, given the close proximity. But a blur from a gray hat and dark hair stepped in front of her.

"Oh, God, no!" Hattie shrieked.

Somehow, Lucinda had managed to stand up and thrust herself in front of Hattie. The sequence of movements slowed to where Hattie could see everything clearly; from the Yankee's angry grimace and battle scream to Lucinda's face in profile... Her mouthed "I love you" was a ghostly whisper just before the long slender blade pierced Private Templeton's heart.

As she fell, Hattie grabbed her Bowie knife from her belt and thrust it into the young man's throat. He fell to the ground, clutching his neck to stop a crimson flow similar to the one that announced the end of Lucinda's life a moment before. The pair sprawled upon the ground made for a meaningless quid pro quo, and the Yankee cheated Hattie from accompanying Lucinda across Death's Veil.

She kneeled next to Lucinda, as she took her last breaths.

Hattie could tell it wouldn't be long. But she wanted to make sure her beloved companion knew beyond any doubt how much she meant to her—how much she would *always* mean to her. But as she opened her mouth to speak again, a fast-approaching shadow loomed from the right in her periphery. Hattie looked up in time to see the rifle butt just before it struck her. A sharp pain ripped through her skull, and the world around her was immediately absorbed into a sea of impenetrable blackness.

* * * * *

The awareness of the agonizing pain atop her head was what first told Hattie she had regained consciousness.

Lying on her back, it took a moment to remember where she was. Things had changed since she received the blow… It seemed quieter. Confederate soldiers mulled around her, while carefully stepping over bodies. Gunshots were still prevalent… but in the distance, and not near as many as before.

The images of what had transpired, and what she had experienced, began to trickle into her mind. In a panic she sat up, looking wildly around her.

How long was I out? It looks like most of the Yankees have moved on... but to where?

The gaping hole in the Federals' breastworks stood less than forty feet away. The fires had died down, but not completely. Confederate dead far outnumbered the silent bluecoats interspersed among them. Then Hattie's gaze fell upon the motionless form lying just a few feet away.

Lucinda!

Hattie scrambled over to her. Lucinda's head was turned toward the ruptured maw in the middle of the Union fortification. The area seemed destined to soon be under Confederate control, but only as a meaningless token. The battle's obvious victors were likely headed north to Nashville.

When she pulled Lucinda's arm to turn her body over, Hattie immediately knew her beloved companion of the last three years was gone. The joints' stiffness told of a life force that had moved on... Unable to bear looking into Lucinda's lifeless eyes that she could detect were slightly open, Hattie reached over and gently closed them, finding it impossible to escape the coldness of Lucinda's face as her fingers grazed against the cheeks and nose.

It was all it took to send Hattie into debilitating grief, and she wept bitterly over her dear friend's corpse. No longer caring about her own fate, she was only partially aware that a small skirmish had broken out on the other side of Columbia Pike, to her right. It seemed to have been sparked by the approach of a handful of mounted cavalry, but ended quickly, with the Union soldiers fleeing up the road.

"Clear the way for Beaufort's men!" ordered a sergeant from nearby. "They might just catch them Yankee sons of bitches up yonder!"

Hattie raised her head in time to see three of the five riders before they hurried off toward the north. Fully visible due to the presence of several lanterns held by the sergeant and his companions, the Negro rider immediately seemed familiar... It took her a moment to recall that she'd seen this man at Chickamauga, though on foot at the time and from a distance. She suddenly remembered seeing a heavily bearded companion with this soldier that day, over a year ago, in profile. The way the bearded one walked as the pair carried what looked like a wounded companion to safety had also seemed familiar at that time, though promptly forgotten until now. She wondered if the pair was still together, even though the notion seemed quite fallacious given how companions in this war rarely lasted, which brought forth yet another dagger to plunge into her defenseless heart after losing Lucinda. Yet, if they had beaten such long odds for so long, why couldn't someone else?

Then he arrived, as the black cavalryman waited. In profile, the man wore a similar heavy beard with his long thick dark hair billowing down past his shoulders. But unlike before, this time he turned his face in Hattie's direction, to thank the sergeant for the volley of shots that gave him and his companions cover, and for the men presently moving enough bodies out of the way for the horses not to stumble.

Oh my God... it can't be!

But it was.

Lieutenant Jonas Grey sat tall and straight in his saddle, a striking figure atop a muscular brown stallion. In the lanterns' soft glow he smiled at the sergeant, lingering long enough for her to detect the dulled light in his once brilliant blue eyes.

This was a broken man, and she wondered if it was from the war itself, or something else.

Does he know I'm no longer in Appleton? If so, did he see the graves and the charred remains of Papa's farm?

Surely, another furlough had been granted at some point in time, and... But then he turned to leave, and the rambling thoughts in her head abruptly ceased. She realized all too late that an opportunity to catch his attention had been lost.

Hattie tried to call his name—to scream for him to stop and wait for her to come to him. Yet, all that escaped her throat was a pitiful croak—one that drew a curious look from the sergeant and his companions, but went unnoticed by the five riders that she now knew were serving under General Franklin Beaufort.

All this time, and I never knew!

The fading sound of hooves galloping away returned her to the despair she'd briefly escaped. But there was also something new that kindled a tiny flame of hope in her desperate soul.

Jonas is alive! I need to let him know that I have survived, too...

A feeling of urgency fell upon Hattie as she gazed toward the north, where the cavalrymen had disappeared into the night. It wasn't just her heart calling for the man she loved more than anything else. It was so much deeper than that... the message to her soul was that he was just as lost without her.

Come hell or high water, she had to find him again... and soon.

Chapter Twenty-Seven

Mid-afternoon, Friday, December 16th, 1864.... Bivouacked

just outside Murfreesboro, Tennessee.

"Lieutenant... you all right, sir? ...Jonas, wake up!"

Jonas Grey awoke with a start. His eyes snapped open in time to catch Levi Jones lifting his hand from his shoulder.

"What in the hell? ...Where am I?"

He sat up in a panic, looking around himself worriedly as if unfamiliar with his recently acquired officers' tent. He shared his new accommodations with two other men, including Levi, who had been promoted to corporal shortly after General Beaufort's Elite Company arrived in Columbia three weeks earlier. After years of sleeping in a much smaller tent—or beneath the moon and stars at night—Jonas was still adapting to the luxury in space and better comfort. Frankly, he didn't know if he could ever get used to this, and looked forward to when Beaufort's cavalry would be on the move again.

"You were dreamin'." Levi smiled compassionately. "We heard you callin' to someone. When we figured out it was a woman's name, Tommy suggested I come check on you, to make sure you're all right... Sounded like a bad one."

Jonas believed he had experienced more than his fair share of nightmares since the war began, with many of the more disturbing dreams being unfairly lucid. The way this one ended made it among the worst he'd had in quite some time.

"Hattie? That's your wife's name, ain't it?"

"It was."

The details from the dream were still fresh in Jonas' mind, and involved memories from deep in the past. Treasured times with Hattie that he had purposely tried to push from his awareness. *Thought I was successful... but now I reckon not so much!*

Most of his dreams the past few months, thankfully, were a milder assortment of meaningless nocturnal journeys. Nothing more than fragmented images he could readily dismiss as mere restless thoughts upon waking the next morning.

This one was different.

He wondered if the experience had anything to do with his decision to indulge in an afternoon nap. He had only done so twice before during the past four years, and both times occurred when away from shelter, leaning against a tree with his hat's brim pulled down over his eyes.

The weather being blustery and inhospitable, this time he heeded Tommy and Levi's suggestion to retire for an hour inside the tent, while the others kept watch. Jonas stretched out on the cot he'd been trying to adapt to for the past week and a half.

But only a goddamned fool would blame a disturbing dream on his surroundings or the time of day he slept!

What bothered him most was how the dream had ended—and it did so immediately when Levi shook him awake. The dream's beginning was innocent enough, and featured scenes that had frequented his dreams until December of 1862, when he'd learned of his wife's murder. *Sweet summertime at Sugar Creek!* He reflected now on how the days seemed to run together in the infancy of their courtship and on through the early years of their marriage. The memories were much the same, although all were precious to him, at least until they became too painful to reflect upon following Hattie's passing.

What he readily recalled from this latest dream experience was laughing with her beneath the majestic oak that towered over their favorite spot—a place frequented so often by them that they had verbally claimed it as their own. Jonas pined wistfully for the images that were already fading from his awareness... Hattie's soft blonde curls bounced gently upon her shoulders as she gazed at him lovingly while they shared a picnic lunch. Her gorgeous green eyes were glistening like emeralds, and her smile enraptured his soul, allowing him to taste a wholeness that had long since died.

The scenes and imagery changed swiftly to those of intimate moments that called to mind precautionary measures they should've heeded, in light of what he had since learned about the nature of men. The images of him and his beloved lying naked in each other's arms beneath the same tree rekindled the blissful longing he had so often felt—even when separated by the early days of the war, until he learned that Hattie was no longer part of this world.

As he reflected further on the dream, after Levi exited the tent to give him time to collect himself, Jonas wondered why now? Why would he suddenly revisit distorted memories from long before the war had begun to strip away his humanity and obliterated his naïve belief in the inherent good of mankind?

Of course, the disturbing manner in which this experience ended needed to also be considered.

Perhaps Levi's interruption had spared him from images he was most familiar with, where his nightmares had often left him with terrifying visions of how Hattie had perished, being stuck inside Rufus Porter's farmhouse as flames engulfed the main floor. Jonas had woken many times in a cold sweat to her bloodcurdling screams as their home burned around her while a gang of Yankee marauders looked on, smiling smugly in their murderous satisfaction.

But this time it was an angelic vision of his beloved wife, in all her innocence and beauty that he had fought so hard to bury in his heart, clinging to his arm. Her entire being was aglow, and yet her lovely smile had faded. She repeatedly glanced over her shoulder, worriedly watching a dark storm cloud that rapidly approached. Thunder soon shook the ground and lightning strikes sizzled through the air above them. All the while, she pleaded for him to not let the storm take her… To his horror, grimacing Union soldiers suddenly appeared by the hundreds, pouring out like rain from the cloud. Soiled by war and screaming threats of harm, they began thrusting bloody bayonets at Hattie while ignoring his cries for them to stop…

He awoke as Hattie's shrill screams were abruptly cut off.

When Jonas stepped out of the tent to rejoin his companions, the winter chill embraced him as if it were a famished and yet uncaring lover. Forced to button his coat up to the neck, his gaze was drawn to the sun peering out from behind a row of dark clouds that again brought to mind the one in his dream. It gave him pause, and for some inexplicable reason he thought of the beleaguered Army of Tennessee. What remained of Hood's once sizable fighting force was supposedly situated somewhere close to Nashville at that very moment. He and the rest of General Beaufort's men had done their part to ensure the Yankee supply lines remained hindered, having battled to a draw against the Union forces under General Rousseau at Murfreesboro just over a week earlier.

Jonas had long since ceased being a religious man, but he felt compelled to offer a sincere prayer heavenward.

Dear Lord, I beseech You to shed Your bountiful mercy upon those who fight nobly under the St. Andrew's cross; and may You allow my beloved wife to rest peacefully in Your bosom. And if I may trouble You, Lord, for one last request... Please, let there be no more tormenting dreams about Hattie until my stay on Earth is over, and she and I can finally be united once again... Amen.

* * * * *

A short time later that afternoon... in Nashville, Tennessee.

"Hold it right there—drop your weapons!"

The voice was menacing; the trio of rifles pointing at Hattie and her four companions appeared even more so. She and the four infantrymen standing to her left regarded one another warily for a moment. Their short breaths from running drifted toward the overcast sky as frigid wisps. Almost all of them cast a longing glance toward the path where the surviving members of the Twenty-Seventh had disappeared moments earlier.

"We *will* shoot you dead if you don't lay down your guns right now!"

Although outnumbering the three Yankees by two weapons, Hattie could tell the enemy was armed with the same kind of

Spencer carbine that Lester had taken from a dead Union cavalryman, just days before his death in Atlanta.

If we don't miss, we might survive… But Amos is over there shaking from fear and the cold, and David ain't exactly the best shot in the Confederate Army. But those guns pointed at us are definitely Spencer repeating rifles….

Hattie knew the chances of the five of them surviving—even if their aim was true—would be slim, since the Yankees might well pull off two to three shots apiece in the time she and her companions managed one. She looked up at the gangly soldier to her right, Jebediah Wilkes, who nodded nervously for them to comply.

"Y'all won't shoot if we lay down our guns?" he entreated the leader of the three blue coats standing less than thirty feet away.

"The chances of you all still being alive get a hell of a lot better the less time we spend talking," said the leader, a sergeant, based on the stripes upon his coat's sleeve. "Time's a wastin', as you slavers are fond of saying."

"We ain't no slavers!" protested Furman, the last member of Hattie's group… a patrol selected to make sure the rear of the regiment that now only numbered thirty survivors made it out of Nashville safely. "None of us ain't ever been able to afford ownin' a single slave—"

"Shut the hell up, Furman!" ordered Jebediah.

"The hell you say, Jeb!"

The report of a gunshot ripped through the air, and Furman fell where he stood. Smoke rose in a thin swirl from the end of the sergeant's rifle, now trained directly on Jebediah.

"I'm not going to say it again," warned the Yankee boss, while his subordinates snickered.

With the odds of survival withering by the second, Hattie's pulse pounded as she and her three companions lowered their weapons and then dropped them on the snow-covered ground.

"See? That wasn't so bad was it?" The sergeant sounded kinder than he had a moment ago. But Hattie hated the look in the man's eyes. She detected deceit, and plenty of it. "Now we have to decide if there's enough rations to feed the seven of us. What have you got there in your haversacks?"

Jebediah looked over at Hattie worriedly, before exchanging anxious glances with Amos and David. She had a few pieces of hardtack that likely wouldn't be enough to get the four of them to breakfast, and figured it was the same for the others.

"Sir, we don't have much food at all—just crumbs left over from the last rations we got this past Monday," said Jebediah. "But we'll give you what we've got, if that's what you want."

He removed his haversack and took a step toward the trio, as if intending to gently toss the bag toward the three Yankees. Before the bag left his hands, the sergeant shot him dead. One of the other Yankees took out Amos with a bullet to his head.

The other soldier had taken aim at Hattie, who dropped to the frozen ground as two shots whizzed past her left shoulder. Barely cognizant of the fact that her small stature had likely just saved her life, she scooped her loaded Springfield rifle and rolled away from the direct line of fire. Realizing there wasn't time to take full aim, she pointed her gun at the Yankee's midsection and pulled the trigger. Meanwhile, David had been hit in the shoulder. At roughly the same time Hattie squeezed off her shot, he somehow miraculously managed to lift his gun from a larger patch of snow left over from a storm that had blanketed the entire area several days earlier, and fired a shot just before being struck in the chest with another bullet.

The blue coat intent on killing Hattie fell to the ground, howling in pain from the wound she'd delivered to his gut. His Spencer carbine flew from his grasp as he absorbed the shot from fairly close range, and it landed less than twenty feet away from Hattie. She looked up tentatively, expecting one of the other Union soldiers to complete the slaughter against her and her companions. The ball fired from David's rifle had struck the sergeant's right knee, and he writhed in even more discomfort than the man she had mortally wounded. That left the third Yankee, who took fresh aim at Hattie, on her knees as he stepped toward her.

The soldier took aim, and she prepared to die... thinking about Papa, along with Lester and Lucinda. Others would surely come to mind in a moment, but she figured it wouldn't matter much, since 'Blissful Eternity' sounded like a very long time. *Plenty of time to come to a reckoning with those I've loved and lost!* But when he pulled the trigger, nothing happened. Confusion gave way to rage as the soldier's further attempts to get the rifle to fire were just as unsuccessful.

What about Jonas? He's alive, and I know he still needs me!

In truth, she understood that either she or Jonas could die at any moment in this brutal and unpredictable war. Yet, the one thing that had allowed Hattie to pick herself up at Franklin and continue to go on living was the fact her husband was verifiably alive. It mattered little that he likely was unaware she still resided among the living, and certainly he was unaware she had enlisted in the Confederate infantry under the guise of being a man. But since that night in Franklin, her heart burned with rekindled faith and the desire to find him—to do whatever it took to stay alive in order to have that chance.

The renewed inspiration to find Jonas was what gave her the strength to take care of the heartbreaking task in Franklin of burying Lucinda. The kind owner of the beautiful home, less than fifty feet from where Private Templeton had taken her last breaths, had allowed Hattie to bury her at the base of the tree that had been shredded by artillery assaults and gunfire. Fountain Branch Carter's son, Captain Tod Carter, had likely taken a mortal wound during the battle, and the tintype image Mr. Carter shared with her was of an officer Hattie had seen occasionally in association with Captain William Powers. Although their connection of profound grief was short lived, Hattie told Mr. Carter that she would always be grateful for his generosity of extending temporary interment of Private 'Louis' Templeton on his property…

The sergeant who lay bleeding offered his rifle for the soldier to "kill the last of the rebel scum." At the same time, Hattie noticed the rifle belonging to the Yankee presently dying from the bullet her weapon had delivered was still lying on the ground, camouflaged by a muddy patch and apparently undetected by his companions. Neither the sergeant nor the other Yankee noticed her scrambling to pick up the other rifle until she had it safely in hand. By the time the lone uninjured Yankee had exchanged his malfunctioning rifle with the one used to kill two of Hattie's recent cohorts, she already had the man lined up in the Spencer's sight. He only had time to look up in surprise as two consecutive shots struck him in the chest.

Hattie only gave his corpse a casual glance as she moved past the other dying soldier to face the sergeant, who had retrieved his pistol. Before he could take aim, she had the rifle poised less than a foot from his head.

"Drop it! Drop it now or I'll shoot you dead too!"

The sergeant nodded and lowered the weapon. But when his gaze shifted from her to the pistol again, she shoved the rifle's barrel just below his nose. That got his attention, and for the first time since crossing paths with this miscreant, he appeared very much afraid.

"Son, you don't have to do this."

"Shhh!"

"I can assure you… no harm will come—"

"Shut the hell up!" she snarled, and his mouth closed. "Had this situation been handled a different way, and my friends had been given quarter as any decent officer is wont to do, then perhaps the chances of you still being alive a minute from now would be quite likely. However…"

"Dear God, please!"

For a moment, Hattie wondered if the fact those were the last words ever uttered by this despicable Yankee would preserve them for when she'd stand before The Almighty at Judgment Day, and become the deciding factor on whether or not she'd be granted a permanent place in Heaven. But the recent images in her mind of Jeb, Amos, and all the other companions she had lost—including Lucinda and Lieutenant Cooper less than three weeks prior—overruled what little capacity for mercy toward the enemy she carried in her bosom.

She pulled the trigger.

After taking one of the officer's handkerchiefs from his coat to wipe away the blood spray from her face and hands, she moved over to her rifle and picked it up. Hattie decided to keep the Spencer for a time, as it reminded her of Lester. And, despite feeling some remorse for the execution of a bad man because he pleaded for his life, she suddenly pictured Lucinda and her ornery smile.

Hattie wondered if somehow Private Templeton's spirit witnessed what had just happened. It was her most dominant thought as she hurried to catch up to her regiment heading south toward Nashville. Another defeat… but this one carried the silver lining that she was no longer afraid of being alone.

She finally could take care of herself without having to depend on someone else to come to her rescue.

Moving forward, when faced with danger, Hattie had proven to herself this day that she'd be just fine.

Chapter Twenty-Eight

Shortly before midnight, Sunday, December 25th, 1864...

just south of Appleton, Tennessee.

On a bitterly cold night, just four days shy of the new moon, the weary and demoralized Army of Tennessee crept slowly in darkness toward Alabama. More than a week had passed since Hattie last expected someone to finally call her bluff and arrest her for deserting the Twenty-Third Battalion. But the distraction of retreating, along with the oppressive mood that had seemingly engulfed the entire fighting force under General Hood's command in the aftermath of the crushing loss at Nashville, bought her an extended reprieve.

The defeat carried such finality to it; made worse by the fact the Confederates were now road weary after fleeing from the Yankees for the past nine days. Caught up in a new desperate race for survival, this time the goal was to simply escape from Tennessee before General George Thomas' forces could prevent it.

Not that the sorrowful flight came as a surprise to Hattie, as she'd watched the army steadily disintegrate before her eyes. Desertions had greatly increased since Franklin. Coupled with high casualties in that battle and again in Nashville, the army that had brought just over thirty thousand troops into Tennessee only five weeks earlier had since shrunk to no more than eighteen thousand men. She and Lucinda had counted over ninety soldiers in Tennessee's Twenty-Seventh regiment when they marched north from Spring Hill on November 30th. But that figure had drastically been reduced by the time John Bell Hood's army fled Nashville, and now numbered just twenty-six. The outfit had become too diminutive to be considered anything other than a small infantry company.

Most of the soldiers around her blamed General Hood for the missteps and oversights that had devastated this once proud army. For nearly two weeks in the debilitating cold, they had held a clear view of the enemy's formidable fortifications surrounding Nashville. What was left of General Brown's division occupied a network of hastily erected breastworks along the crest of a hillside facing the city. Seventy thousand Yankees, ready and eager to resume the war at any time, were rumored to reside behind the fortifications. They greatly outnumbered the Rebels that at the time had been reduced to a fighting force of just over twenty-three thousand men.

We're destitute, hungry, inadequately clothed, and have been so for a long while. Rags for shoes cover our blackened feet, and we have no coats to protect us against the bitter winds that often carry sleet. Then, there's dwindling ammunition to where we must steal much of it from fallen friends or foes... How can we be expected to win anything when facing such dire hardships at every turn?

It seemed as if the entire trip north from Georgia had been an embarrassing disaster for the entire Confederacy, and the tragedy of it all continued to be compounded daily by new travails. In addition to the maladies Hattie considered foremost was the fact that the army was now officially on the run. The Yankees seemed determined to wipe their Confederate counterparts from existence. That threat alone inspired General Hood to charge his generals with making sure the surviving infantry, artillery, and cavalry made it safely out of Tennessee before General James Wilson's cavalry of ten thousand strong could prevent the exodus.

Not only did this mean a potential final humiliation of being routed by a force nearly half the size of the surviving Confederates was on the horizon, but the end of the fight to support the Southern Cause was also inevitable. The resultant malaise that had swept virally through Hood's army had taken a definite toll on Hattie's outlook, too. But she wasn't ready to give up just yet… unfinished business remained.

I am so close to finding Jonas, and just need the right opportunity!

It was the solitary factor that inspired her spirit to continue fighting and hang on. Many of the men around her, though increasingly gaunt and weary, had someone to go home to when the conflict between the North and South was finally resolved. But Hattie's home no longer existed, and the man she loved with all of her heart was likely busy sabotaging the Union efforts someplace less than thirty miles behind her. *Perhaps by now it's only ten miles, or maybe Jonas is even nearer than that!*

The reality of her permanent homelessness had been poignantly realized earlier that evening, when they approached the edge of Appleton while marching toward the state line. Gazing at the few sparse lights, likely from lanterns in windows glowing in the distance, all she could think of was what she had lost so long ago. The pain no longer fresh, a dull ache spoke to the deadness of the place... at least dead to her heart. Only the man that inspired her flight from Appleton remained as something to cling to, or at least the hope of their reunion. That desire still kindled a powerful flame within her bosom, and in the coldest moments offered at least some simmering comfort.

But the agonizing madness of being so close, and yet still too far apart to make a connection with her dear husband, seemed unfairly cruel. Her latest frustration came from the news that General Franklin Beaufort was protecting the rear guard of General Hood's army as it headed south. She desperately wanted to find a way to hang back as part of that brigade, and hoped General Brown's division would be the one chosen to assist General Beaufort in his efforts to stall Wilson's attacks against the retreating Confederate Army.

Hood chose instead to keep Brown's division, presently under General Mark Perrin Lowery's direction, as part of the team leading the retreat. The South's mercurial commander then assigned two of General Edward Walthall's brigades to assist Beaufort's cavalry efforts. Ironically, Colonel Hume Field—whom Hattie had recently served under, both at Franklin and Nashville—had taken over for General 'States Rights' Gist under Walthall, after Gist was killed at Franklin.

If only I possessed Lucinda's brazen nature and could disguise myself as one of those Arkansas or Alabama boys, like she could've done so easily...

Yet, still fearing discovery for the ruse she'd created with Lucinda just a month earlier made that idea too risky. And, if she did get arrested before getting the chance to reveal her presence to Jonas, their reunion might not ever happen.

If he heads out west again, or to some other new place because he still thinks I'm dead, what then?

She had no choice but to bide her time and wait. To *pray* and wait for the right opportunity.

It was all she could do. It became the thing Hattie focused on most as she and the rest of the forlorn infantry trudged along a dark muddy road toward the frigid Tennessee River, and a hoped-for absolution once inside Alabama.

* * * * *

Early Monday morning, December 26th, 1864... Sugar Creek,

Tennessee.

"Here they come, boys... get ready to give 'em hell!"

Just after eight o'clock that morning, Jonas whispered this advisement to a handful of cavalrymen from the Elite Corps who had volunteered to dismount and assist Colonel Field's infantry, set to engage General Wilson's cavalry. Thick fog obscured much of the area, including Sugar Creek itself. Prepared for the enemy's emergence from the soupy haze along the creek's southern banks to happen at any moment, Jonas and his cohorts quietly listened to Union commands to dismount, the words echoing eerily upon themselves.

He and the others had been waiting patiently since dawn, safely tucked away behind breastworks erected in darkness Christmas night. Splashes in the water sounded closer as the cloaked menace attempted to ford the creek. Meanwhile, the combined infantry and cavalry under the direction of General

Beaufort held their fire, as commanded, waiting quietly from three different vantage points within a quarter mile of one another. Each brigade under Beaufort, headed up by generals Sullivan Ross and Armstrong Buford and commanded by General William Hicks Jackson, were primed and ready to take revenge after what had befallen the Confederate Army in Tennessee for much of the past month.

Although Beaufort's men were especially angered and saddened by what had transpired—since General Hood had frequently tied their hands—this was definitely not a defeated army. The rest of the divisions and brigades under Hood might be in disarray, and as such, an unworthy opponent for General Thomas' Union forces. But those who still fought hard for the Southern Cause under Beaufort's direction remained a venomous menace to the Federals and their desire to completely annihilate the Confederate presence in the West.

These Rebels embraced the role of being the perpetual 'thorn in the side' that General Thomas, and his subordinates—including Wilson and Schofield—had come to loathe dearly.

The Union may have thwarted Hood's plans to conquer Nashville and invade the North. However, as long as Beaufort could run amok and continue to sabotage the Union supply lines—or as he had accomplished lately, protect the shattered remains of Hood's army—the war was far from over.

The ten thousand Federals under Wilson's command understood this fact just as readily as the Confederates did. Jonas had seen the looks of disbelief upon many a Yankee face for the past week. He smiled at the thought that their vastly superior numbers over Beaufort's division failed to assure them victory—especially yesterday, when the skirmish ended in a retreat by Wilson's cavalry from Anthony's Hill. No doubt, that experience inspired the extreme caution that the Yankees demonstrated at present.

"Oh, believe me Jonas, I'm 'bout to send a dozen of these sons of bitches to Lucifer's doorstep myself," Tommy shot back in a whisper. "All I'm waitin' on is for Beaufort to give the word."

Levi's chuckle in response to Tommy's comment died soon after its birth. The first of the Yankees emerged on the Confederate side of the creek, less than thirty paces from the breastworks where Field's infantry and the Elite cavalrymen waited. Every man had a finger poised to squeeze a trigger, expecting the order to arrive at any moment to send a barrage of bullets into the line of blue coats materializing from the fog as they scaled the creek's steep banks.

Apparently, the fog obscured the breastworks from the Yankees' view, as Jonas observed widespread surprise among Union infantry and dismounted cavalrymen alike as they climbed out from the haze. The command to fire resounded, and much of the Union line fell away as the Confederate's musketry and rifle shots tore through the Federal ranks. Some fell where they stood, but most stumbled back, vanishing into the thick gray shroud.

Following Beaufort's original plan, Colonel Field and General Daniel Reynolds urged their troops to disband the breastworks and give chase to the Union forces on their heels. Jonas had overheard Beaufort tell General Ross earlier that he would throw the Texan's cavalry upon Wilson's dismounted riders, and Jonas knew that move would soon be coming in order to cut off Wilson's flank. In the meantime, Lieutenant Grey and his Elite companions ran to the creek with Field's infantry, sending forth the most inspired Rebel Yells he could recall hearing since Chickamauga.

Following the path of the frenzied infantry just ahead of them, Jonas, Levi, and the rest of their cohorts stepped into the bitterly cold water that soon came up to their waists. The initial shock was enough to steal Jonas' breath momentarily, as the iciness embraced his body. It left him shivering terribly as he aimed and fired his rifle, taking down a fleeing Yankee from behind. He might've winced from shooting a man in the back if it had been two years ago, but at this point in the war, the rules of honor had largely been abandoned—at least in the heat of battle. Besides, if the conflict's momentum favored the Union instead, then it would be him and his companions worried about catching bullets in the back as they tried to flee. Worse, Wilson's cavalry was largely outfitted with repeating rifles, giving them an enormous advantage that went far beyond having double the fighting force.

As they pursued the enemy to the creek's other side, Jonas recognized the mighty oak and nearby sandbar where he and Hattie had spent many a warm spring afternoon cuddled together. A rush of nostalgia suddenly seized his heart. His chest felt constricted, threatening to distract him dangerously from the task at hand.

If I should die this day, would it not be fitting to have it happen in the place where Hattie and I spent so many happy times? Hell, it's just a mile or so from where she lies in the frozen ground...

The thought attached itself like a leach to his weary mind. His emotional paralysis drew a nudge from Levi, who surely noticed that Jonas hadn't finished reloading his rifle.

He cast an almost absent glance toward Levi, and to Tommy—who shouted angrily at him to watch out for the Yankees reforming on the other side of the creek. Yet, the blissful sensation of letting go grew stronger. To no longer care about the things that had seemed so important just a few minutes ago, such as the welfare of his companions and the defeat of a hated enemy, was intoxicating... It reminded Jonas of a fragrant whiff of lavender and a good strong swig of whiskey all rolled into one… until he saw where a pair of dead blue coats floated near the bank. The bouncing waves drifting toward him were tinted in deep crimson, amid ice that had broken off from the shoreline. Seeing the defilement of a place that was as close to 'holy' as any he knew on Earth allowed him to break free from the Siren's seductive call.

He noticed a tall blonde Yankee lining him up in his Spencer carbine's sight. Fortunately, Jonas was almost finished ramming a cartridge home. The dismounted cavalryman's first bullet grazed the stripes on Jonas' coat, distracting his aim. But it proved to be a most serendipitous miss, and surely the Yankee's next shot would've hit the target straight on, leaving Jonas to look for Hattie beyond the veil of death, if she wasn't already waiting for him in that very place as an invisible angel. But a surge of anger at himself for endangering those around him fueled his determination to quickly line up his aim to ensure it was true.

The bullet from Jonas' rifle struck the Yankee in the forehead, and the man fell over dead, still clutching the rifle poised a second ago to end Jonas' earthly existence.

"Let's push 'em back, boys!" Jonas shouted, leading the way to the shoreline.

Along with the Elite volunteers, Reynolds and Field's men were initially repelled from climbing the bank to engage the enemy. With the arrival of Ross' cavalry that had overwhelmed Wilson's flank, Jonas and his associates were able to climb the bank and assist in the rout of Wilson's army, pushing the Yankees away from the creek. The fight continued for another few hours, until shortly after noon, the last of the Yankees had retreated beyond the reach of Beaufort's guns and artillery.

A feeling of serenity pervaded Beaufort's camp that night, even though to a man they knew more attacks would come until the remnants of the Army of Tennessee had reached its winter destination in Mississippi. Reports received that afternoon from the scouts sent to check on Hood's progress in reaching Alabama were favorable, as part of the army had already crossed into Alabama. The rest of the troops would likely reach the other side of the Tennessee River by evening the next day.

But while Hood and his battered army sought to rest, recover, and rebuild, Jonas already knew that he and the rest of the Elite Company would remain on the move. Beaufort obviously knew better than to believe that Wilson would take kindly to the sound defeat his superior forces suffered that day. The Yankee general's cavalry would return, tracking Beaufort's movements as the "Wizard in the Saddle" sought to keep the Union Army preoccupied with defeating his division, rather than the crumbling fragments of what was now Hood's army.

Despite what had happened to Jonas that morning, his commitment to serving under Beaufort never wavered. He was ready to follow his beloved general to the ends of the Earth, if necessary… just as long as he never had to come back to Sugar Creek, ever again.

Chapter Twenty-Nine

Just before midnight, Sunday, April 2nd, 1865... Selma,

Alabama.

Selma is on fire... we failed to save her!

"We are defeated and utterly so," whispered Jonas, lifting his weary gaze to follow the flames climbing skyward only a few miles away.

Shivering in near darkness, beneath the faint light afforded by a crescent moon nestled upon a bed of feathered clouds, he glanced to where the rest of General Beaufort's Elite Company had gathered near the water's edge. Of the eighty riders from earlier that afternoon, less than half survived the day's assault from General Wilson's army, after the determined and damnable Yankee successfully tracked down what was left of the Confederate cavalry.

In Jonas' estimation, Beaufort had fared much better than most leaders could've done in protecting his cavalry from decimation for as long as he had. Admirable in Jonas' eyes was the fact that Beaufort had also tried to accomplish the same feat for the infantries delegated to his command at the onset of the retreat by Hood's army from Nashville late last year. To avoid capture by Wilson's ever-increasing forces, and the dogged ambitions to destroy the last surviving threat against the Union, Beaufort had divided the vast majority of his cavalry and infantry brigades into regional factions.

Always looking for the simplest solutions to stay one step ahead of the enemy, this time it appeared the ingenious general had chosen this route mostly because there wasn't time for a more complex plan. Pulling on as much homespun loyalty as possible, he arranged for many of the men to return to their birth states as full regiments, where they would then await his orders to return.

It seemed like an excellent idea to Jonas, and perhaps if the Union Army hadn't smelled blood as if they were a pack of wolves circling a wounded elk, there might've been enough time to get situated in Alabama and then regroup for another offensive against Wilson and his troops. Unfortunately, when Wilson elected to descend into Alabama to once again engage Beaufort, the available Confederate troops he had under his immediate command were at an all-time low. He sent couriers with urgent orders to his generals and colonels spread out in three states to bring their men to central Alabama in a hurry.

The regiments that had scored such a sweet victory at Sugar Creek were now hiding in the woods of southern Tennessee, as well as throughout Mississippi and Alabama—and all were largely unaware of the grave danger General Beaufort and his core cavalry would soon face. Of worse concern, though, was the reality that the epidemic of desertion had reached the cavalry, and an alarming number of riders were joining the infected infantry in leaving nearly every regiment under the general's command.

The terrible blight that affected Hood's army has spread to us, and the only cure must come from a decisive victory against Wilson!

In the depths of his soul, however, Jonas believed the chances of such a boon happening was most unlikely. The early months of 1865 had all but ensured the probable destruction of any realistic hopes for a Confederate revival. And by the time everyone should've shown up in Alabama, less than half of the soldiers Jonas remembered from late December made it to where the Elite Company waited, just north of Selma. Meanwhile, word had reached Beaufort that Wilson's army had swelled to nearly fourteen thousand men— nearly seven times the size of Beaufort's current cavalry. And, a sizeable portion of the two thousand Rebels that responded to his call were new to the war effort, consisting of young boys and graying men. *Most of these mismatched men and boys are best suited to walk than ride a horse, and barely so…*

Jonas and his cohorts were disheartened to see the telltale signs that so many good riders and infantry had either ignored the command or failed to make haste in returning to where Beaufort and his most trusted men waited. Still, they resolved to make the best stand possible, hoping that the pre-existing fortifications surrounding Selma would prove sufficient in warding off the Union advance.

"Captain Grey… is that you turning yellow over there?"

Beaufort's words cut like a burning saber through Jonas' heart, and he rose to his feet to face the general, standing less than twenty feet away. Beaufort had been wounded in the fighting earlier that day, and winced as he struggled to remain upright. Jonas detected pained concern written on the faces of the officers standing closest to their leader, in the glow from the lone torch carried low to the ground by one of the few former slaves that had made it to the southern shore of the

Alabama River. The survivors of Beaufort's cavalry were forced to swim for their very lives after the fall of Selma.

"No sir... I will gladly die before I ever surrender to the Yankees," Jonas replied. "I will lay my life down most willingly for *any* and *every* man here, especially you, General. You know it to be true, sir... just as you surely realize we are now without an adequate army to push back the enemy. At least not an army that can stand effectively against such overwhelming odds. We've beaten 'em back when outnumbered three to one, or even four times our fighting force of men as compared to the blue coats. But when outnumbered six, seven, or eight men to one? With only muskets, and our single action pistols and rifles left to volley against a horde of Spencer rifles?"

Jonas waited for a response that didn't come, other than a subtle nod coming from the leader he admired over all others.

"Y'all witnessed with your own eyes what happened back there. The fortifications were damned near useless without an army of at least ten thousand men to patrol the perimeter," Jonas continued, fully prepared for an interruption to come at any moment. "And what about the artillery disparities? Hell, the last few cannons we had until an hour ago are sitting on the other side of the river... It's just us now. With all due respect sir, how do we reclaim the upper hand when this is all that's left to carry on the fight?"

He motioned to the drenched and battered cavalry spread out along the shoreline. No more than three hundred, based upon those he caught glimpses of in the sparse light. Likely, the true total was much lower, perhaps closer to a mere two hundred brave souls.

Beaufort cleared his throat, and Jonas prepared for an upbraiding to follow.

"Jonas… I understand your loss today, and please remember that I lost him too. We all lost friends today—brothers, truly. But that's the way it's been with this war, and despite how things might appear, it ain't over—not yet. Far from it." Beaufort's tone carried an unexpected compassion that softened the wrath Jonas also detected, simmering beneath the confident delivery. The man always carried his emotions and passion—be it joy, anger, empathy, or in this case all three—on his sleeve. "But you're right, son… We won't stand a chance in Hell if all we have are the leftovers of society and an undisciplined militia to work with—the likes of what we dealt with today. We need our boys from Texas and Arkansas that didn't make it back in time from Mississippi. But they're coming… it's the same for General Jackson's group in Tennessee. Maybe other couriers—going both ways—were captured, killed… God only knows."

Jonas nodded solemnly, picturing the easy slaughter that seemed to send the Yankees into a killing frenzy. The combined 'green army' of old men long removed from battle, and boys far too young to carry a musket, and the militia headed up by an overzealous preacher accounted for most of the Confederate fighting force that day. Worrying about the fate of such a rag-tag outfit proved to be a deadly distraction, especially once the Yankees were able to exploit the fortification's weaknesses. Chaos on a level that Jonas had never seen before soon took over, and Levi Jones, Jonas, and several others from the Elite Company found themselves carelessly battling the enemy while trying to keep the inexperienced troops from fleeing in panic.

One moment, Levi was by his side, and then he disappeared. Jonas didn't immediately worry about his closest buddy's whereabouts. When the dust settled a bit, he found him sitting against a stone pillar overlooking the Union's position. At first, Jonas assumed Levi was merely waiting on him, so they could move on together in finding an escape path, covering each other as they sought to elude capture. By then, it had become painfully obvious to Jonas that the dismounted cavalry couldn't hold off the Federal onslaught for much longer.

"You ready to move on out of here?" Jonas had asked him, absently. "If so, we should do it now..."

Levi stared ahead, wearing an expression Jonas had seen a thousand times. Often serious, it was a faraway look that would often be followed by a profound observation delivered in a low guttural tone. Such as when he congratulated Jonas on his recent promotion to captain, after Beaufort had taken a quick straw poll on who the boys of Company C wanted to take over for Charlie May, who wouldn't be coming back after sustaining a serious leg injury at Franklin... It took a moment for Jonas to notice the lifelessness in Levi's hazel eyes and the small trail of blood from where a Minié ball had struck him in his left temple. Even so, Jonas hesitated to the point of endangering his own life... unwilling to accept that his very best friend in the world was dead.

Knowing there wouldn't be an opportunity to give Corporal Jones a proper burial, Jonas fought back tears as he closed Levi's eyes for the last time. Amid increasing gunfire from an advancing Yankee line, he heeded Tommy Means' entreaties to get his ass out of there. Bullets whizzed past both shoulders, and it took all of his resolve to not simply stop and allow a Union bullet to end the misery once and for all. Why? He honestly couldn't say... other than a random thought; a memory from the summer of 1862.

It was the last time he had seen his beloved Hattie alive, and they had shared an intimate night together. Upon saddling up to return to Mississippi early the next morning, to avoid as much of the July heat as possible—despite the presence of Yankee patrols rumored to be in the area—she had grabbed his arm. Her touch was gentle, but effective in distracting him from pulling the reins to guide his horse toward the gates that marked the entrance to her father's farm.

Hattie had motioned for him to bend his head down toward hers, and they'd shared one last kiss. Then she delivered a parting message that he had since tried to forget, after discovering her grave that following December.

"Please be careful, Jonas Grey. Don't you dare die on me, you hear? I love you forever!"

As often had happened during the past few years, this particular memory would rear itself as a painful pinprick and jab its way into his mind and heart when danger seemed to be nearest. He wondered now, though briefly, how many times had that ghostly admonition kept him in the land of the living. *Too many... yea, too many goddamned times!*

Nonetheless, Jonas had escaped with his lieutenant and a handful of others out of the thirty Elite riders that were with him just before the Yankee attack. From there, things continued to disintegrate. Once reunited with Beaufort and the rest of the officers and cavalry fortunate enough to elude capture, the few hundred remnants of a fighting force of four thousand men swam to safety across the river that formed Selma's southern border....

"Captain Grey, we've been left in worse shape before," said Beaufort, his words pulling Jonas from his deepening despair and back to the present. The general had limped several steps closer, and in the dimness he noticed the self-assured smile that for him had separated Beaufort from every other commander he had met during the long, terrible conflict with the North. "We've risen before... we'll rise again. Hell, I've been damned near killed a dozen times since Lincoln made it legal to invade our homeland. But I'm still living, as you can see, and the fire that's always burned in my soul is not the least bit quenched. And, I can see that same fire in you, son.... So, whatever grieving that's needed to be done, let it end by dawn's light. That's when we'll begin rebuilding this army."

Jonas nodded, finding it hard not to return the general's smile. He watched him limp back to where the others kept rifles trained on the opposite shoreline. Although largely useless, the guns were poised in the unlikely event Wilson's victorious cavalry would decide to pursue the last of the Confederate resistance across the river. That prospect seemed increasingly remote, amid the Union's destructive celebration still in progress inside Selma.

He looked away, searching the sky for familiar constellations and maverick stars to focus on instead. But all he could think about was Levi's frozen gaze and the haunting plea from his dear late wife.

Jonas released a low sigh, realizing a long and lonely night awaited him in his personal torment. Try as he might, he couldn't picture things being much different once the dawn's early light finally invaded the eastern horizon. Fixing a broken army this time would be much more difficult than ever before... if not impossible.

Chapter Thirty

Late Friday afternoon, May 19th, 1865... Sugar Creek,

Tennessee.

It's finally over.
The end of killing an enemy and watching friends die... No more blindly following orders and accepting life as a daily existence in perpetual squalor. Everything we did to uphold and defend the Southern Cause is now meaningless.

The Confederacy had lost the war.

Looking for immediate merit in such a brutal and costly endeavor was futile. The haunted looks upon the faces of fellow infantrymen deepened toward eternal despair at the mere mention of the long and hard-fought campaign having ended weeks earlier. The late report that reached Hattie and a handful of other members of the Twenty-Seventh Tennessee in early May had made the news of what took place in Virginia, on April 9th, that much harder to accept; the finality bitter in its rawness.

We stayed in caves high in the northern Georgia hills, and had done so since early March, hoping for a miracle to help us push the Yankee menace out of Georgia and the rest of the South....

But a rescue that could only come from reinforcements never arrived. It wasn't a complete surprise, as more than half of what remained of Tennessee's Twenty-Seventh Regiment had chosen to brave a Yankee gauntlet protecting the border of eastern Georgia, in order to rejoin General Joe Johnston's forces in North Carolina. Much of the shambled Army of Tennessee had made the same decision. Meanwhile, she and the others that stayed behind continued the routines which had filled her days with purpose for the past two and a half years.

Purpose and suffering.

Suffering for two worthy causes: The South's independence and the less-viable dream of an eventual reunion with Jonas. Both had long been her personal reasons for rising each morning and for turning in each night, often exhausted from the stress of fighting to live one more day. Short aspirations based on such ideas were what had made the drawn-out reality of war endurable.

Even if barely so...

But no more.

Hattie had arrived at the southern edge of her former hometown less than an hour ago, her eyes drawn to the battle-scarred banks of the creek where she had experienced her happiest moments before the war took place. A sacred spot she hadn't seen in the full light of day since leaving Appleton, in the fall of 1862. A place now forever tainted by the war's bloodshed.

The details of the last month and a half, many of which she had recently learned, echoed tiresomely in her weary mind... Aside from the bloody conflict between the North and South officially coming to an end at Appomattox Court House in Virginia on April 9ᵗʰ, 1865, General Joseph Johnston followed General Robert E. Lee's lead in giving up the futile struggle for independence seventeen days later.

It wasn't until the end of April that the news reached the hideout she shared with six other soldiers confirming General Lee had surrendered, President Abraham Lincoln had been killed, and despite the latter event, the South had officially given up its battle to secure the right to govern itself autonomously. The reports were met with the same cautious disbelief that had kept her and her associates alive since Christmas... Until the first of many returning soldiers—most being former members of Joseph Wheeler's cavalry on horseback—passed through the area on their way back home. Once these 'newly forgiven citizens' of the United States confirmed the reports as factual, Hattie and her companions surrendered at a Union garrison near Chickamauga several days later.

Upon taking an oath to remain loyal to the United States government, Hattie was pardoned. Pardoned and given a pair of new shoes to replace the latest rags covering her feet. She had kept Lester's suit from when he returned from his furlough the previous spring, and after the first warm bath in nearly a year, she was ready to resume her journey back to Tennessee. Hattie and her associates soon parted ways forever upon reaching Chattanooga. As was the case when she first joined the Confederate Army in November 1862, the trek to Appleton was one she wanted to take alone.

The solace gave her time to reflect on all that had happened since she'd set out for Columbia, and then Murfreesboro, after the tragedy in Appleton. When the beloved creek came into view, after she had first revisited her father's farm in the early afternoon—mostly to retrieve the items she had buried beneath charred boards of the former woodshed, a rush of nostalgia greeted her. With every memory now bittersweet, since all that she'd possessed in this once-magical place was gone forever, Hattie's chest tightened and her legs felt far heavier than they had when trudging the last few miles to return home.

Home? It isn't that anymore, and can only be something else to me from now on...

She moved up to the creek's bank from the rutted road, listening to the soft rush of the water's flow. Spring was in full bloom around her, despite the fact that many of the trees were now mostly barren sticks. Very few had been spared the ravages of the battle that followed Hood's retreat through the area.

A warm gentle breeze swayed the tall grass and wildflowers along either side of the creek, and Hattie's feet pulled her down to the water's edge before her mind fully understood what was happening.

Just one last time… I must have a final look at our favorite spot...

She silently promised to not torture her heart unnecessarily, anticipating the more powerful rush that awaited her arrival at 'our tree', beneath which she and Jonas once lounged carefree. Often, she would rest her head against his chest, listening to his heartbeat and the sound of soothing words rising from his throat. He'd lovingly stroke her hair, and the grazing of his hand against the nape of her neck would send delicious chills along her spine and arousal throughout her body.

But this would be the last time she'd think of it—or at least the end of giving in to revisiting those precious moments never to be relived. This was an oath she intended to impose upon her heart and mind.

She had expected the tree to be gone, since it was a magisterial oak and so many of the taller trees were now stripped of all but the beginnings of rejuvenation. Small branches with tender leaves that would take years to recover—and some of the trees had failed to revive from what happened here nearly five months earlier.

To her surprise, the oak stood largely unscathed, with only minimal damage to one side facing away from the creek. The side standing majestically above the shoreline and sandbar she and Jonas had long favored appeared to have miraculously escaped anything beyond scattered bullet scars. The war's callous wrath had failed to deter the grand old tree from carrying on.

Sort of like me, in some ways... I must continue to live... to carry on, though my heart tells me that I might not make it very far...

Did Jonas survive the war? She had heard that General Franklin Beaufort's cavalry had been spread out near the end, and most were either imprisoned or dead. Some prisoners were released in April, according to an officer who served under General Wheeler, and the same man who had convinced Hattie and her companions to surrender at Chickamauga.

She preferred to believe Jonas had somehow made it through the war safely, and that he also was ready to rebuild his life. But the likelihood that her beloved husband had since visited Appleton and found nothing to confirm she had survived now pummeled her soul.

I should've left something behind to let him know I didn't die here... something to let Jonas know I set out to find him! How stupid and foolish of me to believe I could find him before he'd ever come looking for me!

She'd never dreamed the war, which had gone on for almost two years prior to her joining the Southern Cause, wasn't even halfway over when she enlisted as a man. And, naively, she hadn't planned to stay in the Confederate Army for the duration, believing instead that she would get her revenge on the men who murdered her family and friends and then leave... surely by the summer of 1863.

Plenty of time to find my husband some other way, had I done that... But I could never leave!

Hattie walked up to the side of the tree, unwilling to look beyond to the view of the sandbar. She caught a glimpse of a familiar long branch that stretched out over the creek from high above. *It's still intact!* The sight stirred sweet memories of how she and Jonas loved to look up at it from where they either laid upon a blanket or when cuddled up at the oak's base.

The emotions she had restrained for so long suddenly erupted in a violent torrent, and she slid to the ground while embracing the ancient oak's trunk. It had been so long since she'd been allowed to cry without restraint, and for a moment nothing came out. But as her shoulders heaved and hot tears streamed down her cheeks, an overdue release was about to come... until she heard a horse's nicker coming from the sandbar.

Oh my God, someone else is here!

* * * * *

Captain Jonas Grey had stayed on with General Beaufort up through the general's surrender at Gainesville, Alabama, on May 9th. Like most of the remaining members in Beaufort's Elite Company, Jonas was fully prepared to continue fighting the Yankees until taken by force, or killed.

Selma had scarred them all, including the leader held in the highest esteem by Jonas and his peers. To a man, they would ride through the very fires of Hell, had Beaufort given the order. Yet, the ornery twinkle in the general's sapphire eyes had dimmed weeks earlier, when it became obvious that his returning cavalry gathered from Tennessee, Mississippi, and Alabama was far too small to stand up to General Wilson's riders approaching twenty-thousand strong.

"Sending men to die needlessly, when Lee and Davis have already surrendered, seems foolish," Beaufort had confided to his officers—a rare meeting where Jonas was included in the general's confidence. "It's time for peace and to begin healing, gentlemen. It won't be easy to relieve the animosity that has been fed these past four years by Yankee atrocities we've all witnessed. But I say to you now, and will address the men accordingly, we must divest ourselves of the desire for revenge and be willing instead to extend an olive branch of peace to the enemy."

Jonas recalled how they had all wept with Beaufort, and later stood by him as he made the announcement to the rest of his army gathered before him. Resistance was muted by the overriding deep respect for their fearless leader. Afterward, the dissolution of the Elite Company and the rest of Beaufort's cavalry signaled the end of Jonas' world.

So, now I embrace a new reality. One that offers scant protection from cruel memories of a past I can never experience again, until after my final breath as a dying old man... Unless the Good Lord mercifully reunites me with Hattie long before then.

He worried what would happen when he headed north to Tennessee, and the painful truth that all he had known these last four years was officially in the past. He had hoped to join Levi in a farming venture, and if the war had ended just six weeks earlier that might have been possible... General Beaufort had also offered him employment, working for one of his Memphis plantations in dire need of restoration, after being decimated by the blockades along the Mississippi River.

But all Jonas wanted from Tennessee was to make peace with the past and then move on to someplace new. In his mind, 'new' meant no place he had visited during the war, including Georgia, Alabama, Mississippi, Kentucky, and Louisiana. Texas sounded interesting, and rumors of excellent pay out west beyond Missouri and Kansas were just as appealing, except for the fact he'd have to become a Union soldier.

Maybe I can obtain a land grant and build a farm out west... Someplace like Colorado or Nebraska, new territories mentioned by a few of Beaufort's colonels.

It could all be wishful thinking in the end. Regardless of what he decided to pursue next, Jonas knew he couldn't build a successful future without first laying to rest the demons that threatened to follow him from the war. To do this, he had to return to the place he stated repeatedly he'd never visit again.

Sugar Creek.

His intentions were to avoid visiting the old homestead, which he heard had been left in charred ruins. That update came from one of Colonel Hume Field's soldiers whose uncle, Braxton Carter, was a friend of Jonas' former father-in-law, Rufus Porter. Jonas planned to ignore all of Appleton, save for one location... the scene of his most cherished thoughts and memories of Hattie.

Something to offset the nightmares that have never made any goddamned sense! Maybe I can visit 'our special place' one last time, remember how things were before the war, and then be on my way. I'll head out west, cross the Mississippi and hopefully figure out what to do next...

And, now, here he was... gazing skyward beneath the very same branch he and Hattie would gaze up at. Thin rays from the late afternoon sun slipped through the oak's leaves, the same as had often happened prior to the war, and surely had done so for decades before even he and Hattie were born. It struck him as cruelly ironic that most of the larger trees in this area of the creek had been decimated by the battle he'd participated in just five months ago. Yet, this grand old oak had escaped much of the damage delivered elsewhere.

Hardly anything on this side of the tree had changed, as most of the tree's injuries seemed to have been delivered to the other side, where the Yankees and their careless use of repeating rifles had ripped it up quite a bit. He had noticed the areas where the bark had been torn away by bullets as he guided his prized chestnut stallion toward the sacred spot—a horse that had belonged to Beaufort, who had given it to Jonas after the spotted gelding he'd been riding was shot out from under him by a Union sniper. The gift had come just days before the general surrendered.

Jonas had dismounted soon after reaching the sandbar, and the horse hovered nearby as he squatted near the water's edge. He paused to regard his reflection, wondering if it had been worth it to shave the beard that would likely soon return. Dressed in his captain's coat, he planned to remove and leave it inside one of his saddlebags upon his departure from this place.

Just a few minutes more, and I can leave. No more tears after today. It's time to let her go from my life, even though Hattie will always own my heart... Shit, what in the hell was that?

A noise emanating from behind the tree distracted him... Something was very odd about it, and damn if it didn't sound like a wounded demon of sorts... *Hell, it kind of sounds like a woman trying to hide some serious pain!*

Jonas rose to his feet and quietly stepped to his horse, which nickered as he withdrew his rifle from its holster.

"Shhh… hold steady, Jupiter," he whispered. "I'll be back in a moment."

The mysterious cry abruptly ceased, which heightened his wariness. Jonas had already loaded his rifle in the event he needed to defend himself at a moment's notice—be it a bandit, wild animal, or in this instance a traumatized woman or whatever else lurked dangerously just out of view. He raised the rifle and prepared to take a shot.

"Come out from behind there, and keep your hands up to where I can clearly see 'em!"

* * * * *

The sound of the horse had awakened the survival instincts that had kept her alive when others had perished. Hattie prepared to quietly slip away… to leave this place that had been invaded by a stranger.

But then she heard the voice.

It sounds familiar, yes… but somehow foreign, too.

She wanted to flee; to turn around, scramble up the bank and then run as fast and far as her feet could carry her. To get to the road and keep running, until Sugar Creek and her long lost former home of Appleton were no longer visible behind her.

But something about the voice gave her pause… and she peered her head around the edge of the oak's trunk.

The first thing she saw was the barrel of a rifle pointed in her direction, and she almost obeyed her instinct to duck away and retrieve the Bowie knife she kept in her haversack. But recognition of the longhaired, teary-eyed man holding the gun stopped her.

"Jonas? ... *Oh my God, it's you!"*

She didn't immediately run to him, though every fiber in her entire being screamed for her to do it. His look of confusion made it seem dangerous—especially when pointing a gun at her.

He doesn't know me? But the way he's shaking his head says he does... somewhere inside, he does!

Knowing her being attired in a man's suit further hindered her husband's recognition of a woman he surely believed long dead, Hattie stepped out from behind the tree and removed her cap. She allowed her unkempt hair to fall forward, that had grown to below her shoulders since being cut for the last time the previous summer. And although it had become her habit to walk and conduct herself like a man—or at least a boy in his teens—she approached him in the way she believed he remembered her, with the saunter that Jonas told her had always stirred his soul to watch.

"It's me, Jonas."

"And who would 'me' be, stranger!" he demanded.

The situation moving toward deadly danger, Hattie's mind worked furiously to find a solution. Another step toward him could be her last, and saying anything else seemed equally perilous... Then an idea that could work occurred to her. She slowly brought her left hand to the oak's trunk and her gaze to the spot most often chosen by Jonas when leaning up against it, with her nestled in his arms.

"This is our tree," she said quietly, and turned to face him.

Jonas opened and closed his mouth in silence, as if trying to speak. Tears streamed down his face, and then he dropped the rifle near his feet.

"Hattie?"

"*Yes!* It's me!"

She stepped toward him, but he motioned for her to stop.

"You ain't a ghost come here to torment me? And why are you dressed like that?"

She couldn't prevent a slight chuckle while shaking her head. But then she thought of Lester and Lucinda, and knew she had to push the past aside before it engulfed her and added a volatile element to an already uncertain present.

"It's a long story, I'm afraid," she said, catching herself before falling into despair. She forced a smile that quivered as tears welled in her eyes. "But I'm alive, Jonas, and have been looking for you for going on three years. Three *damned* long years!"

Jonas' lips quivered as he smiled, while the tears continued to flow. He appeared to be on the verge of falling over, and Hattie ran to him.

He wrapped her tightly in his arms, and his embrace ignited warmth that began to melt away the years of bitter sorrow that had come to define her outlook on life. She cried along with him, and traded fervent kisses that brought more tears.

When the deluge finally gave way to peaceful serenity, she allowed him to lift her up on his horse after she reclaimed her haversack. The pair lingered for one last look at this enchanted site that had long ago kindled their love and now witnessed their reunion. Then they turned to leave.

Hardly a word had been spoken, beyond their gratefulness and to express the undying love they held for each other. Hattie's heart and soul were finally at peace, and she had no doubt it was the same for Jonas. There would be time to talk, later; to fill in the gaps of what had taken place in both of their lives since the humid morning in early July 1862, when they had last spoken. So much had happened, and she knew it could take years to share and learn it all.

Hopefully, many wonderful years ahead for us, and in a world much kinder than the one we've recently known...

Upon reaching a fork in the road, not far from Sugar Creek, the decision on where to go next was broached by Jonas.

"You don't want to stay here in Appleton?" she asked.

"Not particularly," he replied, glancing over his shoulder at her. A wan smile tugged at the corners of his lips. "Unless that's what you'd like to do. I'll be fine with wherever.... Just as long as you're there, forevermore by my side."

"That's all I want, too."

"Hmmm."

"What?"

"Would you like to become neighbors with your sister up in Columbia?" he asked.

"Not particularly."

"Well, all right then." He laughed. "I reckon we'll go somewhere else... someplace new. How about we head west and talk about it more once the sun goes down?"

She giggled, loving his drawl that she had dearly missed for so long.

"That sounds delightful."

"All right. Hold on tight, my love."

Hattie wrapped her arms around his waist, cherishing his strength while Jupiter soon sped to a full gallop. It didn't matter where they'd end up, as long as from this moment forward it was together and forever. She offered a silent prayer of thanksgiving for finally finding Jonas, and she offered another prayer as well.

Dear Lord, please take care of those we've lost and who are forever dear to our hearts! I look forward to our eventual reunion... though, may it come many, many years from now.

She thought of Papa, Mary and her family, Jonas' parents, and all the fellow soldiers she had become fond of during the war and who had died. She'd never forget the ornery smile and bravado of Lester Smith, and wondered about the close friends that Jonas had lost as well.

Yet, the one person who came foremost in Hattie's mind was the gal who had many times saved her life, and in truth, helped Hattie become a soldier worthy of being proud of…

I miss you so much, Lucinda, and always will! Wherever you are, may the Good Lord keep you at peace in His loving bosom… and hopefully entertained until we meet again!

Hattie lifted her gaze to the brilliant sunset ahead of them in the distance, while her heart continued to overflow with profound gratitude. Could the years of sorrow and strife finally be over? Only time would tell for certain. But in the very least, hope had been reborn.

A new beginning was finally at hand.

Epilogue

Late Friday evening, December 16ᵗʰ, 1939... Atlanta, Georgia.

The impertinent young man had proven to be relentless.

He had introduced himself gruffly as 'Nathan Spagnola' almost six hours earlier, while trying to confirm that the elderly gentleman at Mrs. Hattie Grey's side was in fact *Captain* Jonas Grey, the last surviving officer to serve under General Franklin Beaufort. At the time, Hattie and Jonas were being ushered into the Loew's Grand Theater with two other Confederate veterans from Tennessee, along with the Greys' great-granddaughter, Lucinda Stewart, who had accompanied her recently deceased grandmother's parents from Memphis to attend the premiere of *Gone With The Wind*.

Mr. Spagnola had shoved a business card into Captain Grey's gloved hand. Jonas promptly crumpled it up and was looking for a trash dispenser just inside the building's entrance decorated as an antebellum mansion, but was interrupted from his task by Lucinda. She gently pleaded with him not to throw it away yet, until after she could see the card first. He reluctantly agreed, gripping his cane as he scowled at her.

"I just want to take a quick look at it. That's all." Her smile carried a familiar orneriness of her namesake grandmother, who had passed away the past September.

Hattie had often regarded her great-granddaughter as aptly named, since similarities between her and Hattie's oldest daughter were striking. Both carried the same obstinate spirit of the late Lucinda Templeton, though neither one had ever been made aware of that fact. Having the younger Lucinda around helped ease the pain of Hattie and Jonas losing their fourth child out of five, leaving just their sixty-five-year-old 'baby boy', Rufus, as the last of their direct offspring still among the living.

"What did the young man ask of you, Papa?"

"Nothing that a damned Yankee would ever understand," Jonas grumbled. But the scowl softened considerably after he exchanged glances with Hattie. No doubt her raised eyebrow had an influence. "Ain't it enough that they won the war?"

"Oh, Jonas, just stop," Hattie lovingly admonished, leaning on her cane as she reached to take the crumpled card from his hand. He didn't resist, and Hattie squinted at it, wishing she had brought her reading glasses with her. She handed the unfolded card to her great granddaughter. "I might still be able to read something that small, but not in this light. And, it looks like they'll be seating us momentarily."

"I don't mind, Nana." Lucinda took the card from her, smoothing out the creases a bit more. "It says 'Nathaniel Spagnola III, Harper's Magazine, New York City, New York'."

"Well... maybe you should've given that poor boy a moment of your time, Jonas," said Hattie. "After all, perhaps his surliness is more on account of the weather than the fact he hails from New York City." She chuckled.

"A little cold might do him some good," Jonas countered, but the twinkle in his pale blue eyes told her that he'd be more cooperative, should any other journalist approach him before they headed home to their farm just outside of Memphis the next afternoon.

A few reporters had already spoken with him during the three-day celebration that had started the past Wednesday. Although the attention was nowhere near what even the supporting characters in the movie had received the past few days, the interview requests from two Georgia reporters and another from the *Clarion-Ledger*, in Jackson, Mississippi, surprised him and Hattie.

"I'd imagine this is like springtime in Brooklyn for him." Jonas gently placed his free arm around Hattie's waist, slowly guiding her toward the theater. "Mr. Spagnola, and his nefarious cohorts that have ventured below the Mason-Dixie line under questionable auspices, will fair all right, I'm sure."

"Regardless of their reasons for being here, I hardly think anyone enjoys lingering in the cold," Hattie observed, dryly. "If we encounter the young man again after the show, you should take a moment to find out what he wants. Surely you agree, darling. Yes?"

He offered a subtle nod that inspired a memory from long ago, when she had said goodbye to him for the last time while living on her father's farm in Appleton. It was the same patronizing expression he gave her after she had urged him to be careful and come back home alive to her. Only, in this case, the shadow of a dark brown beard had long given way to a white goatee. Old age had not robbed him of his comeliness, and he looked dashing in his captain's uniform that admittedly fit a bit more snugly than she recalled the last time he had worn it, at a reunion for General Beaufort's cavalry held in Columbia, Tennessee, nearly twenty-five years earlier.

Hattie's evening gown was also Confederate gray, as she decided to change it from the original black satin gown she had picked out months ago. Lucinda had questioned the last-minute change, but Hattie knew that Jonas understood the underlying meaning that everyone else would miss. *And, Jonas knowing the reasons behind my choice is all that matters.*

"Myron and James are headed inside now." Jonas pointed to the pair of elderly men gingerly moving through the doorway ahead and into the luxurious hall that had been further enhanced for the premiere. "We should do what we can to catch up to them, my love."

Hattie and Jonas allowed Lucinda to lead them up to the ushers, who guided the three of them to their seats. For the next four and a half hours—including the intermission—they were treated to a wonderful romantic fantasy centered on the "War Between the States" that had since been immortalized throughout the world. Hattie figured the true brutality would be too unpleasant for most of the audience to consider, and she wasn't opposed to how Hollywood had greatly toned-down Margaret Mitchell's marvelous novel that had captured much of the war's brutality and effect on everyone in the South, be they soldiers, citizens, or slaves.

She could tell by Jonas' facial expressions that he held a similar opinion to hers. The burning of Atlanta in the distance, in one scene, brought back her memories from the last major battle she participated in while the Army of Tennessee was in Georgia, and she gently nudged Jonas to get his attention.

"I was there," she whispered in his ear, making sure no one else could hear her. He nodded, smiling proudly.

"What?" Lucinda whispered, from Jonas' right. Hattie sat to his left, and Lucinda eyed them both suspiciously. Her response drew several curious glances from other patrons sitting nearby.

"Chickamauga," Jonas mouthed to their precocious great-granddaughter. "I wasn't in Atlanta… We'll talk about it later."

Hattie was grateful for her husband's misdirection. It had been a struggle down through the years to maintain her 'secret'. She had considered revealing the truth about her time serving in both the Twenty-Third Battalion and Twenty-Seventh Regiment of Tennessee. But after the endless ridicule heaped upon several Union women who revealed their exploits as Yankee soldiers, she and Jonas agreed it would be best to keep her secret between the two of them. Yet, now that all but one child had passed, and several grandchildren had also died, she wondered if her efforts to protect her family from her own adventures as a woman pretending to be a male soldier in the war had been the best decision.

Hattie had made a slight reference to participating in the Civil War only once, and it had been at her beloved oldest daughter's hospital bedside the night before she had succumbed to a long battle with consumption. The question about why she and Jonas had chosen the name "Lucinda" had come up, since all of her siblings had been named after ancestors and living relatives from either side of the family.

"Why did you and Pa decide on 'Lucinda', Momma?"

Hattie told her beloved daughter that night it came from a good friend who fought in the Civil War… a good *female* friend. That part, of course, was true. The ensuing account of how she met Lucinda Templeton and became good friends during the war was a rambling lie about meeting her when the 'infantryman' had come to Columbia for a visit, and the two becoming pen pals. Hattie almost broke down and shared the real truth, but her daughter's relief at a time when her health was failing overrode all else.

Hattie thought about the inglorious loss at Franklin and all that had happened during that terrible battle when Rhett Butler mentioned it in passing during the movie. Jonas jolted her from a second movie playing in her head—this one a vivid memory of the 'real' battle on November 30th, 1864. It turned out to be one of the bloodiest confrontations between the Union and Confederacy, and the deciding moment in the war effort that foretold the South's impending demise.

He whispered that Clark Gable's Rhett was as much of a likeable scoundrel as Margaret Mitchell had portrayed this character to be in her book, drawing a wan smile from her, and another perturbed look and head-shaking from the latest incarnation of Lucinda. Hattie forced herself to focus only on the story being played out on the big screen in front of them, wondering for a moment what it would be like to have been someone like Vivien Leigh's Scarlett O'Hara. She pictured Lester Smith's and Private Templeton's reaction to that notion.

"What's so funny, Nana?"

Hattie merely shook her head and mouthed that it wasn't important. She thought again about her former companions and how they might view their shared experiences had they somehow survived. Would they have mellowed to the point they'd prefer a Scarlett O'Hara as the definition of what women in the Old South were like? Or, would they remember the times of poverty that affected soldiers and most citizens of the Southern burned-out lands equally? Especially, Private Templeton, who had become increasingly careless about her own secret status as the war wore on.

Lucinda would've either had to have fallen in line with the prevalent opinions following the war's end, or face being shunned by society.

To my knowledge, no self-respecting Southern gal has ever mentioned such a thing as what we did! Therefore, the decision to let sleeping dogs lie was for the best... Besides, who knows how it would've gone over with the bigoted gentry in

Memphis? They'd likely never have believed it, and God only knows how Jonas would react if I were to be ridiculed in his presence!

Perhaps he'd be dead before the kids were born, since the revival of duels had been a problem that persisted until the turn of the twentieth century along the outskirts of Memphis and down into Mississippi and Louisiana. Jonas had nearly been killed on several occasions by then, after standing up for local black sharecroppers he had befriended.

"The world promised by Franklin Beaufort up and died when the general was laid to rest," he'd lament to Hattie, *following Beaufort's untimely passing in October 1877. "Now that the Klan's stolen his good name, the bastards are worse than ever."*

It soon became too dangerous to express progressive views of any kind in public. The Greys' opposition to injustices toward others had to be handled in a much subtler manner. Then after losing their oldest son, Ezekiel, a career army officer who perished on a French battlefield in World War I, Hattie and Jonas focused their energies on keeping the rest of their family together while maintaining a modestly profitable farm. As the years passed, Hattie's and Jonas' unique past was in danger of being forever forgotten…

Until that wintry night in Atlanta.

The premiere itself was a superb experience, and well worth the two-day trip to Atlanta. By the time Jonas, Hattie, and Lucinda moved to exit the theater, all three had forgotten about Nathan Spagnola.

But he hadn't forgotten about them—especially Jonas.

The reporter stood waiting near the street edge of the red carpet that adorned the theater's columned entrance.

"Captain Grey…. Is it true that General Franklin Beaufort kept forty-four former slaves as part of his cavalry during the war? He is later quoted as saying 'No finer Confederates ever fought.'"

Jonas took a few more steps, ignoring Spagnola until the journalist hurried to catch up and slipped in front of Jonas and Hattie. The Greys' great-granddaughter moved to confront him, but Jonas waved her off.

"He said those words before Congress after the war," Spagnola continued. "Some of your colleagues have claimed that he made that statement in their presence as well."

"Yes, sir… General Beaufort definitely felt that way," said Jonas, after pausing to study this persistent northerner. "The general treated all men equal. Even the Yankee scoundrels we'd capture from time to time. Now if you'll excuse us—"

"Just a few more questions—*please*, sir!" The pain in Spagnola's voice was enough to stop them from trying to step past him. "I've traveled so far, and although you might not believe it, I came down here specifically to speak with you after I saw the guest list."

"Pray tell, why me?"

The young man smiled shyly, revealing dimpled cheeks and a strong jaw line that reminded Hattie of Jonas when he was young. Even his curly dark hair and regal hairline were similar. The eyes, though, were green, and carried a desperate glint.

But he seems okay.

"Because you, Captain Grey, are the highest-ranking officer to serve beneath General Beaufort that's still among us," the journalist replied. "You just now said he felt that way about all men, including blacks. How about you and the other officers? Did you all feel that way, too? Or, do you carry the prejudices that have long marked Confederate veterans who survived the war?"

Well, maybe not... The question is a worthy one, but the look in this man's eyes hints of impetuosity. Is he looking for the truth or just a good story to publish in his magazine?

Jonas studied Nathan Spagnola's face before responding. Hattie could tell he believed the man was baiting him... even if subtly.

"The Negroes that General Beaufort brought along from his Memphis plantations were among the bravest men in our cavalry," said Jonas, finally, after pausing to clear his throat. "That wasn't how everyone felt, though most of the general's officers held these men in the same high esteem as myself... I owe my extended stay on Earth to at least two of these courageous cavalrymen."

"So, they were brave, then? But I doubt you'd ever say they were as courageous as Franklin Beaufort himself... correct?"

Jonas glanced at Hattie, while seemingly avoiding Lucinda's attentive eyes that watched the interaction going on between the two men.

"I lost a close friend in the war... Corporal Levi Jones," said Jonas, his voice bearing a volatile mix of anger and compassion. "I'd say he was almost as brave as General Beaufort, and the bravest of all the rest of us—black or white. However, overall, I would have to agree with your assessment about our leader, since no other commander for either the North or the South could match wits or valor with the general. Truly, it was something you'd have had to have seen and experienced to understand, Mr. Spagnola."

"Then, what you're saying would make *him* the most courageous soldier who fought in the Civil War. Perhaps any American war, huh? Is that what you're suggesting?"

"No sir." Jonas shook his head, seemingly tiring of the various ways the reporter sought to ask the same question. "I can't speak for any other American conflict, since I only fought in one war. But I will say this. Despite General Beaufort being the bravest man I ever personally witnessed fighting in the war, I could never anoint him as the most courageous soldier to fight in the Civil War."

That statement seemed to take Nathan Spagnola aback, as if it were a punch delivered by a heavyweight champion. He chuckled nervously, shaking his head in disbelief.

"So, what? Are you suggesting *yourself* for that honor?

Jonas laughed.

"No sir, not at all."

"Then *whom* are you referring to, sir?"

Jonas tipped his hat toward Hattie. "I believe that's a question better suited for Mrs. Grey to answer. Now, if you'll excuse me. Good evening, sir."

Nathan Spagnola stood slack-jawed, as if unsure what to do or say next. Hattie, meanwhile, wanted to scold her beloved husband for dropping this potential mess in her lap. Jonas seemed to enjoy her discomfort, as if it were an ornery joke between them, perhaps something touched upon occasionally down through the years. He kissed her lightly on the cheek, and stepped over to Lucinda, who looked nearly as confused as the journalist from New York.

"May I trouble you with a few questions, ma'am?"

Nathan Spagnola's question sounded half-hearted in its delivery, and he barely acknowledged Hattie's presence while watching Captain Grey limp with his cane toward the curb where their limousine waited.

Don't think you'll get away with this Jonas Milton Grey! A reckoning is coming in the car, dearest husband!

In the meantime, it was obvious that Spagnola was unsure on how to proceed. Surely, he believed that Jonas had thrown him a knuckle ball to shed his pesky presence. Hattie wished she had thrown that pitch instead.

She waited patiently for him to return his disappointed gaze to her.

"Well, Mr. Spagnola," she said, once she held his attention. "I believe the question as to who were the bravest soldiers is something best left in the past, in the ashes of that terrible war... Good evening, sir."

Before the now twice-jilted journalist could regroup and come at them with more questions, Lucinda assisted Hattie in catching up to where Jonas waited, standing with their driver next to an open car door. Before Spagnola could make one last charge at them, all three were safely tucked into the limousine's rear compartment.

Hattie craned her neck to get one last look through a side window at the defeated-looking young man whose true agenda remained a mystery. Though he seemed genuinely curious about Jonas, Franklin Beaufort, and the brave black soldiers of whom they'd fought alongside, there was also something disingenuous about him. Hattie was ready to ascribe it to the need to make one magazine or newspaper more tantalizing than a competitor, when Lucinda interrupted her private thoughts.

"What was that all about back there, Papa and Nana?"

Her brow was furrowed deeply as she studied them from the seat opposite theirs.

"Just another Yankee finding it hard to believe what General Beaufort told Congress after the war," Jonas replied. "Everything I told him can be confirmed, if he'd just go and look for it. Mr. Spagnola didn't need to speak to me about any of it, but I reckon it's too hard for most folks to believe the general was a good man."

Lucinda nodded, though still frowning. She turned her sullen gaze toward Hattie, again reminding Hattie of her great-granddaughter's true namesake.

"Nana, you're hiding something, and have been doing so for years," she accused. "And, Papa's been enabling you to do so... Papa, you might've been able to fool my dad and my brothers, Jeff and Stanley, but I know you have a lot more stories from your time in the war than the dozen or so that you're most fond of retelling. I bet you have lots of stories that deal with the black corporal you mentioned. And, I'd bet even more that you know Nana's secret. *Please*... just tell me what it is."

Hattie looked away from her, only to find her husband's weary gaze waiting.

"Darling, I think it's time... don't you?"

Hattie began to protest. But he shushed her, gently taking her hand in hers.

"All right." Hattie released a low sigh, and gazed into his eyes, earnestly hoping to draw from his strength. Then she turned toward Lucinda, whose frustrated expression had mellowed.

"As women, we supported our men and nation to the best of our ability..." She paused while squeezing Jonas' fingers. He raised her hand to his lips and kissed it, smiling as he nodded for her to go on.

"Sometimes that meant doing things a bit unconventionally... Sometimes it even meant fighting in a battle now and then."

"Are you saying you actually fought in the same war as Papa?" Lucinda's response was a hushed whisper, as she eyed Hattie incredulously.

"Yes."

Jonas lovingly brushed his hand against his wife's cheek to remove a single streaming tear that marked the edge of a dam that might burst. Then he returned his attention to their beloved great-granddaughter, sitting wide-eyed and waiting for Hattie to continue.

"Your Nana was braver than I ever was," said Jonas. "She set out to find me when I hadn't returned home for many months, and then ended up becoming one damned fine soldier in her own right. Along with friends now long gone—like the woman we named your grandmother after, and whose namesake you carry on—there were no better Confederates than Hattie and Lucinda… Truly, they fought like men."

Hattie had always dreaded the tears that would come if she ever told her story. Tears of pain in reliving the loss of those held dear, and tears from revisiting the joyous and bittersweet memories, such as her reunion with Jonas, when he'd assumed she was dead and she was unsure if she'd ever find him alive again.

But after almost seventy-five years, the time had finally come to share it all with an audience other than her beloved husband, and to do that with someone special—someone who in turn could cherish the narrative and share it further. To make it part of a lasting legacy.

The opportunity, though sudden and unexpected, was perfect.

I hope you'll be proud, Lucinda, wherever you are… I finally have your back!

The End

~~~~~~~~

The authors Aiden James and Fiona Fraser.

About the Authors

Aiden James is the bestselling author of *Cades Cove*, *The Judas Chronicles*, and *Nick Caine Adventures* (with J.R. Rain). The author has published over thirty books and resides in Tennessee with his wife, Fiona, and an ornery little dog named Pepper.

Fiona Fraser played a key role in the shaping Aiden's early novels, including *The Forgotten Eden*, *The Devil's Paradise*, and *Cades Cove: The Curse of Allie Mae*. *Toxicity* was their first official co-authored effort, and *They Fought Like Men* is based on an idea Fiona began tinkering with many years ago.

To learn more about the authors and their interests, please visit the links below:

Website: AidenJamesNovelist.com

Facebook: ManorHousePublishing

Twitter:
@BooksManorHouse
and
@AidenJames3